Praise for the Novels of Naomi Kritzer

## FIRES OF THE FAITHFUL

"This far-from-typical fantasy from first-time
author Kritzer is like chocolate cake: instant
addiction .... With habit-forming books like this,
you can't read just one."—*Publishers Weekly*

"Exceedingly well done. I couldn't put it down."
—Katherine Kurtz

"Entertaining."—*Booklist*

"An engrossing book that tells a thoughtful and
complex story of religious conflict and oppression. I
was completely engrossed in this vividly depicted tale
of ordinary people bravely and hopefully stepping
forward to reclaim their country. I eagerly anticipate
reading the next volume, *Turning the Storm*."
—Laurie J. Marks, author of *Fire Logic*

"Subtly brilliant from start to finish."—*Locus*

"Naomi Kritzer proves that music can indeed
change the world, for those who have the ears
to listen and the heart to follow."
—Susan Sizemore, author of *The Laws of the Blood*

## TURNING THE STORM

## FREEDOM'S GATE

# FREEDOM'S APPRENTICE

## Naomi Kritzer

BANTAM BOOKS

FREEDOM'S APPRENTICE
A Bantam Spectra Book / May 2005

Published by
Bantam Dell
A Division of Random House, Inc.
New York, New York

This is a work of fiction. Names, characters, places, and incidents
either are the product of the author's imagination or are used
fictitiously. Any resemblance to actual persons, living or dead,
events, or locales is entirely coincidental.

Bantam Books, the rooster colophon, Spectra, and the portrayal
of a boxed "s" are registered trademarks of Random House, Inc.

ISBN 0-553-58674-2

Printed in the United States of America
Published simultaneously in Canada

OPM    10 9 8 7 6 5 4 3 2 1

*To my parents,*
*Bert and Amy Kritzer*

# CHAPTER ONE

There was a crumbled spot in the wall around Elpisia. Kyros sent slaves to fix it every year or two, but for some reason—unstable ground, a vulnerability to wind—it was always crumbling there again within a few months. When I was a child and wanted to get in or out of town without being hassled by the guards at the gate, I scrambled over at that spot. Half a year earlier, I had examined that point in the wall while tracking an escaped slave.

Now, I was back, on the other side. I was climbing into Elpisia under cover of night to free one of the slaves that I had once taken back to slavery.

I found handholds easily enough, and scrambled over. Some gravel had made its way into my boot, so I pulled it off and shook it out. Then I wound a scarf around my face and pulled up the hood of my coat. It wasn't cold enough for snow yet, but there was a damp wind tonight. I put my mittens back on.

Nika's owner lived quite close to Kyros, not far from the city gate. I took a roundabout route, trying to stay as far from Kyros's house as I could. The streets were dark and quiet, but a few people were still out. I walked briskly rather than keeping to the shadows; acting like I was trying to hide would only attract attention. The wind gave me a good excuse to keep my head down and my eyes on the hard dirt under my feet. Being a fugitive in my home city was the strangest, most foreign experience I'd had in my life—even more foreign than my first days with the Alashi. If someone had blindfolded me and spun me around, I still could have found my way to anywhere in the city. *It's so strange to be back. To be back like* this.

I turned a corner; there, a stone's throw ahead of me, was the household where Nika had been sold. It was built in the Greek style, like Kyros's house, with a courtyard in the center. The front door would be guarded at night. Well, I assumed that it was guarded; I couldn't see much evidence either way from the street.

The first step was to get inside. The front door, obviously, was out of the question. There were a few low windows that opened onto the street, but they were tightly shuttered and barred from within; besides, the rooms on the other side of those windows might have people in them at odd hours. I circled the house once, keeping to the shadows now, though I couldn't see anyone watching. The street was quiet.

*Right. The first step is to get inside. You were Kyros's most resourceful servant—can't you figure out a way to do that?* Tamar had wanted to come along tonight and I refused. If I couldn't even think of a way to get into the house, Tamar would doubtless offer a dozen different suggestions of ways I *could* have done it if I'd had her with me. I'd insisted that Tamar wait with the horses because I thought that I would have at least a faint chance of talking my way out of trouble if I were caught by myself. If I had Tamar with me . . . When I looked at Tamar, I still saw a hint of the beaten-down slave girl that she'd been when we met. I didn't think I could talk *both* of us out of custody.

The first-floor windows had a sill; maybe I could climb onto the roof from there, and then go over that and into the courtyard. I took off my coat and mittens and stuffed them into my bag; the wind chose that moment to send a gust whipping through the street that left me numb and aching. Before I could change my mind, I climbed onto the windowsill. It was awkward, and when I shifted I knocked up against the shutter. Anyone inside would have heard that, and I froze for a moment, ready to leap off and run if I heard movement inside. But all stayed quiet. If anyone had heard me, they must have thought it was the wind.

Now that I was close enough to make a try for the roof, I realized that it was a good arm's length out of my reach. If I'd brought Tamar, I could have boosted her up onto the roof—but she didn't have the strength or weight to pull me up after her, so I'd have needed both Tamar and a rope, anyway. With freezing fingers, I felt for handholds in the stone and mortar of the house. And found one. Maybe I could swing myself up and launch myself onto the roof . . .

I came nowhere near my goal, but managed to make a wonderful crashing sound as I kicked loose a few tiles that shattered on the street below. I landed on the tiles and managed to bite back a stream of oaths as the shutters banged open.

"—a bird or something."

"I just wanted to check."

"Well, you're letting in a lot of cold air, thank you very much."

I held my breath, making myself as small as possible. I was right in the open. If they poked their heads out to look for what had made the noise, they'd see me.

"It didn't sound like a bird."

"Send one of the men if you're that worried, but close the window before I freeze to the floor."

The shutter closed, but I didn't hear the bar put back into place. The guards would be coming, but it would take a little time—who was in the room?

With the tip of my finger, I eased the window open a crack and peered in. It was the kitchen, and there were two women still there, both Danibeki, and thus presumably slaves. If I offered to free them in exchange for their help, would they leap at the opportunity, or scream to alarm the whole house? Tamar would love to shepherd an entire household's worth of slaves up to the reluctant Alashi, but the practicalities of that were more than a little daunting to me. Besides, even if Tamar were right that there were no slaves who liked being slaves, that didn't mean they'd all be willing to flee to the Alashi. Many believed that the Alashi practiced human sacrifice and other such atrocities.

I hesitated too long; if I'd wanted to speak with them, I'd lost my chance. I sprinted around a corner and hid just a few moments before I heard the crunch of the guard's boots on the street. "—bunch of jumpy girls," a male voice said. "Wanting to hide under the bed from the winter wind."

"Something did knock down a few tiles," another voice said. They had a lantern; I could see the light flickering. "It's not blowing *that* hard."

"Nika's probably right, it was a bird or something."

Nika! Had I looked right at her and not recognized her? Or had she been the one who went for the guards? Probably the latter. So she was probably there, in the kitchen, right now.

Muttering about girls and the cold wind, the guards did a quick search, found a feather that had doubtless been dropped by a bird sometime in the last week, and went back inside. I went back over to the window just in time to hear the bar drop again.

Well, at least now I knew where Nika was. I pressed my ear against the shutter and listened to the conversation. They were up early, not late, baking bread for the morning; the conversation was household gossip, nothing useful or interesting. There were three women working, all slaves. Listening to the chatter and *knowing* that one of them was Nika, I was able to pick her out of the conversation, and figure out which voice was hers.

I could just knock on the window . . .

Instead, I put my coat and mittens back on, rewrapped the scarf that shielded my face, and waited. *There's no hurry,* I told myself. *I can go back to Tamar, talk about what to do, and try again tomorrow. That's probably the best plan right now, take this slowly.*

Still, it seemed like it would be worth waiting. Maybe the other two women would step out for a few minutes and I'd have the opportunity to talk to Nika. So I waited, and just as I was thinking that I'd have to leave to be well away by dawn, one of the women said she was going to use the privy, and another had to go get something out of the pantry; Nika was alone.

I knocked urgently on the shutter. "Nika. Nika!" I hissed.

The shutter opened so abruptly that it almost knocked me off the windowsill. Nika stared at me, white-faced and startled. "Who are you? What do you want?" Her wide eyes searched mine, peering over the scarf. Did she recognize me? Just from my eyes? I saw no anger, so probably not.

"Do you still want your freedom enough to take it? I have a horse and I'll take you to the Alashi."

"Who *are* you?"

"I'm here to free you. What does it matter who I am?"

There was a long moment of struggle on Nika's face, and then she said, "I can't. Not without Melaina."

"Who?"

"My daughter. I can't leave her here. She doesn't have anyone but me."

The other women could return at any moment. I spoke rapidly. "Fine. I'll be back tomorrow night. Figure out a way to get yourself and Melaina out this window, and I'll take both of you." I jumped down to let her swing the shutter closed, and ran back for the city wall.

The sun was rising when I reached our hiding place in the track of the old river. Tamar was letting the horses drink water from a muddy puddle. She saw me approaching and shaded her eyes, looking to see if I'd brought Nika. "Lauria. What happened?" she asked when I reached her.

"She wants to bring her kid. We'll try again tonight. This time I think I want you to wait by the wall with the horses; it'll be slow going with a young child otherwise."

"You're going to leave me behind *again*?"

"Like I said before, if I get caught, I think I can talk my way out. As long as I'm *alone*."

"Oh yeah? What are you going to say: 'Look at me,

I'm Kyros's servant, and this is all part of his plan, just ask him'? What are you going to say when they take you to Kyros?"

"I'll tell him what happened with Alibek, and say that freeing slaves is a ruse to win back the trust of the Alashi. Because I know how important this mission is, Nika's freedom is a pretty trivial cost."

"And when he asks why you didn't come straight to him?"

"The Alashi shamans have strange powers and are friendly with the rogue aerika. I was afraid they might be watching me."

"I guess that might work."

"Maybe. But not if you're a prisoner, too."

Tamar thought this over and reluctantly said, "I want to come along next time."

"Once we're not trying to get someone out of Elpisia," I agreed.

"I didn't join you just to sit around outside and watch horses. I feel so useless."

"Tamar, there's no way I could do this without you."

"You're just saying that to make me feel better."

"No, I'm just saying that because I'm afraid you'll leave me and go back to the Alashi. You *could* go back..."

Tamar took my hand and squeezed it. "You're my blood-sister. We belong together. I'm not going back. Not without you."

*S*ix months earlier, Kyros's slave Alibek had climbed that same bit of wall; I had tracked him down and brought him back. Kyros had praised my efficient work, and then had sent me out on a new mission: to infiltrate the bandit tribes that called themselves the Alashi and lived on the steppes to the north. He thought I would be uniquely suited to this task because I was part Danibeki myself and could pose as an escaped slave. First, though, he suggested that I *be* a slave, so that I truly could escape—even if it would be arranged in advance—and make my way to the Alashi just as a real slave would.

I agreed, and was "sold" to Kyros's friend Sophos, supposedly as a concubine for his harem. Sophos swore that he wouldn't forget that I was a free woman; no one would lay a hand on me. He lied. The memory of what happened still made my gorge rise.

The night that I escaped, Tamar followed me; she threatened to spoil my escape if I didn't bring her along. I told myself that I couldn't risk the delay of my plans, but in all honesty, I already liked Tamar and knew that helping her to escape would be a slap in the face to Sophos. We struggled together across the desert. Although the younger girl had initially forced me to bring her along, by the time we reached the Alashi, we were blood-sisters and friends for life.

We spent the summer with one of the Alashi sword sisterhoods, trying to prove our worth so that we could be fully accepted. I secretly reported back to Kyros through the aeriko he sent as a messenger, but as the summer wore on, my loyalties began to shift. I was angry at Kyros for taking no action to retaliate against Sophos. And I became close friends with some of the Alashi: Zhanna, the shaman, who tried to train Tamar and me to speak with the djinni as she did; Janiya, the leader, who told me I reminded her of her own lost daughter; Saken, who had been kind from our first day with the Alashi. Thinking of Saken, beneath her cairn of stones, still hurt.

At the end of the summer, I decided to defect to the Alashi and never return to Kyros. But I hadn't confessed my true identity to Janiya—I had meant to, but I hadn't done it soon enough. When we rejoined the rest of the Alashi for the fall gathering, I had come face-to-face with Alibek. He had escaped again, and this time reached the Alashi. He unmasked me, and after that, it was too late to confess what I had been. I was cast out. I could have been killed, and if I ever returned, I was under sentence of death.

It still amazed me that Tamar had come with me. She truly had been a slave. Among the Alashi, she had passed the tests with far more grace than I had, and had discovered a natural talent for the bow. Yet she had thrown her vest down with mine, and followed me. I didn't understand, but I wasn't inclined to question her too closely. The last thing I wanted to do was convince her to leave me. I had already lost both my home with Kyros and my home with the Alashi; losing Tamar would be even worse.

"Tell me about Nika," Tamar said now as we sat in the shade, waiting for the day to pass. The day grew warm, once the sun was up. Deceptively warm. In a month or two, we'd be in danger of freezing to death.

"She was about fourteen when I brought her back— your age. That was over three years ago. When I caught up with her, I expected her to cry, but she held herself as rigid as carved stone. She didn't say a word the whole way back to Elpisia."

"What did Kyros do to her?"

"He sold her to a friend in town. I don't know if he

beat her or just sold her. She was young and pretty. He's kinder to his female slaves."

"What's going to happen to Nika and her daughter if you're caught after you get them out?" Tamar asked.

"I'll try to convince Kyros to let me leave with them."

"And if he doesn't?"

"I..." I fell silent, brooding over that. *What if their owner punishes Nika by separating her from her daughter?*

"I think I should come with you. If anyone tries to stop us, we can split up and run in different directions. I can take Nika and Melaina, and try to get them away."

"Tamar. If we tried that, they *would* catch all of us. And then you'd be a prisoner, too, and in far worse danger than either me or Nika."

Tamar fell silent for a while, then asked, "What are you going to tell Kyros when he asks what happened to his djinn? His aeriko, I mean—I guess he'd call them aerika."

"I'll say I have no idea what he's talking about."

Just before I'd been cast out from the Alashi, Kyros had sent one of his djinni to try to threaten me into continuing to serve him. At a loss for what message to send back, I had touched the djinn and spoken the words of banishment that a shaman would use on a troublesome rogue djinn. Though this djinn should have been bound to its spell-chain, it had returned somehow to its own world—free. *Gate,* it had hissed.

I wished that I could have talked to Zhanna about that. She could have told me what it meant...

"So that story you're going to tell Kyros if you're

caught," Tamar said, "about winning the trust of the
Alashi by freeing slaves. Do you think it'll work?"

"I think Kyros will believe me."

"No, I mean, do you think you'll actually be able to
earn back the trust of the Alashi again?"

"No," I said, and swallowed hard, trying to clear
the lump in my throat. "They don't free slaves themselves, and I doubt they'll be grateful to us for doing
so. I don't think there is a way to make them trust me
again." I paused, and managed, I thought, a casual
tone. "Do *you* think it will work?"

"No," Tamar said. "I think you're right. But I think
it's a good story to tell Kyros, if you're caught."

There might be no way to earn the trust of the
Alashi again, but I was still determined to try to free
the people I took back to Kyros when I worked for
him. Nika, Thais, Prax, Burkut, and Uljas. Alibek had
freed himself, but there were five others. And at least
this way I could make amends to the people I hurt. Assuming I didn't fail as completely at this task as I failed
at my last.

*Prometheus and Arachne...Djinni of the Silent
Lands...Let me succeed at this.*

Tonight, Tamar came with me as far as the wall; I
wanted the horses close by. We waited until sundown
and then walked to Elpisia, leading the horses as it was
too dark to ride. "This is where we'll come over," I
said.

"I'll wait somewhere nearby," Tamar said.

I looked at her closely, trying to decide if she was
still bitter about being left behind. "Thank you so
much for helping with this."

"I'm not going back to the Alashi, Lauria, so quit worrying. Now go, already. You don't want to miss your best chance."

Again, the streets were dark and mostly empty. I took a different route, to avoid attracting attention; tonight, my path took me perilously close to my mother's apartment. I wondered if she was still awake. If she was awake, was Kyros with her? When Kyros sent his messenger to persuade me to remain in his service, the djinn had implied that Kyros might threaten my mother to coerce me. *I could warn her. But then what?* I had nowhere to take care of her. She certainly wouldn't be any safer with me and Tamar—far from it. And for her to be caught between her daughter and her lover ... *She would try to keep what she knew a secret. But Kyros is good at spotting that sort of thing. He would know she was keeping something from him. And then he might conclude she was in league with me. If he doesn't know where I am, he can't blackmail me by threatening her, and if she knows nothing, there's no point in trying to get it out of her. Her best protection is to know absolutely nothing.*

So I couldn't visit my mother.

Just as well, really. If I did visit her, we'd just end up fighting again.

I found a hidden spot to wait near the kitchen window and sat down. I couldn't hear the voices of the people in the kitchen here, and I was tempted to move closer, but I stayed where I was. I'd told Nika what to do; I had to trust her to take care of her part.

Then again, if she didn't, how obligated should I feel to free her? If I made a good-faith effort and failed, how many times did I have to try again? *For Nika, I'll have to try at least once more. She'd be free already if*

*it weren't for me. If she doesn't manage tonight, it's be-
cause something kept her.* But what about the others?
Burkut had almost died in the desert; what if he now
balked at the risk? How many times did honor demand
that I return if someone was indecisive?

*I'll burn that bridge when I come to it.*

The window was opening. I moved over to it just in
time to see a pair of soldiers rounding the corner of the
street. *Damn it to hell.* I pushed the window shut
again, hoping that Nika would get the message, and
shrank back into the shadows; the soldiers continued
past without stopping. My heart beat in my chest like a
smith's hammer. I waited for a few moments to be sure
that they weren't coming back. Then I started to knock
on the window, but realized that I could hear the murmur of voices again. Well, at least the soldiers hadn't
walked past as I was helping Nika and her daughter
climb out the window. I waited, clenching my teeth
and knotting my hands into fists.

The window opened a crack, then swung wide.
"Here," Nika said, and swung a small body out the
window. I took the little girl in my arms. She was surprisingly heavy. Nika climbed out after her. With a
day's warning, she'd also found a way to have coats for
both her and the child. "We'd better run, they'll be
back in minutes," she said. She took Melaina back and
swung her up against her shoulder.

We ran. *Prometheus and Arachne, keep us from
meeting those soldiers again!* Melaina clung to her
mother, not complaining, and we made it to the wall
without incident. I scrambled up first, took Melaina,
and gave Nika a hand up. Then I jumped down, she
lowered Melaina to my arms, and dropped down after

me. "Follow me. We have horses," I said, and we found our way to Tamar.

"You got them," Tamar whispered as we approached, her eyes alight. We helped Nika up onto Tamar's horse and handed Melaina up to her; we could lead the horses until dawn.

"I got them out of Elpisia," I said. "We still need to get away."

"They sent only one person after me when I ran before," Nika said.

"If she comes after us again, we'll make her sorry," I said.

Nika sucked in her breath and looked down at my face, still half covered with the scarf. Despite the scarf, and the darkness, *now* she recognized me. I saw fear in her eyes.

"I was wrong before," I said. "I'm trying to make amends." I glanced back toward Elpisia. We didn't have much time.

Tamar reached up and clasped her hand. "Trust us," she said. Nika shifted to meet Tamar's eyes, and Tamar's hand tightened on hers. "I was a slave, like you. She helped me escape to the Alashi, and now we're going to help you and your daughter."

Nika tightened her arms around Melaina and nodded once.

Once the sky lightened to gray, Tamar and I mounted as well; Nika was small enough to ride double with Tamar, and Melaina rode with me. In the daylight I could see that she had dark curls and gray eyes; she was about three, I thought, old enough that Nika had probably been pregnant when she ran. I thought I could see Kyros in Melaina's face. *My half-sister? I always thought myself an only child.* It occurred to me with a jolt that Kyros's wife, the former sorceress, had *eight* children.

We pushed the horses hard; the closest well Tamar knew how to get to was on the Helladia side of the hills. Our horses left an easy trail to follow, though if Myron or someone like him were trying to find Nika, he would completely disregard the possibility that the slave could be escaping on horseback. "What did you tell the other slaves?" I asked Nika.

"Nothing. Well, I told them that Melaina had hit her head and needed to be close to me tonight; that's how I brought her with me to the kitchen. I made her a little bed with the coats, so that's how I made sure we had them. And I made sure to forget something so someone would have to go to the pantry."

"Twice," I said, thinking of the soldiers' untimely arrival.

"I forgot a couple of things, just in case."

"If it was that easy, why didn't you ever climb out that window before?" Tamar asked.

"I knew I'd never get away with a child. And the punishment for running away is severe. I couldn't risk Melaina's safety that way, not with so little chance of success."

We reached Tamar's well at dusk. Like the other Alashi wells I'd seen, it was marked with a cairn of rocks. We took turns hauling up water for our horses, then for ourselves; we drank deeply from the bucket and filled our waterskins. The night was cold. Even knowing that Tamar was on watch, I kept rousing, certain that someone was about to catch up with us. I woke everyone at the first hint of dawn so that we could start again as quickly as possible.

"Even if they follow our trail, we're far enough out

that it would be risky for them to come after us," Tamar said. "They're afraid of the bandits and afraid of the Alashi. It's not worth it, not for two slaves. How stubborn was..." She glanced at Nika, and paused. Since the flash of recognition the night we escaped, Nika had pretended that I was truly a stranger. Tamar was clearly wary of forcing either of us to acknowledge that we'd met before. "How stubborn was *your* old master?" she asked, finally. "How hard would he search for a woman and a child?"

Kyros was stubborn but not reckless. "You're right," I said. "A slave who escaped on horseback would've gotten too far too fast to be worth the effort."

"Did he ever use the djinni to search?"

"No. Bound djinni aren't very good at finding people. There are so many ways to be unhelpful: you can look just in the open and skip over even the most obvious hiding places. If you're told to look *everywhere*, you can waste time checking every mouse-sized crevice. If you don't know exactly what a person looks like, you'll never find them; if they've changed their appearance even slightly, you can pretend not to recognize them."

"Don't they carry messages?"

"This is why you'll send a djinn to 'the commander of such-and-such post' and give a location. Though there are downsides to that approach, too."

"Kyr—*Someone* did find you with a djinn, once, though."

"He knew more or less where I was, and the djinn knew me. Now... it won't be as easy."

"What will he do?"

I bit my lip. I hadn't really wanted to think about

this. "It's a big world," I said. "He'll have to tell the djinn to look *everywhere*. It could take a really long time."

Tamar mulled that over for a few minutes, then asked, "Do you think he'll send a djinn to search, though? Because it probably would find you eventually."

I sighed and glanced at Nika, as reluctant to shatter the pretense as Tamar was. "Alibek told me something once," I said, knowing that Tamar would know this meant *while I was bringing him back to Kyros.* "He said that after his sister escaped, his master took Alibek for his harem instead, then sent a djinn up to the steppes to tell Alibek's sister what he did. And that was just out of pique. He'll *never* give up on finding me. Ever."

It was light enough to ride now, so we mounted up. Nika asked, "If the djinn was able to find the escaped slave to carry a message, why couldn't it just kidnap her and take her back?"

"Moving a person is a delicate task," I said. "Moving an unwilling person is particularly hard, and if the person gets killed in the process, the binding spell is broken. That sometimes kills the holder of the spell-chain and always kills the sorceress, and it frees the djinn. It's too risky most of the time—certainly too risky just to retrieve a runaway slave."

A few more days of travel brought us near to the Alashi fall gathering. We moved in close enough to see the smoke from their campfires and then stopped, helping Nika and Melaina down from the horses.

"Be sure to tell them that you ran away once, and were caught and brought back against your will," I said. "The Alashi don't rescue slaves; they believe those who truly want freedom will run on their own."

"But I didn't get away," Nika said. "What if they don't accept me?"

"They will," Tamar said. "Anyway, you can't stay with us forever."

"They'll call you a blossom and make you pass tests—oh, don't worry. They'll haze you but they'll accept you. Good luck."

"Wait," Nika said, and took my hand. "I thought I recognized you, the night we escaped." She *had* recognized me, even with a scarf over my face; she certainly knew who I was now. "But I was right to trust you. Whoever you used to be, today you are *not* the person I thought I saw. When I reach the Alashi, who should I say helped me?"

Saying my own name, my real name, felt like it would be a rejection of her forgiveness. But I wanted Janiya, at least, to know who'd done it. "Tell them it was two women, one named Tamar, the other named . . . Xanthe." Xanthe, the name of Janiya's lost daughter—the one Janiya had told me I reminded her of. Janiya would know it was me.

"Thank you, Xanthe," Nika said, took Melaina's hand, and turned toward the smoke from the fires.

*W*ell, that went pretty well," Tamar said. "Do you want me to call you Xanthe now?"

We'd ridden west to another well, and had built our own small fire with dung we'd managed to collect. I was still cold. *We need a shelter.*

"No," I said. "That's . . ." I paused; this was personal information, after all. Then I shrugged and finished. "Janiya has a daughter by that name, in Penelopeia where she used to live."

"Huh." Tamar poked at the fire. "If you use another name, will that make it harder for Kyros to find you?"

"His djinni both know who I am. Knew. I guess there's only one of them now."

"If it finds you, can you just banish it like you banished the last one?"

"I don't know. Maybe. It might not work twice." I sighed and wiped my nose on my sleeve; the cold air was making it run. "I wish I could have asked Zhanna about that before I was banished."

"Yeah..." Tamar tossed another chip of dried dung onto the fire. "What if you disguise yourself somehow? You said earlier that if you changed your appearance, a djinn could pretend it didn't know who you were."

"Yeah, that's true. I don't really know what I'd do, though. I would get tired of keeping a scarf over my face all the time. There are people who can change their face a lot with face paint, but I think if I tried I wouldn't look like a different person, I'd look like Lauria trying to disguise herself."

Tamar laughed a little at that, then gave me a long, speculative look. "Well, buy some face paints then, and I'll put them on you. I learned to paint my own face back in the harem. I could make you look older, or something. I think. It's worth a try."

"Huh." I thought it over. "Well, all right. When we pass near a city that isn't Elpisia..."

"So where are we going, anyway? Who do you want to free next? Can we go get Meruert and Jaran and the others in Sophos's harem?"

I took a deep breath and let it out. "I don't know. It would be hard, getting so many people out."

"Well, what would it take? Horses? Sophos has a stable full of horses."

"He also has an entire garrison full of soldiers. One or two people can sneak past. The entire harem—that would be harder."

"Sophos has a spell-chain...maybe we could steal it."

"That would make things a lot easier. You know Sophos better than I do. Is he careless with his spell-chain? If one of us slipped into his house, would we have a good opportunity to steal it?"

Tamar mulled that over. "I've never seen him take it off," she admitted after a little while. "He even wears it to bed, and he is a light sleeper, even when he's been drinking. If someone caught him in an unguarded moment..."

I had seen him in an unguarded moment, once. His knife had been within my reach—but I hadn't grasped it when I had the chance, and he had raped me and sent me bleeding and sobbing back to the harem. I winced at the memory that came back, unbidden. That wasn't the sort of unguarded moment I hoped ever to catch him in again. I pushed the thought away and let out my breath in a sigh. "Think on it," I said. "If there isn't a way to get his spell-chain, then surely there's some other way to accomplish our task."

"If it were easy, then someone would have done it before."

"It might not be easy. But we will find a way."

*I* stood in the center of Janiya's camp: the yurts loomed up around me, but I knew they were empty, and I could hear none of the noises from the horses or camels or dogs that I would have usually heard.

"It was you, wasn't it?"

I turned, and saw Zhanna standing in front of one of the yurts.

"You sent us Nika."

"It was me," I said, but a gust of wind whipped the words away and I was alone again. "Zhanna? Are you there?"

Out of the corner of my eye, I saw movement, but when I turned, it wasn't Zhanna—it was a man riding toward me on a horse. *Kyros.* I wrenched myself awake with a start and stared up at the starry night sky, listening to Tamar breathing beside me. Zhanna had told me that with practice, shamans could sometimes communicate with each other through dreams—was this a dream like that? Was she trying to talk to me? And if so, what was Kyros doing in my dream? He was no shaman. *But he's my father.*

Tamar whimpered in her sleep, but settled when I nudged her slightly. It was almost dawn; I watched as the eastern horizon lightened to gray.

I'd never faced my mother in a dream, though the djinni had sent me a dream once that showed me her past with Kyros. I wondered if she had ever tried to speak with me in a dream. *Surely, if she could harass me in my sleep instead of having to limit herself to my occasional visits, she wouldn't pass up the opportunity.* The last time I'd visited her, she had brushed my hair and nagged me to get married. I ran my fingers through my hair now. *I wouldn't mind seeing her, if only she were somehow temporarily struck mute.*

"We need some sort of disguise," Tamar said, startling me; I hadn't known she was awake. "Not the face paint we talked about yesterday. Some way that we can

move around through places like Elpisia without anyone getting suspicious."

"No disguise is going to get us into Sophos's household unrecognized—not face paint, not a traveling animal show, nothing. You lived there for years. I was
only there briefly, but I still think people would recognize me."

"Yeah." Tamar sighed. "Maybe we should work on
the others first. For practice. When we go to Sophos's,
I want to do it right. I want to get *everyone* out of
there, even Aislan."

"All right," I said.

"For now..." She sighed. "Maybe we could pretend we were merchants?"

I'd thought about that already. "Merchants have
stuff to sell—we don't. And more urgent than disguis-
ing ourselves, really, is money. We need to come up
with some way to pay for food and shelter. Winter's
coming. We have no yurt. We're running out of food."

"Have we got anything at all that we could sell?"

"The horses."

"I don't want to sell them."

"I don't either."

I poked through my packs. They contained what I'd
had with me when I'd been banished: some waterskins,
some food, a blanket, a knife. My sword, the one I'd
stolen from the bandits last spring. Flint and iron.
Women in the sword sisterhoods all carried basic sur-
vival materials with them in case they got separated
from the group—lucky for me, or I'd have died the first
day. Nothing *valuable*, though. Nothing I could sell.
And no money.

There was something lumpy at the bottom of one of
my packs. I dug out the lumps and examined them in

the dawn light. Karenite, two thumbnail-sized pieces of it; they rattled against each other in the palm of my hand. *How did this get here?* After thinking about it for a minute or two, I remembered. Janiya had given us a chunk and sent Tamar and me out to find another piece, as a test to see if we were worthy to join the Alashi. Tamar and I had found karenite, as instructed, but the real test had been whether we'd have the sense to provision ourselves before going out to look. Janiya had refused to take it when we returned, and in my humiliation, I'd tossed both pieces into my pack and forgotten about them, until now.

"Can we sell that?" Tamar asked.

"Probably," I said, looking it over. "I don't honestly know how much we'll get for it, though."

"Do the Greeks even, you know, *like* it? It's pretty, but it's not really a gemstone."

I laughed a little and tucked the karenite back into my pack. "That's not what the Greeks use it for. Karenite is used as the binding stone on a spell-chain; it's needed, I think, as part of the spell." I chewed on my lip. "I think the main reason the Greeks were planning an offensive against the Alashi is that most of the Greek sources of karenite are tapped out."

"There's a lot of it up on the steppe," Tamar said.

"Exactly," I said. "But the Greeks can't go up hunting for it because of the Alashi, and the Alashi don't sell it to the Greeks. That's why I'm not really sure what it's worth." I tilted it in the dawn light, watching the colors shift from gray to luminescent blue-green. "My mother lives upstairs from a gem-cutter, so I know what he'd spend to buy an uncut ruby or sapphire or onyx, and what he'd sell them for after cutting them. But he never touched karenite. I'd never seen it in raw form before coming up to the steppe."

"Could you try selling it to a gem-cutter?"

"It's the sorceresses who want it."

"Do you know where you can find a sorceress?"

"Daphnia," I said.

"Are any of the slaves you need to free down in Daphnia?"

"Yes. Uljas was sold down there."

"Then let's go there next."

*T*ell me about the slaves you need to free," Tamar said that night when we made camp again. I noticed that she never called them *the slaves you took back*.

"There were five," I said. "Now there are four."

"Yeah, and where are they? One was in Elpisia, one's in Daphnia, where are the others? Are they men or women? Are any of them still with Kyros?"

I took a deep breath and listed them. "The one down in Daphnia is a man, Uljas. I think he was sold to a military officer down there. It's a big city, and he may be hard to find. Then there are two other men, Burkut and Prax. Burkut was a house servant who just took off one day; it wasn't clear why. When he ran, he didn't take any water with him, and when I found him he'd just about dropped from exhaustion and thirst, but he still tried to run away, and he started crying when I reached him. Burkut was sold to a farm south of here. Prax was the only one who ever fought me; he had this piece of broken pottery that he used as a knife, and he managed to cut me before I got it away from him. He was sold to a mine. And not because I told Kyros about the knife, either, because I didn't. I know which mine, but I don't know how I'm going to get him out. Then there's Thais. She was sold to someone in Casseia. Casseia is weeks of travel to the south, maybe months, and I don't know the name of the person who bought her."

Tamar let out her breath in a sigh. "Practice," she muttered. "Well, if we can free a man from a mine, and find Thais, then freeing the other concubines from Sophos should be easy."

"It's not too late for you to go back to the Alashi..."

"Not a chance. I don't know if we'll be able to do this together, but you'll have no chance at all without me, I know that already. Even if you knew where to find the wells, which you don't."

I wasn't sure I believed that I *needed* Tamar to do this, and I wondered if I should tell her that I didn't need her and try to send her back to the Alashi where she would be safe. But I was afraid that I might succeed in sending her away. What if she left me? *If she leaves me, I'll be alone.* "I'm glad you came along," I said instead. "I'm glad you're here to help me."

## CHAPTER TWO

*W*e looked down at Daphnia as we approached it. "Arachne's eyeballs," Tamar breathed. "Is all of that the *city*?"

Daphnia was an old city, far older than the Penelopeian Empire; the Danibeki had called it Chach, back before the rivers were bound. Daphnia itself had plenty of water. It was built on the banks of the Chirchik River, and from our vantage point we could see the sparkling web of canals that flowed from the river through the city. The city was walled, though it was far enough from the threat of the Alashi that the wall hadn't been maintained. I felt a slight pang, looking down, that Tamar was seeing the city for the first time so late in the year. The trees that lined the streets had mostly dropped their leaves, and the gardens were mostly brown and dead from the cold fall nights. From above, Daphnia looked almost as dull brown as Elpisia, though at the height of summer it would have been a luminous green.

The houses were crammed together like nondescript

pebbles, but a handful of buildings rose up like trees on a plain, looming over everything else. One, built of the same clay brick as all the rest, was the Temple of Alexander; the other, built of white marble that had been ferried, block by block, by bound djinni, was the Temple of Athena. The white building glistened like a pearl in the bright fall sun, and I glanced at Tamar to see her reaction. She was staring down silently.

"Take a good long look," I said. "You're going to need to act at least a little bit jaded if we're going to pretend we're merchants."

"Yeah," Tamar mumbled.

I had been fretting for the last two days about our horses' tack; Alashi saddles were distinguishable from Greek saddles by even the most casual glance. A slow approach to the city set my mind at ease. There were merchants who rode with Greek-style saddles; there were merchants who rode with Alashi saddles; there were merchants who had horse tack so strange I wasn't even sure what it was for. Even as two women with Alashi clothes and Alashi saddles, we would not stand out. Not in Daphnia, anyway.

There were a dozen different gates leading into the city, and I led Tamar down to the gate I usually entered by when I was working for Kyros. It was watched over by soldiers from the Daphnia garrison, but they were just there to keep an eye on things, and they didn't stop us as we dismounted and led our horses into the city. The walls here were very high. As we passed through, I glanced up to see a flock of sparrows roosting on the wall take sudden flight as a larger bird flapped toward them.

The streets were busy but not crowded. Daphnia was full of merchants during the summer months, but this time of year most preferred the warmer climates. We attracted a brief curious look from a slave out on an errand, but no one else gave us more than a cursory glance. Though the walls of Daphnia were high, the buildings mostly were squat one-story houses made of clay bricks; some of the shutters were open wide to let in the sun, others were closed to keep out the cold wind. Ravens picked through rubbish piles. Even in the cold, the dank smell of human waste rose from the canals. As we crossed a little wooden footbridge over the canal, I spotted a red flower still blooming despite the cold.

I heard a muffled exclamation from Tamar and she grabbed my arm and pointed up. I saw a dot of color, something red and gold. "It's a sorceress's palanquin," I explained. "It's like a box of silk cushions, carried by djinni. Aerika, I mean—we should call them aerika, here among the Greeks. The sorceress rides inside."

One of the gusts of wind that blew down from the steppe caught the edge of Tamar's sleeve and whipped it out like a banner; she caught it and pulled it close around her arm, shivering. "Let's do our business and find somewhere to stay."

My first visit to Daphnia had been with Kyros, the year I was twelve. I'd been overwhelmed by the crowds. Our second day in town, he took me to the marketplace and we got separated. I spent a frantic hour trying to find Kyros again, without success, and finally sat down, in tears, on the steps outside the Temple of Alexander. I had no idea how to get back to our inn—in my inexperience, I hadn't even made careful note of its name, so I couldn't ask for directions, and felt too foolish to ask a priest at the temple for help finding Kyros. The only solution I could think of was to go back up to Elpisia, but

I didn't have my horse, and I had very little money. Fortunately I decided to spend the night in the temple courtyard, and that's where Kyros found me, an hour or so later. I quickly dried my tears, ashamed. Kyros said something kind and led me back to our inn for dinner and wine. That evening, he gave me his ring—a heavy gold ring set with a garnet, and a thong to hold it around my neck. "If you get lost again, or if you ever need help in Daphnia, go to the Temple of Alexander and show my ring."

I'd been to Daphnia many times since. Kyros had dealings with several sorceresses in Daphnia, and had me carry messages fairly regularly. I was no longer overwhelmed by the crowds or the maze of streets. I had a favorite room at my usual inn, which they would put me in without asking if it was available when I arrived. I wouldn't be able to stay there this time, of course. I wondered if there was another inn in Daphnia that had a room with a window overlooking a climbing rosebush in the inner courtyard, and a window on the opposite wall with a view of the Temple of Athena.

"Where are we going?" Tamar asked.

"To a sorceress named Phoibe. I've never met her, but she has a reputation for being relatively calm and predictable, for a sorceress. Also, she has a nice house. I've always kind of wanted to see the inside."

"Are you sure she won't recognize you?"

"Pretty sure."

"Not completely sure?"

"It's possible she saw me from a distance once, and found out my name. But that's true of anyone in Daphnia."

"Maybe we should go to a city you haven't visited as many times."

"We'd run out of food before we got there. It'll be all right, Tamar. She won't recognize me."

Phoibe was also reputed to be trustworthy—not the sort who would steal our karenite and have us thrown back out to the street. Still, I wanted to take only the larger chunk of karenite, and leave the smaller piece with Tamar, who could wait for me a short distance from the house.

But Tamar balked at that. "You left me behind when you went to get Nika. I want to come this time."

"You can come when I go to get Uljas. But I want you to have the karenite in reserve, in case the sorceress reacts badly."

"I think you just don't trust me not to act like a small-town slave girl."

"Well, I *don't* trust you not to act like you've never been anywhere like Daphnia before. We'll just tell people you're new at this job if anyone wonders. But there's no reason you need to come with me right now."

"There is," Tamar said. "I need to start learning more than just how to wait. There will *always* be a reason to leave me behind. But sooner or later you're going to need a second person."

I shrugged at that. Tamar was clearly in a mood to be stubborn, so I decided to bring her along and hope for the best.

Phoibe's family lived within a walled enclosure, much like the ones Kyros and Sophos lived in. There was an outer wall with a gate, and a series of inner buildings, including a large house for the family. The outer wall was brick, like everything else, but well kept—she had a slave who scrubbed it clean seasonally. I'd caught a glimpse through the gate once and seen a fountain built of blue mosaic tile, and a lush garden. I turned to Tamar as we approached the gate, intending to tell her not to gape like she was seeing the land of the djinni, then thought the better of it. If Tamar tried to act like she'd seen it all before, she'd probably look even *more* suspicious.

There was a door in the wall; it was closed. I knocked on it and an elderly male slave opened it and gave me a dour look. "We don't want any," he said.

I shoved my foot up against the door so he couldn't close it. "I'd like to speak with Phoibe."

"What's your business with her?"

"That's not for your ears." When I'd visited a stranger with a message from Kyros, I'd always flashed his ring to the gatekeeper and had been ushered straight in. Unfortunately, I had nothing to show off this time, and he narrowed his eyes and started trying to shove the door shut.

Tamar stepped forward. "Let us in to see your mistress," she said, and slipped something into his hand—a small wineskin. He gave it a suspicious sniff and I saw Tamar raise her chin to give him a level look. He cracked a faint smile—a knowing smile—and opened the door.

"If you'll just wait here," he said, "I'll go see if she's available."

I glanced at Tamar and she rolled her eyes and whispered, "Just because *you* never took a bribe when you were working for Kyros doesn't mean no one else there did."

"What did you give him?"

"Kumiss."

I made a face. "Why *kumiss*?"

"Slaves don't usually have money. We—*they*—trade alcohol for favors."

The courtyard was as beautiful as my fleeting glimpse had promised. A fountain bubbled up at the center, the dark blue tiles shining in the sun. More tile formed a reddish diamond on the ground, and apple trees stood at the points of the diamond. I could see the scrub of a faded flower bed along the sides of the diamond; there would have been red flowers growing there during warmer seasons, but the blooms were long gone and the beds were covered in brown leaves. Though the streets of Daphnia smelled even more foul than Elpisia, Phoibe's enclosure was scented with lemons and sweet incense.

"This is pretty nice," Tamar said casually. I looked at her. She had the offhand voice right, but her shoulders were hunched, and her wide eyes darted around the interior courtyard, trying to covertly take in everything at once. I suppressed a smile, but didn't say anything. As a "merchant" who wouldn't have known to bribe the door guard without assistance, I was hardly in a position to complain about Tamar blowing our cover story.

The servant returned a short time later and said, "Phoibe will see you."

When I had visited other Weavers in Daphnia on behalf of Kyros, I had nearly always been taken into a receiving room, with a desk and comfortable chairs. But Phoibe's servant ushered us into her workroom. A huge mahogany loom stood at one end, with a half-completed tapestry on its strings. There was a chair beside the loom, but it faced a workbench; on the bench I could see tools and wire and beads, the pieces of a spell-chain not yet assembled. Phoibe rose from the chair as we entered.

"My servant tells me that you may be of interest to me," Phoibe said, "but that you refuse to state your business."

I bowed. "We have something that may be of interest to you," I said, and drew the karenite out of my pocket.

Phoibe sucked in her breath and crossed the room in a few long strides. Sorceresses were always mercurial and tended to get worse over time; during my years working for Kyros, I'd learned to tell whether a sorceress was melancholic or touched by the cold fever. *Cold fever,* I thought, looking at Phoibe. *But at least she's not as frantic as some I've seen.*

She clasped my wrist to study the karenite in my hand. "Beautiful," she murmured under her breath. She released my hand and whirled to pour a cup of tea from a pot that sat on her work table. She had not prepared for visitors, so offered me her own cup. "Thank you so much for coming to me," she said, a little breathless. "Where did you get that?"

"We are merchants," I said, and hesitated; I'd planned a story before coming here, but now I wasn't certain how much I wanted to try to tell. "This was a find, however, not a purchase."

She took my wrist to study the karenite again and then went to look at her work table. "How much do you want for it?"

That, of course, was an excellent question. I had only a vague sense of the price karenite brought to the Alashi; I thought it would probably be higher here but I wasn't sure how much. The sorceress's excitement implied strongly that it would fetch a very good price indeed. "I know you will make me an excellent offer," I said. "Better than the offer I had elsewhere."

She looked at me with narrowed eyes, trying to gauge whether I really did have another offer, or was just trying to drive up the price. I kept my face neutral.

She licked her lips. "Two hundred alexanders," she said.

*Two hundred alexanders.* My mask slipped; I knew she saw the shock in my eyes. *That would pay for everything.* Everything! *I could practically* buy *everyone out of slavery with that kind of money.* I got it back into place and said, "My other offer was for nearly twice that."

She laughed, and I knew I'd given myself away. "Yet you came here, and I'm sure you know it's because I'm more trustworthy than the other sorceress. Two hundred and twelve."

"Three hundred," I said.

"Two hundred and twenty-five, and that is my final offer."

"Done," I said, wondering how much I was underselling myself. *But look on the bright side—all that money! And another piece yet to sell . . .*

Phoibe went to her workbench, unlocked a strongbox, and counted out the coins. Then, with a little bit of a flourish, she took out a drawstring bag made from thick patterned linen and gave that to me as well. I knew looking at the way she touched it that she had woven the cloth. At her nod, I put the karenite on her work table. "Be sure to come to me the next time you . . . run across something like this. If my gate guard gives you any trouble, show him this." She took a silver brooch off of her own collar and pinned it to the bag. It showed a silver bird, wings spread. "My maid will show you out." She gave me the bag.

Back out in the street, Tamar blinked a little in the sunlight. "Let's go find somewhere to stay," she said. "Somewhere *really* nice." She dropped her voice and hissed, "*Two hundred and twenty-five* alexanders? Can we go buy Uljas and the others?"

"It would be suspicious, just knocking on someone's door to try to buy a slave. Did anyone do that with Sophos?"

"Aislan's officer tried to buy her once, but other than that, no."

"We can think about it. Remember, we have to live on this money for a while. We need a tent, horses... If we use it to buy Uljas's freedom, and Prax's, we'll be pretty much back where we started."

Tamar shrugged. "Or we could get robbed on the road as soon as we leave Daphnia and be back where we started, too."

"True enough." I glanced at Tamar. "We'd better buy nice lodgings tonight like you suggested, just in case. Imagine how stupid we'd feel if we saved our money, stayed somewhere cheap, and *then* got robbed tomorrow."

The best inn in Daphnia would have been too conspicuous, but we found one that made my old favorite look shabby. From the outside, it looked like a Greek household, with a wall and an inner courtyard, but the gate guard was rather more welcoming. We brought our horses into the courtyard and looked around. It wasn't as opulent as Phoibe's courtyard, but it was a whole lot fancier than Kyros's. There were trees, with

wicker benches under them for hot summer afternoons, and a fountain—though this one had no mosaic. The water trickled down over an upturned
tortoise shell, as large as my two cupped hands. In the
corner of the courtyard, I saw a palanquin draped with
blue velvet and gray silk. A sorceress's palanquin.

"Let's get inside," Tamar said, shivering.

The innkeeper welcomed us graciously, though he
did ask to be paid in advance, and became even more
gracious when he caught a glimpse of my purse. He
ushered us up to a very comfortable suite of rooms, as-
suring us that our meals would be brought up. The
rooms made me think of the inside of an Alashi tent.
The floors were covered with thick wool rugs, red and
orange and deep golden yellow—though Alashi rugs
were usually felt and these were pile. Of course Kyros
used rugs for warmth during winter, too, but like most
Greeks, he preferred more subdued colors. The walls
were hung with tapestries: broad stripes of brown and
yellow, little green and blue diamonds, a huge sun-
burst, a picture of Alexander's helmet. There was a
fireplace in the sitting room, with a roaring fire already
built. A copper pot sat on a brazier if we wanted to
make tea. I took a quick look in the bedroom. The bed
was soft, the quilts were thick and piled high, and I
trusted that the innkeeper wouldn't risk offending
wealthy guests with bedbugs. "We'll take it," I said.

"There is a bathhouse down by the courtyard," he
said.

"We'll use it right now, if that's convenient," I said.

"I'll send word down," he said. "Would you like
your dinner at sundown?"

"That would be lovely."

We checked on the horses before we went into the

bathhouse. They were unsaddled and groomed. I felt a prick of uneasiness, despite my earlier confidence that our horses wouldn't attract attention. What if they noticed, and suspected? *I suppose we could take the horses now and take off* . . . But the prospect of a bath, a warm, comfortable night, and a hot meal were far too tempting.

*Besides, our horses were trained with Alashi equipment. It's not as if we can just go have Greek saddles made and slap them on. We would have this problem everywhere.*

Our horses seemed content enough in their accommodations, so we went to find the bathhouse.

The door opened directly onto the courtyard, so we closed it and locked it behind us. A young woman was pouring in a bucket of clean water as we entered. The bath was built from large blocks of smooth marble; it was knee-deep, with shiny copper buckets to wash with. A roaring fire kept the bathhouse itself warm enough to be almost too hot; the young woman was dressed in a very light shift. Tamar gave her a stricken look, and I realized that the young woman was undoubtedly a slave owned by the innkeeper.

"Would you like to take turns washing, or should I send for another assistant?" the slave asked.

"We can take turns," I said.

I shed my filthy clothing and gave it to the slave to send to be washed; again, it occurred to me that it was made in the Alashi style, but undoubtedly some merchants wore foreign styles. I stepped into the water, which had been warmed but was still chilly enough to make me glad of the heat of the room. The slave poured water over me. I took the soap from her to scrub my own body and hair, and then she poured more water over me to rinse with. The towels were warmed. I dried myself, put on a linen robe that had been laid out, and then combed out my hair while Tamar had her bath.

The last time I'd been assisted in a bath, it had been Tamar assisting. It was strange to watch Tamar accepting assistance now—especially as she was clearly uncomfortable with it. She was shivering, despite the warmth of the bathhouse, and kept glancing nervously at the slave, who had her eyes fastened on Tamar's feet even as she was pouring water over her hair. *A merchant should know that she's supposed to just ignore the slave,* I thought, and started talking, to try to distract Tamar.

"I hope we'll make it back to Daphnia next summer," I said, and told her a bit about the last time I'd been in Daphnia, about the gardens and green trees from the canals that flowed through the city. I rattled on as Tamar soaped herself up, talking about some of the other cities I'd visited, what they were like, how Tamar would get to see them now that she was my apprentice, alluding a little to the adventures we were going to have. Clean, Tamar dried herself as quickly as she could and put on a robe. "What are they going to do with our clothes?" she asked.

"They'll wash them and press them and send them back to our room. For now we can borrow these." I gave Tamar the comb. She ran it quickly through her short hair, scowling as she realized that the ends of it came almost to her shoulders when it was wet. "Now that we're back in the Peneleopeian Empire, though, maybe we should buy ourselves new clothes." I glanced at the slave myself. "Have you seen clothing like ours before?" I asked.

The slave hesitated, then said, "Most merchants wear clothes of the local style while they're here."

"On our last expedition, this was more practical. However, we need some new clothing now. Please send word to have a tailor sent to our rooms tomorrow." Our Alashi clothing was worn anyway; we would need replacements soon or we'd find ourselves in rags. I wanted men's garments, though. It was far more practical for our current occupation, which could probably be most honestly described as urban banditry.

We were clean, dry, dressed, and combed. "May I be of further service?" the slave asked, her eyes on the floor.

"No, I think we're done," I said.

Tamar and I hurried back to our room; someone had built up the fire in our absence, and there was hot tea and a plate of sweet cakes waiting for us. I settled down in a cushioned chair beside the fire, poured myself tea, took a honey cake, and sighed with faint satisfaction. Life with the Alashi definitely lacked certain amenities. The honey cakes were perfect, even better than the ones Kyros's kitchen made: crunchy on the outside, moist inside, and rolled in sesame seeds. I took another. "You should have one of these," I said to Tamar. "I'm going to finish them all if you don't stop me."

"Help yourself," she said. She unlatched the shutter to look down at the courtyard.

"What are you doing? It's freezing out there and your hair's still wet."

"I want to take her with us, too."

"Who?"

"The bath slave."

I didn't need to ask why. It was quite clear what

other "services" she was sometimes called upon to provide.

"We need to find Uljas first," I said.

"But we can take her with us when we go, right?"

"What are you going to say if I say no?" I glanced at Tamar and met her furious glare. "Yes, then. If she wants to come. We'll think of some way to get her out."

The sun was setting when the innkeeper knocked on our door with dinner. Servants brought in trays of food and a clay jar of wine. "Please send for me if anything is unsatisfactory," the innkeeper said, "or if you need more wine. Someone will be back later to gather the dishes."

I looked out the window; a light still glowed in the window of the bathhouse, and I could see someone ambling away from its door. I closed up the shutters, tossed another stick onto our fire, and sat down to eat.

The food was excellent—a blend of Greek and Alashi flavors. There was lamb marinated in olive oil and lemon juice and broiled over a fire; there were strips of juicy broiled eggplant; there were hard-cooked eggs in a sauce with ginger and garlic. The bread was fresh and hot and as light as a feather pillow, and crisp wedges of apple finished the meal. I poured myself some wine cautiously. The last time I'd tried to drink Greek wine, the very smell had swept me back to the room where Sophos had raped me. Tonight I sniffed it carefully, but somehow my awareness of the possibility kept it from happening. I took a cautious sip, then another. I didn't really want a second cup, though, and Tamar took no wine at all.

"We could ask the bath slave if she knows where to find Uljas," Tamar said as we were finishing.

"Why would she know? I doubt she ever leaves the inn."

"If you want to find honey, ask the bee, not the bear."

"Yeah, but if you're looking for a particular *bee*..." I shrugged. "Well, if you want to ask her, go ahead."

Tamar looked out the window. A thread of light gleamed under the bathhouse door, but it was shut up tight. "Tomorrow," she said, and turned toward the bed.

*A*fter months of sleeping on the ground, stretching out in the bed was delightful. There was no shifting and tossing to try to get comfortable; I just lay down. The sheets were linen, and there were thick wool blankets and then quilts, and the room was still warm from the fire. "I could get used to this," Tamar mumbled, and then I fell asleep.

I dreamed of Zhanna again. The first time, I had woken quite certain that it was a *true* dream—that Zhanna had come to me from her dreams to mine. Tonight, though, I wasn't sure whether she was trying to dream of me, or if it rose from some corner of my own soul. She said nothing, and I said nothing, but we stared at each other for a long time across a fire, alone in an Alashi camp. Then the fire flared a little higher and my eyes burned from the smoke, and when I had finished rubbing them, she was gone. And then I remembered that I was banished and would never see her again. The steppe was dark around me like the depths of a mine, and I wrapped my arms around myself against the cold wind.

I had been a misfit child. There were other free

Danibeki families in Elpisia, but their children avoided me. I realized thinking back that this was probably because I was Kyros's child, but at the time I thought it was because my mother liked to pretend we were Greek. We weren't Greek, of course, so I didn't fit in with the Greek children, either. When Kyros had arranged for me to come work for him, I had a purpose and a mentor; I even developed friends among his other servants. Still, I had truly found peers and equals for the first time in the Alashi sword sisterhood. And then I had been cast out. *Alone.* I ached with loneliness.

*But you're not alone,* I heard Zhanna whisper, and this time I thought the message really came from Zhanna. *You're never alone.* She meant the djinni—Zhanna, like Tamar, still worshipped the djinni far more than Prometheus and Arachne. But I thought of Tamar when I heard her words, and smiled, and sank into dreamless sleep.

*H*er name is Zarina," Tamar said. "The bath slave, I mean."

"Does she know where to find Uljas?"

"No. You were right, she doesn't leave the inn much."

Another slave returned with our clothes as we were finishing breakfast. They'd been scrubbed clean and ironed dry; they were perfectly pressed and still warm, with a scent like fresh rosemary. I laid them out to get dressed; the laundering only made it more apparent that we needed to see a tailor. The style made us too distinctive, and the cloth was worn thin.

To my surprise, as soon as we were dressed, Tamar

laid out a set of pots and brushes. "Sit down by the window, where there's light," she said. "I'm going to paint your face."

"Where did you get those?"

"From Zarina, of course." She opened the pots. "Look up. Now hold still."

When she was done, she ran down to the bathhouse to borrow a hand mirror, so that I could inspect her work. The effect was subtle, but definite. She'd made me look older, and more foreign. She'd also used the paints to make it look like I had a healed scar under one eye. "Why did you give me a scar?" I asked.

"It'll draw attention away from the rest of your face. Anyone who knows you well will still recognize you, but people who've met you only a few times, maybe not."

A tailor knocked on our door shortly after Tamar had finished. Zarina had sent for him, we gathered from his murmur as he came in. "You'll be wanting something less conspicuous," he said. "But warm. Practical. For *merchants* such as yourselves. Would you care to pay the rush fee?" We weren't in any particular hurry, but that could always change, so after he took our measurements, we agreed to pay the fee and he assured us that the clothes would be ready within a day.

"Well," Tamar said, staring after him as our door closed. "I was planning to ask more slaves where to find Uljas. I even secured some wine to use as payment."

"We still need to buy a tent," I said. "And horses..."

"How conspicuous *are* these clothes?" Tamar asked, plucking at her trousers.

"With our coats on, no one can really see them. Let's go buy a tent."

The tent maker was able to sell us a tent on the spot. He said that it would hold six people, though looking at the circle of fabric I thought that it might hold six children, if they were small, or six adults if they were stacked on top of each other. At least it would hold the two of us plus Zarina and Uljas, assuming that we all made it out alive, and some of our gear. We'd need a shelter for the horses, as well, before too long, but for now they'd be all right outside.

Tamar was able to slip away and speak quietly to the tent-maker's slaves, offering small bribes of wine in exchange for anything they knew about Uljas. Back out in the street, she told me that one man had thought Uljas's name sounded familiar, but couldn't remember where he'd heard it. "If we can't find anyone else, maybe we can stop back here and see if he remembers..."

"I suppose," I said, hoping that it wouldn't come to that.

It was midday and I was getting hungry. We bought food from a street vendor, skewered pieces of mutton drenched in lemon juice, grilled over a little brazier on the street. When we'd finished that, we bought some apples. The skin was red and gold, the flesh white and crisp. They were small, so we bought a half dozen and ate three apiece.

"Where do we go to buy horses?" Tamar asked as we licked apple juice from our fingers.

"There's a big market near one of the gates—it's where all the itinerant merchants go. Fruit dealers, horse dealers..." Slave dealers. I paused, wondering if Tamar was going to insist that we steal every last slave she laid eyes on.

"Only the rivers' return can free them all," she said. The logic of faith: I'd heard the same statement from my mother when I'd asked her why we were free people when most of the other Danibeki in Elpisia were slaves. When I'd pressed her—because it didn't make sense to me—she had explained that to defeat our people, the Sisterhood of Weavers had bound the northern great river, and had redirected the southern one, using aerika to dig a long tunnel to send the water to Persia. *Yes, but if the rivers came back, how would that free people?* She'd sighed and said that she didn't know, it's just what she'd always been told. Then she amended: "If the rivers *did* return, it would change things. It would mean that the power of the Sisterhood of Weavers had weakened. So maybe it's not so much that the rivers would free the slaves, but that whatever freed the rivers would also free the slaves."

I wasn't going to argue the point with Tamar. Under the circumstances, I was still afraid she'd see a child who reminded her of herself, or some other impossibly tempting target. Fearing that same possibility, too, she kept her head down as we entered the market. That didn't last, though; there were too many interesting things to see.

Kyros had paid me a small salary, and I'd saved it up to spend during trips to Daphnia. On one of my first trips to Daphnia by myself, I'd decided to buy a gift for my mother and wandered the marketplace for hours. I'd been most impressed by the exotic textiles—there was a heavy indigo linen with gold threads running through it, a gauzy cotton that looked like it would float away in the breeze if it weren't rolled up, and silk the color of embers. I'd spent hours examining the different fabrics, running from vendor to vendor in indecision. I'd finally worked up the nerve to begin the bargain, only to find that all were far more expensive than I could afford. The merchant had called after me, "Wait, I'll give you a better price! How much will you offer?" and I'd turned back with an apologetic shrug, sorry to have wasted his time.

In the end, I had bought my mother a silver clasp for her hair. She'd been wearing it the last time I saw her.

Tamar and I made our way past a merchant selling copper pots and sharp knives; the next merchant was selling songbirds, the next sold carved jade bracelets. "Is there anything in particular you want to look for?" I asked when I saw Tamar staring at the bracelets.

She shook herself. "I don't need a bracelet," she said. "We need food, right? Should we start with that?"

The food vendors were in a cluster not too far away. We bought sacks of rice and lentils, dried meat, a small bag of raisins, apples. There were other supplies we were running low on, and we restocked those as well. For good measure, I bought some nice rope in case that came in handy for breaking in and out of houses, and coats and sturdy clothes for Zarina and Uljas. We could barely carry it all, and I started thinking about buying a pack horse as well, if we could afford it. I couldn't remember how the market was laid out, but we heard the whinney of a horse and I followed the sound.

Greek horses and Alashi horses were different. The Alashi horses were smaller, and, I'd realized during my time with the Alashi, hardier. I wasn't sure whether we'd be able to buy Alashi horses in a Greek market, but if we could, that's what I wanted. There were at least a dozen different horse dealers, I saw as we approached; they appeared to specialize. Most sold Greek horses, but a few sold Alashi ones, and there were others who sold horses different in appearance from any I'd seen before. One sold ponies so small that my first thought was that they were meant as mounts for young children; then I saw one whip its head back. Definitely not for children.

I wandered past the pens, mulling over my options, trying not to look too closely at any one horse lest I attract the attention of the dealer. I knew I wanted mares, since both Tamar and I were riding mares already; also, I wanted the sort of sedate, predictable horses that could be trusted with beginning riders. Then I heard a loud nicker and turned to see the most beautiful horse I'd ever seen in my life. She looked like a cross between the Greek and Alashi breeds. She was chestnut, with a coat that shone in the late afternoon sun, and she had just dumped a chagrined Greek officer on his ass in the dust. *Zarina can ride Kara*, I thought instantly. *I want that one.*

The chestnut horse's name was Krina. When I approached her, she looked me in the face for a long moment, and then gave a demure sniff. It was nice to think that she knew just looking at me that I was a better rider than the Greek officer, but some horses just prefer women. For that matter, some horses just prefer men; I tried to avoid riding those.

We bargained for Krina; the same dealer was also able to sell us a gentle, trustworthy older mare for Uljas and a pack horse. This would be quite a herd of animals to take care of, but after we took Zarina and

Uljas up to the steppe, Tamar and I could use the spare horses as remounts like the Alashi did, and travel much faster. From a nearby vendor, we bought some grain so that if we wanted to travel fast, we didn't have to stop early in the day to let the horses forage. That done, we led our new train of horses through the streets to the inn where we were staying, and got them settled in the stable, paying the extra fee and tipping the stable hands for the extra work.

The sun was setting; our errands had taken all day. I felt quite satisfied with our purchases, though. We were already in a far better situation than we'd been when we entered Daphnia. We had a tent so we wouldn't freeze, at least not for a while. We had horses. We had food for our journey up to the steppe. Our parcels were heavy but I felt lighter as we headed up the stairs to our room. Then Tamar opened the door and fell back a step, nearly running into me. "There's someone in our room," she hissed.

"Come in, come in," the voice was saying. "Look, I paid well to get in here; I don't want that wasted. Close the door before someone sees!"

Trapped by the urgency of the voice, Tamar stepped inside; not wanting to let her face whatever or whoever it was alone, I followed her. It was a sorceress, not one I'd ever seen before, pacing our rug. I could almost see the cold fever hovering around her like a swarm of insects, it was so palpable. As soon as we were in the room she darted to the door and closed it.

"Now, where is it? You have more, I'm certain of it. You'll sell to me. Certainly you'll sell, if we can settle on a price. I'll give you a better price than that chiseling cheat you dealt with yesterday. Double whatever she offered."

*Karenite*. "We don't have any more," I said. This was an excellent opportunity to sell our second chunk, but I didn't trust this sorceress. She had bribed her way into our rooms. If discretion was warranted—and surely it was—she was not the person to sell to.

"But you *did* have some! No more means you had it, ah ah ah!" She barely restrained herself from pouncing on me. "You have to sell it to me," she said, her tone wheedling. "How much did she give you? Double. Triple! Whatever you ask!"

"Why are you so desperate?" Tamar asked.

Her eyes grew wide at that and she beckoned us closer. "I know things I'm not meant to know, and I think the Sisterhood suspects. It has been well over half a year since they sent me any for myself. I need to know what they're planning; I need to know who's against me. But for that I need an aeriko, and for that I need soul-stone—do you see my dilemma?"

"Don't you *have* aerika?" Tamar asked.

"Yes, yes, but they're busy." She pulled back and glared at Tamar. "You're being deliberately dense. I don't have time for this. Are you going to sell to me or not?"

"We have nothing to sell," I said.

"It's possible she's telling the truth," she murmured to herself. "It's possible she sold all she had to the first one. She's stupid enough to make it possible, her and her companion. Look," she said, and she was speaking to me again. "If you happen to come across any *more* of it, come to *me* next time. First. Here." She unpinned a brooch from her coat and placed it on our table. It was silver, worked into the shape of an apple tree. "Any silversmith in town should be able to direct you to me if you want to find me." She rose and left. The door swung shut behind her, and this time Tamar barred it.

"Weavers," Tamar said with a faint groan. "Why couldn't we have found something of value to fruiters or silversmiths or horse dealers or *anyone* other than Weavers!"

"They're not usually this difficult," I said. "She's in a particularly bad state."

"They all get bad eventually."

"How many have *you* met?"

"Some of Sophos's slaves used to be owned by Weavers. You want to know how bad a Weaver can get? Ask a slave."

I decided to drop the subject.

When our dinner arrived that night, one of the servants slipped a tiny bottle of scented oil to Tamar. "Zarina thought that after your errands and exertions today you might be interested in a bath."

"Yes," Tamar said immediately. "Tell her we'd like to come down as soon as supper is over."

"What's that about?" I asked as soon as the slaves were gone.

"I asked Zarina to send us a message if she was able to find out anything about Uljas. She's not supposed to leave the bathhouse, so she said she'd send us a message if she had anything to tell us."

"Huh." I took a bite of dinner. It was as good as the previous night's. "Why is she doing us favors?"

"I bribed her."

We went down when we were done eating. Zarina was watching for us anxiously. Tamar passed her a small wineskin, which Zarina put away somewhere safe. "I don't have any information about Uljas but there's something else you should know," Zarina said. "You're being watched."

My first thought was that our interest in Uljas had attracted attention, but Zarina went on to say, "*Are you soul-stone merchants?*"

"Why do you ask?" Tamar asked.

"That's what the Weaver this afternoon thought, but you don't seem to know the protocols..." Zarina looked from Tamar's face to mine, and then slowly raised an eyebrow. "Please tell me there's no soul-stone in your packs." Tamar glanced at me, and we looked back at Zarina.

Tamar passed her another small wineskin. "Tell us what you think we ought to know."

Zarina put away the bribe. "According to the law, all soul-stone is the property of the Sisterhood of Weavers. The High Ones own most of it, and give pieces of it to the rest, but in the last year or two they've gotten a lot stingier with it. The bandits in the north have it, but they don't sell it to the Greeks, so it falls to go-betweens, the soul-stone merchants, to sell it on the black market. Of course there are plenty of sorceresses willing to pay a lot of money for the unofficial supply. But discretion is important, and many sorceresses, especially when they're in the grip of the cold fever, are not particularly discreet."

"What is the penalty for selling black-market karenite?" I asked.

"Soul-stone. Don't call it karenite, or they'll *really* think you're a bandit! The punishment is severe. Death by dismemberment. That's why discretion is important. It's not just selling soul-stone that's illegal, but also just having it, if the Sisterhood didn't give it to you. They don't like executing other sorceresses, but they don't hesitate when they catch a merchant. It's considered theft from the Sisterhood if you have any."

"What about people who just *find* it?" I asked.

"Well, you always have the option of turning it in," Zarina said. "The Sisterhood does give a reward to those who bring Athena's property to her temple and turn it over. It's not nearly as much money as you can get for selling it, but no one will execute you."

Tamar was pale. I thought I probably was, too. "So what do we do now?"

"Well, that depends on whether you have any soul-stone with you right now or not. If you try to sell to a sorceress, you'll likely be followed; any sensible sorceress will refuse to let you in, and a crazy one, well, you run the risk, the *big* risk, of selling to someone the Sisterhood would just as soon dispose of. Then they might come in and arrest all of you. If you try to leave Daphnia, you'll be stopped and searched, and if they find any soul-stone in your bags you'll be executed."

"How did they know to start watching us?" I asked.

"You arrived from the north with nothing obvious to sell and then a day later you had enough money to stay at an excellent inn and buy yourself a nice tent and a couple of horses. *Someone* was bound to notice."

I nodded, feeling extremely foolish.

"Thank you," Tamar said.

"You really ought to at least get wet," Zarina said. "If you come out of the bathhouse as dry and dirty as you were when you went in, *I'll* fall under suspicion."

We stripped off our clothes and let Zarina pour water over our heads; I scrubbed my face and hands, at least, then we dried off and got dressed again. Tamar lagged behind me as I was getting ready to leave; I thought she probably wanted a private word with Zarina, or maybe to pay her another bribe, so I stepped out and lingered for a moment in the courtyard.

Tamar joined me a moment later. "I asked her if she wanted to come with us when we left."

"Did she?"

"No." Tamar paused. "She said she thought we were both likely to end up dead; that if we were lucky we'd be run through with a bandit's sword rather than cut into pieces slowly by a city executioner, and she had no particular desire to share that fate. There are worse things than slavery, she said."

"I can't really blame her."

"Me neither. But we have *got* to get better at this, Lauria, or Uljas and Prax and all the rest are going to feel the same way as Zarina."

We discussed the situation quietly late into the night, and decided that turning the soul-stone in at the temple was our only reasonable option. "We're not doing this to make money," Tamar said. "We're doing this to free slaves. We can't do that if we're dead. And we have enough money right now to last us a while, if we're careful with it."

We went out in the morning with the soul-stone in my pocket. It was easy enough to find the Temple of Athena; we could glimpse the glimmer of white marble like a snowcapped mountain from a long way away. Up close, it resembled an enormous swan's wing, curving upward and coming to a peak. There was a sort of courtyard in front of the temple, also paved with white marble, with a fountain built of white marble in the center. I had visited the temple on previous trips to Daphnia and had found it beautiful. This time it made my stomach tighten in fear. I glanced at Tamar; she was looking around in frank amazement. After a long look, she said, "A white *floor*? It must take about a hundred slaves scrubbing all the time to keep this place clean."

And sure enough, when we went up for a closer look at the vast gates of iron and silver, I saw two Danibeki women polishing them. I'd never noticed them before.

The gates stood open this time of day; the iron and silver bars were bent into the outline of an olive tree on one side of the gates, and a loom on the other. Women and a few men streamed in and out with offerings: chickens, honey, elaborate woven tapestries rolled and tied with ribbon. *If I look around, will I be able to spot the watchers that Zarina said were there?* I decided I didn't care quite enough to try. We'd made our decision.

We went in through the gates, following the press of the crowd. I put my hand in my pocket and touched the cold, rough pebble. *Hard to believe all the trouble we could get into for a little piece of rock.* The temple was as busy inside as out. Visitors left offerings at the altar, then paused to speak with a priestess—to ask for prayers, to receive a blessing, to get some advice. I wondered how we did this. Did we just drop the stone in front of the altar like a jar of honey? Or were we supposed to give it directly to a priestess?

"Good morning," one of the priestesses said to me. *Ah. I guess we really are being watched.* "Are you here for a blessing? To ask for advice on something?"

"I have, um, some property of Athena's which I would like to return," I said. I dug in my pocket. "Am I supposed to give it to you?"

"I think you need to see the high priestess," she said

with a broad smile; I could see her eyes go briefly to someone near us, then back to my face. "Just come with me."

She led us back along the edge, past acolytes that knelt at looms, past little rooms where you could sit to have your dispute mediated, if that was what you needed from the Goddess of Wisdom. The high priestess had an office in the back, apparently; it was much like Kyros's office, complete with a plate of honey cakes to offer visitors. "These young women have something that belongs to Athena," the junior priestess said. The high priestess set aside whatever she was working on and gestured for us to sit down.

I was really hoping to just hand over my karenite, get whatever reward they offered, and *leave*, but I sat. So did Tamar.

The junior priestess smiled and left. The high priestess waited.

I took the karenite out of my pocket and dropped it on the desk. "Is that yours?"

The priestess looked at it. "Yes," she said. "That is ours. Thank you very much for returning it. I'd like to reward your honesty. Will you wait for just a moment?"

She withdrew to a back office, and came out with a small bag—coins, presumably. I doubted they were alexanders. Like the bag we'd gotten from Phoibe, it was beautifully woven cloth; I thought it had probably been made by one of the acolytes we'd seen outside. We'd handed over the karenite, we'd gotten the reward. Was there anything else we needed to do before we got the hell out? "Thank you," I said, and stood up.

"If I may ask," the high priestess said. "Where did you come across this?"

"We found it on the ground while traveling," I said.

"And yet you knew to bring it here. Have you seen a spell-chain up close in the past?"

"We picked it up as a curiosity," I said. "It wasn't until recently that we discovered that it was the property of Athena."

"Where were you traveling?"

I thought for a moment that she suspected we were Alashi. But it would be terribly foolish for the Sisterhood to offer amnesty and then not fulfill their promise; if they did that, nobody would ever bring their karenite in again. *She probably wants to know where they should go look for more. They are running out, just as the rumors say.* "Near Elpisia," I said. "At least, that was the first town we came to once we headed back to civilized parts."

The sorceress nodded. "You may go," she said, so we picked up our bag of money and fled. I didn't look in the bag until we were out of the office. Five alexanders. The price was, indeed, much better on the black market. *It doesn't matter. We'll have enough money to do what we came to do.*

There were a few Weavers coming in to make offerings as I left; one had brought in a huge, elaborate rug she'd presumably woven herself. It was slung across the back of a horse. I glanced over at the slaves, wondering if Tamar could approach them while their mistress was in the temple, and realized that the man holding the horse's bridle was Uljas. In my excitement, I almost stumbled right into Tamar. "Over there," I said when I had regained my composure. "Holding the white horse. That's Uljas."

Tamar looked at him and nodded. She was starting

to say something back when I heard someone—not Uljas—shout, "Lauria!"

Tamar instantly fell back into the temple. My hands turned to ice. *It would be worse to flee—whoever this is, I can probably talk my way out of it, but if I run I'm done for.* Tamar was already pretending not to know me, so I stepped quickly away from her and looked for whoever had called. "Lauria!" the voice called again, much closer this time, and I turned around to face... Myron.

Myron was one of Kyros's *other* trusted servants. One of his *Greek* trusted servants. Myron and I had been sent out together to look for Alibek, a lifetime ago, though I'd found him myself; Myron, as usual, had been more of a hindrance than a help. He had a tendency to act as if I worked for him. I summoned an amiable smile as he clasped my arms. He might be slow-witted, but he hadn't been fooled by the face paint.

"Lauria, it's been *months*!" he said. "Where have you *been*? You wouldn't believe how cagey the old man's been, but then, it's been a rough time for him lately. Let's go get a drink." I started to protest and he said, "Oh come *on,* first round's on me!"

I thought about breaking away from him, claiming that I was still on some mission that couldn't be interrupted, but it occurred to me that I could probably get some useful information from Myron. *But did he have instructions to detain me, and send for Kyros, if he found me?* He didn't have that sort of guile in him, I decided after a few moments of thought. "One drink, Myron, then I have to keep moving. Kyros's instructions didn't mention getting drunk with you."

"An oversight, of course," Myron said. "How could he know we'd run into each other?"

Myron led us quickly through the streets; I suspected that any city he visited, he always knew the closest place to go get drunk. The tavern he dragged me into was reasonably clean, at least. He found us a table and ordered wine. "So where did you get that nasty scar? And tell me where you've been!"

"Sorry, I can't," I said, resisting the urge to finger the scar that Tamar had manufactured for me. "It's still confidential. But I'd love to hear what *you've* been up to."

Myron had never needed much prodding to get him to talk about himself. He'd spent the summer running various errands for Kyros, the sort of thing I'd used to do. He'd carried messages to garrisons, sorceresses, and merchants, and brought home messages and observations to Kyros. He'd audited someone's books, purchased a set of horses, and delivered a sealed pouch. To my disappointment, he didn't seem to know anything that would be of use to me; it had been a very busy summer (not surprising, since I'd been gone—he was doing his own job and mine as well) and he'd barely seen Kyros.

"You said things had been rough for him," I said. "What's been going on?"

"His wife took a turn for the worse." I knew what that meant: Kyros's wife had been gently cut loose from the Sisterhood of Weavers because her moods became erratic so quickly. "Then Kyros did, too. I don't know why Kyros is so changeable—*he's* no sorceress."

"It's the spell-chains," I said.

"Oh, that reminds me, another thing that went wrong—one of his spell-chains just quit working! He sent the aeriko out and it never came back. Isn't that the strangest thing you have ever heard?"

"Well, that explains why I haven't heard from him," I said. "Are you heading back to Elpisia soon?"

"Yeah, probably tomorrow."

So if I wanted to send a message to Kyros, Myron would be a good carrier. I sipped my wine and debated whether to send one. The trouble was that any message I sent, even false information, would likely teach Kyros *something*. The most important thing was going to be to get away from Daphnia as fast as I could. I wound up just smiling mysteriously over my wine, which had the benefit of irritating Myron more since he figured it meant I knew some secret he wasn't in on.

As we were getting up to leave, Myron leaned forward and whispered, "He has you tracking down the black marketers, doesn't he? The soul-stone merchants."

"What do you know about that?" I hissed.

"Not much." A self-satisfied grin spread from cheek to cheek. "I do know that the high-muckity-muck Weavers think they should be the only source of the stuff, and want to squash the competition. And Kyros is always looking for ways to be friends with the Weavers. So that is what you're doing?"

"I can't tell you," I said coolly, and we stood up to go.

*I* took a roundabout path back to our inn as soon as Myron was out of site. No doubt Uljas was long gone; I hoped Tamar had followed him. I checked one more time to make sure Myron hadn't followed me before stepping inside the gate. Tamar was waiting in our room. "Who was that?" she asked.

"Someone I used to know."

"An old friend?"

"No. Well, I always had to *act* friendly, but he wasn't a friend. His name is Myron, and he's an idiot, which is just as well. Did you follow Uljas?"

"Of course. He belongs to a Weaver named Kallistrate. She's only a short walk from the temple; she must've brought the horse along to show off what a big, heavy rug she was offering to Athena."

"We need to come up with a way to get Uljas out *tonight*."

"I can show you the house. Or you can find it yourself—it's near the Temple of Athena and uses a lot of the same marble. There's a big carving out front that looks like an eagle, painted to be lifelike. I don't know how you'll get Uljas out, though."

"We should settle up with the innkeeper and get the horses out of the city," I said.

"I wanted to talk with Zarina..."

"She made her choice, didn't she?"

"I hoped..." Tamar shrugged. "You're right. She made her choice."

We paid the innkeeper, took our string of horses, and left the city. If anyone was still watching us, they made no attempt to stop us or search our bags. "I'm going to need you to wait here..."

"Lauria!"

"I'm not just trying to run off without you. Look, *someone* has to wait with the horses. Leaving them tethered right outside the city is just about asking for them to be stolen."

"I want to risk it. I think you need me."

"I don't even know what I'm going to do."

"That's why you need me."

"I need you to guard the horses. What are we going to do if they're stolen?"

"Walk? We walked the first time we went to the Alashi. Oh, all right. But I'm going to hire an assistant to hold the horses if you ever try to use this excuse again." Tamar dismounted and pulled several things out of her pack. "This wineskin is spirits of wine. It's better than wine—stronger. If you need to bribe a slave, this is what you should offer. As for the gate— just remember, the fastest way out of any city after dark is to bribe the guards."

Sundown was close. I made it back into the city just before they shut the gate. The temperature was falling fast, and my pulse quickened. I had no idea how I was going to manage this. Well, the first step was to find the house...I went back to the Temple of Athena and walked around until I found the place Tamar had described. It was shut up tight. If I knocked, someone might answer, but then what? Hand over the spirits of wine and ask for the doorkeeper to turn a blind eye for ten minutes while I made off with Uljas? That seemed....risky.

*This will be easier under cover of darkness. I'll wait awhile.*

I found a quiet spot in the shadow of a nearby building. The sorceress had neighbors, of course: some closely packed houses, a locked up silversmith, and—a few doors down—a neighborhood tavern. I could smell meat roasting. My mouth watered. I'd forgotten to bring food with me to eat while I waited, and I was tempted to go into the tavern to buy dinner, but what if I ran into Myron again? Better to keep hiding. I was nervous enough that I'd have had to force the food down anyway.

True night fell and the street became quieter. I had plenty of ideas, but they all seemed bad. *I could climb over the wall and go look for him in the stable. I could bribe someone to pass him a message and see if he could make his own way out.*

I was freezing cold; my feet were starting to become numb. I bounced up and down in place. I should have gone for dinner earlier in the evening, just to stay warm. I found myself thinking about the time Zhanna, the Alashi shaman, had tried to teach me to meditate. I had closed my eyes and breathed deeply, and gotten so itchy and twitchy that Zhanna had started laughing at me. Tamar had fallen asleep.

"Lauria."

Not Myron's voice: this voice was a hiss, like a snake. I turned and saw a shimmer in the air. *A djinn. Kyros's djinn.*

My heart began to knock in my ears so hard that my head hurt. *I thought it would take longer to find me than this. Much longer. And with the face paint—it must have wanted to find me.* "Are you alone?" I asked, my voice trembling. "Or did Kyros send another djinn to watch us?" It was silent—unhelpful. I clenched my teeth and willed my voice to steady. *I can banish it. It won't return to Kyros, so I have nothing to fear. He hasn't found me.* "Did Kyros tell you what I did for your fellow djinn? Because I could do the same for you. But I want you to answer me."

"Kyros tells me nothing," the djinn said. It paused, and then added, "But there are no others at close hand."

"Good. What message did Kyros send?"

"Kyros sent this message: *Lauria, please tell me your status. I know something has gone wrong. Please reassure me that you're still alive.*"

Well, at least it didn't sound like Myron had been able to send him a message yet. Rather than sending a message back to Kyros, I stretched out my hand and touched the shimmer in the air. My hand prickled, as if it had fallen asleep. "Return to the Silent Lands, lost one of your kind, and trouble us no more."

The last djinn had screamed; this djinn whirled in the air for a moment, silently, then I felt it slip through me into darkness like water swirling down a pipe into a vast reservoir. *Thank you,* it whispered. Then, an even fainter whisper: *Kyros doesn't know yet that you have left his service. But he will soon.*

Darkness again, and quiet. As my panic ebbed, my hands and feet felt even colder. *I need to act. If I can free djinni, then surely I can free Uljas—if I have the courage to act, and not stand here freezing in the dark.*

Something fluttered overhead and I ducked, my heart pounding again. As it sailed off, I got a good look at it. It was a white owl on the hunt. The priestesses of the temple kept owls, to honor Athena; I was near the temple, so it wasn't surprising. *It's an omen,* I thought, and then resolutely told myself: *No, it's just a temple pet. If it's a message, it's from the djinni. You have nothing to fear from the owl, because you are not a mouse. You have nothing to fear from Athena, because you belong to us.* The wind brought the scent of acrid smoke from the sacred fire burning deep inside the temple, and that gave me an idea. *Fire and venom against our enemies.* Perhaps I could set the house on fire.

It was too bad that I had no fire arrows like we'd

used on our raid of the Greek garrison when I was riding with the Alashi Sisterhood...but surely I could find something that would burn well. I dug quickly through my bag. Would spirits of wine burn? Perhaps, but lamp oil would burn better. I ripped some loose cloth off my old shirt and wet it with the oil. It would need to be wrapped around something that could be thrown. I found a crumbled piece of broken brick in the street and wrapped the greasy cloth around it.

I went to the upwind side of Kallistrate's household and considered whether I could throw well enough to get it over the wall. *Ha. I should have brought Tamar after all. She could get it over a wall three times this high and right through the sorceress's bedroom window besides.* Well, I'd just have to take my best shot. I muttered a quick prayer to Prometheus and Arachne, echoing the words that Janiya had said before our raid: *as a sacrifice in their honor, we use their gifts.* I was using fire, at least. *Give me the spark I need. Carry my gift over the wall.*

I took out flint, iron, and tinder; the tinder caught readily, and I lit the cloth. It flared up immediately, almost burning my hand, so my throw was panicky. For a moment I thought it would bounce off the wall and drop back down onto me, but it cleared the edge by inches. *Hopefully it will land on something that will burn.*

I waited. *Maybe it landed on something that won't burn. Maybe it went out as it flew over. How long should I wait before trying again?* But I realized quickly I already saw smoke—and sparks. *Uh-oh.*

I'd thought that I would just wait a few minutes and let the sorceress's household discover the fire on their own, but my spark had apparently fallen on ready fuel—dry straw, lamp oil, I had no idea, but I could see the flicker of flame and the shadow of smoke boiling up from it. In a minute or two, this fire could easily burn out of control. I ran to the front door and pounded on it with my fists. *"Fire!"* I shouted. *"Fire! Your house is on fire!"*

Inside, I could hear a shouted oath and running feet. *"Get out, get out!"* I shouted. "You could all be killed, get out of there!"

Someone inside believed me; the door banged open and terrified slaves and servants spilled out into the street. "Get buckets," someone was shouting. "No, not back in there, run to the neighbors! Has anyone seen Kallistrate? Surely her aerika . . ."

The people spilling out now were coughing, rubbing eyes that streamed from the smoke. Slaves and servants, women and men; I didn't see the sorceress. But Uljas? *There.* He'd already drifted to the edge. I approached him and caught his arm. "Would you be free?" I hissed into his ear. "I can take you to the Alashi. But you have to come *now.*"

He was clearly half blinded from the smoke, but he closed his fist over my wrist. "I'll come," he said.

I led him swiftly away from the burning house. *I hope I didn't hurt anyone. I didn't* mean *to hurt anyone . . .* Uljas said nothing as he followed me. After a few minutes I stopped and took out the extra coat for him to put on. When I looked up, he was staring at me. Like Myron, he was not fooled by the face paint; he clearly knew who I was.

"I thought maybe Burkut had gotten away, and sent someone," he said. "But it's *you.*"

"What I did was wrong," I said. "I was wrong to take you back to Kyros. I'm trying to make amends."

"I swore that if I ever saw you again, I would kill you."

I fell back a step, though he was unarmed and I was not. "We don't have a lot of time. I'm here to take you to the Alashi, if you still want to go." He looked furious. I didn't remember him looking this angry even when I took him back to slavery. "Do you want to come with me, or do you want to stay? I'm not going to try to drag you out of Daphnia."

"I'll come," he said, through clenched teeth.

The walk to the gate seemed to take a terribly long time. *Surely the sorceress will be distracted by the fire. Surely they won't suspect yet it was started by arson. Surely Uljas isn't going to pick up a brick and hit me in the back of the head. Surely.* Tamar was right, the fastest way out was to bribe a guard; these walls were too high to climb easily, especially in wind like we had tonight.

The guard post was quiet; the gate, of course, was closed. I banged on the door to wake the guard. He looked out at us dubiously. "We received an urgent message and need to leave," I said.

He came out, yawning. "Gate opens at dawn."

"We can't wait that long. Surely there's a fee . . ."

He named a sum, I paid, and the gate was opened a crack for us to slip out. *That went more smoothly than I expected.* The part of me that had once been Kyros's willing servant thought, *That went more smoothly than it should have. Well. It's not my problem anymore.*

We found our way to Tamar. It was too dark to ride, but with lanterns we could lead the horses and put some distance between ourselves and the city. "How did it go?" Tamar asked.

"I set a fire," I said. "It proved an effective distraction."

I had wondered if Uljas would stay with us once we were out of Daphnia, or if he'd immediately go his own way. Tamar, however, simply handed him the reins of one of the horses and set off, and Uljas followed her. *I guess he's coming.* I brought up the rear, feeling some relief at not having my sworn enemy right behind me.

I was just starting to think that it was getting light enough to ride when Uljas spoke. "So, Lauria. What made you decide to get into the business of stealing slaves?"

"*Freeing* slaves," I said.

He turned and gave me a long, guarded look. Tamar edged closer to me.

"Look," I said. "You can go wherever you want. We'll take you to the Alashi, if you want to go there. Do you?"

"What if I don't?"

"Go where you like. I'm not going to stop you. You're free."

"What if I go to Kyros and tell him where you are right now?"

"You'd be a fool. He'd send you back to the sorceress." Uljas's face twisted into a faint smile at my words. No, not at my words; at my eyes. He'd seen that the idea frightened me.

"Does he know where you are right now?" Uljas asked. "Perhaps he'd pay well for that intelligence. Buy me back from Kallistrate, take me to the temple, and set me free before the priests, so that I could truly go anywhere. Like you."

"What do you want?" I asked.

"I want to know what you're doing. And why."

"Can we talk about this later?" I asked, with a desperate glance back toward Daphnia. "They must have missed you by now, and they will send out searchers. We need to get farther away from the city to be safe." He was still giving me a skeptical look.

"If you're going to betray Lauria to Kyros, you'd better start by getting away from Daphnia," Tamar said, her voice exasperated. "*I* don't want to be executed for freeing you, so Lauria and I are going to get on our horses and ride right now. If you want to come along, we have a horse for you. If you want to stand here all day, go right ahead, but *I* am riding." She mounted. I'd expected Uljas to need help, but he'd apparently learned how to ride while working in the stables; he mounted without difficulty. *I guess he's coming along. That means he trusts us. Surely that's a good sign.*

It was difficult to have a conversation on horseback, especially when traveling quickly, and Uljas needed to devote his attention to riding. I spent the day fretting about Uljas, and about the djinn Kyros had sent after me. I needed to tell Tamar about that, but not now, not when Uljas could overhear; he knew more than enough already. How much longer until Kyros knew for certain that I was no longer serving him? And once he was certain, what would he do? Would he realize that I was the one making his djinni disappear? If he did, the only logical course would be to send a djinn to *watch* me and report back with my location, since having the djinn approach me to carry threats would mean losing that djinn.

Of course, that was assuming he was able to get another spell-chain. He'd had two, and I'd freed both of

those djinni now. Would the Weavers give him another? Would they forbid him to send it out looking for
me, or would the strangeness of the situation—djinni
didn't just go *missing*—mean that they would give him
a dedicated searcher? How long till it found me, if they
did?

Dusk fell and we made camp. I thought we were a
good distance from Daphnia. Chances were good that
the sorceress would assume Uljas had seen his opportunity and run; her searchers would be in an area near
the city. Tomorrow we would have an easier ride.

Tamar fixed a cold dinner and the three of us shared
it. Uljas ate quickly, as if he thought we'd take it away
from him. "So you want to take me to the steppe," he
said when he'd finished.

"If you want to go."

"Then what?"

I wet my lips. "When I worked for Kyros, I took six
slaves back to him. You, Nika, Prax, Burkut, Thais,
and Alibek. Alibek freed himself a second time. I found
Nika and freed her and her daughter, and I got you
out. That leaves Prax, Burkut, and Thais."

"So you're half done." His voice was mocking.

"I guess."

"How are you going to get Prax out? Wasn't he sold
to a mine?"

"Yes. And I don't know."

"Burkut was sold to a farm south of here."

"I was going to free Burkut next."

"Next? You're going to take me up to the steppe,
then ride all the way back down here for him? You'll
be waist-deep in snow by the time you're back at the
steppe. You'll all freeze."

"The Alashi spend all winter on the steppe."

"You're not Alashi."

"What would *you* have me do?"

"I don't care what you do," Uljas said, "unless you kill Burkut trying to drag him up to the steppe just to atone for your own past mistakes. I like Burkut. We used to be friends. I'd rather he not freeze to death in a snowstorm while his failed-bandit rescuer insists that she knows what she's doing."

My face burned so much that I started to sweat. "You have a point," I said, the words sticking in my throat. "It would be easier if I go to Burkut's farm next. But it could be dangerous. I guess I didn't want to make you come along."

"I thought you weren't *making* me come anywhere."

"Do you want to *walk* from here to the steppe? It's a long way."

"No," Uljas said. "I want to help free Burkut."

I glanced up at him; his eyes glinted a little in the dark. "All right," I said. "We'll head back south tomorrow."

It took a long time to go to sleep that night; Uljas snored. When I finally fell into a doze, I found myself by the fire in my room back at the inn. Zhanna sat across from me. "What an interesting place to find you," she said.

"It's the inn I stayed at with Tamar," I said.

"Are those cakes? And tea? My goodness, it's warm in here." She looked around. "I guess I didn't need to worry about you after all."

"Well, I'm not here *now*. This is just where I stayed for a couple of days. Then we had to leave."

"How are you doing?"

"I'm not alone," I said.

"Who are you with?"

It wasn't Zhanna's voice. I looked at the chair again, and Kyros was there. "Wait, wait, don't go," he said, as if I was going to disappear like Zhanna had. "This is such a comfortable spot, so warm." I *did* feel warm; the fire leapt on the hearth, casting strange shadows on the hangings that covered the walls. "Let's chat for a few minutes."

"Send a djinn," I said, backing away.

"Yes, yes, but I need to know *where*."

"I don't want to talk to you," I said. "This is *my* dream, I shouldn't have to talk to you if I don't want to."

"With whom would you prefer to speak?"

"No one," I said.

"How about your mother?" Kyros was gone, and my mother waited in the doorway of her apartment.

"Come here, darling," she said. "Let me comb your hair."

I touched my hair, shorn to chin length. "There isn't much to comb."

"That's all right. Come here, darling, and let me comb it." I settled myself warily at my mother's feet. She took out a comb of carved bone and began to run it carefully through my hair, making little fussing noises over the dirt and sweat and tangles. She pulled me back against her, and whispered in my ear, *"Do not trust Kyros, even here, even when you think we're alone. He watches, he always watches. He hears my words."* She raised her voice to a normal pitch. "Darling, I miss you, please come back to me. Kyros says you can. Come back. Come back."

"I can't," I said. "Tell him I can't. Tell him he has to trust me." I caught her hand in mine. *I need to warn her.* "I think Kyros will use you against me if he can. Don't trust him."

"When has Kyros not done right by you?" She was combing my hair again, speaking loudly like she thought she was being overheard. "Just come back. I'm sure we can sort this all out."

"How did you get here? I've never dreamed of you before. Who brought you here?"

"I'm always here. Always," my mother said, but her hand was slipping away from mine. I felt a feather-light kiss brush the top of my head and then I woke to the sound of snoring in my ear. *Let it be morning, please,* I thought, and it was.

# CHAPTER THREE

*B*urkut's farm was in a temperate area south of Daphnia, along the Chirchik River. Canals diverted some of the water through fields that grew lush and green even in the worst heat of summer; this time of year, the farms along the Chirchik were the muddy green of plants that were getting plenty of water but not enough warmth. Soon, though not yet, they'd be covered in snow.

Burkut's farm, like many in this particular area, was owned by the Sisterhood itself, and managed by a steward; its fruits were used to feed the garrisons along the northern border. There were enough other people on the road that we attracted no special attention. I had ridden this route any number of times for Kyros, but for the first time I found myself noticing every slave I saw: the muddy column of men and women marching under guard from the market where they were purchased, the line of slaves chopping frost-killed vegetation in the fields so that it would rot and enrich the earth for next year's growing season, the slaves in an orchard gathering up the wind-fallen apples. The guards looked different to me, too. I noticed their weapons, and found myself nervously avoiding anyone's gaze. There was no reason to expect to run into someone I knew, but I still worried about it every time we passed soldiers.

The trip took several days. We were fortunate enough to have a spell of beautiful fall weather. The sky was blue and cloudless, the sun warm, and the breezes gentle. I wanted to conserve the grain for our trip to the steppe, so we stopped each day in midafternoon to let our horses graze. Krina was busily showing the other mares that she was boss; that was fine with Kara and Kesh, who'd been anything but dominant back with the Alashi herd. Still, Kara seemed to miss me; I had Uljas ride her, and used the other horse we'd bought at the market to carry some of the food.

It was a quiet trip. Uljas was not inclined to talk to either of us. Instead, after we stopped for the day, he would go for a walk, apparently just to avoid us. After the first day, I found myself wishing that Uljas would ask me again *why*. I wanted to tell him my story. I wanted him not to hate me, and I knew that he did. *Maybe after I get Burkut out...*

We moved off the road as we got close and camped about an hour's ride from the farm where Burkut had been sold. I knew right where it was, though not what Burkut was doing, exactly, or whether he was even still owned by this farm.

I'd carried messages to this farm for Kyros a couple of times. The steward, Lycurgus, was Kyros's cousin. He was also a habitual drunkard, though I didn't imagine that his superiors were acquainted with that fact. Kyros was fond of him mostly because they'd played together as children, and had me visit occasionally to keep an eye on things.

The farm itself wasn't walled in, but there were guards. If I approached Burkut during the day, they'd notice. During the night, the slaves were shut in to windowless bunkhouses. If I tried to get Burkut out of a bunkhouse, that would also be noticed. My instinct was to try during the night; that's when I'd freed Uljas and Nika. But in Burkut's case, it might actually be easier to get him away during the day.

There were always occasions when the guards' attention wandered. They were thinly spread. With a little luck and a distraction, I could approach Burkut and get him out without anyone noticing, probably until the next head count. On the other hand, my luck had been mixed so far. If I asked Tamar to create a distraction and things went badly, we could *all* end up caught. And head counts of field slaves were pretty frequent, since the opportunity to simply walk away—as Burkut had already done once—was there.

I mulled my options as I watched the horses graze. The last time I'd come, I'd ridden Zhade, first of all, and I'd come with a letter from Kyros. Lycurgus had treated me as a guest rather than a visiting servant because he knew Kyros liked me, and he wanted to stay in Kyros's good graces. We'd had dinner together, and although he'd tried to impress me with his competence, he'd gotten himself so completely drunk over the course of the meal that he'd had trouble standing up by the end. I'd wondered just how drunk he got when he *wasn't* trying to impress someone, and had said as much to Kyros. Kyros had responded by dispatching the competent son of a friend to be an "assistant" to the steward—someone young enough not to try to get the steward removed, at least not for a few years, but old enough to run the place on his own. Solon, that was the name of the assistant. I'd never met him.

*What if I went and asked Solon for a job?*

Working for them—at least for a few days—would give me the leisure to figure out exactly where on the farm Burkut worked. I could approach him without exciting suspicion and probably even take off with him and no one would notice until evening. The risk of being recognized by anyone other than Burkut, even without face paint, was low. Certainly lower than my chances of being caught if I simply approached Burkut in the field and attempted to spirit him away. I'd steer clear of Lycurgus, just in case, but as he would probably be drunk most of the time, I didn't expect that to be too difficult.

I chewed on my fingernail. My hands were filthy. I would need different clothes; mine were too new to fit my story. Maybe I could trade with Uljas. His showed about the right amount of wear. The big farms preferred to hire Greeks as guards, but free people of mixed Greek and Danibeki blood, like me, often found themselves in positions like the one I was going to ask for.

I took Tamar aside to tell her my thoughts. "How are you going to let us know if you need help?" Tamar said. "You might want us to create a distraction."

"I'll slip away, I guess. Unless you think you'll be able to come talk to me in my dreams—Zhanna said we ought to be able to do that."

"I'll give it a try, but I've been trying to talk to Zhanna and it hasn't worked yet," Tamar said. "Are you going today or tomorrow?"

I looked up at the sky; the sun was still pretty high. "Today," I said.

"Riding or walking?"

"Walking. I need to look poor." I turned toward Uljas. "This will work better if we trade some of our clothes," I said. "Shirts, at least, so that not all of my clothing is new."

Uljas looked me over, then shrugged. I'd expected him to step into the tent, but instead he pulled his shirt over his head and handed it to me. His scars, in the afternoon light, stood out in sharp relief. They were bad scars, the kind that would go down through the skin and ache when you did hard labor. He didn't have to say anything for me to know that they were from the beating he was given after I had brought him back. I swallowed hard, then pulled off my own shirt for him to wear.

My coat was old; my boots were reasonably well worn. I put my coat on and started digging through the saddle packs. A person looking for work wouldn't show up utterly empty-handed; I needed a reasonably convincing travel pack. I put in a blanket, one of the cooking pots, a little food, and a few coins from the remaining money. The rest of the money would stay with Tamar. "Take good care of the horses."

"Good luck," Tamar said, and gave me a tight hug. "Prometheus and Arachne go with you."

I felt perfectly calm, and at the same time far more nervous than I'd felt when I'd gone after Uljas and Nika. *This isn't like going to Sophos's,* I told myself. *I was posing there as a slave.* My stomach was still churning. I squeezed Tamar's hand and started back toward the road.

*A* rutted wagon track led from the road back into the farm. There was a little shack for a guard post, but it was unmanned. I walked along the wagon track, trying to stay out of the mud, and reciting my story to myself as I went. *My name is Xanthe. I'm out of work and need a job. I used to work for a sorceress in Daphnia, but she killed herself in her melancholia and her nephew who inherited her estate didn't want to hire me. I don't have any references because of that, but I'll work for room and board through the winter and if you don't like my work, you don't have to keep me on in the spring...*

"My name is Xanthe," I said when I was shown into the office of the assistant steward. It had to be Solon, I thought. He was young, sober, and a bit harassed-looking. "I need a job."

"Where are you from?" he asked.

"Daphnia. I used to work for a sorceress there."

"Did she fire you?"

"No, she died." I bit my lip. "It was sudden. She—well, you know how sorceresses are. And her nephew didn't want to keep me on."

"Was she killed by an aeriko?"

"No, she killed herself." I flushed and swallowed hard. "Her nephew kept me on while he settled the estate and then let me go. I've been looking for work ever since." My hand strayed to my nearly empty purse, and I firmly put it back at my side.

"What can you do?" Solon shoved aside his stack of papers and looked at me with some interest.

"Well, I can use a sword and I ride well. I've managed slaves, both in the house and in Hypatia's stable. I can keep accounts. Almost anything, really, though I don't know a whole lot about farming itself." He was still looking a little skeptical so I added, "I really need a roof over my head right now. I'll work for room and board through the winter, so long as you promise to feed me well and give me a bed somewhere warm."

Solon's eyes brightened. "You're hired. The account books are in that room." He pointed to a door. "The head steward has been... Well, his handwriting isn't the best. If you can make any sense out of them by spring, I'll keep you on permanently."

The door led to a room crammed with shelves full of paper. Account books, ledgers, lists of purchases, bills of sale...all crammed together in an unsorted heap. Just looking at the mess gave me the beginnings of a headache. I tried to look undaunted; glancing back, I could see that Solon was looking at me. I summoned up a confident nod for him, and he chuckled to himself and went back to his own stack of papers.

What I really wanted to do was start looking for Burkut. In an hour or two, I'd tell Solon that I wanted to walk around the farm and get a sense for what they grew, how big it was, and so on—that seeing it would help me make sense of the books. Which was true, actually. *But first I should probably at least poke through the mess a little bit*. I pulled down one of the books at random. This one had been neatly kept and was easy to understand, but from the dates it was several years old. I looked at the book next to it on the shelf and it was much more recent, and utterly haphazard. Well. It had been obvious that Lycurgus had been going downhill.

I looked through the rest of that shelf. Things were in no particular order. *If I were doing this for real...* I felt a weird pang. If I *had* been the cast-off faithful servant that I was pretending to be, I would be truly grateful to Solon. Unraveling the messy accounts would be tedious but satisfying. And my life would be so very much simpler.

*Well, if I were doing this for real, I'd probably decide that only the last two years were really important. And that's probably when things really started to go downhill.* I pulled everything down from that shelf and started to sort. Older than two years went back on the shelf, newer went in a pile for me to sort through later. I was startled to realize that I was having to strain to see the books; I had gotten so absorbed in my task that the afternoon had slipped away. *Damn.* Well, I would go out to survey the farm early in the morning. I hoped the weather would be fair, or at least dry.

I came hesitantly out of the room. "How's it coming?" Solon asked.

"I think I should at least have everything *sorted* in a month or two," I said.

He laughed shortly. "That's farther than I've ever gotten," he said. "Why don't you go have some dinner? There's a meal hall in the next building over, the one with the brick. Most of the guards will be eating soon. Why don't you go join them? As for sleeping . . . I don't want to put you in with the guards for the night; half of them snore. There's a little room over the kitchen that should be pretty warm. It's used for storage. Take a pallet out of the guards' bunkroom and put it up there for now. We'll figure out something better tomorrow."

"Thank you," I said, and headed off to get something to eat.

The clamor when I opened the door was almost overwhelming; I paused for a moment to get my bearings. Both guards and slaves ate here, apparently; slaves filled most of the tables, but a table of Greek and mixed-blood men near the kitchen were obviously the guards. It was a big stone hall, with rough walls of dirty plaster and a floor made from even dirtier wood; the tables were equipped with long benches, and the guards ate the same fare as the slaves, though their table was closest to the warmth of the hearth. The hall was well lit with oil lamps, and the clamor was just the sound of cheerful conversation. It was overwhelming only because I'd spent the afternoon in a nearly silent closet, and the last few days on the road. And because it had been a long time since I'd taken a meal in such a loud, crowded, raucous environment, unless you counted my beer with Myron.

If Burkut saw me, he might recognize me. Well, he had no reason to know that I wasn't here on Kyros's behalf. And I remembered him as being fairly timid. I thought it was unlikely that he would draw attention to himself by shouting my real name out in the meal hall.

I tried to slip quietly into the kitchen to ask for some food, but that effort was doomed to failure; I was new, and a stranger. "Hey lady!" One of the guards stood up as I passed by. "We heard you spent the afternoon in Solon's office! Is he as stiff from the waist down as he is from the waist up?"

*This will go better if I can laugh it off convincingly.* "All I can tell you is, he's not much of a bookkeeper," I said with a cheerful shrug. "Can you tell me where to get something to eat?"

"I'll show you." The dirty-minded guard stepped over the bench and offered me his hand. "I'm Demetrios."

I shook his hand. "Xanthe," I said.

"The kitchen's this way." We went through a

doorway; the kitchen was warm and smelled like goat stew and fresh bread. A young girl jumped up to fill a bowl for me and tear off a piece of bread; Demetrios filled a cup of cider for me from a large barrel, and re-filled his own cup while he was at it. I investigated the stew with my spoon and found meat, cabbage, carrots, and beans. "Solon may be wound tighter than a bow-string, but he feeds us well," Demetrios said. "Come sit down."

The guards scooted over on the bench to make a spot for me; I found myself wedged between Demetrios and his neighbor. "I heard you came from Daphnia; how'd you end up *here*?" someone asked. I gave them an edited version of my story; they nodded sympathet-ically and some of them chimed in with stories of their own. I made sympathetic noises and then bent my head over my food, listening to the conversation as I ate. It turned to the harvest; it was mostly in, but the rain had delayed some of the fall work. Not all the apples were picked yet, and windfall apples were rotting on the ground because no one had had time to gather them up. Demetrios thought that Solon would probably send everyone to the orchards in the next day or two. Once all the apples were in, it would be time to start making cider, which was good news to the guards, as supplies from last year were running low. I took a sip of my own cider. It was sour and strong, and I put the cup down. I'd need to finish it or Demetrios would comment, but I'd have to drink it slowly. I wanted a clear head.

I tried to discreetly look over the tables of slaves, wondering if I could spot Burkut. I didn't see him, but it would have been hard to see him in this crowd. The slaves were damp and muddy but warmly dressed, and the kitchen slaves came around several times with the pots of soup to refill bowls; it wasn't just the guards who were well fed.

"I heard that Solon was the assistant steward," I asked during a lull. "Is there someone else who's actually in charge?"

There was a lot of derisive laughter at that. "Lycurgus is the name of the steward," someone said. "He's in charge if you can hang him up and dry him out long enough to get anything sensible out of him. Solon doesn't usually bother."

"Solon is *wise*," someone else said. "He'd run this place better drunk than Lycurgus did even when he was sober."

"I'd pay money to see Solon drunk."

"What do you suppose he'd be like?"

"He'd probably be a cool, responsible drunk. He'd take off his own boots and settle down on his bed before he even started drinking."

"Well, and Lycurgus does that, doesn't he?"

"Not ever getting *out* of bed is not the same thing."

It didn't sound like I needed to worry about running into Lycurgus.

"Speaking of beds, where are you sleeping?" Demetrios asked with a leer.

"If I decide I want visitors I'll be sure to let you know," I said, which elicited a round of reasonably friendly laughter. "Solon said I should take a pallet out of the bunkroom, though. If someone could show me where that is, I'd appreciate it."

"Let's give her Damon's bed," someone muttered, inspiring more laughter.

I trailed along with the guards as they escorted the slaves back to the slave bunkhouses. The slaves slept in a single long house; I caught a glimpse of the interior and they were packed tightly, but that seemed to be more for warmth than to save space. I thought I saw Burkut, but when I turned for a better look I realized it was someone else. *What if he got sold to another farm?* I bit my lip and refused to let myself reflect on that. *If he was sold, then somewhere in the financial records it should say where.*

The slaves were locked in for the night, and the guards retired to their own bunkhouse. It was warmer and more spacious, and immaculately clean; no doubt it was the responsibility of some of the slaves to clean it, but Solon must have to lean pretty hard on the guards to get them to keep their belongings so orderly.

Demetrios found me an empty bed and let me gather up the bedding. "You'd be welcome to sleep in here," he said with another leer.

"Solon already warned me that you all snore," I said, "but thanks ever so much for the offer." I headed back to the kitchen.

The storage room was easy enough to find and, as Solon had said, quite warm. I made my bed, shoved a barrel in front of the door just in case someone had guessed where I was sleeping and decided to make a late-night visit, and lay down, pulling my coat over myself. It was a warm bed, and though it was harder than my bed at the guesthouse in Daphnia, it was a great deal softer than the ground.

I was bone-weary and my head hurt from trying to decipher Lycurgus's spidery handwriting all afternoon, but I was too tightly wound to sleep. I kept running through the events of the day, thinking about all the things that could still go wrong. Also, I felt guilty for my deception; Solon had treated me quite fairly and it hurt to poison the cup of his trust.

*Kyros betrayed me, and Sophos betrayed me, but Solon has played fair with me, at least so far. I'm the one betraying him.*

I couldn't think about this right now or I was going to mess something up. But my doubts kept eating at me, keeping me wide eyed in my bed. At least I never slept deeply enough that night for Kyros to meddle with my dreams, but Tamar couldn't visit me, either, even if she was trying.

I woke stiff and sleepy while the kitchen slaves were making breakfast, and picked my way downstairs, yawning. One of the slaves sympathetically waved me to a spot in the corner of the kitchen and gave me some tea and porridge with honey.

I ate my breakfast and watched the farm wake for the day. Solon wandered into the kitchen a short time after I did, his hair damp and neatly combed. One of the slaves loaded up a tray to be taken elsewhere—I suspected that was for Lycurgus. Solon followed the servant with the tray; I wondered if he made a daily report to Lycurgus even if he was still passed out unconscious on his bed. A short time after that, the guards brought in the slaves and everyone else had breakfast.

Since no one had made any attempt to shoo me out of the kitchen I stayed where I was, drinking tea. As they were finishing breakfast, Solon returned and gave the guards their assignments for the day. I could overhear him from the kitchen, and it sounded like everyone was being put to work in the orchard, as the guards had expected. I drained the last of my tea and decided it was time to get to work. I reached the office a few minutes before Solon did. When he arrived, he was clearly pleased to see me already at work.

I was determined this morning not to let my job distract me from my real task. At midmorning, I would ask for permission to go out and survey the farm itself. It was a sunny day; I'd just keep an eye on the angle of the sunshine.

I started to step out just as someone was coming in to Solon's office. I ducked instinctively back inside and watched cautiously from the shadowed part of the room. *Lycurgus. So much for thinking he'd just stay holed up in his bed while I was here.*

"—offer you a chair," Solon was saying. I heard a puff of air as Lycurgus's unsteady butt landed on the cushion. I held my breath, working quietly in the part of the room that Lycurgus couldn't see, and trying to overhear whatever I could. Unfortunately, the conversation itself was quiet and difficult to catch, at least until Lycurgus lurched to his feet and bellowed, "I am the steward here! I am. Me! Not you."

"Of course," Solon said, completely unruffled. "I'm so sorry not to have discussed this with you previously. Let's step out and get some fresh air; it would be a nice day for a walk." Lycurgus grunted. "Well, or I can follow you back to your room, and we can talk there, whatever you prefer." Another inaudible mutter. "After lunch, then. I look forward to it."

The door slammed shut.

There was a pause, then Solon called, "Xanthe?" I poked my head out and he gave me an amiable smile. "Were you listening to that?"

"Of course not," I said.

"No, well, did you overhear anything accidentally?"

"Not really. You were speaking, um, pretty quietly for most of the conversation."

"Well. Lycurgus heard I'd hired someone to look over the books and took exception to the idea. Don't worry, I can handle him, but if he sneaks in sometime while I'm out and harasses you, just apologize a lot and delay him until I get back. If he sends you packing, just go wait in the kitchen and I'll straighten it out later."

"But if he's the steward..."

"He's a drunk who keeps his post because he's well connected," Solon said with a shrug. "It's hardly a secret; you must have caught some of that from the guards last night. Anyway, I was put here to keep things from falling apart, and that's what I'm doing."

I gave him a hesitant smile. "I was thinking about going out for a look around the farm, if you don't mind—I think the accounts might make a little more sense if I saw the whole place."

"Oh, absolutely. It should keep Lycurgus out of your hair, too. I'll see you this afternoon."

I went out, feeling guiltier than ever for my deception.

# CHAPTER FOUR

The sun was very bright and the air was crisp; I shivered when I stepped out and briefly considered going back for my coat. I could smell wood smoke and the faint whiff of rotten apples in the air, and when I looked around, I saw some of the slaves hauling wheelbarrows loaded with apples into a low-roofed stone building. I wandered over; I would have to duck to go inside. "Xanthe," the guard greeted me. "Need something?"

"I'm just trying to get a feel for the farm," I said.

"This is the cider hut," he said. "Folks inside are peeling the apples and getting them ready for the press—that's what we do with the apples that are bruised or bird-pecked. Lucky for us a lot got knocked down in the last storm." He winked. "The apples that will keep best, those go over in that hut." He pointed to another low-roofed stone building. "We ship them to Daphnia, and they get sent up to garrisons from there. Say, want one?" He poked through the wheelbarrow that was sitting by the door of the cider hut and turned up an almost unblemished one.

"Thank you." I took it. "Which way is the orchard?"

He pointed. "Just watch for the wheelbarrows."

I passed a house with glass windows and a floor of tile mosaic; that was where Lycurgus lived, and I ducked my head and quickened my step going by. Then I was striding through the open fields, picking my way over mud and cut stubble. I bit into my apple; it was tart and crisp, and the juice dripped down and made my fingers sticky. *What a beautiful day.*

Demetrios spotted me as I approached the orchard and came over to say hello. When I told him that I was giving myself a tour of the farm, to better understand the accounts, he winked and laughed and then insisted on guiding me around the orchard, pointing out guards, varieties of trees, and particularly noteworthy slaves. "That's Sabir—he has six fingers on his right hand. Hey, Sabir! Show Xanthe your finger." Sabir grimaced a little and then gamely held up his hand; the sixth finger stuck out at a right angle from the rest of his hand, as immobile as a dead twig. I gave him an apologetic shrug and he shrugged back, then returned to picking apples.

I didn't see Burkut anywhere. Convinced that I must have missed him, I told Demetrios that I wanted to try to learn the guards' names and we made another circuit of the orchard, but I still didn't see him. "Is this really *all* the slaves from the farm?" I asked. "It doesn't look like as many as I'd have expected, for a farm this size."

"Well, we bring in extras during the height of the harvest. There are men who own teams that roam around the Empire; they go up north at the end of the summer and move south, hiring the teams out for the harvest as they go."

"Even beyond harvest... the kitchen slaves aren't out picking, are they?"

"Oh, that's what you meant? Of course not, they're in the kitchen. Oh, also, there's the work detail that's making cider with the windfalls. If a slave gets injured they go on light work for a while to recover. There are a couple who got hurt during the harvest, including one clumsy oaf who fell out of a tree he was picking apples in. They're all in the cider hut. And of course there are the stable hands; they're in the stable. And the house hands who clean... but all the farmhands are out here or in the cider hut today, I think. We run an efficient operation."

The cider hut. That was certainly worth a try; Burkut actually seemed like the sort of person who might fall out of a tree while picking apples. I thanked Demetrios for his help; he handed me an apple (this one fresh-picked and unblemished) and I walked back to the main farm.

The door to the cider hut was standing open. I knocked on it as I stepped inside. "Are you looking for Nikolaos?" one of the slaves asked. "He went to the privy."

"I'm just nosing around some more," I said cheerfully. The slave by the door was peeling an apple in a long spiral; so were two more sitting beside her. Another slave was cutting away bad chunks, and another was cutting fruit away from the core. The fruit was going into one barrel, the waste scraps into another.

"They'll feed that to the pigs," the talkative slave said, pointing to the waste barrel. "The good parts will get put through the press."

I still didn't see Burkut, until I turned and spotted a slave lying down on a bed in the back of the cabin, sleeping. The talkative slave followed my gaze and shook her head with a cluck of her tongue. "Burkut was sick last week with his stomach. Amazing he didn't make everyone else sick. Anyway, he's still weak so we're letting him take some extra rest."

I hardly heard what she said; relief was flooding over me, just knowing that he was *here*. And now I knew where to find him. I just needed to figure out how to get him away.

I thanked them and stepped back outside, greeted the guard who had just returned from the privy, and went back in to my office.

It was clear that the slaves here were not guarded all that closely. They were far enough from the steppe that it would be an arduous trip, and they were treated well enough that most of them were unlikely to consider the risks to be worth it. I could buy us some time, though, if I could come up with a reason that I needed him with me. *I could probably request an assistant. Someone who'd be on light duties anyway.* I pulled a ledger down and looked at it; that one appeared to be a mix of new and older information. *What a mess.* I put it in the "new" pile.

"What are you doing?"

I looked up. Lycurgus stood in the doorway, swaying slightly back and forth and steadying himself on the frame. His eyes were bloodshot and his face was puffy, but he looked more alert than I would have liked. "Good afternoon, Steward," I said, and bowed politely, which not coincidentally gave me the opportunity to duck my head and keep it lowered so that he'd have a harder time seeing my face.

"Who the hell are you and what are you doing?"

"My name is Xanthe—I lost my old job and came

here looking for a roof over my head. Solon was kind enough to promise to feed and shelter me if I'd work on sorting through these papers. I've done clerk work before."

"We don't *need* any help with those papers. Get out, shoo!"

I sidled out, keeping my eyes on the floor. *Delay.* That's what Solon had asked me to do. "Is there some other work I can do here?"

"No. We don't need any *clerks* nosing through *my* papers. I'm the steward here, not Solon!" He grabbed some of the books out of the piles and held them close to his chest. Despite myself, I found myself reevaluating what was probably in them. *Those are the books he wants to hide. If I can get them back, I'll put them somewhere safe until I can go over them and tally every last stray mark.*

With his hands occupied with the books, he was having a difficult time keeping his balance. "All right, all right," I said, making my voice as soothing as I could. "I'm terribly sorry, it's clear that I should have demanded to see you to ask for a job, and not let them shunt me over to Solon. Let me help you get back to your room; you're clearly tired from all the stress you're under."

To my surprise, he let me put my hand under his arm and steady him on the walk back over to the big house. "You look familiar," he mumbled as we crossed the mosaic tiles.

My stomach knotted but I thought I hid my fear adequately. "A lot of people say that," I said. "Almost everyone seems to think I look like their niece, for some reason."

"Not my niece. You look like someone else."

"Well, if you think of who I look like, let me know. Maybe it will turn out to be some long-lost kinswoman of mine."

"Where are you from?"

"Daphnia," I said. "I used to work for a sorceress there, but then she died." We walked up the narrow stairs and into Lycurgus's bedroom. I helped him sit on his bed; he dropped the books beside him on the sheets and reached for his wine cup. "Let me refill that for you," I said, and fetched the wineskin from a shelf, filling his glass to the top. He drained it in a gulp and then lay back against his pillow, muttering about resting his eyes for just a minute.

When he started snoring, I carefully extracted the books, and flipped through them. *Ah.* It didn't take me long to find the pages that made me suspicious. He'd miss the books, but as long as they were by him when he woke up ... To do this properly I needed a sharp knife. Lycurgus's room was a terrible mess, a heap of dirty clothing, books, papers, random household items, empty wineskins, and personal items all jumbled together. I poked through a pile and dislodged some dirty dishes and a live mouse. *Lovely. No doubt he thinks anyone cleaning is also usurping his role as steward.*

I poked through the personal effects on a table; there, an ornate sheathed knife with semiprecious stones studding the sheath—the sort of thing you might get as a gift from someone like Kyros, if you were a kinsman he didn't have a whole lot of respect for. I drew it from the sheath and ran my thumb cautiously along the edge; it might be jewelry rather than anything useful, but right now it had a nice sharp edge. I lay the book down on the table and delicately cut out the suspicious pages. I was pretty certain that if

Lycurgus went looking through the books and didn't find what he wanted, he'd think he must have left the books back in my office. Admittedly, that might mean that I'd get another visit from him. I sighed. *I'm letting myself get distracted. I'm here to free Burkut, not to find out if Lycurgus is embezzling.* But I'd already cut the pages out. I closed the books and quietly slipped them back onto the bed. I put the knife back in its sheath and left it back at the bottom of the pile on his table; I folded the pages I'd removed and put them in my sleeve.

Someone was coming up the stairs two at a time. I slipped quickly out of the room to meet Solon, who gave me a look of alarm. I held one finger up to my lips and whispered, "He's sleeping." Solon nodded and followed me back downstairs and out of the house.

"What happened?" he asked when we were outside. "The servants said they saw him stumble over to the office, and a little while later they saw you helping him back to his house."

"He wanted to fire me," I said cheerfully. "But he picked up two books in particular when he was yelling at me not to touch anything. I figured those books probably had information he wanted to hide, so I made sure to go with him and then I cut out some of the suspicious pages once he was asleep."

"You really were sent by Athena," Solon said. "Although Lycurgus may very well have grabbed two books at random."

"I don't think so," I said. We were back at the office; Solon pulled up a chair for me, and I sat down and smoothed the pages down against the desk.

"I think these are the pages he wanted to hide," I said. "If you were going to try to embezzle from the farm,

you'd probably underreport your produce to the Sisterhood, and then you'd sell the extras and pocket the difference. This looks like the real numbers regarding the
bushels of apples from last year, and the year before last.
Somewhere in that mess, no doubt, is the information
that got reported to the Sisterhood." I glanced up at
Solon. "Do you *want* to catch him embezzling? Because
I will leave these here and if they get lost, well, who
could really expect to find anything of substance given
the mess Lycurgus has made of the records?"

Solon smiled. "If you find the other piece of the puzzle, I'll decide what to do after that."

I nodded and got up to go back to the records room.

"Xanthe."

I looked back at him.

"I'm raising your pay. You've shown your worth
since you arrived, and it wouldn't be fair to keep you
here over the winter without paying you." He drew a
small bag out of his desk drawer and tossed it to me.
"Thank you, and I'll do my best to keep Lycurgus from
bothering you again, though I'm sure I'm doomed to
fail."

"Thank you." I hesitated, then said, "Can I have an
assistant?" Solon raised an eyebrow and I hurried on:
"One of the slaves from the cider hut, maybe. I'm just
thinking that if Lycurgus comes looking for me again,
it might be helpful to have someone who can create a
distraction or something..."

"Ah. Good idea." Solon mulled it over for a minute
or two and then said, "I'll send word that you can borrow Burkut. He was sick last week and needs a lot of rest
right now. If you can arrange for him to infect Lycurgus,
that would solve the problem another way."

*Well. That was simpler than I'd expected.* "Thank

you," I said again, and went back into the records room.

Guilt hit me like a stack of sliding papers as I began to sort through the ledgers again. Solon reminded me of Kyros at his best. But Kyros, I knew now, was my father; he had his own special reasons to be kind to me. To Solon, I was a homeless vagabond who'd asked for charity and had unexpectedly turned out to be useful. From what he knew of me, he had no reason to believe that I'd leave before winter unless he threw me out. The only reason to pay me was his own sense of fairness and justice. I peeked inside the bag; it was ten athenas, a fair wage for a clerk.

*Maybe if I can find the information on the harvests, at least I'll be able to leave behind some information that he can use.*

But who was I trying to fool? There was nothing I could do that would make him not hate me for my betrayal when I took Burkut and left. I needed to remember why I was here: to free Burkut. That was the only reason.

"It's about time for the midday meal," Solon called from his desk. "If you want to go pick up food for both of us and bring it back here, I wouldn't complain."

I walked over to the kitchen. The meal hall was empty except for a couple of house servants eating bread and cheese; in the kitchen, bread, cheese, and casks of cider were being loaded onto a small wagon, presumably to be hauled out to the orchard. One of the kitchen slaves caught sight of me as I came in. "Do you need lunch?" she asked.

"For myself and Solon," I said.

She nodded and pulled down a tray from a shelf, then quickly loaded it with bread, cheese, some apples, and two mugs of cider. I carried it back up to the office as the wagon creaked off toward the orchard.

Solon waved me to a chair near the desk as I brought the food in, and I put the tray down on a cleared space on his desk and sat down. I broke off a piece of bread and crumbled some of the cheese on top. The bread was crusty and chewy, still a little warm from the oven; the cheese had a mild, sour taste. *I wish I could bring some of this to share with Tamar.*

Solon tossed aside his papers and set his pen down, then took bread and cheese for himself. "Tell me more about your job working for the sorceress," he said.

*Ugh.* The bread hardened to a lump in the back of my throat as I swallowed. I washed it down with some of the cider. "What do you want to know?"

"Well, what you did for her, for one."

I tried desperately to remember what I'd told him before. "It depended on the week," I said.

"Were you her household manager?"

"Not officially, but I did a lot of that sort of thing. I was also usually the one who made sure she ate. During the depths of melancholia, she wouldn't want to, and of course when she was taken by the cold fever, she'd forget to. She had no husband or children. It was her nephew who was her heir." *That* much of my own story I remembered; I'd put together quite a mental picture of the heartless nephew who'd cast me out into the chill of approaching winter. He looked sort of like a younger version of Sophos.

"That nephew was a fool," Solon said.

"Thank you."

"So you kept accounts, you made her eat, sometimes you used a sword—was there anything you *didn't* do?"

I thought about it. "Well, I didn't ever have to actually shovel the horse shit from the stable; she had slaves to do that. I'm not much of a cook—we had a very good cook, fortunately for all of us."

"Where were you born?"

"Oh, I was born in Daphnia. My mother is a freewoman there. She works at an inn."

"Why didn't you go back to your mother when you lost your job?"

I made a face. "She wouldn't leave me to starve or freeze, but we don't get along all that well. I preferred to take my chances and hope I'd find a job, rather than counting on an entire winter sharing a room with my mother."

Solon let out an appreciative laugh. He was almost done with his lunch, I noted with relief. "What was the name of the sorceress, again?"

For a moment of blind panic, I couldn't remember. Then it came to me: "Hypatia," I said, hoping that my panic hadn't showed on my face.

Solon nodded. "Don't worry about the tray, one of the servants will come get it," he said, and went back to his work.

I went out to the cider hut after lunch; someone would no doubt bring Burkut to me later, but I wanted an opportunity to talk to him out of Solon's earshot. I needed to know how soon he'd be able to travel; tonight, if I could, I would sneak out and walk to Tamar's camp to let them know what was going on. Someone saw me coming, and Burkut was getting slowly out of bed as I came in, looking worn and disgruntled. "Do you need me to come with you now?" he asked.

"I can come back later," I said.

"No, it's all right. I'm awake anyway, I might as well come now."

Burkut followed me out, blinking a little in the bright sun after the dimness of the cider hut. "Come on, I want to go somewhere to talk for a little while," I said, and led him to a sunny spot on the far side of the slave sleeping quarters. No one was around, I looked carefully to be certain of that.

"Do you recognize me?" I asked.

Burkut stared at me for a long moment. He had circles under his eyes, and his shoulders were slumped. "Should I?" he asked, finally. He was avoiding my eyes, but I saw the glint of recognition.

"I used to work for Kyros. The time you ran away, I brought you back."

"I've never run away," he said, sounding confused.

"Yes, you did," I said. "You ran away once, but you didn't get very far. You didn't bring water with you, and then you cried all the way back."

Silence, then a grudging nod. "I remember you." There was a pause. "Why are you here?"

"I'm here to free you."

An even longer silence. Finally I added, "If you still want to be free."

Burkut's jaw tightened a little, but he didn't lash out at me like Uljas had. Of course, it would have been dangerous for him to show anger toward a guard, or toward Lycurgus or Solon. From where he stood, I looked like one of them, no matter what I said I was here for.

"Where do you want to take me?" he asked finally.

"To the Alashi," I said. "That's where you wanted to go, wasn't it?"

"I guess." He looked up, for the first time, and gave me a long stare. I was expecting suppressed anger, but mostly Burkut looked puzzled and suspicious; he also looked sick. Finally he said, "What do you mean, you're here to free me?"

"I'm here with Uljas," I said. A light flickered in Burkut's eyes at the name. "We have horses, food, and water. We can help you escape, and then take you up to the steppe." Still no response. He'd looked down again. "If you *want* to."

"I'll have to think about it," he said.

"How sick are you? When would you be able to travel?" I asked.

"I'm feeling better than I was," he said. "I don't know when I'll feel like traveling, though."

"We can't wait all that long," I said, beginning to feel desperate. "We have *horses;* you won't have to walk. But we need to leave soon, so that you can be safe with the Alashi before the snows come."

"I need to think about it," he said.

"Well, think fast. For now, anyway, Solon has you working as my assistant. If you come up to the records room, you can rest there while I work. Call me Xanthe."

I made Burkut a little pallet to rest on in the corner of the records room; he lay down and closed his eyes. I clenched my teeth as I sorted. Of all the various problems I could have encountered, a reluctant slave who couldn't decide whether he *wanted* to be free was not what I'd planned for. *If he wants to stay here, then fine,* I told myself, but my stomach knotted with frustration at the thought; I wanted him to be free. I wanted to undo what I had done. *Of course, Burkut is the one who'd have been dead without me.* I glanced at him, resting on the pallet with his eyes closed. *And that, I'm not going to try to undo.*

Lycurgus didn't lurch in to interrupt us, and Burkut slept the rest of the afternoon away. At dinnertime, I walked him down to the meal hall and sat down with the guards again. I barely heard the conversation that flowed around me tonight, as I was thinking over the conversation with Burkut and all the things I *should* have said to him. *I'm sorry. I was on the wrong side of the fight, but now I'm not. Please trust me. The Alashi will take you in—the stories you've heard were lies. Uljas is eager to see you again.* I looked toward Burkut as I went to the kitchen for seconds, and spotted him tonight since I knew where he was sitting. He was alert and cheerful in the company of his friends; he looked much healthier than he had in the records room.

After dinner, as the guards were lining up the slaves to take them back to their bunkhouse, I found myself near Burkut. He saw me and caught my eye, and mouthed a single word: "No."

My stomach sank, but the signal had been very clear. I went up to my room over the kitchen to wait for the quiet of the night.

*I* slipped out in the dark quiet around midnight; I took everything with me because there was no reason to stay any longer. *I can't blame him for not wanting to run. He has friends here. Solon is a decent man, a kind master—the sort of person I'd want to be owned by, if I were a slave.* Though another part of me insisted, *I would never* want *to be owned by anyone. I might not be able to escape—I, of anyone, should know that it's not always possible to 'take your freedom'—but if I were offered a chance at freedom, I would never choose slavery,* never.

*But it is his choice to make, not mine.*

It took me about an hour to walk to the campsite. Everyone was asleep when I got there; they all woke up as I came into the tent.

"Do you have him?" Tamar asked breathlessly.

"No," I said. "He didn't want to come."

"He what?"

"He didn't want to come," I said again.

"I don't believe you," Uljas said.

The tent was too dark to see anything, but I shrugged anyway. "I can't help that. He said he didn't want to come. Would you have me kidnap him? Drag him to freedom like a stolen horse?"

"Did you ask him why?"

"I couldn't. We'd talked privately earlier, but when he gave me his answer, there was a crowd of people around."

"Did you tell him I was here?"

"Yes." I heard Uljas let out his breath in an angry hiss. "I told him you were waiting."

"So now what?" Tamar asked.

"Now I guess we head back to the steppe."

"No." Uljas's cold hand closed around my wrist. "*I* want to talk to him." When I didn't answer, he tightened his grip and said, "Burkut was my best friend once. Let me talk to him."

I was tempted to tell him no; I'd offered Burkut his chance, and if he refused it I wasn't going to try to convince him to change his mind. Especially since I had no idea how I would bring the two of them face-to-face. But I was working out a way to do it even as I tried to think of a way to say no to Uljas. "Everyone should be in the apple orchard again tomorrow. Uljas, there's a field fairly close to the houses where they grow cabbages.

Find that field, hide, and wait for us. I'll try to bring Burkut to you sometime during the day. I'll probably just tell him that you want to see him. You can say your piece when we get there. I'll warn you, he's been ill."

"He's always ill," Uljas muttered. "That doesn't mean he can't travel if he wants to."

"If you get caught, tell them that you're a freeman and used to work for a sorceress named Hypatia in Daphnia. She killed herself a few months ago and you were discharged by her heir, a nephew. You heard a rumor that Xanthe was coming here and you were hoping you might be able to find a job here as well. You ran Hypatia's stable, we knew each other, and if you make up any outlandish details, try to give me some hint as to what they are so that I can back you up. I'm going back to *try* to catch a few hours of sleep."

I crawled back out of the tent and walked back toward the farm. *I'm going to want to join Burkut on his pallet tomorrow.*

A gust of wind blew back my hood and rattled the dry leaves around my feet. I started to pull my hood back up and saw a shimmer out of the corner of my eye; I turned and saw a djinn in the air beside me.

*Kyros,* I thought, and started to reach out to banish it, but it flickered away from me.

"I am not a slave," it said. "I do not need your favors."

I dropped my hand, wondering why it had approached me. Well, I could always ask it some questions of my own. "Are any other djinni following me?"

"No."

That probably meant *not at this moment,* unfortunately; if Kyros had a djinn stalking me, it might not be here right now. "Why are you here?"

"To look on you."

I shivered in the blast of cold wind. "Do you know Zhanna?" I asked.

"No," the djinn said.

"Why did you come looking for me?"

"I'd heard stories from the slaves you freed."

For a moment I wondered why the djinn had been talking with Nika; then I realized what it meant. *Kyros's djinni. And maybe the one from the bandits' spell-chain.* It struck me that if I wanted something from a djinn, now would be a good time to ask for whatever favor I needed, but nothing came to mind. Finally I asked, "Do you have anything to tell me?"

"Arachne is not Athena's only restive apprentice," the djinn said.

"Arachne was never Athena's apprentice," I said.

"No? Then perhaps Athena is not Arachne's only restive apprentice. Either way, both of the sisters have put their hand on the lovely rock they found, and they will fight to the death over it."

"Do you mean karenite?" I asked, but my only answer was to see the shimmer melting away into the darkness.

When I got back to my room over the kitchen, I was so tired I could barely see straight, yet I was so tightly wound I lay awake even as I heard the kitchen slaves stirring downstairs, lighting the fire and starting the morning bread. *It's no use,* I thought. *I should probably just go ahead and get up. Maybe I'll just lie here and rest my eyes a few more minutes, though . . .*

*Lauria!*

I was up on the steppe; it was dusted with a light covering of snow, and Zhanna was standing by the

yurt, warmly wrapped. "You came," she said with relief. "I'd almost given up waiting."

"I—" I didn't know what to say to that. "It's good
to see you."

"I need to ask you a question. Rumors are flying up
here about the Greeks and the offensive they're supposed to be planning."

"The Weavers need karenite," I said.

"They what?"

The sun was rising over the horizon, but it was coming up far too fast, flying up and up into the sky like a
bird taking off. Zhanna's voice sounded far, far away,
and I screamed, to try to be heard, *"Karenite. The
karenite is the key."*

Someone was shaking me gently. "Would you like
some breakfast, miss?"

I struggled back to awareness, feeling like I needed a
good night's sleep. One of the kitchen slaves knelt next
to me, her hands still on my shoulders. "Did I say
something?"

"You called out a name as I was waking you.
'Zhanna.' I brought you some tea." Satisfied that I was
up, she headed back downstairs. My tray waited for
me on the floor, steam rising from the tea. I downed it,
hoping that it would clear my head, and tried to remember what I needed to do today. *Figure out what
Lycurgus is up to. No, that's not it. I need to take
Burkut to the cabbage field so that Uljas can try to talk
sense into him. And if he can, I guess I'll need to get
Burkut out. Ugh.*

Burkut was waiting for me when I got to the records
room. If he was surprised to see me, he didn't show it;
he just blinked at me sleepily and lay down on his pallet after I nodded hello.

I thought I'd better spend some time with the records before I took Burkut out to talk to Uljas, so I continued to work on sorting, keeping my eyes open for the other piece of the puzzle I'd handed Solon— records of the harvests and where, exactly, they'd been sold. I found all sorts of records, but for different years, or different crops, or some other piece of the finances. *I'm glad it isn't really my job to untangle all of this. Especially on no sleep.*

Toward midmorning, I found a page from a letter tucked inside a ledger and flipped it open to read it.

*—shipment in hand; please update regarding shipment of rice. According to our records, you promised us the following:*

Numbers followed; as far as I could tell, Lycurgus was selling someone apples and then using the money to buy rice, which was shipped to the farm and then to parts east. I started to leave the letter on the top of the pile, then hesitated; Lycurgus would no doubt take it if he saw it. Solon was working at his desk, so I handed him the letter. "Found this," I said. "It looks like it might be important."

Solon frowned at it, then looked up sharply. "Where did you find it?"

"In a ledger—"

"I'd like that ledger, please."

I fetched it for him and he tucked the letter back inside. "I'm going to put this somewhere safe," he said, and strode out.

Well, it was a good time to go find Uljas. I woke Burkut and he got up and stretched, then shambled after me out to the field. It was a crisp, sunny day again; it would be perfect for travel, if we could just resolve this situation and get moving again. Out to the cabbage field we went. If Burkut was curious about our destination, his face gave no hint of that. He looked as bored and apathetic as ever until Uljas stepped out from behind a bush.

He might not have recognized me, but... "Uljas," Burkut whispered. "You *are* here. What are you doing here, with her?"

"I'm here for *you*," Uljas said.

There was a long pause as the two men looked at each other. Then Uljas looked at me and said, "Would you go away for a few minutes? Please?"

I shook my head. "Burkut's supposed to be with me. If someone sees me without him they might wonder where I left him. This is risky enough already."

Uljas fumed silently for a moment, then turned back to Burkut. "She had some sort of message from the gods that she's supposed to free slaves now instead of hunting them down. She got me away from the sorceress who owned me, and now we're here to free you as well, to take you to the steppe. Why did you tell her no?"

Burkut's eyes filled with tears. "Why didn't you come earlier?"

Uljas shook his head. "I couldn't. What difference does it make?"

"I've been sick, so sick..."

"The steppes will heal you."

"You don't understand. I'm always weak, my stomach hurts, I'm hungry and yet I can hardly eat—at least here I have regular food. They let me rest when I'm feeling ill. They take care of me. But I'm still sick half the time. What would *happen* to me on the steppe when I got sick? Who would take care of me?"

"*I* would take care of you," Uljas said.

"What if something happens to you?"

"Do you think the Alashi would just leave you to die? Surely they get sick sometimes, too." Uljas glanced at me, a little uncertainly.

"The stories about Alashi cruelty are mostly lies," I said. "They would take care of you when you were sick."

"But just to get there," Burkut whispered.

"We have horses," Uljas said.

"I would have to ride for... how long?"

Uljas looked at me again. I cleared my throat. "Probably three weeks," I said. "You would have to ride with the Alashi as well, but not for long hours every day, not right now, anyway." I wondered if they would really send Burkut out with a sword brotherhood. *Probably*.

"I can't do it," Burkut whispered.

"Yes, you can," Uljas said fiercely. "Burkut, when you saw your opportunity for freedom once, you struck out on *foot*, with *nothing*. You could have done it then *and you can do it now*."

"I was a fool," Burkut said. "I would have died in the desert before I ever saw the Alashi."

"No. You'd have made it. And you can *do this*. Say yes, Burkut," Uljas pleaded. "Come with us. *Come with me*. Don't think of the trip, don't think about the hardships; you can endure those as they come. Think about living in freedom. *Together*."

"I need to think about it," Burkut said.

I was afraid that if he thought about it again, he would back out again, just as he had before; Uljas clearly had the same fear, but didn't know what else to say. He glared at me for a long moment, then reached out and clasped Burkut's hand between his own, pressing it tightly like something treasured. "Think for a day," he said. "Come here tomorrow and give me your answer then."

Burkut followed me back to the records room. Solon was out somewhere. Burkut settled himself back on his pallet and closed his eyes. I wanted to talk to him, but I couldn't decide whether I wanted to urge him to come with us or quietly encourage him to stay. On one hand, I was quite certain I could get him out. On the other hand, shepherding a sick, melancholy, reluctant man to the steppe and leaving him to the mercy of the Alashi was not a prospect I relished. I settled for poring over the books some more.

Toward midday I found a page from another letter. *No,* I thought as I looked it over. *It's the first page from the letter I found earlier.*

*Lycurgus—My younger sisters greatly appreciate all your past support and assistance. According to my information, there is a shortage of rice currently in the Persian provinces. We need your apple harvest as quickly as possible in order to make the trades that will be most beneficial to both of us. I can promise you an excellent price, far better than our older sisters would be able to give you. I would prefer not to give specifics in this letter, but has my generosity failed you in the past? Think it over. We will remit payment immediately once we have your*

*Once we have your shipment in hand,* I thought, remembering the other page that Solon had taken with such interest. *According to our records, you promised us the following . . .* I studied the page I held for a few moments longer.

*Younger sisters. Older sisters.* The words of the djinn came back to me, about restive apprentices. There was a split in the Sisterhood. A rival faction. Before, their differences were easily smoothed over, but now there was a shortage of karenite. Now they were all desperate to lay hands on what power was left to grab. *The lines are being drawn, and people are taking sides. People like Lycurgus, and no doubt Kyros as well.* This letter was from a year ago; a year ago I had come here to spy on Lycurgus, and shortly after that, Solon came to take over. Was Kyros on the side of the Weavers? Or their 'younger sisters'? Or was he making sure he had good friends on both sides of the line, so that whoever won, he'd have a pleasant position when the dust settled? *That certainly sounds like Kyros.*

Solon clearly knew about this, in detail, even if I hadn't. He knew that the first letter was a big clue. This letter would be the other piece he needed. And why not make sure he got it? *If the sorceresses fight among themselves, so much the better for the Alashi.* And I liked Solon. If I could give him a parting gift at no cost to myself...

Was he back yet? I poked my head out the door of the records room and found myself face-to-face with Lycurgus.

The letter was still in my hand; I thrust it blindly into the stack of ledgers just to the right of the door. *I'll find it again later.* I started toward Lycurgus. "Steward, I can't believe you dragged yourself out of your bed when you're this ill. Your devotion to your duty should start with keeping yourself healthy! Come, take my arm and I'll help you back to bed."

Lycurgus pulled back from me, staring into my face with his watery bloodshot eyes. "I know you," he said, and my heart sank. "You're *Kyros's* spy, here to snoop through my papers. *Kyros's spy!*" He raised his voice to a bellow and advanced on me. "Does Solon know *that* or are you spying on *him* as well, you filthy, sneaking rat?"

My hands went hot and cold. I heard Burkut stir behind me and sit up, though he made no particular effort to come to my rescue. "I don't know what you're talking about," I said, my mouth so dry I could barely speak. "My name is Xanthe, I don't know a Kyros, I came from Daphnia and I'm not spying on anyone."

"*Spy!*" he shouted again; I could smell the reek of his breath, sour with far too much cider and other indulgences.

I thought I could hear someone's foot on the stairs below, so I dodged past Lycurgus and skidded into Solon's chair with a crash, screaming piercingly as Lycurgus swung around to stare at me. "Help!" I shouted. "Lycurgus, don't hurt me!"

Solon burst into the room a moment later, having come up the rest of the stairs at a run. "Thank Athena," I said, and shrank back into the corner, away from Lycurgus, letting my breath catch in a sob for good measure. "Lycurgus tried to attack me."

"Attack you?" Solon stared at Lycurgus's red face, and then at mine. "Why?"

"He wanted the letter."

"She's a spy!" Lycurgus shouted.

"He kept saying that," I whimpered.

"No, listen to me, Solon," Lycurgus said.

"No, you listen to me!" Solon shouted, turning on him. "You may *not* attack my staff. I made the decision to hire Xanthe, and while she's here she is under *my* protection."

"But she—"

"If you have a problem, you can take it up with me. *At a later time*." Solon slammed his hand down on the bell he used to summon a servant; someone must have been paying attention, because rather than house slaves, the bell was answered by two of the guards. "Assist the steward back to his room and bring him his lunch there. I will be with him shortly."

"You'll be sorry!" Lycurgus said. "You should listen to me, Solon. Don't trust her, she's a spy . . ." His shouts faded as the servants "helped" him away.

Solon turned to me as soon as he was gone. "Letter?" he said.

"Let me get it," I said, and started for my room. Even as I was moving, though, someone else came pounding up the stairs—not Lycurgus, as I'd expected, but Demetrios.

"The kitchen is on fire!" he shouted.

"Zeus's bloody eyeballs," Solon said in his calm, measured voice.

"We're already bringing buckets," Demetrios said, already running back down the stairs.

Solon turned to me. "Get Burkut and come help carry water; we need everyone available. Even you, Burkut," he said, raising his voice to be heard in the next room. "I know you're sick, but get up anyway— we need you."

Burkut shuffled down the stairs after me; Solon was running toward the kitchen, toward the group of slaves and guards hauling buckets of water from the well. "Form a line," he was shouting. "Pass the buckets along." There weren't enough people to form a proper line but they began to sort themselves out under Solon's guidance.

"This would be a great time to get out of here," I said to Burkut.

He looked at me in horror. "My *friends* work in the kitchen. What if someone's *trapped* in there?"

So we took our spots in the line, Burkut at my side, swinging the heavy pails of water. We fell quickly into the rhythm: two steps to the right to hand off the bucket, two steps to the left to grab the next one. A few people were running with empty buckets back to the well, since those could be carried easily. Burkut rallied, despite his misery, and kept up the pace. Down the line, I could see Demetrios; once the line was working smoothly, I saw Solon running buckets back to the well, too.

Black smoke was pouring out the door of the kitchen; I wondered what had started the fire, and tried not to think about my pallet above the hearth. At least I hadn't left my coat up there. Everything I needed was with me. All I needed was for Burkut to make a decision—and the opportunity to run for it. *He can't have until tomorrow. I need to get out before Lycurgus convinces Solon to sit down and listen to him.*

Despite the buckets, the fire was getting larger. I could see flames now when I swung my bucket to the right. My body was beginning to ache, from my cramped fingers to my knees. Then we heard shouts— the slaves were arriving from the orchard. Solon arranged them into a second and third line, these lines more tightly spaced, and then told us to take a short break while he packed our line more tightly and added people. Burkut gasped for breath beside me, bending over to rub his hands together. "Are the kitchen servants safe?" I asked Solon as he passed.

He nodded. "Everyone got out. We're hoping to

save some of the building, and keep it from spreading. Pray for sudden rain."

"Do you have a spell-chain?" I asked.

"Lycurgus does. He keeps it hidden in his room. I think this would be a bad time to try to get him to use it, unfortunately; he was feeling distinctly uncooperative, and the servants all have instructions to get him as drunk as possible when he's like this."

*I hope they succeeded, or he's probably already using it.* I suppressed a groan and stood up with the rest of the line, ready to start passing buckets again. My arms and legs were trembling from exertion; I thought about the night I'd drawn water for the Alashi sisterhood, as we camped in the desert, and thrust the thought from my mind. *I need to be Xanthe right now. Xanthe, but in a hurry to get out of here. I need to trust that I'll have an opportunity, and hope that Burkut will have made a decision.*

There was no sign of rain; the smoke boiled up into a clear blue sky. A gust of wind blew the smoke toward the well and everyone started coughing. I glanced at Burkut, but he recovered and continued to pass buckets. Now that he knew that his friends were safe, I wondered if his resolve might falter, but he seemed to have fallen into a rhythm.

*Surely,* I thought awhile later, *surely the kitchen must be ashes by now.* I could still see flames; had the fire moved on to the main dining hall? Were we going to just let it burn while pouring water on the surrounding buildings in the hope that the fire wouldn't spread? In the crisp fall day, I could feel the fire's heat, and shivered in my sweat at the thought of how hot it must be closer in.

Around me, someone exclaimed and pointed at the

sky, even though this threw off the rhythm of the line. I looked up and caught a glimpse of scarlet: a sorceress's palanquin, trailing a veil of red silk as it flew overhead. It came to a stop and slowly descended, the sorceress's djinn lowering it to the earth like hands lowering a pitcher of thin glass. It tipped a little as it touched the ground, then steadied, and a moment later the sorceress stepped out, her hands already going to the chains looped around her wrists and neck.

We paused in our labors, watching the sorceress. *Lycurgus must have summoned her. Probably to deal with me. But even so, surely she won't let the fire rage.* She was dressed in scarlet robes of pieced silk and velvet; a vivid ruby the color of wine held a black cape where it spilled around her shoulders. Even from a distance, I knew that the cold fever had her tightly in its grasp; it was as palpable around her as the cloak. The air shimmered around her briefly: the djinni. *Aerika.* Then the shimmer moved and was lost in the bright fall sun.

"Out of the way!" someone shouted, and everyone backed away from the well.

I craned my neck to see what was going on. Water was pouring upward into the sky, forming a shimmering, rippling column. Then the column lifted up and flattened out, and became a giant lake in the sky. The lake sailed over our heads like the palanquin and centered itself over the burning kitchen; everyone backed away from it.

As if from a punctured waterskin, water began to pour down in a narrow stream from the lake in the sky. The fire hissed and for a moment leapt even higher, then began to die. I craned my neck for a better view, then left the bucket line completely to watch. The kitchen was a charred mess, but the meal hall looked like it might be salvageable, thanks to the sorceress's intervention. I clasped Burkut's arm and began to back up, trying to move discreetly to the edge of the crowd.

The lake in the sky circled slightly to pour water down on every part of the kitchen and the meal hall. When every spark appeared to be truly out, the much-smaller lake went to hover over the well, and a single line of water came down again until it had drained completely back into the well. *And Burkut and I are almost gone from here...*

Someone seized me roughly from behind by the shoulders. *"Spy,"* shouted Lycurgus. "Melissa, this is her—Kyros's spy!"

I let go of Burkut, jerked myself free, and turned to glare at Lycurgus. "What made you think Kyros sent me to spy on *you*?" I hissed furiously. "You've probably ruined *everything*. Oh, let's just get up to your office; bad enough to have this conversation outside where everyone can hear."

Lycurgus fell back a step, his grip loosening, and I stalked toward his rooms, letting both steward and sorceress follow in my wake. *Arachne give me wit*, I thought. *And don't let me get caught in my own web.*

# CHAPTER FIVE

*I* went to Lycurgus's room. If he had an office somewhere that was better kept, I didn't want our meeting there. I wanted the sorceress to see the disorder here; it would cast doubt on anything Lycurgus said in a way that no words of mine ever could. I strode into the middle of the room, then whirled to face the sorceress as she came in. "Do you know Kyros?" I asked her.

"I haven't met him," she said. The scent of her perfume mixed with the reek of unwashed clothes and spilled wine that permeated Lycurgus's room.

*Thank the gods for that.* "I work for him. This is the second time he's sent me here. The first time was a year ago; after that, Kyros arranged for Lycurgus to be sent an assistant, since it was clear he wasn't entirely competent. I'm sure that's evident to the Sisterhood, as well." Melissa's face furrowed slightly, and on impulse I added, "*Especially* its *younger* members."

"Indeed," Melissa said.

Lycurgus came in, panting for breath. "You're a spy, a foul—"

"Of *course* I'm a spy," I hissed, turning on Lycurgus. "I was sent to spy on *Solon,* before you threw any chance I had of success onto the flaming kitchen and danced on the ashes."

"If you were sent to spy on Solon, why wouldn't you have told me?"

"Because," I said, "you are a drunken, sodden *fool* of a steward and Kyros knows better than to trust you with *any* information. You're only in your position because you're his cousin. Everyone knows not to trust you."

"But the papers—" He turned to the sorceress. "She was going through my *ledgers,* giving information to Solon—"

"It was only a matter of time before Solon went through the papers himself. *Someone* had to clean up your mess." I turned to the sorceress. "He kept *letters,*" I said, my voice dripping scorn. "Letters that mentioned his *younger sister*."

"You *what?*" Now Melissa turned on Lycurgus.

"If you could have just trusted me," I said. "Or waited until we could talk *alone* instead of attacking me in Solon's office..."

Lycurgus looked from me to the sorceress and then said, "You're *lying.* Kyros would never cover up for the Younger Sisters."

"Why would he tell *you* where his loyalties lie? He knows you're not trustworthy."

Outside, we heard shouts. Lycurgus went over to look out the window and then backed away, his face pale. "There's—there's another sorceress out there. I only sent for you, Melissa."

Melissa peered out the window and then stepped

away, breathing hard. "Solon. Where did Solon get a spell-chain?"

"He doesn't have one," I said. "If he did, he'd have used the djinn to put out the fire earlier." *I should have said aeriko, not djinn. Maybe she won't notice.*

Lycurgus's hand crept to his wrist and his face went even whiter. The sorceress was already running down the stairs. I followed; behind me, I could hear Lycurgus's slow tread.

"Phaedra," Melissa said, her voice surly. "We meet again."

Phaedra wore white—brilliant, shining white like the polished marble of the Temple of Athena. Her hair, too, was white; she was much older than Melissa. "Melissa!" she said with warm welcome. "My sweet little Melissa. How good you look. Come here and give me a kiss."

*I need to find Burkut.* Whatever those two sorceresses did—whether they kissed and declared their bonds of eternal friendship, or fought to the death—I did not want to be around for it. Particularly once the dust settled and someone remembered to ask about that Xanthe or Lauria who had been the cause of all the trouble. *Let's just get out of here.*

Both guards and slaves were clustered near the ruins of the kitchen; some had come out to stare at the two sorceresses, while others were poking at the smoking debris and speculating about the cause of the fire. Burkut was staring at the wreckage, and I touched his arm and drew him aside.

"You have to choose," I said. "Now. I can't wait any longer." He *still* hesitated, and I said, "Look, you could rally the strength to pass buckets of water for an hour, trying to put out a fire. You can ride to the steppe, too, *if you want to*. I think Uljas would like you to, but it's your choice."

Burkut nodded, finally. "I'll come."

I felt a moment of triumph, followed immediately by the knowledge that this would make things even more complicated than they already were. "Follow me," I said.

We walked away from the wreckage of the kitchen, across an open field, and then we were over a small rise and out of view of the farm. No one stopped us; everyone had other things to worry about. As we reached the very edge of the farm, Uljas fell into step beside us, his face alight. "You came," he said, and embraced Burkut.

"Did you start the fire?" I asked Uljas as they broke apart. *And did you get the idea from your own escape?*

Uljas looked at me, then at Burkut's face, and gave me sort of a half-shrug. *Yes.* "No," he said. "I saw smoke from here, though. What burned?"

"The kitchen," Burkut said. He fell into step behind me again, Uljas at his side.

"Must've been a spark from the fire," Uljas said.

"Burkut had friends working in the kitchen," I said. "We helped try to put the fire out, but our buckets didn't do much. Then Lycurgus summoned his djinn."

"Was anyone hurt?" Uljas asked.

"We didn't stay long enough to find out," Burkut said. His voice sounded frighteningly weary. "All my friends seemed to be safe, though."

With Burkut, it took much longer to walk back to our campsite. We stopped to rest a few times; as we grew close, Uljas urged him to keep going. "It's just a little bit farther, I promise. We're almost there."

Tamar jumped to her feet when she heard us coming, and grabbed me in a hug. "You did it," she said. "Do we need to get moving?"

I shrugged. "I have *no* idea what's happening back at the farm right now. If they're looking for me—well, there are two sorceresses with an awful lot of djinni. If the Weavers want to find me, I think they'll probably be able to."

"Get in the tent," Tamar said. "Both of you, get under cover. The djinni can't find you if they don't see you, right? You've told me before how bad they are at looking for people..."

I went into the tent; Burkut lay down on the blankets and Uljas sat down beside him to rub his shoulders. "I'll bring you all some food," Tamar said.

I lay down and covered my eyes. I was so tired; I couldn't remember ever having been so exhausted. I couldn't decide what I thought would come of the standoff at the farm. What happened when sorceresses fought? They couldn't make their djinni kill each other. They could, I supposed, kill each other with their own hands. I'd met a number of Weavers, in my days working for Kyros; all were quite accustomed to giving orders, either to their djinni or to human slaves and servants. None were fond of getting their hands dirty. It was hard to imagine one of them committing bloody murder against a fellow sorceress. *I can always hope. It would certainly solve some of* my *problems.*

Tamar came in with bowls of lentils and rice. I shook my head. "Eat," she said. When I still made no move to take the bowl, she said, "Eat or I'll *feed* you if I have to."

I took the bowl and started eating. "We should probably start moving," I said. "Keeping me and Burkut under cover and out of sight is a nice idea, but we're too close to the farm. We need to get moving. I just wish I had time to sleep for a little while first..."

"It's too late in the day to start out," Tamar said. "By the time we got the horses loaded, the sun would be setting. We're going to have to hope for the best tonight and start our journey very early tomorrow."

I should have been worried, but mostly I was just relieved that I wouldn't have to move. I closed my eyes, just to rest them for a moment, and forgot to open them for a long, long time.

I dreamed of Solon that night. "Such a lot of trouble to go to, to steal a worthless slave," he was saying. We were sitting in Kyros's study, but Kyros was nowhere to be seen. Solon's feet were on the desk and he leaned back against the cushions in Kyros's chair, sipping from a cup of tea. There was a tray of honey cakes on the desk; he took one, nibbled at it experimentally, raised his eyebrows in approval, and took a large bite. "Slaves like Burkut are a problem. You can't sell him, because no one wants to buy a dying slave. A mine owner might, but you'd have to get him to a mine and he probably wouldn't survive the trip. You could force him to work if you whipped him enough, but that's demoralizing to the *rest* of the slaves. It makes them angry. And angry slaves don't work as well. They're more likely to have 'accidents' that can cost you a lot of money if they break the wrong thing. I never knew whether to think Burkut was really sick or just lazy, but the other slaves believed he was sick. There was no *good* option, but letting him lie around pathetically was the best one I had. I'd have *given* him to you if you'd asked. He was a useless stomach, nothing more."

"So you're not going to come after us?"

"I might have to, just to ask you a couple of questions," Solon said. "Where is the letter you spoke of yesterday? That's what I really need to know."

"I had to hide it quickly when I saw Lycurgus. I was facing the door, holding the letter in my right hand. I thrust the letter into the stack of ledgers closest to me; you will probably find it on the third shelf from the bottom, in the stack of ledgers closest to the door. The letter spoke of *younger sisters* and was very incriminating."

"I see. And Kyros. You *do* work for Kyros, don't you?"

"I... did. If you tell Kyros that you've seen me, he will be eager to hear more. Much more."

"I see." Solon finished his honey cake and refilled his tea, knocking some of the papers off of Kyros's desk.

"So you suspected all along that I worked for Kyros?"

"Of course I knew. Did you take me for an idiot? I'd *hoped* that you would take word of Lycurgus's number-juggling back to your master, so Lycurgus would be removed and I'd be left out of it. It complicates things considerably that you're not working for him anymore. Well, at least you've taken Burkut off my hands. That's worth something. Here..." He held out the tray of honey cakes. "Have a cake..."

I recoiled and turned to look over my shoulder—was Kyros here?—but no one lurked in the doorway. Still, the dream was fading away. "Don't worry about me," Solon called as the darkness and fog swirled around me. "Kyros chooses sharp tools."

The phrase puzzled me, and for a moment I wanted to turn back to ask Solon what he meant, but the office was gone. I was suspended somewhere between sleep and morning. There was no road under my feet, no walls against my outstretched arms. "Solon!" I shouted. "Solon?"

A hiss, and a swirl of dazzling light. "Here. You have come."

It wasn't Solon.

The djinn whirled around and around me like a fly. Its words were coming too quickly for me to understand—like a sorceress in the iron grip of the cold fever. It stopped suddenly and faced me. Here, in this dark place, the djinn looked very different: like a brilliant flame instead of a flickering shadow. Though I saw no eyes, I had a clear sense that I was being *looked at.* "Hello," I said.

"I've heard of you," it said, much as the djinn on the road had. It began to whirl again; trying to watch it gave me a headache.

"Would you do me a favor?" I asked.

It stopped cold and waited.

"Go to Solon, on the farm just west of here, with a message."

The djinn flared brightly, and interrupted me. "I am not your errand-boy. But I'll give you *this* . . ." For a moment I felt as if I was falling; then I was sitting on the floor of my mother's apartment. It was raining outside, a cold, steady rain. My mother was awake, by lamplight, knitting. The apartment was quiet; if Kyros was here, I could neither see him nor hear him.

I thought my mother might be able to hear me if I spoke. I tried to think of something I could say, knowing that she might pass on any word to Kyros. *I'm safe* was a lie. *Don't worry about me* was a useless thing to say to a perpetual worrier like my mother. *Take care of yourself.* She had always taken care of herself quite well.

I waited too long; the dream was fading, someone was shaking me. I heard Tamar's voice, felt her small hands on my shoulders, and then I was awake.

*I* saddled the horses and loaded our gear onto the packhorse; Tamar woke Uljas and Burkut. Uljas looked fully alive for the first time since I'd seen him; he kept looking at Burkut as if to confirm that Burkut was really there. Burkut, however, did not look good. He had the misty, glazed look of someone facing a forced march. I helped him mount. "Do you know how to ride?" I asked.

"No," he whispered.

"I'll teach you," Uljas said, taking the reins of his horse in hand. "It's really not that hard."

*I hope my dream last night was one of the real ones—that my message got to Solon, that Burkut was worthless to him and he doesn't want him back.* It made sense. Kyros would have brought Burkut back, even as sick as he was now. But Kyros also would have whipped him into working, no matter how angry it made the other slaves. In any case, we wouldn't be able to outrun his guards, if Solon made a serious attempt to catch us—not with all our gear and a sick, inexperienced rider. I'd assumed that Burkut's illness was mostly a ruse to avoid work, but he didn't look good this morning.

Still, he seemed to rally as we got farther from the farm. Uljas rode beside him, speaking quietly just to him; I thought that was probably giving him strength. Tamar, at least, was in an excellent mood as we rode out. The sun was shining, she was on horseback with her friends, we were headed for the steppe, and best of all, we'd completed another rescue.

I wondered what had happened back at the farm; I'd seen no flying palanquins overhead as we rode, so were the sorceresses dead? Injured? Or had they simply headed in the other direction, or left in the night?

We camped in midafternoon to let the horses graze. We had bought grain for them back in Daphnia, and feeding them grain would let us ride longer days, but Burkut looked exhausted. *We'll need to start riding longer days soon, if we're going to get up to the steppe before the snow starts*. Well, in my experience there was nothing like time on horseback to condition you for time on horseback. I wished I had some of the salve that Maydan, the Alashi healer, had made over the summer; Burkut no doubt was on his way to developing saddle sores, and the salve would help.

Uljas, at least, rode without complaint. He brought Burkut his dinner each evening and fed it to him if Burkut lacked the strength to finish the bowl himself.

It wasn't until we'd been riding for a week that I realized that Burkut was getting worse, not better.

He had been perilously thin when I first saw him at the farm; now his skin seemed to hang loosely on his bones like a too-large shirt, and his eyes were sunken. "You need to eat more," I said that evening, and dished him out a larger bowl of food, though that meant less for everyone else. But Burkut seemed to find it painful to chew, and left much of the bowl uneaten. The next day I started the meal earlier and cooked his lentils for twice as long, then mashed them with some water so that all he had to do was swallow them. That went better; he ate a bit more of his dinner, and I went to bed that night feeling more confident that he would regain his strength as he traveled.

But the next day, as I was packing up the blankets and the tent, I found a handful of black hair on Burkut's blankets as I was rolling them up. My first thought was that someone had cut off some of the hair from one of the horse's tails, and I wondered why they would have done that. But when I gathered up the handful of hair, I realized that it was Burkut's. His hair was falling out.

I had seen people lose most of their hair before, when seriously ill. Also, once when Kyros's wife was in the grip of the cold fever, she'd shorn all her hair off and then taken a razor to her scalp, removing every trace; the hair had been scattered across the courtyard. I remembered averting my eyes and stepping over the handfuls on the step into Kyros's office. I shook out the blanket, scattering Burkut's hair onto the ground. *Now that he's eating more, he'll get better,* I told myself. I saw Uljas watching me; he wiped his hands against the legs of his trousers, as if he could still feel hairs clinging to them.

When we called a halt that afternoon, Uljas settled Burkut down to sleep and then came to find me as I groomed the horses. "He's getting worse, not better," he said.

"He needs to eat more," I said.

"He's eating as much as he can. As much as his stomach will hold. We need to find better food for him—some meat, maybe. Olive oil. Honey." He gripped my arm. "I told him we would take care of him."

"I'll go look for a farm later this afternoon," I said.

"Once the horses are settled. I'll see if I can find something."

I knew Uljas was watching me as I finished grooming the horses, resenting every moment I took caring for the horses rather than finding more food for Burkut. I clenched my teeth, thinking, *This isn't my fault. Uljas was the one who convinced Burkut to come along. Yes, I took him back to slavery the first time, but he would have* died *if I hadn't. Uljas thought Burkut was faking his illness. If Burkut is getting worse on the road, it's Uljas's fault. Not mine.* I heard a footstep near me and turned to glare at Uljas—only to see Tamar, bringing water for the horses. She saw my furious, defensive look and quickly lowered her gaze, getting out of my way as fast as she could.

I kept my word once the horses were settled, finding a small farm and handing over some of my dwindling supply of money in exchange for a jar of honey, a jar of oil, and some dried meat. It was dark by the time I got back to the camp. I handed all three packages directly to Uljas, silently. He stirred oil into Burkut's lentils and rice, mashing it in; he fed him some of the honey directly from the jar.

The honey seemed to help Burkut rally. I thought I could see a hint of color returning to his cheeks, and he smiled more often. But there were still hanks of hair in the blankets when I shook them out in the morning, and Burkut shook with cold even in the warmth of afternoon. Still, I believed that the honey was helping; that all we needed to do was get Burkut up to the Alashi and, as Uljas had promised, the steppes would make him well again. When the honey started to run out, I stopped and bought more.

That evening, Uljas fed spoonfuls of honey to

Burkut until Burkut turned his face away and closed his eyes. In the dim light of the tent, I watched as Uljas covered Burkut with the blankets, tucking them in gently around him for extra warmth. There was a faint tender smile on Uljas's lips as long as Burkut was looking at him, but once Burkut's eyes were closed, his face slipped into bleak despair. A tear dripped down his cheek; he turned his face away so that it wouldn't drip on his friend, and he swallowed his sobs so that Burkut wouldn't hear him.

Looking at Uljas, I knew what I should have known looking at Burkut: Burkut was dying.

We kept riding, because what else could we do?

To add to Burkut's misery, winter was truly approaching. None of us left the tent at night; sunny days were still cold, and cloudy days were truly miserable. My hands were stiff inside my mittens and the warmth from the fire never seemed to get deeply enough into my bones to truly warm me. We needed somewhere to stay for the winter. Somewhere with four walls and a roof. Uljas was right; we were not Alashi, and we didn't know how to live on the steppe through the winter.

Each morning, Uljas would wake Burkut as gently as he could, and as soon as he was out of bed, Tamar would step behind the yurt to shake out the blankets, to keep him from seeing all the hair he'd left behind. Uljas helped him mount his horse, and helped him dismount when we would stop to rest. I'd bring out the honey when we stopped to let the horses graze. "Eat all you like, we can always buy more," I said each day. Later, when we had dinner, I would stir olive oil into Burkut's lentils before giving them to Uljas. "This will put some meat on your bones," Uljas said each night as he settled down to feed Burkut his dinner. Burkut struggled to sit up and said, "The Alashi *eat* the slaves who come to them, haven't you heard? I want to stay thin, deny those nasty bandits a good meal." Uljas would chuckle and say, "Don't you worry about that. Anyone who eats you will die poisoned from your bad attitude."

Burkut made it to the very threshold of the steppe. We were well beyond Helladia, the last outposts of the Greeks; the wind battered at our tent at night. On the last morning before I thought we'd be able to say that we'd made it, Uljas was unable to wake him. He was still breathing—I could feel his breath on my hand when I held it under his nose—but even shaking him brought no response. "We're almost there, Burkut," Uljas said in his ear. "We're so *close*." When nothing woke him, Uljas wrapped him in his blankets and carried him in his arms to rest in the sun. In early afternoon he put him down, cold and still. The wind whipped across the plain, but Burkut no longer felt it.

Silently, Uljas gathered together a bag of food and water. I thought perhaps he would want to bury Burkut, but instead, I realized as he tested the load he'd decided to carry, he was going to take Burkut's body with him. To be buried by the Alashi, I supposed.

"We can take you closer," I said, but he gave me a look of such venom that I fell silent. I watched with Tamar as he finished gathering a bundle together and then came over to face us.

He stared into my face for a long moment. I wanted to say something like, *This wasn't my fault,* or *Please forgive me,* or *The Alashi will be lucky to have you,* but instead I swallowed hard and looked back at him. He took a half-step back and then punched me in the stomach as hard as he could. I fell down, gasping for breath; Tamar grabbed him before he could hit me again. She managed to knock him away from me, and then drew her knife. She wasn't very good at close-quarters fighting, but she had a knife and he didn't, and he fell back a step.

"If I ever see you again," he said to me, "I am going to kill you."

He picked up his bundle, and Burkut's body, and walked away across the plain.

It took me awhile to catch my breath. The ribs that had been broken last summer ached anew, and it felt like something had been bruised deep inside me. By the time the ache in my gut had mostly subsided, Uljas was gone.

"Let's mount up," I said to Tamar, my voice still hoarse. "We can ride Alashi-style now, and switch mounts when the horses get tired. It'll make things go a lot faster."

The darkness around our camp seemed very empty that night; Tamar avoided my eyes as she tended the campfire, making me feel even lonelier.

"We need to find somewhere to spend the winter," she said. "We were lucky the weather stayed nice as long as it did. It's going to snow soon."

I nodded.

"Who's left?" she asked.

"Prax. Thais. Sophos's harem." My head ached. "Prax is probably already dead. Thais is months of travel to the south. And I still have no idea how we're going to free Sophos's harem." I had a blanket wrapped around me; as I shifted, some of Burkut's hair, still caught in the fold of the blanket, slipped into the fire. It sizzled and smoked. "It doesn't matter who's left."

Tamar opened her mouth to say something, then paused. A few minutes later, she said, "Human lives aren't beads on a string, you know. It's not like you can collect all five and just be done with it."

"I know that," I said, and found myself blinking back tears. Rescuing Nika had gone so perfectly. She'd still wanted freedom, I'd gotten her out so easily, and she'd been strong and willing and had forgiven me. Was it so much to hope for, that this could happen four more times?

A gust of wind made our campfire flicker and flare wildly. "I hate to say this," Tamar said, "but we should wait until spring for the harem. It could snow, *really* snow, any day now. They'll be safe and warm where they are. If a storm starts while we're walking north, we could all die." She tapped her finger against the side of her bowl. "Prax, though . . ."

"If he's even still alive, I still don't know how we're going to free him, either." I batted at the tears in my eyes, embarrassed. *Why are you crying* now? *Nothing has changed.* Burkut's face swam into my mind's eye, sunken and wasted; I thought of his smile, the smile he summoned from the last of his reserves when he looked at Uljas. My stomach ached, and I covered my face with my hands, trying to stop the tears.

Tamar looked down. "Could we make it to the city where Thais was sold, before the snow got too deep to travel?"

"Casseia?" I drew a deep, shaky breath, and tried to think about that for a minute. "Maybe. It's where the Oxus turns south . . ."

"The what?"

I looked up at her, surprised that she didn't know this. "The Oxus is what the Greeks call the Amu Darya. The second of the two great rivers."

"I thought it didn't flow anymore, like the Syr Darya."

"No, it just doesn't flow in its old course. The Sisterhood of Weavers used djinni to bottle up the Syr in a valley in the mountains. I've never seen the reservoir, but I've heard stories. With the Oxus—the Amu Darya— they had djinni construct a channel to turn it south. They built a tunnel under the mountains. The waters flow down toward Persia now. Casseia is the regional capital for that part of the Empire. Daphnia is also a regional capital, but Casseia is a new city—every brick, stone, and hinge put there since the rivers were bound."

"Have you seen it?"

"Kyros took me there once."

"Did you ride there?"

"We were guests of a sorceress. She sent a palanquin." I'd been very young then, even younger than Tamar was now—it was perhaps a year after Kyros took me into his service. I had been fascinated by every detail of the trip, from the silk covering the seats of our palanquin to the splash of the fountain in the sorceress's courtyard. "It was warmer there, which will be nice this time of year, but it's a long way away."

"I don't think we can free Thais and bring her up to the steppe until spring. But we have to winter somewhere. We've got four riding horses and a packhorse— we ought to be able to travel pretty fast. Do you think we can do it? When you say *months,* are you taking all our horses into account?"

I thought about it, calculating days and distances. "If we buy grain, so that we don't have to spend so much time grazing the horses . . . with the extra horses for remounts . . ." *Without Burkut to slow us down . . .* "You know, I think it would actually take us less than a month. We could do it."

Tamar nodded thoughtfully. Another gust of wind made her shiver, and she said, "Maybe we should go after Prax first." I started to ask her how in all of Zeus's lost hell I was supposed to manage that, and she went on. "You could just buy him. Better that than leaving him down where he is."

I thought this over, staring into the black night beyond the embers of the fire. The mine slaves probably slept at the bottom of the mine. I wondered what they used for light—lanterns? Oil lamps?—and whether they ever saw daylight. I wondered how cold it was, under the ground.

"If we ride up and say we want to buy a slave, they'll be suspicious," I said. "Especially if we insist on seeing the slaves that are normally down under the ground."

"Can we pay them enough money that they wouldn't care?"

"We're running out of money," I said. But I was thinking up a story, even as I said that. We could say we were merchants, if they asked—representatives of a larger caravan who'd split off. We'd had to leave our slaves behind when we crossed Alashi territory, but now that we were back in Greek territory we wanted someone to do the nastier chores, and the sooner the better. We wanted to see the slaves from the bottom of the pit because we thought they'd be stronger. Or because we thought they'd be so grateful to be out that they wouldn't try to run away.

*They'll still be suspicious.*

*But I have to try.*

"Do you know which mine he's in?" Tamar asked.

"I know where he used to be. If he's still alive."

"Well, let's go there and free him next, then. Even though we have to buy him. Because Meruert and Jaran and the rest will live until spring. Prax might die." *Like Burkut,* she didn't have to add. "I know, I said that they're not beads on a string, but I know how much it means to you. You could free a hundred others, but if you can't free the ones you sent back to slavery..."

I nodded and didn't say anything, because I could feel the tears still hovering at the back of my mouth, and I hated crying.

It took us another day of riding to get close to the mine. As we approached, I tried to straighten my shoulders and look like Kyros's most trusted servant again, instead of a harried fugitive. I looked at Tamar. She still looked like a defiant slave girl, but I thought she'd probably always look to me like a defiant slave girl. *She didn't look that way to anyone in Daphnia. Of course, they immediately guessed that we were rogue karenite suppliers...*

When I'd visited the iron mine with Sophos, I'd felt the heat from the furnace to purify the iron. This was a gemstone mine, not an iron mine; I felt no heat as we approached. Also, the iron mine had an open camp around the hillside, spilling out from the entrance to the mine. Here, there was a brick wall surrounding everything, and a tower by the gate with a guard standing watch. *Shit.* Well, I might as well give it a try. I didn't see any good way to *break* him out...

"Stop!" the guard shouted as I approached. "What do you want?"

I held out my empty hands. "Is this a bad time?" I asked.

The guard signaled for another to take his place, and came down from the tower and through the gate, out to the road. He was lean and twitchy; one hand kept straying to the hilt of his sword, while the other worried at the edge of his belt. "Who are you?" he asked.

"My name is Xanthe and this is my associate Zosima," I said, indicating Tamar. "We're with a group of merchants and we'd like to buy a slave."

"Does this look like the Elpisia market?"

"Well, no," I said. "But are you sure you won't sell us one? We'll make it worth your while."

"We're always buying, never selling," the guard said, and turned away.

"But—" *But I didn't even get to use the story I came up with to explain why we need a slave.*

"But what?" He whirled back to face me, giving me a look that chilled me even more than the wind.

"Nothing," I said, falling back a step.

"That's what I thought," he said, and stomped back through the gate, slamming it shut.

"Elpisia is only a couple of days away," the other guard called down as we walked away. "There are always slaves in the marketplace there. Buy extras. Bring some up here. We're *always* buying!"

O ur fire that night was small; we were running low on fuel. We huddled close to the flames in silence, and moved inside the tent as soon as we were done cooking our food. I shivered in the darkness, counting my failures again and again. *Burkut is dead. Uljas will never forgive me. I have no idea how I'll free Prax and I don't know if I'll even be able to find Thais. I don't know how I'll keep my promise to Tamar, and free Sophos's harem.*

*It's not that I expected this to be easy. But I thought it would be* possible.

The darkness of the tent made me think again about the darkness at the bottom of the mine. *I condemned him to that.* Prax was one of the ones who probably would have gotten away, if it hadn't been for me. He'd had the knife; he'd had water, as well, and a little food, and he'd even stolen some boots. He'd planned his escape well. Prax could have made it. He *would* have made it. Now...I didn't know if he was even still alive.

I felt cold fingers against my cheek, and when I flinched away, Tamar muttered an apology and stroked my hair instead. "I think the djinni will forgive us our failures if we attempt with a good heart," she whispered.

*But Prax is still in darkness.*

*D*arkness.

I wasn't in the tent. It was colder, and the ground underneath me was harder. *Prax's mine.* I stood up and looked around. There was a light burning, an oil lamp, that cast just enough light that I could see the huddled bodies at my feet, dozens of people wrapped in blankets and sleeping a thin, exhausted sleep. A strange smell nearby made my nostrils burn and my eyes water. There were no guards. At the bottom of the mine there was nowhere to escape to, and in the middle of the night, there was no need to make them work.

Someone stirred and sat up; he limped over to a bucket in the corner and peed into it, then stumbled back to his place and lay down to sleep again. His eyes were hollow, but I recognized the cast of his jaw. Prax was alive. He might die before spring, before I could come and try—somehow—to get him out, but if I was seeing truth with this dream, he was at least still alive.

I wanted to shake him by the shoulder and tell him that I was going to come for him, but when I put my arm against his he didn't move. I had as little substance here as a cloud. I leaned as close to his ear as I could and spoke into it. "I'm coming for you, Prax. I swear before the djinni, I swear by Prometheus and Arachne, I am coming for you. I *will* get you out of here. No matter what it takes, no matter what I have to do."

His eyes were open, and he turned his head as if he'd heard me. For a moment our eyes met. "I'm coming for you," I said. "I swear to you, Prax. *I will get you out of here.*"

# CHAPTER SIX

We broke camp quickly in the morning; I'd had many disturbing dreams over the last half year, but this one truly felt like it had sunk talons into my heart. Looking into Prax's eyes in the mine, my vow was the only thing I had that I could offer him. But I still had no idea how I was going to get him out, and in the daylight I found myself thinking that this only meant I would add vow-breaking to my list of crimes.

*If only I had a spell-chain,* I thought. *Then this would be easy. Well, maybe not easy, but* possible. *To free Prax and the harem slaves both. We could even have it carry us to Casseia to look for Thais.* As I saddled the horses, I thought about the spell-chain that lay broken and useless in Saken's grave. Kyros had owned two, but I'd freed both those djinni, and I had no idea if the Sisterhood had given him another one. Sophos owned one. *If we could kill Sophos and take his spell-chain . . .* I shook my head. Sophos had guards, walls, friends, weapons. Tamar and I had walked out once, because our escape had been arranged in advance—or mine had, and they couldn't stop Tamar without stopping me. Getting in and committing murder—well, if it were *that* easy, more slaves would kill their masters.

Krina sniffed at my hair as I saddled her, and snuffled my hands to check for hidden treats. "I'll try to find you apples once we're back in civilized parts," I murmured to her, stroking her neck. "We don't have anything right now. I know, I know, you've given us your best and what do we have to offer you? Not even particularly fine grass." She nuzzled my head a little anyway and let me tighten the girth of her saddle. Then she dipped her head to sniff at something on the ground; I looked and saw a glint of blue. *Karenite.* I snatched up the grayish rock and tilted it in my hand, back and forth: it was karenite, no question about it, a chunk the size of my thumbnail.

"What have you got there?" Tamar came over to look and her face lit up. "Well, so much for our money worries! There's probably more near here. Gulim told me once that you tend to find it in clusters—like someone had dropped a clay pot onto stone, and the pieces had gone everywhere."

We spent a little while hunting for it and came up with three more pieces. We each tucked two pieces into pouches under our clothes.

"Do you want to sell these when we get to Casseia, or earlier?"

"Casseia," I said. "We've got enough money to get down there, and I don't want to stop in Daphnia."

"If we can sell it without getting caught, that will easily be enough to live on during the winter. Surely we'll be able to find Thais and free her once it's warm enough to travel again. I think we should have a cover story this time, though."

I was already thinking about this. "Gems," I said. "I grew up over a gem-cutter's shop, I even know something about gemstones. I'll buy some on the way down..."

"Will we still have enough money to get down there?"

"If you don't know anything about gems, a garnet looks pretty much like a ruby. If I buy a nice sack of oiled linen with cushioning inside, and fill it with small garnets, the sack will be the most expensive part."

"I bet all the karenite merchants pretend to be gem sellers," Tamar said.

"You're probably right. I think we should unload the karenite as fast as we can. If they don't catch us with it..." If we fell under enough suspicion, they'd find an excuse to execute us anyway. But they couldn't execute too many suspicious gem merchants or they'd scare all the other legitimate merchants away. "We'll keep our heads down," I said.

"And keep some money handy," Tamar said. "In case we need to bribe the gate guards on our way out."

*T*hough I'd traveled with the Alashi across the steppe using remounts, I was still shocked at how much more ground we could cover with two riders and four horses. We bought grain for the horses, and I was chagrined to discover that I grew sore from our longer days riding. Krina was getting to know me, but Kara, I realized on the second day, was not happy about being relegated to "remount" status. She'd willingly carried Uljas up to the steppe, since obviously Uljas needed *someone* to carry him. But now it was just me and Tamar, and she resented the fact that Krina was my first choice.

That first day, I kept wanting to look back over my shoulder, at the steppe. When I'd ridden down to Elpisia and to Daphnia, I'd known that I would be heading back toward the territory of the Alashi as soon as I could. Even as an outcast, I would at least be near them. I tried to tell myself that I would be returning in the spring, but that was many dark months away. *What does it matter? I was cast out. I can return to the steppe, but not to the Alashi.* Not surprisingly, that thought didn't make me feel any better.

We skirted Daphnia, not wanting to get too close; I found a gem cutter in one of the larger towns just beyond Daphnia who willingly sold me a sack of garnets. He had a white silk cloth that he spread out before laying them out for me, one at a time, then weighing all of them: they glittered in the sunlight that slanted through the open door. Our negotiations were quick, and the gem cutter was also able to sell me a nice sack to keep them in. It was padded and lined with silk on the inside; on the outside, it was dirty, scuffed leather, designed not to attract attention. As I'd predicted, it cost more than the garnets. If the gem cutter thought it was odd that I was buying such a nice bag for such cheap stones, he didn't show it. I drank a quick glass of tea for courtesy's sake and we were on our way again.

"They may look like rubies at a quick glance, but if someone gets suspicious of us and tries to scratch stone with one of them, they'll know for sure that we're up to something," Tamar said.

"We can take payment for the karenite in real rubies," I said. "And leave the garnets with the sorceress."

As we lay down in our blankets that night, I thought

about Zhanna. Though I'd been a reluctant apprentice, I missed Zhanna more than Janiya or Erdene or any of the others. I wished I could talk with her, not least because I had so many questions, and no way to answer them for myself. *Shamans can talk to each other in dreams. I think some of my dreams have been Zhanna coming to me ... maybe I'll try to talk to her tonight.* I really had no idea how to go about doing that, but the first step was no doubt falling asleep. I tried to focus my thoughts on Zhanna as I waited for sleep to come, but of course that just made me wide-eyed and restive even as I heard Tamar fall asleep. My thoughts began to drift from my desire to talk to Zhanna to Zhanna herself: her raven-black hair, the quirk of her willing smile, her unabashed laugh. I was thinking of her laugh when sleep finally claimed me.

*Lauria, Lauria, stay here, I need to talk to you ...*

That was Kyros's voice. I looked around, but didn't see him; part of me wanted to jerk myself into waking, but I forced myself to take a moment to look around and see where I was. I was enveloped in darkness, and as I tried to understand my surroundings, I realized that it wasn't a simple matter of standing on a dark road or in a dark room. *This is foreign,* I thought. *This is something very different.*

*Lauria ...* The voice was farther away.

On occasion, I'd seen burning clouds—the rippling flames in the sky that appeared most often on very cold nights in the depths of winter. As I looked around, I could see something like that now—cold flames, white and yellow and red, rippling around me like water. Around and around, above my head and below my feet, and now that there was light, I realized that it gave me no illumination: I couldn't see my hands or feet.

*Lauria . . .*

I couldn't see my hands or feet, but I could *taste* the colors, I realized after another moment. The white flames tasted like honey-sweetened tea; the yellow flames tasted like unripe apple. The red flames tasted like fresh mint leaves, chewed to keep the mouth moist, and when blue flames washed over the others for a moment I tasted kumiss.

*I need to find Zhanna,* I thought. *She can explain things to me. Surely all of this is familiar to her.*

But then I felt hands seize my wrists and whirl me around, and suddenly I faced Kyros. We were in a room—*my* room, I realized, back in Kyros's house—but as I protested inwardly, *no, I want this to be on my terms, mine* we stood in a tent instead, an Alashi yurt, filled with red and black felt rugs and hand-stitched tapestries of horses and glittering hangings that looked like glass mosaics.

*Zhanna,* I thought, but I knew she was nowhere near me. I was not at the Sisterhood's camp. *I made this. Kyros came to me.*

"Where are you?" Kyros demanded.

"Penelopeia," I said. The tent started to shift again, and I grabbed the tapestry behind me with my hands, as if to hold it in place.

"Why are you lying to me? Why are you hiding?"

*I need to convince him that I'm still on his side.* "How can you think I would lie to you? You don't trust me anymore," I said. The words were bitter in my mouth, but I forced them out.

"Then come back to me. You can't possibly be in Penelopeia; you can't have gotten that far. Come back to Elpisia and tell me what's going on."

*I've got a better idea, Kyros. Why don't you search out*

*Zeus's lost hell and move there, you cold bastard?* I choked the words back, but the room around us was changing, and I realized with horror that it was taking the form of a cave, Zeus's lost hell where Alexander had imprisoned him after conquering Olympus. Would Kyros realize where we were? With a wrench I turned my thoughts to Elpisia, and found myself standing in Kyros's office.

"I can't come back right now," I said. "I'm pursuing a project that *might* win me back into the good graces of the Alashi, but I have to assume I'm being watched." *They could be watching us right now.* The room was becoming an Alashi tent again, and I decided to let that particular bit of panic slip out. "They could be watching us here!"

"No, listen—"

"They have shamans! They could—you have to leave! Now!" Kyros started to back out of the tent and I ran after him, shouting, "Don't contact me again! Don't try to speak to me! You could ruin everything, *everything*!"

I was back in the rippling darkness. "Zhanna?" I said, but my voice scratched in my throat, and I knew I'd woken myself. Well, I hoped that conversation with Kyros would throw him off the scent a little longer. Maybe. If I was lucky. *Or perhaps I will be unlucky, and Zhanna heard the conversation and thinks I'm still working for Kyros.* It was a risk I had to take.

On our tenth day riding south, Tamar grabbed my arm and pointed. Black clouds were approaching. "We need to find shelter," she said.

We urged the horses to a faster pace; it didn't take much encouragement, as they could smell the storm approaching and wanted to get to shelter even more than we did. The first flakes were spitting down when we saw a roadside inn. Tamar reined Kesh in. "It's got a stable, four walls, and a roof," she said.

"We could attract suspicion. Arachne help us all, we could run into *Myron*."

Tamar looked at me with long-suffering patience. "Lauria. Do you have any *better* ideas? Because camping in a snowstorm isn't one."

The innkeeper couldn't give us a room, but was willing to let us stay on the floor of the common room with all the other latecomers desperate to get out of the storm. There was room in the stable for our horses. We led them through the yard as a gust of wind swept down hard enough to almost knock me off my feet. *Yeah, it's winter,* I thought. *Somehow I always forget just how much cold wind can hurt.* The stable boys opened the door with some reluctance, as a gust of freezing wind came in with us. Once the door was shut it wasn't too bad. "We'll groom our own horses, you've clearly got plenty to do," I said. I wasn't making our horses *wait*.

We unloaded the horses and stripped off their tack. I groomed Kara, since I'd just been riding her, then Krina, who made it clear she thought I should have groomed her first. Tamar worked over her own horses, and I groomed the packhorse as she finished up, brushing away sweat and dirt.

"Do you think we could just stay in here?" Tamar asked. "It's plenty warm in here, and we won't run into anyone... It's not like they'll have any beds inside."

"Good idea." The stable master grudgingly gave me permission and we settled down near Krina.

"There's hot stew inside," one of the stable hands

told us as he passed, but wind rattled the door of the stable even as he said it, and I shook my head.

"It's not worth going out in *that*. I'll trade you some wine for some of whatever you're eating."

"Are you sure? There's no meat in ours. For wine I could maybe run in for you . . ."

"I'd just as soon you not open the door," I said. "I don't want meat that badly."

"I'll be right back," he said, and a few moments later he returned with two bowls of soup and a hunk of bread. It was decent enough vegetable soup, I thought: mostly root vegetables and beans, with a few withered remnants of the fall harvest tossed in. Tamar measured out a generous portion of wine to trade for it and we settled down to sleep.

We woke early, roused by the stable hands bringing in food and water for the horses. "Hey," said the slave who had brought our food last night. "You made a good choice. Everyone who ate the inn's stew last night got sick."

"Really?"

"Yeah, half of them stumbled out and puked all over the courtyard in the night. One drunk soldier died, choked on his own vomit. Did *you* do something to the stew?"

I blanched. "No! We barely even set foot in the inn. We paid for a place to stay and then stayed here."

"Lucky," he said. "Well, the cook'll probably get blamed again. She always does . . ."

The snow was still falling too hard to go out onto the road again. "We should go inside," Tamar said reluctantly. "If everyone's sick, they may need the healthy people to pitch in and get water and tea for the sick people . . ."

"What if *we* get sick?"

"Just don't eat any of the food."

"Probably a good idea."

Not quite everyone was sick, as it turned out. The inside slaves had eaten their own food, like the stable hands, and were all feeling fine. As I passed near the kitchen, I heard shouting, and looked in to see the innkeeper backhand the cook so hard that her head hit the wall. She pressed her hands to her cheeks, sobbing silently and shaking as she shrank into the corner. The innkeeper heard us come in and turned around to look at us. "Do you need something?" he asked.

I wouldn't have eaten or drunk anything coming out of this kitchen if you'd paid me in karenite, but I said, "Tea," hoping to distract him from beating the cook.

It worked, more or less. He glanced at the cook, said, "She'll get you some," then stalked out.

"Next time poison him, not the rest of the customers," I said as one of the cook's assistants brought out hot water and started to make more tea.

"She didn't do *anything*," the girl said, her eyes filling with tears of sympathy. "He *always* blames her."

Always? "How often does this happen?" I asked.

"Every now and then. Maybe twice a year."

The cook stood up, rubbing her cheek as she started preparing the next meal. When the tea was ready, I took a cup, stepped outside into the courtyard, and poured it out on the ground.

"The innkeeper blames the cook," I said when Tamar joined me. "Apparently this happens every so often. The other slaves in the kitchen swear the cook had nothing to do with it."

Tamar let out a dry chuckle. "The master always blames the kitchen slaves for this sort of thing. My mother got blamed once, when I was a child, and we spent a month scrubbing floors before he decided it couldn't have been her and put her back in the kitchen."

The one good thing about the day was that the snow seemed to be tapering off; I thought we'd be able to travel the next day, if we were stubborn about it. The slaves were healthy enough to care for the sick guests, so we returned to the stable.

"I want to take the cook with us," Tamar whispered as night fell.

*Of course,* I thought, but I didn't argue.

I rose before dawn, told the stable hands to get our horses ready, and trudged back into the inn and poked my head into the kitchen. As I'd expected, the cook was awake, along with one of her assistants. She had a black eye from the blow she took yesterday, and a bruised, swollen cheek. I leaned forward to whisper in the cook's ear.

"My companion and I would help you escape, if you would like to be free."

The cook gave me a look of disbelief, squinting at me with her bruised eye. "Where would I go?"

"We're going to Casseia, for now. In the spring we could help you go to the steppe . . ."

"Me, join the bandits? At my age?" She seemed both taken aback and genuinely amused. "I can't even ride a horse."

"You'd learn. It's not that hard."

"The snow is waist deep out there. What a favor, freedom in the middle of winter." She laughed again. "Come back in the summer and you might convince me, girl, but for now I like slavery better than freezing to death."

"Even being blamed every time someone gets sick?"

She touched the bruise on her cheek gingerly. "It's not so bad. He's a fine master when things are going well, and that's most of the time. I've had worse. If I ran and he caught me, I'd have worse again."

I bowed slightly, acknowledging her refusal. "Good luck to you, then," I said.

"It was kind of you to offer," she said, sounding a little apologetic.

I went back to Tamar. "She's not coming," I said.

"Really?" Tamar sounded shocked.

"She thinks we'll let her freeze to death. She might be right, too. Only the rivers' return can free them all. Are you ready? I want to get out of here before anyone gets sick again."

The cook hadn't exaggerated by much: there were drifts up to our hips. The storm was over, though, and the sun had come out; the feathery snowflakes caught the sun in tiny, dazzling sparkles. My eyes watered in the brightness. Krina snorted beside me and twitched her head up as if she were admiring the blue sky. I decided to ride her first today, even if it annoyed Kara.

"Hey," Tamar said as we mounted up. "When you said that only the rivers' return could free all the slaves—do you really believe that?"

I glanced at her. "I was afraid you'd want to stay and try to convince her yourself. You'd quoted that old line about the rivers back when we were in Daphnia. I figured it might persuade you. I don't know if I believe it. I've never really understood it."

"My mother told me that the great river would sweep away the Greeks and their Empire. But where we lived, I think if it had come back it might have swept us away, too."

"You grew up worshiping the djinni, didn't you?" I asked.

"Yes. Did your mother worship Arachne?"

I shook my head. "Athena."

Tamar laughed at that. "Did anyone ever tell her that she can worship Athena all she wants, but Athena's never going to make her Greek?"

"I don't know. My mother makes me crazy—I've said lots of things to her, but last time I visited I was still pretending to be Greek, too."

"Well, it's the djinni that promised that the rivers would come back, and that this would free our people. I really don't know what the Alashi and the other worshippers of Arachne and Prometheus make of that. It's not how I grew up."

We had to take it very easy that day, with plenty of breaks, and due to the snow we couldn't just let the horses forage. I didn't want to stop at another inn because I was superstitiously convinced that it would make us sick, so we bought oats at a farm for the horses and then camped, digging a big hole in a snowdrift and pitching our tent inside. I knew, of course, that if caught outside in a snowstorm the best way to survive was to dig a hole in the snow and crawl inside—you didn't have to be Alashi to know that—but when traveling for Kyros in the winter I'd always stayed at inns or with military garrisons and I'd never been caught out in a storm unprepared. I hadn't realized just how well it worked. With layers of wool felt underneath us and the snow insulating the sides, I woke in the night feeling *too* warm. I took my coat off and lay back down, enjoying the sensation of warm hands and feet, and fell deliciously back into deep sleep. And dreamed, decisively, of Zhanna.

We were on the steppe, in a yurt; it was warm and comfortable inside, and Zhanna sat on a pile of wool felt rugs. She was meditating, her eyes closed; she held something black in her hands, and I realized as I approached that it was my vest. The black felt vest of sister cloth that I'd embroidered over the course of the summer—that Janiya had taken away from me when I was banished. I wondered if Janiya knew that Zhanna had saved it.

Zhanna's eyes opened and she looked straight at me. "Janiya has a question for you," she said.

"Janiya knows you talk to me?"

"I am a shaman," Zhanna said calmly. "Janiya wants to know why you are sending us freed slaves, men who didn't free themselves."

"Uljas freed himself once, but I hunted him down and brought him back to Kyros," I said. "I'm trying to atone for my past mistakes. His companion—" I winced. "There was another man whom I also took back to slavery. Burkut. He died just as we reached the steppe."

"Without your intervention, would Uljas have reached the Alashi that first time?"

"How can I possibly know what *would* have happened?" I said. "I always told myself that Burkut would have died without me. But no one can know what he might have accomplished."

"Who else do you plan to send us?"

"No one before spring." I caught her hand. "Zhanna, I have a question for you, too. Why can I free bound djinni? I've never heard of anyone being able to do this before. Have you?"

Zhanna shook her head. "But there are many different gates to the country of the djinni."

"Gates. That's what the djinn said when I freed it, it said, *you are a gate*." I knew that I was staring at her like a puppy, expecting that she'd be able to give me the answers I wanted so badly. But she shook her head again.

"Lauria, I am a *young* shaman. A very, very young shaman. I was an apprentice myself until last year. I don't think I ever told you that last summer...I will ask the wiser shamans what they know about this."

"And then come to me again. I'm only here because *you* wanted to talk to me. When I've tried to talk to you..."

"It helps if you can hold something that connects us."

"I don't have anything of yours."

"It doesn't have to be something that *belongs* to me. Just something that makes you think of me will do."

I wondered what Kyros focused on to dream of me. The thought made me fear that he was near, and I turned and lurched into wakefulness. Tamar muttered in her sleep and rolled over beside me; she flung out her hand to rest gently on my hair, and I settled back down again to try to sleep.

# CHAPTER SEVEN

The first time I had visited Casseia, I had approached it from the air, like a high-flying bird, in a sorceress's palanquin. It was a fascinating and baffling way to see a city—the streets and houses spread out below me like toys arranged on an elaborate rug, the canals like glittering silver chains. I'd knelt on the silk pillows and clutched the railing as I looked, hardly daring to peer out the window. Kyros had smiled indulgently as he leaned back against the cushions. I'd thought him very worldly, not to want to look. I had later realized that he didn't like flying at all; it made him feel sick.

Now, the city was blanketed with white snow. Everything, as I'd told Tamar, was new, including the wall around it. I hoped I wouldn't ever find myself needing to climb this one, as it was in much better repair than the walls around Elpisia or even Daphnia. The bricks of the wall formed a pattern: huge diamonds chased each other around the city, outlined in reddish-gold bricks against the gray, with blue-black forming a dark center. A weaver's pattern. But then, this was the Weavers' city. I should have been ill at the thought of living here—the Weavers were the enemies of the Alashi, and *my* enemies, after all—but instead I felt myself beginning to smile with reckless delight at the thought of living in a city, a *huge* city, with no mother, no Kyros, no one to tell me what to do.

"What's that?" Tamar asked. She was pointing at a narrow white tower that jutted up, impossibly high, over the city.

"That's a tower attached to the Satrap's palace. They built the city with djinni so they could build really tall. That's the tallest thing in the city. I think they may have just piled stones on top of each other until they were afraid it would fall down if anyone breathed on it."

"Does anyone actually go *up* there?"

"There aren't stairs. You need a palanquin to get to the top. But yeah, I think sometimes people do. There's supposed to be a room. They call it the Needle."

This time of day, the gate was watched but not really guarded. Even in the snow, a press of people were going in and out of the city: merchants, soldiers, farmers, travelers. Two vast statues were carved into the wall beside the gate: Athena, her owl on her shoulder, and Alexander, his horse Bucephalas at his side. Each statue was six times the height of a tall man and painted to be lifelike; I cringed a little as we approached, as I couldn't quite shake the feeling that they were looking straight at me. The snow had melted underfoot from all the people walking over it; Krina lifted her feet high and snorted at the mud. I stroked her neck. "You'll be clean and dry soon, I promise," I murmured.

We dismounted as we approached the gate, leading our string of horses. We attracted only an incurious glance from the guards at the gate, and passed easily into the city.

"Now what?" Tamar asked. "Do we start by finding an inn?"

I hesitated. We were almost out of money. "I think we need to go sell some of our gems first."

"That could attract attention . . ."

"Trying to go through an intermediary has its own risks." Being inside walls again made me itch to get the karenite out of our pockets as fast as possible.

"Do you know who you're going to approach?"

"No." I planned to avoid the sorceress I'd met while traveling with Kyros. She might not even be alive and probably wouldn't recognize me, but there was always the chance. That left hundreds of possibilities, though.

Someone was coming through with a large wagon; Tamar tugged gently on Kesh's reins so that she sidestepped out of the way. "Let's get off the main street," Tamar said.

I nodded. "This way."

We led our horses through a courtyard filled with old women selling scarves, hats, and other warm clothes; beyond, an alley curved and then joined with a path that led past some high, crowded buildings, stairs running up the outside wall to each apartment. The shutters were all closed up tight.

"Where do the Weavers live?"

"They're scattered all over, but the most influential live near the Temple of Athena."

"We probably don't want one of those."

"That's what I was thinking, too."

The tower was the tallest building in Casseia, but

the whole city was tall; I felt like a mouse in a stable crammed with horses. Daphnia had started out as Chach, pieced brick and stone by the Danibeki inhabitants long before Penelope had figured out how to summon and bind djinni. Casseia had been built by sorceresses, or rather, by their djinni. Unfenced by scaffolding, unconstrained by the difficulty of lifting heavy blocks, they could go ridiculously, impractically high on a whim, which was more or less what had happened with the tower. No one really wanted to have to climb thousands of steps just to get home to bed, plus very tall buildings could be unstable, so the ordinary buildings were much shorter—but most were still six stories high, and some were ten. The tall buildings, packed together, crowded out what little sun there was on the cloudy winter day.

Under the gray sky and the sloppy snow, Casseia didn't look as fresh and new as I had remembered. I found myself noticing crumbling mortar, broken shutters that had been patched but not painted before winter, a block of houses that had fallen victim to a bad fire and stood empty and roofless in the snow.

"This looks like a sorceress's house," Tamar said. The street we were on had forked. Set into the fork was someone's home, with a surrounding wall forming a neat triangle. The door was built into the point of the triangle, with pillars on either side; the door itself was closed. A carved statue of an owl stood beside the door; the knocker was shaped like a wreath of olive leaves.

"Not this one," I said.

Tamar shrugged, and we continued on.

We passed another sorceress's house a few minutes later. This one had had her wall painted to form a pattern like the city wall; the paint had been freshly applied before winter, because it was still bright and fresh. I could see smoke coming from a chimney inside the compound, and I found myself thinking about how nice it would be to get inside again. This sorceress had no statuary. I looked at Tamar; she was looking at me. Her look said, *I'm not going to tell you how to do this. If you want me to walk all over the city, all afternoon, I'm not going to say a word. Not me.*

I lifted my hand to knock, then changed my mind. "Maybe we'll come back," I said.

Tamar shrugged and followed.

I bypassed the next one as well, and the next. And the next. I almost knocked once at the one with the beautiful statue of a horse by the door; the horse even looked a bit like Krina. But no smoke rose from within, and that gave me a bad feeling, so I passed it by. Tamar shrugged and said nothing, though I knew she was wondering what, exactly, I was looking for. *I* was wondering what I was looking for.

*It shouldn't be that hard to sell this. I need to just choose someone and be done with it.*

Just as I was starting to think that I needed to choose and choose now, we passed another house with statuary—a waist-high pillar with an exquisitely carved statue of a mouse. The mouse was sitting back on its haunches, holding something in its paws and nibbling away. Unlike the horse and the owl, it was actually life-sized, and for a moment I thought it was a real mouse.

*If I were a sorceress, that's the statue I'd put up,* I thought. "This one," I said, and thumped the knocker against the door before I could change my mind.

The door swung open a crack and an elderly female

slave looked both of us over. "What do you want?" she asked.

Tamar handed me a wineskin and I slipped it into the slave's hand. "I'd like to speak with your mistress."

She took out the stopper of the wineskin and sniffed at it, then swung the door open and let us in, along with our horses; the wineskin vanished somewhere while we were distracted. "Asem," she shouted, and a girl came to hold our horses while we went inside to speak with the sorceress.

Tamar leaned close to the slave and asked, "Is she in a good mood right now?"

The slave shrugged. "She hungers but forgets to eat; work is the most important thing to her right now. The cold fever can be a brutal mistress, but I've seen her far worse."

That was about the best I could hope for, I decided.

The sorceress's compound was built much like the others I had seen: an outside wall, an inner courtyard with a garden (now faded and covered in snow), and a building. In Daphnia, the sorceress I had visited had several small buildings within her walls; here there was a small stable just inside the door, and then a single large house that rose several stories up. We followed the slave into a receiving room on the first floor. It was warm and very comfortable, with several pillowy couches draped with blankets, and a big rug. The windows were covered with parchment to keep in warmth while allowing daylight. The doorkeeper brought us cups of tea, gestured for us to take off our coats and make ourselves comfortable, and went to find her mistress.

"We're selling all four, right?" Tamar said. "Don't forget to demand payment in gemstones." She pulled the little pouch out from under her clothes and put it in my hand. It was warm from being next to her skin, and I put all four pieces of karenite into my hand and looked at them for a moment in the muted daylight. They looked like little gray pebbles, until the the fire flared higher for a moment and caught the spark inside of one. It flared blue-gray and I had a sense, just for a moment, of looking into that wash of color in the sky that I'd seen in the dream. The taste of kumiss was on my tongue, though I'd avoided drinking it even when I was with the Alashi. I swallowed hard and slipped all four pieces into my drawstring bag.

*Zhanna thought I had the potential to become a shaman. Could I become a sorceress, instead?*

"I hope you're bandits, like my servant implied. You certainly look dirty enough. Do you have anything to show me?"

The sorceress stood in the doorway. She had dark hair with hints of red in it, and wide violet-blue eyes. I could see the cold fever in them, but today it was like a lurking predator rather than a roaring flame. She was very thin, with long, bony fingers. Her skin was very clean, and I suspected that she might forget to eat, but she seldom forgot to bathe. She was *young,* compared to the other sorceresses I'd met—no older than thirty.

Maybe it was the mouse statue, or her relative youth; maybe it was my years observing people for Kyros that told me in my bones that if I had to trust any sorceress, she was probably the one to choose. I glanced at Tamar, waiting. *I hope she's not too angry about this. I don't have time to ask her what she thinks.*

"You're hoping I have something like this?" I asked, drawing out one piece of the karenite. The sorceress caught her breath and looked at it with open hunger, but made no move to take it. There was an etiquette here, and I wished I'd asked Zarina about it when I'd had the chance. "I'm not here to sell, exactly. I want to trade."

"Horses? Slaves?" She glanced at Tamar, who met her gaze with a faint smile. "My servant tells me that you don't lack for horses, at least. Shelter through the winter?"

"That would be part of the arrangement. I want to be your apprentice."

Tamar caught her breath beside me, but did not interrupt. The sorceress looked at Tamar, then dismissed her; she was not the one holding the karenite. "For a single piece of soul-stone?" the sorceress asked.

"I have four pieces. Three for you, one for me."

"That's not much, for what you're asking," she said, but her eyes narrowed and I could see calculation, and hunger.

"Should I go ask someone else?"

"I'll tell you what will happen, if you do," she said. "You'll find someone who will take you on and promise to teach you, who will take your soul-stone and not teach you anything. *That* I'd be happy to do for you. Let you live here, and let you watch me work, and put you off with pretty promises about teaching you the mysteries of spirit binding when you're *truly ready* and not before." She rubbed the back of her neck with her hand. "And admittedly, that's more or less what my mistress did with me, when I apprenticed. Some knowledge is always stolen knowledge."

"Well, all right then." I shrugged. "Three pieces of karenite, and in exchange you will let us stay here through the winter, and you will let me watch you work." She liked to talk. That was good. If I sat in her workshop every day, I thought I'd probably learn something of value.

She hesitated, then held out her hand. I gave her three of the pebbles. "My name is Xanthe," I said.

"My name is Tamar," Tamar said before I could come up with another name for her.

The sorceress looked from Tamar to me, then at the karenite. "My name is Zivar," she said. "And before I agree, there's one other thing. I need to know that you are both women. Drop your pants."

"I'm your apprentice, not Tamar," I said.

"You might be planning to teach her," Zivar said. "I want to know before we begin that you're both women. Besides, I'll have no men in my house."

I sighed, then untied my pants and lowered them. Very reluctantly, Tamar did the same. Zivar didn't touch either of us. She just looked us over, gave a curt nod, and let us pull our pants back up. "I'd like to get back to work," she said. "One of the servants will show you to a room where you can stay."

"I'll come with you and watch you now, if you don't mind," I said.

"Don't you need to get your horses settled? My servant said you had an entire equine herd."

"Yes, *Xanthe*," Tamar said. "If we're staying here, there are a few things we'll need to take care of."

"The servants will show you to my workroom when you're ready," Zivar said. The door swung shut behind her.

I took a deep breath. "Tamar—"

"Have you *completely* lost your mind?"

"We'll be able to free Sophos's harem if we have a spell-chain. And Prax."

"We don't need a spell-chain! We can do it ourselves."

"I haven't thought of a way. Neither have you. If we have a spell-chain—"

"Then we'll be holding a djinn as a slave! *You* will be enslaving the djinni."

"Just one. And I'll set it free once we've freed Prax and the harem." Tamar looked sick. "I was going to sell Zivar all four pieces of karenite! Do you think she's ever going to free her djinni? You didn't say a word about not selling the karenite!"

"I know," she said, her cheeks scarlet. "This is different."

"Look, at the very least, we'll be here through the winter. We'll be under her protection, in a sense—not attracting attention as possible rogue karenite dealers. I don't even know that I'll be able to learn how to do it. I held back one piece of karenite. If I can't learn how to make a spell-chain, I will give you the karenite and you can decide whether to sell it, or to destroy it so that it can't be used to enslave a djinn. Does that sound fair?"

"Lauria," she said. "You could have discussed it with me first."

"I didn't even think of the idea until we were sitting here. I swear to you, Tamar, if I'd thought of it earlier I'd have told you and we could have talked about it."

"Very convenient, that you found such an unusual sorceress."

"I was just looking for a sorceress who wouldn't turn us over to the Sisterhood."

"Yeah." Tamar bit her lip. "I'll go get the horses settled, Xanthe. You go on and follow Zivar. I'll see you later."

That was the closest thing to approval I was going

to get from Tamar, so I nodded and tried to force a smile to my lips. Outside the sitting room, a slave waited; she led me up a narrow staircase, through a hallway, and then up another narrow stair to a small room at the top of the house, where she bowed, and left me. The workroom was round, like the city tower, but a bit more practical. A loom gathered dust in a corner, strung with thread but with only a handful of rows completed; Zivar was a weaver in title only and didn't bother to hide it. The room had a large window fitted with many small panes of actual glass, and despite the winter gray, the room was bright. Layers of rugs kept the chill off the floor. They were plush with ornate designs like huge cut gemstones, very different from the felt rugs the Alashi used. Each rug had its own colors, but together they created a colorful jumble like a spilled jewelry box. The one by the door had a dark blue background and rows of green diamonds with gold circles at the centers, and made me think of swirling spring water.

Zivar had arrived only minutes before. As I came in, she used tongs to open the door of a brass stove, shoved in a couple of sticks, poked the fire a bit to encourage it, and then closed the door again. Then she took out one of the spell-chains that was tucked under the fabric of her dress. There was a key tied to the end, which she used to unlock a metal padlock that secured a box that appeared to be built directly into her wall. Out of the box came a velvet bag; she tucked two of the pieces of karenite into the bag, pulled it shut with a drawstring, put the bag back in the box, and locked the box again. The remaining piece was still in her hand. She sighed faintly and turned her attention back to her desk, ignoring me completely.

There was nowhere for me to sit. Zivar didn't seem to consider that her problem, so I stood.

Zivar took out a set of files and laid them out on her worktable, side by side. Working from the coarsest file to the finest, she began to smooth down the rough edges of the karenite. The process took a long time. Bored, I looked around the room. Shelves above and behind Zivar's worktable held beads. Beads of all colors and kinds were jumbled together in bowls, in teacups, in metal goblets, in what appeared to be the shell of a large tortoise. There were beads as large as my thumb and beads as small as a grain of rice; there were beads made from gold and silver, beads of carved stone, beads of painted clay, glass beads, wooden beads. No karenite beads, of course, but that was clearly what she was making.

There was not a great deal of daylight left when she began working. As the sky on the other side of the glass darkened from gray to dusk, a servant came up with a tray of food and a lamp. Zivar ignored the food, but moved the lamp to a holder above her table, and worked in the narrow circle of light. I could barely see what she was doing. After hours of filing, she seemed to consider the edges adequately smooth. She rubbed it clean with a polishing cloth.

It was still much rougher looking than the karenite beads I'd seen on spell-chains in the past, but I'd only seen a handful of those up close. Zivar fixed the karenite into a small vise, and then took out a tiny drill with a bit so narrow it looked like a needle. She stood up to do this, working quickly and precisely. A few minutes later, she blew dust off her bead. It was complete.

Out of a drawer she drew a tiny silk pouch, with a drawstring closure. She put the bead into the pouch, pulled the strings to close it, and then tied it snugly around her neck so that it rested in the hollow of her throat. A woven scarf was quickly arranged over that, as if to conceal it, and then she turned toward the door, hesitating when she saw me, as if she'd forgotten I was there. "You should go get something to eat," she said. "The servants should already have brought food for your companion."

"Are you going to keep working?" I asked. "Because I'd rather watch you work." My stomach growled.

"I'm going to go take a bath." She sniffed. "Oh yes, that reminds me. Have the servants draw you a bath before you come up here again, and wash your clothes. You smell foul."

I wasn't sure how I'd find my way to the room where Tamar and I would be staying, but a servant was waiting at the bottom of the stairs when I came out of Zivar's workroom. "Lady Xanthe," she said with a slight bow. "No doubt you'd like something to eat." She flicked her hand, and a younger girl came to join us. "This is Mysia." Apparently the older servant was going to continue to wait for Zivar to come down; Mysia, lamp in hand, showed me down another hallway and up a flight of stairs to a guest room.

"Zivar wants me to take a bath," I said.

"Yes," Mysia said. "I'll have more water drawn and heated, and come get you when it's ready."

Tamar had already bathed and was wearing borrowed clothes, presumably while her own dried. She was wearing a dress, and it occurred to me that it had been a very long time since I'd seen her in Greek girl's clothes. She looked nervous and on edge, refusing to relax into the pillows while she ate her dinner, but she didn't immediately try to convince me to leave as soon as I walked in the door, which I took to be a good sign. "The horses are all settled," she said. "I'm going to try to sell the packhorse tomorrow, so that we have some money if we need it."

"That's a good idea," I said.

"What did you do this afternoon?"

"Watched Zivar."

"Do you know the secrets of spirit binding now?"

"No. All she did this afternoon was to turn one of the pieces of karenite into a bead. It didn't look like a particularly magical process. She locked up the other pieces, in a box built into her wall. She put the bead into a pouch that she tied around her neck."

"Huh."

"Anyway, if I'm going to make a spell-chain, I'll need tools. She used files today, and a really delicate drill."

"The packhorse isn't going to bring enough money for that," Tamar said.

Mysia came in to tell me that my bath was ready and I went down. Zivar had a bathing room, rather than a bathhouse, at the bottom of the house near the well. There was a tub full of water, but this wasn't nearly as luxurious as the bath back at Zarina's inn; the water was barely tepid and quickly cooling off. I scrubbed my hair and body with scented soap, then dumped water over my head and inspected the results. My hands and nails were still grimy from ground-in dirt and my hair still felt gritty; my feet were hideous, with blackened, broken toenails and scaly skin. I soaped up again and rinsed again. At least my body looked clean now, aside from my hands and feet, and I thought that I probably didn't reek like yesterday's refuse anymore. I washed my face again and my hands and feet one more time, rinsed off, and—shivering—put on the warm robe that had been left for me and dried off. Mysia had whisked away my clothes, and returned a little while later with a clean, pressed dress to loan me while my own clothes dried. I pulled it on. It didn't fit me quite right, and in any case I felt very strange in a dress. I stepped on the long skirt as I was going back upstairs and almost fell down.

"You look cleaner," Tamar said when I came in. She was curled up with a wool blanket by the fire. "They brought you some food a little while ago."

A tray was waiting for me. I picked up my bowl. "Zivar's servants are very efficient."

"She doesn't have a family, does she?"

"No."

"There was a saying that I heard back when I was a slave—sorceresses make the best mistresses, and the worst, and usually both at the same time. A slave never has more autonomy than when she's owned by a sorceress with no family. This household is run by the senior slaves, not by Zivar."

"Why are they also the worst mistresses?"

"They're unpredictable, especially when the cold fever has them. Dark fevers are the worst. Sometimes a sorceress will become convinced of strange ideas—like her servants are trying to poison her, even if no one's so much as become sick. She'll drag everyone out and threaten to flog someone to death if no one confesses. And if someone steps forward to take the blame, to save the innocent victim, she'll flog *that* slave to death, even if she'd done nothing, either." Tamar shook her head. "My mother's worst fear was being owned by a sorceress, or having me sold to one."

Zivar seemed so kind, and so calm—for a sorceress, at least—I found it difficult to imagine her doing anything like that.

Tamar seemed to be following my thoughts, because she added, "They all get worse over time. All of them. Zivar is young, so she's probably not as crazy as someone more experienced."

"But Kyros's wife was sent away from the Sisterhood because she grew so frantic so quickly. And that happened when she was sixteen."

Tamar shrugged. "All I know is, if she'd stayed with the Sisterhood, she'd be a lot crazier now."

Zivar's guest room was much like her receiving room, equipped with soft cushions, warm blankets, and a thick rug. Tamar or one of the servants had shuttered the window for the night and covered it with a curtain for extra warmth, and the fire warmed the room nicely. My food had been left on a low table near the fire, and more wood was stacked neatly in the corner. There were wool hangings on the walls—woven tapestries with row after row of tiny blue diamonds, interlaced with green triangles. It reminded me of the pattern outside. I wondered if Zivar had woven these or if she'd had one of her servants do it, or if she'd simply purchased them. Maybe a friend had given them to her. If she had any friends.

I'd heard that the Sisterhood of Weavers usually started out by demanding that apprentices learned to *weave*. I'd expected to have to spend the first part of the winter hunched over a loom. I wasn't sure whether it had anything at all to do with their magic, but it was traditional. Zivar showed no particular inclination to teach me weaving. I wondered if this was because she didn't like weaving and knew it had no value, or if it was because she wasn't *really* teaching me magic.

The next day, Tamar took the packhorse out to find a horse dealer. I borrowed a stool from the kitchen and a cushion from the guest room and carried them upstairs to Zivar's workroom. She barely looked up as I came in, arranged the stool and the cushion, and sat down to watch her work.

This morning, she was gathering up beads. Some of the beads seemed to be chosen almost randomly. She would run her hands through a bowl of glass beads and pull out a small fistful, then select a half-dozen from there. I could hear the faint click as she would swirl them around in their bowls, like uncooked rice spilling out into a pot. Other beads took a great deal of thought. She would roll them between her fingers, smell them, or even pop them into her mouth briefly to taste them. I realized after a while that the large pile scattered across her desk was the discard pile. The chosen beads went into a bowl. She had a faint smile of satisfaction on her face as she worked.

"Can you hear them?" she asked me after a few hours.

I could hear the beads rattling faintly in the big glass bowl, so I nodded yes. She raised her eyebrows and muttered, "Maybe you're going to learn something after all," and went back to picking through her beads.

At around noon, one of the servants brought up food—two trays, one for each of us. Tamar must have befriended the servants, I thought; I couldn't imagine that Zivar, who frequently didn't even see to her own food, would have arranged for food to be delivered for me. Zivar stretched her hands, put down her bowl of beads, and took a break. There was bread and cheese, and cured olives, and a little bit of salted meat, and watered wine. Since Zivar was away from her worktable and didn't object, I went over to look in her big bowl of beads. She'd selected several dozen; they seemed to have nothing in common with each other. Some were glass beads of swirling colors; there were also some wooden beads, carved stone beads, and a few sparkling faceted beads.

"Can I touch?" I asked.

"Don't take any out," Zivar said.

I stroked my finger through the beads, half expecting to feel warmth like a hearthstone, or some sort of strange vibration. But no, they were only beads, after all; they clinked gently against the side of the glass bowl, and smelled like nothing other than glass and stone to me.

Zivar was at my side, so I handed the bowl back to her and went to eat the food on my own tray, only to find that Zivar had eaten it while I was distracted. My stomach growling, I sat back down on the stool and watched as she continued to work, silently, for the rest of the afternoon.

When darkness fell and I went down to find Tamar, she had bad news for me. "No one wants to buy pack-horses this time of year. It makes sense, if you think about it; no one's heading *out* right now. Buying a horse means you just have to feed it through the winter." She hesitated, then added, "I *could* have sold it, for a loss, and we'd have had some money. But we're going to want the horse again in the spring, aren't we? To get back up to the steppe?"

"Yeah…"

"If we don't, the price of horses apparently goes way up in the spring. We could sell it *then* for a profit.

Since it sounds like Zivar will feed all five of our horses without complaining..." Tamar shrugged. "I started asking after Thais, as well. Fortunately it's cheap to bribe slaves. What does Thais look like?"

"Beautiful," I said. "At least, she was beautiful when I knew her. Beautiful but cold. Did I tell you that Kyros tended to go easier on the beautiful women? She was sold far away because when I brought her back, she spit in Kyros's face. He couldn't let that go."

Tamar let out a very faint snort. "What kind of beautiful? Back in Sophos's harem, Aislan was beautiful. So was Meruert. But you'd never have mistaken one for the other."

"Thais was more like Aislan in personality, but more like Meruert for looks. Black hair, really long, a little curl to it. Long eyelashes. Round breasts, curvy hips. That kind of beautiful."

"She's probably in someone else's harem."

"Unless Kyros punished her by selling her to someone whose harem was all boys, and would set her to work scrubbing floors."

"I'd have been happier scrubbing floors."

"Not Thais."

"He really took her all the way down here?"

"In a palanquin. They didn't ride down."

"Hmm. Well, I'll keep inquiring about her. Discreetly. We've got a few months, after all."

There was food waiting for me and I ate heavily, ravenous from another day watching Zivar work. "I had them send up food for you," Tamar said, watching me. "Didn't you get a chance to eat?"

"Zivar ate my food."

"Really? I'll have to tell the servants that. They usually can't get her to eat during the day at all."

The next day, two trays arrived at noon, just as before, but this time the servant caught my eye and glanced at the trays and Zivar. I took the hint and wandered over to examine the beads as I had yesterday, while Zivar took a break to eat. The bowl of beads was perhaps a quarter full now: one by one, she'd added a handful of faceted red stones. She'd discarded another two handfuls. I looked at the identical beads in the bowl and the pile; I could see no difference. They felt the same under my fingertips, as well. I was tempted to try tasting them, like Zivar, but she'd again asked me not to take any out of her bowl, so I refrained.

She'd eaten half the food on my tray when she stood up, but not all of it. As I sat back down, I saw the servant lurking at the top of the stairs with a *third* tray, which she slipped in to me with a smile. Zivar was absorbed in her beads again and didn't notice.

And so it went for several more days. Zivar picked through her beads. The bowl grew fuller, and the discard pile grew larger, until the beads from that rolled off the table and scattered across her floor like sand, making me wince as tiny faceted gemstones scattered into corners. No doubt one of the servants would set it all to rights when Zivar was done with this spell-chain, but I wondered how many precious gems were hidden under the rugs in this room. It occurred to me that I could steal them, if Zivar ever stepped out of her workroom and left me unsupervised, and she would probably be none the wiser. Her servants, though—they were another matter.

When Zivar had filled her bowl, she took out a length of silver wire and new tools: pincers forged from hard steel, their tips as slender and delicate as needles. She chose a bead from her bowl, slipped it onto the wire, and bent the end into a hook, then a loop. She cut loose the wire and bent the other end into a loop. From her cluttered shelf, she pulled down a new empty cup, and dropped the link in; I heard the clink like a tiny muffled bell. Another bead on the wire: loop, snip, loop. *Clink.* Another bead: loop, snip, loop. *Clink.*

This process seemed to require less concentration than selecting beads. She'd clearly twisted many, many links of wire, and as long as her eyes were on the project her mind could be elsewhere. "Where are you from?" she asked the first day she began her new task.

"Daphnia," I said. "Where are you from?"

"Lysandreia." It was a Penelopeian city, but far south of Casseia, down in Persia. She twisted another loop. "So just how close are you and Tamar, anyway?"

"We're friends."

"Yes, but are you summer friends?"

Her eyes were still fastened on the wire she was looping. I took a moment to compose myself. *We've spent time on the steppe. Of course we've encountered the Alashi. Where else would we have gotten the karenite? But we probably still don't know their customs.* "I don't know what you mean," I said.

"Lovers. Are you lovers?"

"None of your business."

"Why did the Alashi cast you out?"

*How did she know that?* "What are you talking about?"

A long pause. Then she shrugged. "If you don't want to talk about it, I won't try to wrench it out of you." Another long pause. "But really. You show up with a string of Alashi horses, cropped hair like Alashi sisters, soul-stone in your pocket, and you expect me to believe that you just happened to wander down off the steppe?"

"We went up there and traded for soul-stone and horses."

"Traded what?"

"Why do you want to know that? So you can go trade yourself for more soul-stone?"

"After you learn my secrets and leave? Yeah, of course I want to know."

"I don't think they'll trade directly with a sorceress."

"I'll chop off my hair and pretend I'm just a 'merchant,' like you." She looked up from her work to look me over. "Maybe I'll trade clothes with my housekeeper and tell them I'm an escaped slave. They like escaped slaves, right? I'll tell them I'm an escaped slave who wants to take up karenite dealing."

"I don't think that would work very well," I said, knowing that my own voice was faint and a little shaky.

Zivar put her tools down and looked up to fix me with her green eyes. "Look, Xanthe or whatever your name is. One mouse is not going to give another mouse to the owls. Do you understand me?"

I wasn't sure whether I did or not. I licked my dry lips and said, "You may have a statue of a mouse at your doorstep, but I think I see an owl in front of me."

Zivar sighed and went back to her work. "Fine. But remember, I have information *you* want."

"You already told me you're just going to give me vague promises and empty platitudes."

"So I did. That's all we bargained for, after all." She looked into her cup full of links and then shook them out onto her worktable. "Patience, young weaver," she intoned. "To truly understand the arts of Athena, one must pursue her wisdom as well as her power." And she closed her mouth and said nothing more for several hours.

All the beads were on links; now she began to connect the links together. That went faster than I expected; it wasn't a great deal longer before she had a long line of links, almost as tall as she was. Finally, she took the karenite out of the pouch, threaded it onto the wire, and fastened it to one end of the chain. A single loop of wire could turn it into something that *looked* exactly like a spell-chain. She placed it on her worktable, held it in her hands, and closed her eyes.

Nothing happened for a very long time.

Then she opened her eyes, and I saw a faint strange glint in them, like a djinn looking out from the eyes of a shaman. But she was the one who possessed the djinn, I knew; not the other way around. A quick twist, and the chain was closed in a circle.

"It's done," she said. I'd guessed as much. "I'm going to go take a bath."

So she just closed her eyes, and it was done?"

"She meditated, I think. Like Zhanna, but without a drum, or dancing, or anything."

I was slumped against one of the pillows, a cup of tea in my hands; Tamar sat beside me, staring into the fire. "So do you have any idea how she did what she did?"

"No."

"Have you learned anything in the last week?"

"Yeah. I know how a sorceress makes the necklace

now. I just don't know how she imprisons a djinn in it."

"That seems kind of important."

"Yeah, I think so, too."

"Could you maybe get her to talk about it?"

"Maybe." I thought about our conversation about the Alashi. "Zivar asked yesterday why the Alashi cast us out. She was convinced that we'd been with the Alashi, and that was how we got our horses."

"Oh, great." Tamar sat bolt upright. "Do you think she's going to turn us in?"

"No. She said that a mouse wouldn't feed a fellow mouse to the owls."

"So what's that supposed to mean? She's a sorceress, isn't she?"

"That's what I said to her. And then she quit talking. If I tell her more about the Alashi, maybe she'll tell me more about sorcery."

"Be careful, Lauria. You're a really trusting person. Don't tell Zivar anything you wouldn't want Kyros, or someone just like him, to know."

*I* woke up in the morning to the sound of unaccustomed activity; the servants were rushing around in a panic. Curious, I went downstairs to see what was going on, only to find myself shoved into a closet by one of the servants. "You mustn't be seen," she hissed. "Stay here! I'll see to Tamar."

The closet shared a wall with the receiving room. I pressed my ear against the wall and listened quietly.

Footsteps. Then Zivar's voice, low and respectful. "Ligeia. You honor my house."

"Zivar, child." An older woman's voice. I heard a sisterly kiss. Another sorceress, no doubt.

"Let me just send for tea." Zivar stepped out of the room, and I heard her hiss to a servant in the hall, "Keep them out of sight. Oh, and bring us tea and something to eat, whatever the kitchen can find to send up."

I had no desire to make trouble for Zivar with the Sisterhood; that definitely would not be to my advantage. Listening, on the other hand...I settled in with my ear against the wall.

"How is your health?" Ligeia asked as Zivar stepped back in.

"I can't complain," Zivar said.

"Still no husband?"

"I don't want a smelly man about the place."

"Hmph. It's not good for a Weaver to be alone."

"My servants take good care of me."

"They'll bleed you dry in your dark weeks, if they think they can get away with it. A Weaver needs family."

"It really touches me to know you care, Ligeia. You're like a mother to me."

*Ugh. At least my mother's nagging is out of love.* I kept my ear against the wall.

"Will you be staying long?" Zivar asked. "I can have the servants ready the bedroom..." A rustle, as if she were edging toward the door.

"Oh, no, I wouldn't think of putting you to the trouble. No, I'm really here on business, though of course I'd like to catch up with you, first. I won't be staying long. Tell me, how goes your weaving?"

Zivar said nothing. Ligeia sighed heavily. "You are a stubborn one. Well, it makes you a better sorceress, I suppose. Here."

A pause, then, "What do you want?"

"A spell-chain, of course. Or rather, the Sisterhood wants a spell-chain. The spirit must be bound tightly enough for the chain to be given outside the Sisterhood."

"You've only brought one piece."

"That's right. You're only making one chain."

"Shouldn't you have brought a piece for *me,* as well?"

"Not this time." Ligeia's voice was crisp, but with an edge of defensiveness. "Perhaps next time." A creak as she moved toward the door. "We need it soon. You'll need to start work today, and we need it as soon as you can get it done." I heard Ligeia's footsteps retreating, back out to the courtyard, where presumably her palanquin waited. Zivar stood frozen in the hallway. When I was certain that Ligeia was gone, I eased the door open a crack and looked out to see her staring at a piece of karenite in her hand.

She looked up and saw me; she looked tired and sad. "Back to the workroom," she said, and headed upstairs.

Though it had only been a day since she'd finished the spell-chain I'd watched her make, the servants had been busy. The workroom had been swept, every bead picked up from the floor and from the heap of discarded beads, and sorted into a bowl or vase or box. They had swept the corners and polished the worktable; they even appeared to have taken the rugs out and beaten the dust out of them before spreading them back out onto the floor. A fire waited for us. *They do take good care of you,* I thought. *I hope you don't ever do like that sorceress Tamar talked about; they deserve better than that.*

Zivar took down a metal chalice of polished silver and dropped the karenite inside. This piece had already been cut into a bead, drilled, and polished. She set the chalice back up on her shelf—apparently karenite from the Sisterhood didn't need to be locked away. She saw me watching and said, "If anyone steals this one from me, I'll complain to the Sisterhood and they'll have the thief make the spell-chain instead. It's not as if I'll get to keep it."

She took down a bowl made from a dried shell of a gourd, cut in half. The beads inside were mixed glass beads of different colors; she raked her fingers through them. "You want to be a sorceress. Have you ever seen one die?"

"No."

"I have." She plucked out a bead, blood red, and set it on the table in front of her. "You probably know that you shouldn't tell a bound aeriko to kill someone. It breaks the spell that holds them here, and back they go to the shadow world. If someone else held the chain and gave the order, sometimes they're killed; the sorceress who made the chain is *always* killed. When I saw it happen, it was because—" she took out another bead, also red "—some pompous inflated fool of a military officer, some dim-witted, self-important little cockroach, had been given one of her chains to hold, and in a moment of panic, gave the order to kill. The aeriko didn't kill him, though of course the Sisterhood did, later. For Mila, there was no warning; it was like an arrow out of nowhere. She was at dinner, and for a moment I thought she was choking. But then she began to scream. I don't think it took all that long, but the screaming seemed to last for hours. There was a rug on the floor, and grabbing it in her agony, she wrenched a hole in it. We watched her die, helpless." Out came another bead; this one was broken, and had a ragged edge. It had cut the edge of her thumb. "I hated Mila. I've never once missed her company. But even in my darkest dreams I never would have wished that sort of death on her."

My mouth was dry. I didn't know what to say, so I said nothing.

"For some reason it's seldom hard for a sorceress to remember not to tell her aerika to kill someone. Even when we *haven't* seen a sorceress die that way, it's just not something that we tend to forget. I think the certainty of painful death tends to focus the attention. But when the chain leaves our hands..." She threw her own hands out, empty. "I wish I at least knew who this chain was going to."

I wondered if it was going to Kyros, of the two misplaced aerika.

"Ligeia doesn't much like me. That means that if they *have* to give a spell-chain to someone unpredictable, someone they don't entirely trust, I'm one of the ones they'll have make it."

"Can you just refuse?"

"Of course not." Out came more glass beads: blue, yellow, black. "I could run away, I suppose. I could take my own spell-chains and palanquin and have my aerika take me to the ends of the earth, far outside the Empire, but then what? The Sisterhood owns the soul-stone— most of it, at least. What's galling is that they expect me to work for free. To bind for *them*, and they didn't give me a piece of the soul-stone to use for *myself*. I've heard rumors that they're running out. I don't believe it, though. I think they're just realizing that the less they give away, the more power they can control themselves. I think they started a rumor that they were running short of soul-stone so that we wouldn't assume they were being stingy just to control things." She dropped a handful of beads on her worktable, sorted through them quickly, and brushed all but two into her new discard pile in the corner. "It's not a good idea, though. Now people are buying their soul-stone from traders, secretly, and the Sisterhood has even *less* power. In some ways."

"But they can still tell you to make a spell-chain, and you'll do it."

"It's not worth the trouble of running away." She took down a pottery jar with a swirling red glaze and began to line up glazed clay beads on her table, like a giant multicolored centipede.

"You talk about the 'Sisterhood' like you're not in it," I said. "Aren't you a member of the Sisterhood of Weavers?"

"Well, of course." She put the last bead in place and began to stroke the beads gently with one finger, pulling out a half-dozen as she went down the line and sweeping the rest into the corner. "But I'm not part of the inner circle, the ones who run things. I'm a novice, a youngster. Someday I suppose the inner circle will be made up of women who are novices now, but I won't be one of them. I'll be an old, bitter, crazy outsider."

"You seem quite sure of that."

"Well, Mila *died*. If you're going to find yourself in power in Penelopeia, you need to apprentice yourself to someone who will open the door for you."

"You weren't apprenticed to Ligeia?"

"After Mila died, I went to Ligeia and asked her to finish my training, and she did. So she acts like I was her apprentice, but I wasn't, really, and she doesn't treat me as one of her own unless it's to her advantage." From one of her shelves she pulled down a new bowl. "Do you know what this is?" she asked, and handed it to me, a faint smile on her face.

I held it up and looked at it. It was one of the strangest bowls I'd ever seen. It was heavy, like clay; the inside was smooth, a pearly pink color. The outside was rough and ridged, with horned bits that jutted out. They felt a little like rock, or like bone, but I'd never seen a bone that looked like this before. "Carved stone?" I guessed.

"It's a seashell. Penelopeia is near the sea, too, but this is from the great southern ocean, beyond Persia. These wash up on the shore, sometimes. There are creatures who live inside the shells, but the creature from this one died a long time ago. I use it for beads." She put the handful of beads she'd chosen inside, and set it on her table, balancing it on three of the spines. "Have you ever seen the ocean?"

"No." I wanted to touch the shell again; I wanted to run my fingers over the smooth inside. "Have you?"

"Yes, long ago. But I didn't find the shell, I bought it from a trader."

Zivar pulled out a teacup full of star-shaped metal beads and began to sort through them. "What are you looking for?" I asked.

"I'm listening for the ones making the right noise," she said. "The soul-stone makes a noise—" she hummed, a single high note. "I need beads that sing that note. When I'm making spell-chains for myself, I like to choose beads that sound nice together even if they aren't all singing the same note. When I'm working for the Sisterhood, I just want beads that sing the same note. Why try for beauty?"

*She has to be making this up,* I thought, but her eyes were on her work, her face serious. She wasn't watching for my reaction, just describing what she was doing. *Beads that sing? Great, I'm going to fail at this, too.* Though as I watched, I remembered the dream I'd had with the burning sky full of colors that tasted of apples and mint leaves. I'd never experienced anything like that *awake,* though.

Zivar sped up as she worked; imperceptibly, at first, but as the day wore on I realized that beads were being scattered across the floor like thrown sand, and when she spoke out loud—sometimes to me, sometimes to herself—I could barely understand her. When our food came, she didn't touch it.

Night fell and I expected her to put her work down; instead, she shouted down the stairs for her servants, who brought up a dozen lamps to provide light. The servants returned each hour to replenish the oil, as Zivar sleeplessly hunted through her beads. I was tired, but propped my chin on my fists and kept watching. She was in a more talkative mood than she'd been before, and I was reluctant to leave when she might tell me something useful, like how to "hear" the beads or—for that matter—how to actually bind the aerika.

"None of these," she muttered as she hunted through one cup. "None of these. Oh, these are terrible, *terrible.*" Her hand shook and they scattered over her rug. "Oh, *no!*" she shrieked. "No, I don't like their song, and now they're *everywhere.*"

The waiting servant hurried in. "Clean them up," Zivar said, pointing at the rug, her hand shaking. "No, no, that's not going to be fast enough," she said as the woman started to pick up tiny beads one by one. "Just roll up the rugs and take them out, all of them! Out!"

The servant rolled up the rugs without question and took them downstairs. A few minutes later another servant brought up new rugs and rolled them out, silently, on the floor.

"Ligeia," Zivar murmured under her breath, and then began to sing the name. "Ligeia, Ligeia, Ligeia. Mila Mila Mila Mila Mila. Ligeia Mila Ligeia Mila."

Her bowl of beads was full around dawn. Now she got her tools back out, and her wire. "I'm going to need more wire," she murmured, and shouted down instructions to her servants again. She sat down and began to make links, as she had before: thread on a bead, loop, snip, loop. The cold fever—for that was certainly what I was seeing—didn't interfere with her efficiency. She worked with a ferocious concentration, occasionally launching into a strange monologue that I might have been able to understand if she'd been speaking either Danibeki or Greek.

When the last of her links was done, she put down her tools and briefly stretched her cramped hands. "It's not fair," she said, quite distinctly. "Every binding makes us a little bit worse. The cold fever becomes colder, the dark days become darker. To sacrifice that for the Sisterhood . . ."

"But running away is too much trouble?"

"It's not just the trouble. There's also the danger that I'd be caught. Soul-stone is *always* the property of Athena, you know." She took up her tools again. "Maybe next time they demand a binding from me, if they don't bring a piece of soul-stone for me, too." She bent her head over her work; it was time to start linking the pieces together.

I'd lost track of time. The servants were lighting lamps again. I was so tired that my vision blurred and I saw two Zivars instead of one. *I need to just rest my eyes,* I thought as I lay down on the rug near her feet. *Just for a few minutes, so that I can keep watching.*

I could hear the *click-click-click* of the beads, and then something else—a low hum, like a hundred voices singing the same note. *Oh, now I hear them,* I thought, and dropped into sleep.

The night I'd tried to find Zhanna, to speak with her, I'd found myself under a sky of burning clouds. Tonight, I realized, I was surrounded by a circle of dancing flames, but it wasn't clouds, it was a net. I could still hear the hum I'd heard as I was falling asleep, only now I thought I heard words, or the edges of them—voices singing *something* that I could almost understand, but not quite.

*It's the spell-chain.*

Where was Zivar? She was here, I knew, but I couldn't see her.

Suddenly, the colors around me flared up bright and new. There was an aeriko here, trapped within the circle of flame. Looking at it here, I saw not the indistinct shimmer, but the figure of a woman made of fire. "Run," she whispered to me, and her despair hit me like freezing water, icing around me even as the noose of colors tightened close around both of us. I couldn't run, or even move, and for a moment I thought that I would be trapped in the spell-chain, too, forced to obey Zivar's orders. The dark sky, the open emptiness, those were gone. I could see nothing but the brightness, hear nothing but the hum, and then at the last moment I felt something push me, and I lay on the floor, awake.

Zivar stood over me, the spell-chain draped over her hands. "There," she said. "You were lucky. Now you've seen how it's done."

"The woman of fire—"

"Yes, she's mine now. The aeriko." Zivar dropped the spell-chain to the floor beside me. "I need to be sure the aeriko will obey orders from someone who isn't me. Summon the spirit."

I picked up the spell-chain. The karenite bead was warm, from Zivar's hand or the spirit's presence I couldn't say. "Show yourself," I said, and there she was, a shimmer in the air, like a pale, miserable echo of the woman of fire I'd seen just moments earlier.

"Tell her to do something."

What I wanted to do was to set her free. But I couldn't do that, not with Zivar watching me. "Fetch me a feather from one of the birds that flies overhead," I said.

The djinn vanished; a moment later it was back, and a single white feather drifted slowly to the floor.

"Good enough," Zivar said, taking the spell-chain back from me. "Go to Penelopeia, to the home of Ligeia. It's a brick house, painted with a huge green bird on the wall outside. Ligeia will be the pompous woman in a bright green robe, white haired, a sorceress with many spell-chains. Stay out of sight, but follow her quietly until she's asleep, or better yet, having sex with her husband. Then disturb her loudly and tell her that you come from Zivar to tell her that the spell-chain is done. If she asks you what your instructions were, just tell her that you were told to find her. Then come back here." Zivar looped the spell-chain around her wrist and tucked it inside her sleeve. "I need a drink," she said. "Come on." It took me a moment to realize that she was speaking to me now, and not the djinn.

I followed her down to the kitchen, trailed by one sleepy servant who'd been left with a lamp to keep a watch for Zivar when she was done. The servant clearly understood the routine. We sat down at a table near the stove and the servant brought wine cups and a decanter. I could smell it even as she was pouring and realized that it was spirits of wine, not wine itself. This could make us *very* drunk very quickly.

And that in fact seemed to be Zivar's intention. She raised her cup in a brief salute, then drained it and poured herself a fresh cup, shooing away the servant with a flick of her wrist. I took a cautious sip. It burned my throat and tasted like I'd always imagined scorpion venom would taste, drunk straight. Zivar didn't seem to mind it. The servant appeared again, this time setting out bread, already sliced, along with cheese and cold meat. I gratefully took some of the bread and cheese. Zivar ignored it.

"I watched Mila for years before I first saw the borderland," Zivar said. "You're better than I was."

"Did she train you, or just let you watch her?"

"I watched. She didn't tell me much of anything, but that night I saw the borderland, I knew everything I needed to know. Good thing, too, as she died not long after that." The servant had unobtrusively filled a plate for Zivar and slipped it in front of her; she took a piece of cheese, absentmindedly nibbling off a corner before she put it down. "That's what the *weaving* is all about. It's supposed to make you open to going to the borderland. That's how Penelope got there, so she thinks that's how everyone's supposed to go there. Never really did anything for me."

"Do you think I'll be able to bind spirits now?"

"Well, you've at least seen how it's done. Whether you'll be able to do it, who knows. Some can, some can't. Some destroy themselves trying. Really, if I could send an aeriko back with a message to myself, ten years ago, I would tell her not to bother. It's not worth it. What's power, when you lose yourself?"

"Have you lost yourself?"

"I lose another piece every time I go to the borderland. And so will you. Sometimes it's a big piece, sometimes it's a small piece, but the aerika always claim their share."

"What about shamans? They go to the borderland. Do your slaves have a shaman?"

"Shamans, ha. They're a different breed. The aerika let them come and go more freely, because they don't seek to bind, only to touch. Still, they get strange, too, after a while." She poured herself more of the spirits of wine. "Mila, now. Once we had to wrap her in a sheet to keep her from harming herself, just as she was emerging from the dark days. Another time we had to wrap her in a sheet to keep her from killing someone else, when the cold fever was at its worst. This is why they say a sorceress needs a husband to look after her, because your slaves can't be trusted, any more than your aeriko can."

"What about your apprentices?"

That was very funny, for some reason. "Oh, yes. Thank Athena for apprentices. Will you bind me in a sheet if I want to throw myself off my tower, Xanthe? Will you? I think not. I think the task will fall to Nurzhan over there." She indicated the servant standing in the shadows by the hearth.

"How many spell-chains do you need, anyway?"

"You'll always need one more than you have," Zivar said, dreamily caressing the new spell-chain with her fingers. "The new one I made, that aeriko spends almost all his time guarding the karenite I have hidden in the wall, in case one of the other sorceresses sends an aeriko to try to steal it. I used to worry night and day about someone stealing from me. Now I need a spell-chain so that I can send an aeriko out to look for someone I want to find. Aerika are terrible at finding people—at finding anything, really, because if someone sent you into my workroom to look for a particular bead, and you didn't wish to be helpful, you could search for centuries and never find it. They will look, though, if you tell them, and sometimes they find the person you sent them to look for. Of course I could send one of the aerika I already have bound, but then I'd have to pull it away from its tasks. Do you see how it works? You never have enough."

*Kyros made do with two,* I thought. *But if he'd had the ability to make more . . . No, he'd never have had enough.*

*But I only need one.*

"Do you see the darkness coming?" Zivar asked me.

"What?"

"The darkness is coming, like a bird the size of a temple. I can hear its wings beating in the air above us; it's settling in the courtyard, even now, folding its wings over the roof." Her voice was still conversational and eerily calm.

"Perhaps you hear Ligeia, returning?" I strained my own ears.

"No." She rose, unsteady from the drink; Nurzhan stepped swiftly to her side to catch her arm, supporting her. "Let the lights be put out, let the fires go cold," she murmured. "Night is coming."

Nurzhan looked back at me. "Stay out of sight when Ligeia comes back," she said. "I don't think she's supposed to know you're here."

The kitchen was very quiet, with Nurzhan and Zivar gone. I took another sip of my spirits of wine, but it burned my throat again and I hated the taste. It was a shame to waste alcohol, but I had no doubt the servants would put it to good use. Leaving my cup on the table, I picked up the lamp and went to find the guest room, Tamar, and bed.

*I*n the morning, the whole house seemed weirdly quiet. Ligeia had apparently arrived, collected her spell-chain, and gone away again, leaving Zivar to her personal darkness. Zivar was still in bed. The servants seemed to think she would probably be there for days, or possibly weeks. "It's the melancholia," said the girl who brought up our breakfast, with a shrug. "She's a sorceress. She'll get over it in a few weeks."

"What's the longest you've ever seen a melancholia last?"

"For Zivar? Probably two months. Though my sister serves a sorceress who once spent an entire year dark."

Kyros's wife still had regular melancholia, but hers seemed to be mostly just tired sadness, not bleak despair. When I tried to approach Zivar, I was gently but firmly turned away by the servant at her door. "It will only agitate her to see you. This morning she seemed to think that you were planning to sell her secrets to the Sisterhood. She's dropped the idea of cutting your throat, but it's best if you don't remind her of your existence right now."

*Cutting my throat.* Well. "Thanks for not handing her a knife and showing her the way to where I was sleeping."

A shrug. "Don't mention it."

Tamar was down in the kitchen, helping knead the

bread. Apparently she'd been coming down daily for the last couple of days. I was surprised to see her so eager to help with a slave's labor, but after pulling up a stool and sitting for a while I could understand why. It was warm in the kitchen, and the company was amiable. Everyone seemed to like Tamar a lot; I was accepted as her hanger-on, and I realized that the kindnesses the servants had shown to me—the extra trays of food, for instance—were because they liked Tamar.

They had all heard that Zivar had wanted to cut my throat at some point during the night, and seemed to view it as very funny. "Don't worry, we'll keep her in her room until she's her right self again," one of the women said, patting me on the shoulder.

"Remember the time she thought the squirrel outside her window was a spy sent by a Persian sorceress?" one of the other servants said. "Or the day that her fever told her that we all needed new clothes? She rounded up every servant, including the stable hands, and herded us all to a tailor's shop on the other side of town. We came home dressed in velvet. Very impractical."

"Where does she get the money for that sort of thing?" Tamar asked.

"She backs a merchant company; she gave them the spell-chains they need so that djinni can carry sky-boats loaded with fruit from Persia and bring it up to Daphnia. That sort of thing. She provided the djinni; they take care of operations and give her a cut of the money. That's what keeps us in silks and velvets." Everyone laughed again.

It was snowing outside again; I went to visit the horses for a few hours, taking the time to groom Kara and Kesh and Krina. The stable hands were all girls—no smelly men about the place, as Zivar had put it. It should have been reminiscent of my days with the Alashi Sisterhood, but it wasn't. Things were too strange, and Zivar was too crazy. I wondered if she would stay melancholic for the whole of the winter.

The next day, again, she stayed shut up in her room—and the next, and the next. My days began to fall into a routine: morning with Tamar and the servants in the kitchen, afternoon in the stable with the horses. They desperately needed some exercise; perhaps when the snow stopped I'd take them out of the city, one by one, for a proper run. Tamar made it clear that she was glad to have my company again. As long as I was keeping her company, the household of a rogue sorceress was not such a bad place to spend the winter, after all.

"Have you found anything out about Thais?" I asked Tamar one morning. "Is there anything I can help you with?"

"Oh." She bit her lip and looked down. "I've been meaning to tell you about that."

"Tell me what?" I jumped immediately to the worst possibility I could think of. "Is she dead?"

"No—well, not so far as I know." Tamar sighed deeply and turned up her hands. "It turns out she was sold to a sorceress—to a household without a harem, in fact; you were right. She did menial labor for the sorceress, scrubbing the floors and walls to keep them clean. As you noted, though, she was quite beautiful, and she caught someone's eye. He made the sorceress an excellent offer, and Thais was sold. The buyer wasn't local, though, and no one knows where he was from. Once you described Thais, I was able to track her down remarkably fast, and I even talked to the other slaves owned by that sorceress! But they couldn't tell me the buyer's name. He was a Greek officer. That's all they know."

I closed my eyes and shook my head. The trail was cold. But I was already thinking of ways to find her. There were a lot of Greek officers. But officers were easy for a djinn to find. If I had a spell-chain, I could find her. Without a spell-chain . . .

I didn't have wire, tools, or beads. But Zivar did. The servants probably wouldn't stop me if I just went up to her workroom and started making a spell-chain. *I've wasted enough time. I've made enough excuses.* Tamar didn't want me making a spell-chain, but she'd do what she could to protect me—she'd have the servants warn me if Zivar suddenly left her bed. And as long as I was out of the workroom by the time she arrived—I'd seen how she worked. She'd never notice a little wire missing, a few beads.

That afternoon, I headed for the staircase to Zivar's workroom instead of the stable. I was still afraid, but I had to admit that I was afraid that I would succeed and become a sorceress, with all that meant. And that, I knew I was right to fear. *But it's why I came here. It's what I'm here for. No more excuses.*

The servants had cleaned. Once again, every bead had been picked up and put away; the old rugs had been beaten clean and rolled back out on the floor. Looking around, I thought I saw the shimmer of the djinn that Zivar had set to guard her karenite, but when I turned for a closer look I realized it was just the winter sunshine filtering through the glass window and reflecting off a row of glittering beads, laid out on her shelf.

My hand stole to the pouch I carried under my clothes. She had set one djinn to guard her other pieces of karenite. The purpose of the pouch around her neck suddenly dawned on me: it was to make it too danger-ous to have someone else's djinn steal it. I opened a drawer and borrowed a pouch. Then I pulled out Zivar's chair and sat down. Her tools lay beside my right hand, a long thread of silver wire lay to my left. Well, then.

The first step was to make a bead. I took out Zivar's files to smooth down the rough edges of the stone. I had not used a file much in the past, but at least this was fairly straightforward—monotonous, but not something that required exceptional skill. I wondered if I could leave the karenite rough—did it *have* to be filed down and polished? Zivar's was much rougher than the karenite bead she'd gotten from Ligeia, I was certain of that. *Best to just copy what Zivar did.* I worked for hours, until I was satisfied that it was as smooth as Zivar's had been.

Now it was time to drill. I tightened her vise around the stone, realizing that I didn't know how much pressure would make it crack. The drill was easy to find, but not easy to use. It kept slipping to the side, scratching the stone without actually making a hole in it. Finally I got enough of a hole started to provide a little groove for the drill itself, and once that held the drill in place, things went fairly quickly.

There. I had a bead. I held it in the palm of my hand and blew gently to chase away the dust, wondering if there was any magic in those tiny scattered bits.

A sound from the doorway startled me; I jumped off the stool like I was going to pretend I'd been polishing Zivar's worktable. Nurzhan regarded me, a little amused, a lamp in her hand.

"How is Zivar?" I asked, trying to pretend that I hadn't been startled.

"The fever has ebbed," Nurzhan said. "The dangerous part is past, we think. We will keep watch to make sure the darkness doesn't drive her to harming herself, but she's no longer likely to harm others." She placed the lamp in its holder. "Should I send up a tray of food for you?"

"Will Zivar be angry, when she comes back to herself, and finds that I was up here, and that you were helping me?"

Nurzhan shrugged. "She won't be angry at us. If she's angry at you..." She shrugged. It wasn't her problem.

"I've heard that sorceresses are either the best masters, or the worst," I said. "Were you frightened when you were sold to her?"

Nurzhan leaned back against the wall and gave me a long, meditative look, sizing me up. I had asked a rather personal question, I realized, and a strange one, inquiring about a slave's personal life. Perhaps they expected that of Tamar; it was probably obvious to the slaves that Tamar had once been a slave. But this was a strange question, and one Nurzhan clearly wanted to consider for a moment before answering.

"*Do* you know Zivar's secret?" she asked, after a long silence.

I stared at her; this was not the answer I had expected.

"This is why we are servants, not slaves," Nurzhan said. "We hold her secrets. All slaves know secrets their owners wish they didn't, but Zivar's secret is far more dangerous than most. Perhaps living here, you should know it as well. You and your companion." From the look she gave me, I thought she was probably more concerned about protecting Tamar than protecting me. I still didn't know what she was talking about though, and she said impatiently, "She did *tell* you, I believe, in almost so many words, that night before the darkness took her. When you drank together, and spoke of who would bind the mistress when she was in a frenzy."

"She said *you* would do it." Nurzhan continued to stare at me like I was a very stupid child, and I suddenly remembered the other thing she had said: *Mila, now. Once we had to wrap her in a sheet to keep her from harming herself . . . This is why they say a sorceress needs a husband to look after her, because your slaves can't be trusted.*

"Yes," Nurzhan said. "Now you see. Mila was not a teacher, but a master. We've pried the full story out of her, in bits and pieces over time. Zivar was a slave down in Persia, owned by one of the lesser Weavers, Mila. She spied on Mila and learned her craft. When Mila died, she had learned enough that she was able to go to Ligeia and claim that she'd been Mila's apprentice, and persuaded Ligeia to finish teaching her. And so the mouse became the mistress."

"What would the Sisterhood do, if they knew?"

"We don't know. But they could kill her easily enough; they hold several of her spell-chains."

"Would you ever tell?"

"And risk being sold to a sorceress I had no hold over? Unlikely."

"Have you ever been owned by another sorceress?"

"Yes, I was born into the household of a sorceress. One with a family. It was . . ." She thought it over. "During the dark fever, in her frenzies, her husband would usually seek to control her, up to a point. But he feared her—I think the husbands of sorceresses fear them almost as much as their servants. And sometimes he would try to placate her by giving her what she wanted, at least up to a point. When I was still a child, she became convinced that I was spying on her for a rival sorceress. She wanted me killed. Her husband prevented that, but he did arrange to have me sold, very quickly. I had time to say good-bye to my father, but not to my mother, before I was whisked out of her household and into another."

"When Zivar bought you, were you worried?"

"Yes. I would have been worried even if she hadn't been a sorceress, though; it's always frightening to go somewhere new."

"Have you ever thought of spying on her and learning magic, just as she did with her own mistress?"

Nurzhan looked at the bead in my hand, and then back to my face. "I have seen Zivar's darkest days and her wildest frenzies. When the dark fever has her, she believes that the entire universe has united together to torment her. Thank you, but no, I would not become a sorceress for any price. I think Zivar must have wanted power very, very badly to study as she did."

I closed my hand around the bead, then slipped it into the silk pouch and tied it around my throat, as Zivar had. "Are you going to clean up Zivar's tools if I leave them out?"

"Not unless Zivar stirs herself and seems better."

I nodded, and went to the stairs. "Good night, then." *I will not work through the night. That's fevered sorceress behavior. And I am not a fevered sorceress.*

*Not yet, anyway.*

Nurzhan snuffed the lights behind me as I left.

Tamar was sleeping when I returned to the room, but stirred and sat up as I came in with my lamp. "Where have you been?"

"Making a spell-chain." I took off my slippers and crawled under the quilt. "I decided to come get some sleep."

"Good," Tamar said, and pulled the quilt back up to her ear. I lay back against the pillows.

I had expected to slip easily into sleep, but instead I lay awake for a long time, tossing and turning and listening to the faint whistle of the fire. Very late, I heard the wind suddenly pick up. It was probably snowing outside again. When I closed my eyes I could almost see the whirl of flakes, like a million falling stars, or the glittering crystals of a spell-chain.

*Lauria.*

It was Tamar's voice—but I had fallen asleep, I realized, and stood in the strange borderland of whirling colors. *Lauria.* Her voice caught me like a bird in a net, and I found myself standing on the summer steppe. Her cheeks were flushed, as if she'd just been riding. I fell back a step; it had been her voice, but it made no sense for Tamar to try to talk to me this way when she could simply wake me up.

"It worked!" she said, delighted.

"What worked?"

"I got you. I found you!" Tamar gave me a hug. "I've been trying to do this for weeks—no, months. And it worked. It worked! I came to the borderland, I called you, and you came."

"Do you think you'll be able to do this again?"

"I know I will." Her eyes were alight. "I'm a shaman now."

# CHAPTER EIGHT

*I*n the morning, I checked with the servants to make sure that Zivar was still indisposed, then went up to her workroom. It was snowing hard outside, and the workroom's light was veiled, her window half-covered with snow. The fire in the little stove had been built up for me, and the room was warm and comfortable. I looked around at the shelves of jars full of beads, then pulled one down, choosing one at random. The jar held beads of carved jade. I tipped them into my hand and looked at them. Some skilled person had carved each one into the shape of a tiny animal. There were dogs, cats, horses. No mice. I wondered if Zivar, of the stone carved mouse guarding her doorway, had used up any carved mice on past spell-chains.

Zivar had talked about the beads singing to her, and having tasted the swirling colors of the borderland I visited in dreams, I had a faint inkling of what she meant. I closed my eyes, holding the beads, but heard nothing. I popped a bird-shaped bead into my mouth, but it tasted like a slightly dusty piece of rock. I spit it out and stared at it, perplexed. After a moment, I took the karenite bead out of the silk bag at my throat and set it in my palm as well.

Something about the color of the karenite seemed to match with a carved jade horse. I set the horse on the table and tipped the rest of the beads back into the jar.

The next jar I chose held glass beads: tiny swirls of color, crimson and yellow and azure blue. I thought about Zhanna's meditation lessons, when she was trying to train me as a shaman: I tried to slow my breathing and to focus, just for a moment, on the beads. My ears still heard nothing but I decided, after looking at them for a long moment, that one of the beads went with the horse the way the horse had gone with the karenite. It was striped yellow and blue. I set it beside the horse and poured the rest of the beads back into their jar. I put the karenite back into the pouch around my throat.

The next jar held metal beads, and four of those seemed to fit, somehow. And so it went. I realized after a while that I needed some way to keep my chosen beads together. The giant shell from the sea that Zivar used was empty, so I took it carefully down from the shelf and put my beads inside.

Choosing perhaps twenty beads had taken me hours and I still wasn't sure I was doing it right. I would need at least twice this number to make myself a single loop of a reasonable length. If I wanted a nice long strand that could be looped two or three times around my neck, I would need eighty beads or more. I reached for another jar.

As the day wore on, the pile of beads began to grow. Even in the muted, snow-filled daylight it sparkled; I dug my fingers into the pile and let the beads trickle out like sand, listening to the sound they made. It was a sleepy day; I felt tired, half-asleep as I worked, but that didn't seem to make it harder to choose the beads I wanted. By nightfall, I had enough, I thought. I looked at the pile; it would make a nice long chain, big enough for two or three loops around my neck, or many more around my wrist. I wondered if more links made a more secure spell; intuitively it seemed like they *should,* since I had never seen a spell-chain big enough only to be a bracelet. Kyros had looped one of his spell-chains around his wrist, but it had been a many-stranded bracelet. *Perhaps I should add more beads. No. This is enough.*

I was tired and hungry, but reached for the wire and tools anyway. I had watched Zivar do this, over and over, and now I tried it myself: thread a bead, twist the end of the wire into a loop, and then cut that link free. But when I tried to bend the wire into a neat little circle, it was a gruesome, misshapen thing. I tried to straighten it out to try again and only made things worse. I tried a few more times and finally snipped off the end of the wire; it was bent and weakened past repair, the metal wasted. I tried again, and this time created a fragile-looking loop. I snugged the bead against the loop, snipped the wire free, and bent another loop. My loops were nothing like the perfectly balanced circles of Zivar's. Like selecting beads to go in the chain, this was harder than it looked. *I'll work on this tomorrow, when I'm fresh,* I thought. *But what if Zivar wakes from her stupor?* I took a bag and poured my beads into it, tightening the drawstring and putting the shell back where it went. *If Zivar wakes, I'll wait for the next time she goes into darkness to make the rest of the chain.* I dropped the twisted end and the single link into my bag as well, put everything else back where it belonged, and went down to have dinner with Tamar.

She was eating alone, staring pensively into the fire. "Are you done?" she asked as I came in.

"No." I described my day's accomplishments. "I'll get back to it in the morning. If I'm going to teach myself how to bend wire, I think I want good light for it."

"Fair enough." She pushed aside her half-eaten dinner.

"What's wrong?"

"The snow is making me restless."

"How deep is it outside?"

"Haven't you looked?"

"I haven't set foot outside since . . ." Days ago. "For a while."

"Well, maybe you should go look. Don't annoy Zivar, because we're stuck here until spring."

"If she tries to throw us out, I could threaten to expose her secret."

"That might work for her servants. I think she'd just kill you."

"What, with her bare hands? With a sword?"

"She'd think of a way, if she thought she had to."

I crossed the room to the shuttered window and cracked it open, peering down in the last of the evening twilight. The snow was falling outside very gently, but it looked really deep. I closed the window and shivered a little. "I'll be careful, then."

"You're using her tools, her beads . . ."

"Do you have a better idea for getting Prax out of the mine? For freeing Sophos's harem? For finding Thais?"

"I've been thinking about the harem," Tamar said. "Jaran is a shaman. I found you in a dream, I could probably find him. We could plan something. If the slaves worked together, if we were on the outside to help them get up to the steppe once they were out . . . I don't think we'd need the spell-chain. I think we could do it ourselves. I think *they* could do it."

"You're assuming that no one would rat them out. Aislan is in the harem! How is everyone else going to plan something and keep it a secret from Aislan?"

"That would be up to Jaran."

"And what about Prax? If there's a shaman down in the mine, I don't know who it is."

"You don't even know if Prax is still alive."

"Yes, I do," I said. "The djinn showed him to me. But I don't know how I'm going to get him out without a spell-chain."

"There's a way. There *has* to be a way. But you're not going to see it unless you turn away from what you're doing now. You're focused on the sorcery, on learning to make spell-chains; if another way is right in front of you you're still not going to see it."

"Even if you're right, what are we going to do for the rest of the winter? As you pointed out, we're buried in snow. We're stuck with Zivar until spring."

"So we stay here. Until spring. That doesn't mean you have to accept anything other than her hospitality."

"I'm never going to have this chance again," I said. "If I put away my beads, and throw away my karenite, I could be throwing away the one chance I'd have to do what I've promised to do."

"You are the most pig-headed stubborn goat of a *fool* that I have ever met," Tamar said. "What if you grab this chance, and the darkness the sorceresses walk along eats you like an owl eats a mouse? Gauhar, one of the servants here, used to work in the home of one of the big, important Weavers, a woman with a lot of apprentices. Do you realize that out of ten apprentices, five are sent away because the melancholia grabs them so strongly? And of the rest, three might end up killing themselves in a fit of dark fever? And of the two remaining, one might end up so mad that her spell-chains are taken away and she's kept somewhere quiet and safe, forever? The powerful sorceresses *don't make their own spell-chains.* They have apprentices who work in exchange for karenite. Zivar is probably hoping that you'll complete a spell-chain so that she can steal it from you."

"She can try," I said.

"Ask Gauhar what happens to the apprentices who fail, if you don't believe me," Tamar said. "Even one attempt at making a spell-chain can do it. Even a *failed* attempt. You're so busy grasping at your one precious chance that you don't realize that you could fall into the middle of a raging river in spring flood. *Look where you're going.*"

I was too infuriated with Tamar to stay in the room, and too infuriated to go to bed, anyway, so I turned around and went back up to Zivar's study to work on making necklace loops.

The workroom was dark when I reached it; I lit the lamps and bent over the desk again, bending the wire into tiny circles, over and over and over. It was tedious work, and my mind went back over my conversation with Tamar again and again, the way you might touch a bruise. I clenched my teeth together, steadying my hand against the table and squinting to focus my eyes. When I could barely keep my eyes open, I laid my head down on the desk—*just for a moment, to rest my eyes*—and found myself drifting, like a feather in a snowstorm.

*Here we are.*

I was in a room full of women. My first thought was that I was seeing someone's harem, but these women looked Greek, and many of them were old or unattractive. Still, they were dressed much like the women in Sophos's harem, in loose white shifts of thin linen. Some of the women were slumped in corners; one paced furiously. Then I noticed that some of them bent over small looms, and I realized that I was seeing some of the failed apprentices.

*See.*

One of the women could see me, I realized. Slouched in a corner, she had raised her chin slightly and was gazing directly at me. I wanted to say something to her, but I had no idea what to say. "Where are we?" I asked, finally.

"Hell," she said, her voice conversational. "Or maybe Penelopeia. I can't remember."

"How long have you been here?"

"Who knows?"

"Whose apprentice are you?"

"I was apprentice to Ligeia."

"How many spell-chains did you make?"

"Five," she said. "All for my mistress." She turned her head and spat on the floor.

The room was fading around me. *See,* the djinn whispered in my ears, again. *See see see see see.*

I lifted my head from Zivar's worktable and began to bend wire again. *Five spell-chains. I only need to make one.*

*S*ometime after sunup, I heard footsteps on the stairs; the servants moved almost silently, so my first thought was that it was Zivar. I leapt off the stool, stuffing my nearly complete chain under my shirt, and then saw that it was just Tamar. "Good morning," I said, trying to collect my scattered nerves.

"It's afternoon," Tamar said with a shrug.

"It is?" I realized suddenly that I was ravenous. No one had brought me anything to eat. They'd fed me as a courtesy to Tamar, so no doubt now they'd stopped bringing me food because Tamar had asked them to. I sat back down and picked up the tools again. "Any word of Zivar?"

"She's sleeping, apparently." Tamar sat down on the rug. "Are you almost done?" I held out the necklace. Tamar stared at it bleakly, then shrugged. "How many more beads?"

I did a quick count. "Ten. Plus the karenite."

"And once it's done, is that it?"

"No, I have to go get the djinn. That's what I saw Zivar doing."

"Ah."

She showed no inclination to leave, so I went back to work. A few more minutes and I had a long single strand. I drew the karenite out of the silk bag and made a link for it: the circle was almost ready to be closed. I spread the necklace out and looked at it for a moment. *All that glittering color.* If I closed the circle right now, anyone looking at it would think it was a spell-chain. The potential seemed to hum in the air; I could hear the singing of the beads again.

I remembered my glimpses of sorceresses in the past, draped with glittering spell-chains. *I could make a dozen necklaces out of nothing but beads, dress up in fine clothing, and almost everyone looking at me would take me for a sorceress. Though they might wonder why I traveled by horse, rather than palanquin, if they saw me on the road.*

Well, this was a real spell-chain, or would be shortly. I looked up and saw Tamar watching me still.

"Now I'll have to meditate," I said. "I think I'm going to do this in our room, if you don't mind. I don't think it matters where I take the necklace, and up here I've been jumping every time I think I hear Zivar."

Tamar shrugged again and got up as I put away Zivar's tools, all but the one set of pincers that I would need for this final step, which I tucked into my pouch with the spell-chain. Then she trailed me down the stairs and settled herself down on a cushion near the fire, watching me.

During the summer, when we were apprenticed to Zhanna, she had tried several times to teach us to meditate. Some shamans opened their minds to the spirits through dancing or drumming; apparently the sorceresses did it through weaving. I'd never been able to meditate properly in my lessons with Zhanna, but after following Zivar to the place she called the borderland, I thought I might be able to find my way there again. The fire reflected against the glass beads like sun on water. I held up the necklace and let it spill down from one hand to the other, back and forth, back and forth, watching the play of flames against the glass.

I could hear the smooth click of the beads. Then, faintly in the distance, I could hear a hum, the voices singing the same note. *Yes,* I thought, and I followed the hum.

I was not surrounded by a circle of dancing flames tonight; I held it, I controlled it, and I could fling the net out across the dark plain that surrounded me. *I'm here,* I thought, *I came here on purpose and I brought the spell. I am a Weaver! Or I will be, if I can take an aeriko.*

Of course, I had to find one first.

I turned around and around, and then realized I could see a faint glow in the distance. Remembering the woman of fire that Zivar had captured, I started toward the light. As soon as I thought about movement, I began to move, gliding over the shadowed plain like a diving eagle. Approaching, I could see the aeriko. A man, I thought, shining like a star, or like white heat.

"No!"

The voice was in my ear. I turned and saw nothing but the dark plain; the voice was in my real ear. "No!" Tamar's voice said again. "I'm not going to let you."

The man had seen us. He was moving, fleeing. I started after him, my movements sluggish and distracted. Then something cold and wet slapped me across the face. The darkness shattered around me like a dropped jar, and after a moment of intense nausea and a blinding pain in my head, the world settled around me and I was sitting, still, in front of the fire. Tamar stood in front of me, a wet rag in her hand and a faint smile on her face. Our eyes met for a long moment.

I said nothing, just closed my fist around the necklace and walked out.

*I can avoid her. Or wait her out.*

But Tamar was friends with the servants, and Zivar's servants were everywhere. Had she passed along word to dump water on my head if it looked as if I was meditating? The sickening pain of being dragged out of the borderland wasn't something I wanted to relive if I could avoid it.

Maybe I could pretend to sleep. Not real sleep—though I sometimes went to the borderland in my dreams, I didn't think I would be able to bring along the spell-chain. Of course, Tamar would guess that if I were "sleeping" somewhere other than my own comfortable bed, I might really be meditating. Well, perhaps I could go back to the room and lie down. *Not tonight. Tonight she would guess. But maybe tomorrow.* For now... for now, I realized, I was hungry. I didn't want to go back to the room because I thought that if I had to face Tamar's smirk, I would slap her. I headed for the kitchen.

The kitchen was busy. It was time for the evening meal, and even if Zivar was uninterested in eating more than a few sips of broth, the servants were all hungry. Food was loaded onto trays and carried up to Zivar, up to Tamar, out to the stable. Someone dished me out a bowl of chicken stew and I sat down at the kitchen table to eat it, mostly ignored by the busy staff. Someone ladled in more when I finished what I had, refilling my bowl until I pushed it away. There was a cup of wine, as well, though I barely touched that, and bread. When I'd finished, I slipped back out.

*I should make another attempt tonight.* Tamar would be expecting me to try again, and might stop me. But once she'd stopped me twice, she might begin to relax a little. I would have a better chance tomorrow—or even later tonight—if I let her stop me again now. I headed for Zivar's workroom.

It was quiet and dark, but when I stepped inside to light the lamp I heard someone say, "Stop, I like it dark." *Zivar.* Trembling, I turned. In the dim light I could just make out her shape, slumped at her worktable.

"It's Xanthe, isn't it?" she said. "Or Lauria. Tamar calls you Lauria, some of the time."

I shivered. "It's me," I said. "Lauria is a... nickname."

"Of course. So is 'Zivar'; I'm sure you guessed as much. The servants have given me to understand that you also know my secret now." She leaned forward. "They seem to think that you *own* Tamar; that I would kill you to protect my secret, and keep Tamar with them. They favor that idea, as they are fond of Tamar. But I am fond of you. Is Tamar your lover?"

"None of your business."

"We both know a few things that are none of our business, I think." I heard her let out her breath in a faint, dry chuckle. "Have a seat."

I sat.

"I've been well shadowed for a while now, but that hasn't stopped me from listening. It's a matter of habit, I suppose. And it's always stood me in good stead. Who is Prax?"

I shivered. "A slave that I would like to free."

"What if he doesn't wish to be free?"

"I don't think he'll refuse. He's in a mine."

"I see."

I wished she'd let me light a lamp. I couldn't make out her face in the darkness at all.

"So you plan to steal him, then free him, using the spell-chain that you made. That you *almost* made."

I tightened my fist around the necklace. "Yes. Are you one of the Younger Sisters?" I didn't really care about the answer to that question, I just wanted to push back.

"No. They're as cliquish as the High Weavers, in their own way. I had no sister-apprentices, in my 'studies' with Mila. In fact, I avoid Mila's old apprentices rather assiduously. There is one of them who might recognize me."

"Only one?"

"Mila had seven apprentices, and four of them never looked twice at Mila's slaves. Of the three who did, two are now dead. The one who remains knew my name, though. If she saw me, and looked past my robes and spell-chains to my face, she would probably know me." Zivar began to crack her knuckles, one by one. "Fortunately, she lives in Penelopeia."

"What is it that you want, Zivar?"

"From you? I wanted your karenite. Are you happy with our bargain?"

"Yes."

"As am I. Good. You're welcome to stay until the snow melts."

"But what do you *want*? Not from me. From... magic. From the djinni."

"I wanted freedom. I wanted power. Now... Now, I suppose I would most like to see an end to my own darkness. And perhaps..." She laughed, a little roughly. "I don't like the Sisterhood. I don't like the Younger Sisters. I would like to see magic scattered throughout the world, not controlled like gold coins from a locked chest. It's why I agreed to let you watch me. Every sorceress that the Sisterhood does not control is one more mouse in the granary."

"Yet you still checked to make sure I was female."

"I won't have a smelly man about the place." She paused, and I heard her sigh in the darkness. "I like that rule," she admitted. "Sooner or later, a man *will* learn magic, and the Weavers won't find out in time to have him killed, and then things will change. But for now... men have their swords, their shields, their horses, their armies. Alexander conquered the world with those things. But this is *our* power, the power of women."

I remembered thinking something along those lines, about sorceresses, a long time ago. A very long time ago.

"Lauria." She used my real name. "What do *you* want?"

"I want to free Prax, and the others I've sworn to free. And then as many more as I can."

"Only the rivers' return can free them all," Zivar said. Her tone was sarcastic.

"You don't believe that."

"I don't believe the rivers' return would matter. Ligeia has seen the spell-chain used to bind the Jaxartes—yes, there's a spell-chain for that. It's a single loop, so long that if you unwrapped it and held it out to its full length it would be taller than my house. It could be worn around someone's neck, if you looped it enough times, but it would be heavy. The beads are mostly blue, apparently. And it has hundreds of pieces of karenite, since it takes many, many aerika to keep the river bound."

"It's just a spell-chain that binds the rivers?"

"The Jaxartes. The Oxus—well, it took a great deal of aerika to build the tunnel under the mountains, but once the channel was built, it doesn't actually require any magic to keep it flowing. The Jaxartes, though, is bottled up in some valley in the mountains. It's not natural. It's held there by aerika who do nothing else."

"Have you ever seen it?"

"No. I haven't traveled a great deal. Flying makes me nervous."

"If it's bound with a spell-chain, though . . ."

"Yes, the binding stones could be broken, one by one. You'd have to lay hands on the spell-chain to do that, though, and it's not as if the Sisterhood leaves it just lying around. I think that's what the worshippers of Arachne are getting at with their story. Haven't you heard this one? They say that Arachne has ordered her servants the spiders to find the secret heart of the Weavers' power. When they find it, Arachne will destroy it. Then the rivers will return and the Danibeki will be free, because the power of the Weavers will have been broken. That's why the Greeks kill spiders."

"I always thought that was just to dishonor Arachne."

"It is. And there's no secret heart for the spiders to find, just a spell-chain that could be remade if it were ever stolen and smashed. Why doesn't Tamar want to let you finish *your* spell-chain?"

"She doesn't want me to enslave the djinni. Tamar didn't grow up worshipping Arachne—she grew up worshipping the djinni."

Zivar let out a dry chuckle. "If they are gods, why can the Sisterhood enslave them?"

"Well, right. But Tamar doesn't see it that way."

"What are you going to do?"

"Wait. And keep trying."

"Good luck," Zivar said, and fell silent. After a few moments, I edged out of her workroom, and went to find somewhere else to meditate.

I settled down, finally, in the downstairs sitting room where Zivar had first received us. I saw one of the servants, from the corner of my eye, as she passed by; no doubt word would be passed to Tamar. Well, there was nothing for it; I didn't really expect to succeed this time anyway. I meditated on the beads, but for whatever reason, I wasn't able to find my way to the borderlands this time. After a while I kicked off my slippers, pulled my feet up, wound the chain around my neck snugly enough that any meddling would wake me, and went to sleep on the cushions.

I slept peacefully, somewhat to my surprise; a tray waited on the table for me when I woke the next morning, with fresh bread and steam rising from the glass of sweet tea. I felt slightly hung over. I couldn't remember how long it had been since the last time I'd slept, woken, and eaten breakfast at a proper hour.

I looked out the door and saw a servant quietly sweeping the immaculate hall. Tamar knew I was awake, or would know, soon enough. How to avoid the eyes of the servants? It would be an almost impossible task. I sat down and ate my breakfast. This was a large house; perhaps this morning I would take the time to explore more thoroughly.

I spent the morning confirming that this was indeed a very nice house. In addition to the rooms I'd visited—the workroom, the guest room, the sitting room, and the kitchen—I found a number of others. There was a narrow room with a long table, presumably used for formal parties, if Zivar ever held them, which I doubted. The servants appeared to occupy a large set of rooms on the ground floor; I poked my head in and withdrew quickly when I was met with a stony glare. They were large and comfortable, fit to house the keepers of Zivar's secrets. The most interesting room was the library. It had a large window for light, and a shelf of books. The window was unshuttered, and the room was extremely cold; it probably got more use in the summer. I was intrigued enough to look through the books, but nearly all were in a strange foreign script—Persian, I guessed— and I couldn't read them. Of the volumes in Greek, one was a travelogue from someone who had wandered quite far beyond the territory of the Alashi, and one was a book of instructions for proper sacrifices to Athena.

I tucked the travelogue under my arm and closed the door behind me. The servant polishing the floor never so much as looked up. I bit my lip and went back downstairs.

The servants undoubtedly had instructions to tell Tamar if I took out the necklace to meditate; they might have been warned to tell Tamar if I lay down to take a midday nap. But would she have told them to tell her if I sat down and started reading? I might as well try. I curled up by the fire in the sitting room, lit a lamp for extra light, slipped the necklace into my lap where it was hidden by the folds of my tunic, and opened the travelogue.

The author had clearly wanted to save money on paper, because the handwriting was so tiny and cramped I had to squint to make out some of the words. In places, water or wine had been spilled, rendering it illegible. Still, it was interesting enough that after a few pages of pretending to read, I had started reading in earnest. The traveler was a man named Photios who worked for a merchant company with an aerika caravan. Except instead of sticking to the established trade ports, he seemed to spend a great deal of time using the aerika to explore. The travelogue was more of a long letter than anything else; he was reporting back on what he'd found. Zivar backed a merchant company, the servants had said. Perhaps she had backed the exploration mission. It seemed quite possible that this had been a letter to her.

On the trip he described, Photios had gone to the very edge of the world, beyond the people who sold silk and tea, to an island. The people on the island had little contact with magic, beyond employing rudimentary shamans to keep the aerika from causing trouble, but they had the most excellent metalsmiths that Photios had ever seen. He lacked the funds to buy a sword to bring back, and noted that on a modern battlefield, they hardly posed a threat to the Sisterhood of Weavers. Still, if magic were somehow removed from the equation, he thought they would be a remarkable foe. He finished with the regretful note that they were unfriendly and suspicious of foreigners, and that it would not make a comfortable place to retire.

So she was looking for a place to run away to. I turned the page; the next place Photios described was in the other direction, a cold land with mountains and pale barbarian warriors. *Enough of this.* I gripped the necklace. It was fascinating, but ... *I have work to do.*

I set the book aside for a moment, stretched, took a sip of tea, nodded at the servant who was replenishing wood in the fireplace, and bent my head over the book again. But I wasn't looking at the text now; I looked at the sparkling crystal in my lap as my fingers ran over the tiny carved horse, over and over again. I knew the note to listen for, and listen I did, until I could follow the sound to the borderland like one would follow the trickle of water against rock to find a stream ...

And there I was, in the singing darkness. I eased the pincers out to my lap, where I could use them.

*I need to work quickly,* I thought. *It won't take*

*long*. But as I turned, searching for a spirit to bind, I felt a sharp blow against my chest. This time, however, the force came from within the borderland itself, and a moment later, I could see Tamar standing beside me. "You're going to ruin everything," I said.

Her eyes were bright, like stars against the twilight. "I'm not going to let you," she said, and pushed me again.

The blow coming from the borderland itself didn't force me out the way the wet rag had. I pushed her back. "I am a sorceress," I shouted. "You can't tell me what to do here!"

"You may be a sorceress, but I am a *shaman*," Tamar said. She raised her hands, palms toward me—and though I felt no blow, I found myself abruptly back in the sitting room. *You are not permitted here*, her voice echoed in my ears.

I threw down my book and leapt to my feet. "Tamar," I shouted, no longer caring who heard. *"Tamar!"*


Tamar was waiting for me in our room. "Leave me alone!" I shouted as I came in.

"What makes you think—"

"I'm not stupid, Tamar. I know you've been having the servants watch me, and I know you just pushed me out of the borderlands!"

"Nurzhan has told me that when the cold fever has Zivar, she sometimes thinks that people are conspiring against her. Perhaps you're beginning to catch that fever yourself," Tamar said, primly.

"Leave me alone, or I'll, I'll—"

"Hurt me?" Tamar stood up. She was short, barely up to my shoulder. "Kill me? Your blood sister?"

"Don't be ridiculous." I turned away. "Who do you think you are?"

"I'm a shaman," Tamar said. "And what you want to do is wrong."

"Are we going to free the *horses,* too, while we're at it?"

"The djinni are not like horses. You know that perfectly well. And we will never free any djinn you bind, you know that perfectly well, too. Just as Zivar will never have enough spell-chains, you will always have one more thing you *need* that djinn to take care of for you, *always.*"

"No, Tamar, listen to me . . ." I had expected her to interrupt me, but instead she turned toward me, waiting, listening to hear what I said. "What do you want from me?" I asked.

"I want you to give up on the idea of becoming a sorceress."

"I'm not going to do that."

"It's not just because you'll be enslaving djinni," Tamar said. "I've had the chance to hear stories about Zivar from her servants. Lauria, *you don't want to do this*! There will be no going back, do you understand that? Don't go through this door."

"What if I take one week to think about your advice?" I said. "If I promise to think about it for a week, if I give you the spell-chain to hold while I think about it, at the end of the week will you promise to back off and let me do what I've decided to do?"

Tamar thought it over. I took the spell-chain out of my pocket and held it out so she could see it.

"All winter," Tamar said. "If you let me hold it all

winter, and you still want to do this in the spring, I'll agree."

"That's too long. How about two weeks?"

"No."

"Three weeks."

"All winter or nothing," Tamar said, and reached for it.

I snapped the necklace out of her grasp. "I'll wait you out," I said, spun on my heel, and walked out of the room.

My head ached, and I felt as sick as I had when Tamar had slapped me with a wet rag to drag me back from the borderland. But this time it wasn't the shock of the sudden return that had caused it, but my anger and frustration with Tamar. *I thought I could trust her. She's supposed to be my sister, my ally, someone I can turn to . . .*

We had argued almost since our escape from Sophos, but we'd never fought before, not like this. Fear caught at the corners of my mind, as well. *After I bind the spirit, will she refuse to speak to me? All winter? Will she turn her back on me come spring?*

Downstairs, there was a servant dusting the dustless sitting room. I started to sit down, to read the travelogue a little more, but I was too angry. *I need a walk.* I went to the front door and looked out. The snow was deep, up to my hips, but there was a well-trod path out to the stable. *The stable, of course!* How long had it been since I'd seen my horses? *Too long.* I sent a servant to get my boots so that I didn't have to see Tamar, pulled them on, and ran across the courtyard to the stable.

The stable hands leapt to their feet as I came in; their morning chores accomplished, they appeared to have been gossiping over a dice game. "Just pretend I'm not here," I said, but they skulked off to various tasks, looking busy even if they weren't. I shook my head and went to groom Krina.

The horses were happy to see me. *Happier than I deserve.* I hadn't even provisioned myself with treats, so I took some carrots from a sack in the corner of the barn to feed my horses, then brushed their coats. They didn't need brushing any more than the sitting room needed dusting, but they appreciated the attention. "You're going to be fat and soft by spring," I scolded them as I worked.

"We take them out for exercise whenever we can," the stable girl near me said. "The weather's been bad lately."

The stable smelled of straw, horse, and wood smoke; it was warm and dimly lit. After a while, the servants sat back down again and resumed their game; I worked my way to the back of the stable and found a comfortable spot, half hidden behind sacks of grain and polished horse tack. The servants were paying no attention to me at all. *Either Tamar forgot to tell them to keep an eye on me, or they're too busy with their game to remember that they're supposed to.* Tamar was much closer friends with the kitchen staff; the stable hands were their own little circle, not one that was as kindly disposed to her. *Now, perhaps, is my chance.* I glanced at the servants one more time, then laid out the unfinished spell-chain and the pincers that would let me close the circle.

I found my way to the borderland quickly, and no unseen hands shoved me out or caught hold of me. Catching my breath, I looked around and saw a spirit shining in the darkness like a candle flame. *I'll have you. You are mine.*

My spell-chain was in my hand, and I flung it out, encircling the spirit. I heard a scream of despair. I could see the lights, encircling the spirit like a net, like a cage; inside the circle, I could see the spirit. It was male. My first impression was of a blazing bird, like an eagle on fire; then of a vast cat, the kind that could eat a man as its prey. The aeriko flung itself against the imprisoning circle, jerking it like a fish against a line. I held on, wondering what would happen to me if the spell didn't hold. But it did.

I twisted the necklace, making the circle smaller. Within, the aeriko became more frantic, more desperate, like a landed fish fighting against the air that drowned it. I twisted again, and the aeriko screamed again, then began to weep, as Burkut had.

*I have to do this.* I twisted again, again, making the circle smaller and smaller. Finally the aeriko faced me, its hands bound against its sides, held prisoner by the spell. I looked across the chain of fire into my prisoner's face, into its eyes.

"No," it whispered, looking at me, and for a moment, I saw Alibek's eyes, as he'd begged me not to take him back to Kyros.

*Don't let it sense your weakness!* I urged myself, but I stood frozen.

"Not you," the djinn said.

I saw Thais's eyes, cold and distant; Nika's eyes, proud but terrified; Burkut's eyes as he collapsed, weeping to the sands. I saw Uljas bow his head to refuse to look at me, the day that I took him back to Kyros.

*You don't talk about freeing horses. Are horses*

*slaves? Horses don't talk. Only people talk. People and djinni.*

The djinn raised its hands and stretched them toward my face; I felt a shiver run down my back like a drop of melted snow as it touched me.

*I can do this. I can. I can take it, it can find Prax and get Prax out for me, and I'll let it go.*

I heard the hiss of Prax's breath as he drew his improvised knife and attacked me with it, in his last desperate bid for freedom. *I'll die before I go back there.* I had taken the knife away from him with barely a scratch, and brought him proudly home . . .

All that remained was to close the circle.

I dropped the chain. "Not today," I said to the djinn. "Go in peace."

The light vanished. The chain vanished. And I fell from the darkness into the stable. It was dim, and I could hear the servants laughing over their game. Before I could change my mind, before Zivar or one of the other sorceresses could steal the chain and the karenite from me, I grabbed a hammer off the wall, threw the chain onto the stone slab of the floor, and smashed the karenite on the necklace into dust.

*I hear the bird,* I thought as nausea suddenly overpowered me. *The bird that Zivar spoke of, the dark vulture of vast size that settled on the roof, shadowing her with its wings. I think I know now what she might have been talking about.*

# CHAPTER NINE

*I* walked back into Zivar's house. My anger toward Tamar was gone, but exhaustion weighed me down with every step. I did make it up to Tamar's and my room before collapsing into bed, my boots still on. Tamar was sitting by the fire. "I'm tired," I said, and tossed the necklace onto the floor, lay down, and closed my eyes.

I heard Tamar pick up the necklace; I could hear the soft click of the beads as she turned it over in her hands. "What happened?"

"I couldn't go through with it."

"Good," she said. I wondered if the beads would still be singing, if I saw it in the borderland. "Good." Another rattle as she put it away somewhere. "I'll get you some lunch."

"Don't bother," I was going to say, but it seemed like too much effort.

*I* expected to feel better the next morning, but I didn't.

It was strange, the bone-weariness I felt. It went so much deeper than mere exhaustion.

Tamar nagged at me to eat.

There was an ache, somewhere beyond my heart. I wanted to make it go away. Carving out my heart with a sword was the only thing I could think of that seemed as if it might help.

*U*p. Up!" Someone shook me violently. It wasn't Tamar. I curled up, resisting, but the hands only shook me harder. "Open your eyes, you lazy girl. Up!"

It was Zivar. I let her drag me out of bed. There was a hollow where I'd been lying, like a bird's nest.

"I have discovered the secret of flight," she whispered to me. It made no sense, but I didn't care enough to ask for her to clarify. "And that will cure your melancholia. Come on, out out out!"

My boots were gone; Tamar must have pried them off my feet. Zivar dragged me downstairs in my socks, then out into the snow. The sun was shining, and the air was still but very cold. Zivar was shivering, but her cheeks were flushed as if it was midsummer. "Now run," she said. "Run back and forth! If only we can get up enough speed, we'll be able to fly by ourselves, no aerika necessary. Come on!"

She was dragging on my arm, so I stumbled after her, blinking in the dazzling sun. Back and forth across the courtyard we ran. My hands and feet ached in the cold; we slipped and slid on the packed snow and skidded into the wall of the stable.

"This isn't working," Zivar said after a time. "All right, back inside. I'll have to think of something else."

The servants had gathered to gape, and Tamar met

me with a warm blanket to wrap around my shoulders as she hurried me back upstairs and sat me down in front of the fire. Zivar trailed behind her, still talking.

"....melancholia," she was saying as I sat down.

"But I broke the spell," I said. "I smashed the binding stone. Why..."

"You heard the cry of the aeriko," Zivar said. "You looked into its eyes and knew its hate. I think perhaps that's what does it. That's why I always work as fast as I can."

"Is that really the reason?"

"Who knows? It's what I tell myself when I work. Anyway, we'll cure you yet. Let me just think..." And out she went.

Tamar held a cup to my lips. I drank, expecting tea, but it was broth, salty and very strong. I spluttered, then drank it anyway.

"You're wasting away," Tamar said.

"There's plenty of me left."

"Will you eat? I'll send for food," she said, but by the time the food had arrived, I had gone back to my nest.

*B*ut now I couldn't sleep, not the way I'd been sleeping. Night came, and I still couldn't sleep, staring into the darkness and thinking of Prax. *I failed you. I had a chance, and threw it away.*

My failures lined up in front of me like soldiers on parade, and I counted them, from failing Kyros to failing Burkut to failing Prax, Thais, and Sophos's harem. The ache beyond my heart overwhelmed me, and I knew I deserved to be punished. I thought of Uljas's scars from his beating at Kyros's hand: *I deserve no*

*less. I deserve worse. I deserve to be sold into a mine,
like Prax, to be forced to work in darkness, not knowing whether it is morning or night.*

For some reason the thought was almost appealing:
driven to work myself to death, at least I would probably be distracted from the unending ache that swallowed my days. I wondered if I could persuade Tamar
to sell me—*we're always buying, never selling*—so that
in one way, at least, I could finally pay for my crimes.

And if she sold me to Prax's mine? If I were face-to-face
with Prax, what would I tell him then? *I've made myself
one of you. I'm here with you, do as you like to me.*

My thoughts were thick; I tried to imagine what
Prax would say to that, and couldn't. Perhaps like
Uljas, he had sworn to kill me, which was what I de-
served, after all. *We are both in darkness,* I thought.
*And I see no way out.*

*I* did sleep, finally.

*I* dreamed, some nights, when I was asleep, but I had
none of what I'd come to think of as my "true"
dreams. Zhanna didn't come find me; neither, fortunately, did Kyros. My thoughts, during the waking
hours, were slow and muddled. Thinking about anything felt like wading through hip-deep mud. I would
get stuck with each new step and lose my way. I settled
into imagining the mine, which for some reason was
easier. The heaviness of the stone; the darkness of the
pit; the constant hunger, the exhaustion.

*I will be unable to ride there in the spring if I don't
get out of bed soon.*

I rose, and sat by the fire. *I will be the world's most useless slave, more useless than Burkut.*

*I*t was dark and I couldn't sleep, and thought again of the mine, seeing myself face-to-face with Prax as I'd faced Uljas. *I am one of you now. Do as you like to me.*

*And?* asked the Prax of my dark imaginings, surprising me. *And? This helps me how?*

*I am an offering. You can kill me. Have your vengeance.*

*I don't want your sacrifice. I want to see the sky again.*

*But...I have a confederate on the outside,* I thought earnestly to Prax. *A friend who can help us escape.*

*That's it.* My blood went cool, suddenly, as I turned the idea over and considered it. *If I have nothing to lose, if I'm willing to risk slavery, beating, death... why not?*

Prax was not a shaman, nor were we connected through blood, so I couldn't communicate with him in dreams. But Tamar and I could talk, by night, even over large distances. *Even if I were there, how would I get them out?* The slaves would outnumber the guards, but the guards had fear on their side, and weapons. They were strong, not worn almost to death from the work in the mine. And by night, they put all the slaves down below, so that they couldn't run.

Opening my eyes where I lay, I saw a shadow skitter across the wall—a spider. *Venom,* I thought. *Arachne's weapon makes us strong.* The Alashi tipped their arrows with venom, giving themselves an advantage in fights against the Greeks. The slaves would have no weapons they hadn't managed to wrest from the guards. Then I remembered the cook at the inn, the innkeeper who beat her when everyone became ill. *The food at the mine will be cooked by slaves. The pots are scrubbed by slaves. And the guards and the slaves probably do not eat the same food. I could bring something...a little bit of spoiled meat, to add to the guards' stew.*

*The guards are not likely to be very effective when puking their guts up.*

*Tamar could wait until the guards were ill, then come to help us out of the mine...*

*It would be easier with help. Perhaps we should free Sophos's harem first...*

I lay awake through the night, thinking.

*I* was tired in the morning, but I felt as though I could see daylight again. *I just needed to think of a way to free Prax,* I thought. *Now that I have a plan, of course I feel better.* I got up and stretched, shook out the covers to air the bed, and helped myself to a cup of tea from the kettle by the hearth. Tamar came in a few minutes later and stopped in the doorway, looking as if she'd seen a ghost. "You're out of bed!"

"I had an idea," I said. "Is that food on that tray? I'm starving."

"You *are* starving!" Tamar set down the tray and lifted my arm, encircling my wrist with her fingers. "You've barely eaten in weeks. Here, eat what's on the tray. I'll go get more."

There was a cup of broth, which I ignored in favor of the bread, cold meat, and yogurt. I was finishing it off when Tamar returned. She dumped more food on the tray and sat down to eat her own. "There. Eat up. Are you feeling better?"

"This tastes really good." How had I never noticed before how good cold roast mutton could be? "*Really* good."

"Mmmm-hmmm." Tamar eyed me a little nervously as she ate her own bread.

"I had an idea. About freeing Prax."

Tamar leaned forward. "Tell me."

"Well..." I finished a mouthful of food and washed it down with tea. "Remember at that inn we stayed at, how sick everyone got? The meat must have gone bad. What if we let some meat spoil on purpose and used it to poison the guards' food, up at the mine?"

"Hmm. I suppose that's the start of a plan," Tamar said cautiously. "How would we get the spoiled meat to Prax?"

"We'd ride up there and you'd pretend to be selling me as a slave. I'd have it with me."

"Are you *crazy*?" Tamar slammed her bread down on to her tray. "Or maybe you're just joking?"

"We can talk to each other in dreams. I can't talk to Prax, or anyone else down in the mine. If I'm there, and you're on the outside, we could make plans... once all the guards are sick, you could come in and help us get up out of the mine."

"All by myself?"

"Well, I was thinking maybe we'd free Sophos's harem first. Do you think you could convince the slaves from the harem to come help you?"

"No. I don't think they'd do it. So this plan isn't going to work." She turned away from me. "Think of something else."

The shutter rattled and I jumped. "Oh, yes, it's

snowing again," Tamar said with a shrug. "So we've got some time to come up with a better plan. You spent a month in bed—"

"A *month*?"

"—but there's still months of winter left. We're not going anywhere soon."

*I* was ready, I thought—ready to load up our horses and head north, ready to do whatever it took to get Prax out. But it was the coldest part of the winter; an ocean of snow would have to melt before we could travel, and there was nothing I could do just now except wait.

Fearful of slipping into another bleak melancholy, I threw myself into activity. I got up every morning to groom our horses and take them out for some exercise if it wasn't snowing hard; the snow in the courtyard was trampled down now and the horses could move. In the afternoons, I would put on my boots and all the clothing I owned and go for walks through Casseia. After snowfalls, they would have bound djinni scoop up the snow from the streets and dump it outside, so that the residents could walk around the city without too much trouble. It was appallingly cold, however, and even after a short walk I would be shivering, my toes numb and my face aching.

After my walk I would join Tamar in our room. I had told her about the travelogue and she was curious, so I had begun to read it to her. "Reading really isn't that hard, you know," I said, putting the book down one day. "I could probably teach you your letters, and then you could read to yourself."

"Eh." Tamar sounded deeply dubious. "I might be

able to puzzle words out, with practice. It's easier to have you read to me."

"What if it comes in useful, once we're working on freeing Prax and the harem?"

"It will be more useful if you're really good at the dream speech. When are you going to start practicing?"

"I'd have to go to the borderland again."

"That's right."

I shrugged. "I'd rather not do that until I have to."

"If it's going to send you down into the darkness again, wouldn't it be better to find that out now?"

"Eh," I said.

Tamar rolled her eyes. "Fine, then. As long as I can find you in the night, we should be fine. Right?"

"I'll try it," I said. "Tonight."

If I was going to try to speak to someone in my dreams, though, it seemed silly to take the risk just to talk to Tamar. After all, I could talk with her in the night just by waking her up. No, if I were going to travel to the borderland and visit another shaman in the dark hours of the night, I wanted to see Zhanna. She hadn't visited me in a long time. I wanted to know why. I wanted to be certain everything was well with her.

The last time she had visited me, she'd told me that it would help me to find her if I could hold something of hers, or something that reminded me of her. I didn't have my vest anymore, of course, though it made me feel strangely warm to think that Zhanna had kept mine. Zhanna always smelled of incense; the smell clung to her hair, especially. *If I could find some incense* . . . It was too late to go hunting for it.

When I thought of Zhanna, there were a lot of memories that came to mind: her matter-of-fact response to my nightmares, her laughter when Tamar and I had tried to learn how to meditate, her face as she chewed thoughtfully on her lip, trying to decide how to answer a question. But thinking of an *object* that reminded me of Zhanna, that was hard. She'd had cropped hair and plain clothes and a black vest, like every other member of the Sisterhood, plus a box of feathers and other items for her shamanic rituals. The embroidery on the back of her vest had been flowers, nothing special. No, that wasn't true; I pictured Zhanna working on her vest and remembered the exact picture. She'd done flowers down one side, and then a larger picture of a hawk. A feather, perhaps? I didn't know where to find one of those, either, not this time of night, in the dead of winter.

"Do you have any feathers?" I asked Tamar, who was getting ready for bed as well.

"Yeah, of course," she said. There was a small wood box on the table; I'd barely noticed it, but out of the box came a soft leather bag, and a bundle of feathers, large and small feathers from all sorts of birds. She selected a small gray feather and handed it to me. "Will this one be all right?"

"I don't know why Zhanna bothered trying to train me," I said, taking the feather. "Of course you have feathers. You were a shaman's apprentice. It never occurred to me to pick up feathers over the summer."

"You'd make a fine shaman. You just needed a chance to learn more. You didn't grow up with a shaman, so you don't know the rituals. Why would you think to pick up feathers?" She yawned and stretched. "I'm going to bed. Maybe I'll talk to you in a bit."

I lay down beside her, my hand curled around the feather; I closed my eyes and thought of Zhanna.

*I*t was winter on the steppe, but the yurt was warm, even with just me and Zhanna inside. "Zhanna?" I said, hesitantly, not certain I'd truly found my way here.

"Lauria." Her face lit up.

"You haven't come..."

"I was forbidden to seek you out. But no one can forbid you to come to me."

"Who forbade you? Why?"

"You troublemaker," Zhanna said with a joyful laugh, and gave me a hug. "They cast you out, and you keep making trouble. Tamar was not the only Alashi who disliked the rule about not freeing slaves. But the two you've sent could have been born Alashi; this has given strength to those who want us to free Danibeki slaves more often. Uljas wants to form an army, a strong army. And we've heard the Penelopeians are moving against us."

"I think they are," I said. "They want to wipe you out. They want your karenite; they're almost out of their own, or so they say. Still, it's the foundation of everything they do. Without it the Sisterhood is nothing."

"Will you be sending us more slaves?"

"I hope so. But not until spring."

"Lauria." The dream was fading, and Zhanna grabbed my hand with all her strength, as if she could keep me from leaving. "You are the gate. You were chosen. I believe you cannot fail at your task, so draw your sword without fear."

I woke to daylight and Tamar shaking me. "Where were you? Where are you? We need to go. Nurzhan brought a warning. Zivar means to kill us both."

"Go where?" I scrambled out of bed, pulling my boots on, my coat. "It's winter, it's snowing..."

"She's going to hide us. Zivar will calm down soon."

Down the stairs, into the servants' quarters, through a door, and down more stairs...there was a cellar I hadn't seen when I'd explored. Tamar had a lamp; it flickered wildly, then settled as she put it on a shelf. I looked around. We were under the kitchen; I could hear footsteps above our heads, and the voices of the servants. The cellar was used for food storage. Sacks of flour, grain for the horses, carrots, cabbages, rice...There were clay jars in the corner that probably held wine or spirits of wine. Another shelf of jars probably held honey.

"She won't think to look here?" I asked. "I'd look here, if I were Zivar." I looked around. "And there's no way out."

"Yes there is," Tamar said. She opened a cabinet against the wall; the sounds from the kitchen abruptly grew much louder. "This cabinet goes up, if you pull on a rope from the kitchen. It's how they get the heavy things up and down. If Zivar comes down, we jump in and go up."

"She won't notice?"

"It's what Nurzhan suggested, and I didn't have any better ideas."

"The stable?"

"That's the *first* place she'll look."

"Maybe we should just leave..."

"It's snowing hard, and the temperature is dropping."

"Maybe tie her up in a sheet?"

"If it comes to that, I think they will, but they'd rather just hide us. Don't argue, Lauria; they know what they're doing."

"Yeah." Hearing my real name from Tamar made me think of Zivar *listening* from her bed, however she'd managed that—djinni, servants, some secret Persian magic left over from her days as a slave girl, I had no idea. I wondered if she was listening to us now, and all this sneaking around and hiding was a farce. *They know what they're doing.* If anyone here knew what they were doing, it was the servants. If anyone could trust them, it was Tamar. If they wanted me dead, they'd have separated the two of us ...

Tamar blew out the lamp and we sat down in the darkness, our backs to the open cabinet, listening to the voices of the servants in the kitchen.

Sitting in the darkness, I began to feel jittery. I found myself thinking about the day Zivar had dragged me outside to learn to fly. Running as hard and as fast as I could sounded strangely appealing. I stood up, shifting from foot to foot. "Do you need to relieve yourself?" Tamar whispered.

"No. I need ... I don't know. I need to move a little." The floor was hard stone, very quiet; so long as I didn't knock over a cask of wine my steps should be soundless. I groped my way to the wall and felt my way along it, just to be able to pace. Three steps in each direction. It wasn't enough. I tried jumping up and down in place. It felt like I had a kettle of boiling water inside my heart, with nowhere for the water to splash as it bubbled out of the spout, and no one to take the kettle off the fire. I sat back down and tried to steady myself, but found my thoughts racing. *Calm down*, I told myself, but it didn't help.

"Lauria," Tamar whispered, and closed her hand gently over my wrist. "Come here."

She drew me against her and had me lie down with my head in her lap. "Think of the river," she said. "The snow will begin to melt soon; think of the Arys, of the snowdrifts turning to the spring flood." She ran her fingers through my hair, stroking my scalp and my temples with her fingertips. "Think of the white foam on the water, the branches caught in the rush, the sound of the snow beginning to drip . . ."

I could see a river in my mind's eye, but it wasn't the Arys at spring flood. It was the Jaxartes—the Syr Darya—its bonds cut as if with a sword, crashing down from the mountains and into the dry riverbed. The sky was a cloudless blue, but the rush of water sent a cloud of water up to the sky like smoke from a wildfire. *As they flowed once.*

Tamar was still whispering, her hand warm and comforting against my face. *Draw your sword without fear,* Zhanna had told me. *Why stop at slaves? I will free the rivers, both of them. They were bound; they can be unbound. It was done; it can be undone. This is my task, this is what I was born for, to find the spell-chain that Zivar described and free the djinni within it. Zivar thinks it could be remade, but she doesn't realize how scarce karenite is becoming. Besides, if the rivers returned, people would* believe *that they were free. They would rise up against the Greeks—slaves and Alashi together.*

I felt a swell of elation, as if the task were already completed, even though I had not the faintest idea how I would do this, where to begin, how to even *find* the spell-chain that bound the Syr. It seemed perfectly clear, however, that Zhanna was right. I was chosen, I couldn't fail, so why not set my sights on the ultimate goal? I settled back against Tamar, willing to wait, just for now. Spring was coming. I would free Prax, I would find Thais. It would all work out because I could not fail.

Tamar suddenly went rigid, her hand freezing against my hair. I could hear someone's feet above us, quite close. "Into the cabinet," Tamar whispered, and I scrambled in after her. We had to pull our knees up against our chests to fit in; Tamar swung the door shut, and then we were going up, up, and when the door opened again we were in the kitchen. "Hurry," someone whispered as we scrambled out.

"Which way?" Tamar asked breathlessly.

"The stable..." We started to follow, but a shimmering light abruptly blocked our way. "Shit," the woman muttered and fell back a step from us as if to distance herself from our doom.

Zivar stood in the doorway to the kitchen, her eyes alight and an unsheathed knife in her hand. "And this is why they say that a sorceress should have a *family*," she spat, striding toward us. "Someone she can *trust*."

The servants bowed their heads and avoided her eyes. Some of them edged away from the knife.

"Instead, I have a house of spies and liars."

Nurzhan appeared in the doorway, her face anxious. "My lady," she said. "What's going on?"

"Are you here to pretend to me that you didn't know? To speak to me soothingly, lock me somewhere safe, tell me that it's all the fever talking?"

Nurzhan approached her hesitantly, keeping a wary eye on the knife. "Well, my lady, I *don't* know what you're talking about, and whether it's the fever talking or your true heart, the fever's kept you from eating

much in days. What do you say to lunch?" It seemed
an absurd proposal, but Zivar seemed to be consider-
ing it. "Look, whatever you want to discuss can be discussed in the dining room—when was the last time we
even used the dining room?—and we can all have a
good meal. Then if you decide to execute all of us we'll
go out with a full stomach."

"As soon as I put down my knife you'll be after me
with a sheet to force me to bed."

"Well, let's think about this. Maybe you can sit at
one end of the table, where no one can reach you before you can pick your knife back up, and Xanthe and
Tamar can sit at the other end."

"Her name isn't Xanthe, it's Lauria."

"It's agreed, then." Nurzhan nodded to some of the
other servants, who hastily began to carry food and
dishes into the dining room.

The dining room had probably not been used in
years, but it was immaculate and well kept by Zivar's
servants. One had already spread out a cloth, and another was setting out plates and bowls and serving
meat and cheese and bread. Zivar settled into an arm-
chair at the opposite end, her back to a wall, and maintained a vigilant grip on her knife until her meal was
served. I wondered if the servants could wrestle away
the knife from her if they were truly determined to do
so. *If she were threatening one of them, they'd probably be more inclined to take the risk.* Tamar and I sat
at the other end of the table, well out of reach, and
Nurzhan and a few other servants clustered in the
doorway. "Eat your food," Nurzhan whispered to us.

Tamar tucked into her food; I ate a few nervous
bites. Zivar was also eating, a wary eye on the rest of
us. No one said anything for several minutes.

"Now then," Nurzhan said. "Did you have plans for the afternoon, my lady? Shopping, perhaps, or planning an improvement to the house?"

"Killing the spies," Zivar said. "And anyone who tries to stop me."

"We're not spies," Tamar said.

"Oh, you *pretend* to be outcast Alashi, to be a couple of fugitives, but I have ears in a lot of places. A *great number* of places, and so I know all about your little arrangement with the Sisterhood. You're trying to trap me. You probably think you *have* trapped me."

"What little arrangement? I honestly don't know what you're talking about," I said.

"Of course you're going to say that. What are you going to say? 'Why yes, Zivar, we were sent here by the Sisterhood to lure you into exposing yourself...'"

"Listen to me, Zivar," I said. "If the Sisterhood wanted you dead, they wouldn't waste their time getting you to expose yourself. They hold your spell-chains. They could arrange for someone to accidentally free one of the djinni so that it came back through and killed you. They don't care about your secret because you're useful to Ligeia. You said yourself she can have you make spell-chains that she knows will be at risk, because she doesn't care whether you live or die."

Zivar's hand tightened on her knife; her jaw clenched. "Then what *are* you doing here?"

"We came to Casseia to find a slave."

"And why did you smash your own spell-chain, you foolish, stupid girl? What were you *thinking*?"

"I was thinking that I never want to enslave anyone, ever again, and that the djinni deserve freedom as much as you or me or Tamar."

"You're as sentimental as a little girl."

"Yes, you're probably right."

She thought it over. "No, this makes no sense."

"What doesn't make sense?"

"I *know* that you are Kyros's daughter," she said. "Ligeia spoke of a Lauria, and it was clear from the description that she meant you."

Tamar choked on her meat and I almost spit a mouthful of wine back into my cup. "Ah," Zivar said. "*This* is true, if nothing else is. You *are* the daughter of Kyros."

"Bastard daughter," I said, setting my cup down very carefully. "The child of his mistress, a former favored slave."

"Then why does Ligeia think that you work for him?"

"Because Kyros is lying to her, I guess, or else I've lied to him better than I thought."

"Who *is* Kyros?"

"You know I'm his daughter but you don't know who he is?" I shook my head, considered lying, then shrugged and said, "He's the commander of the military garrison at Elpisia, near the northern border. I was supposed to go infiltrate the Alashi. You correctly guessed that we were cast out. Now I'm dodging his djinni."

"What did you do to the first two?"

"I don't know what you're talking about."

"That's it," Zivar said, and she snatched up the knife and launched herself at me. "I'm going to cut your lying throat."

She knocked me backward in my chair to the floor; my head knocked against the wall and my ears rang from the impact. I brought up my knee, kicking her as hard as I could. Tamar leapt onto her like an angry dog, biting down on her wrist in an attempt to slow her arm.

Despite Tamar, I felt the knife score my shoulder; Zivar's breath was hot in my face, her eyes utterly wild.

Then she was off me, in the hands of the servants, the knife clattering to the ground. "Spies—liars—" Zivar shouted, struggling. The servants pinned Zivar against the wall. Someone had a sheet and they were binding her in it, pinning her arms, her legs. She screamed like they were hurting her, though they had a practiced air and I doubted that they bound her tighter than was necessary. Tamar watched with horror. Zivar writhed as they carried her away, still screaming.

"Well," Nurzhan said, as Zivar's cries faded. "That was unpleasant. You're leaving in the spring, aren't you? I think having strangers around makes it more likely that her fevers make her violent, rather than making her want to dress all her servants in velvet or buy fifty perfectly matched white horses." She shook her head and returned to her work.

We went back to our own room; Tamar sent for water and a soft cloth to bandage the cut Zivar had left on my shoulder. We didn't expect to hear anything from Zivar for a time, but a few hours later one of the servants knocked on the door. "Zivar wants to speak to you," she said to me. "She will not be refused. She's bound, so she can't harm you." She gestured, and it was clear that this was an order, not a request.

I hadn't seen Zivar's bedroom before. It was chaotic, despite the best efforts of the servants, with stacks of books and heaps of clothing. I wondered how much of the mess came just from the last day. Zivar lay on her side on the bed, her face flushed, her body wrapped in the sheet like a fly in a spiderweb. "Tell me one thing," she said. "Kyros. Will he misuse my spell-chain? Will he be the death of me?"

"He won't forget he can't have his djinni commit murder," I said. "Ever. That's not Kyros."

"But," Zivar said. "I hear a *but* in the way you say that."

"But if the Weavers order him to have one of the djinni kill someone, risking death himself to kill you and commit the assassination—he would probably do it."

"Ah." She smiled faintly. *"Probably."*

"The penalties for misusing a spell-chain are severe. He would want some sort of assurance that they wouldn't turn on him once he'd served as their tool."

"A wise man."

"Were you going to try to take away my spell-chain, if I'd completed it?"

"Only if you were stupid and let me do it. No, I have two pieces of karenite right now. I was going to try to get you to make me a spell-chain. I was planning to try to persuade you to do it, but I'd have given you a piece for yourself if I'd had to. Now..." She blew out her breath. "Not likely, you silly girl."

"Was that all?"

She shifted a little in her binding, striving for a more comfortable position. I wasn't sure whether to offer to help her move herself, or just to keep my distance. "You have been reading Photios's letters to me, or so I heard."

"Letters—oh yes, the travelogue."

"As he has time, he explores new lands, looking for new trade goods. Alas, when he finds interesting things he seldom has the ready cash to buy them for me."

"I thought he was looking for a place for you to re-tire to."

"Well, that, too. But it's quite hard. If it's far enough from the Sisterhood that I could go and not be found, the languages are all foreign and the people rather barbaric." She sighed. "And no matter how far I went, there's always the spell-chains I made ..."

"Why can't you have one of your own djinni snatch them back before you left?"

"They're no better at finding spell-chains than finding people. Besides, if you let an aeriko touch soulstone, sometimes they find a door back to where they came from, and ..." She blew once, gently, as if chasing away a feather. "Gone."

"So why do you hide it so carefully? Why the lock, the guard ... ?"

"Well, you never know." She paused. "Would you like to read more of Photios's letters? I will trade."

"Trade what?"

"Your own stories of lands far away, for him to go look for."

"I don't know of any."

"Sure you do. You must. Everyone does. You heard them from your mother, from soldiers, from traders." Her voice turned coaxing. "Think it over. You can take one of the letters with you now; they're stacked by the window." Sure enough, there was a pile of books on a table, all in that cramped handwriting. I chose one with a dusky green cover. "Think about it, and come back when you have thought of one."

I nodded and tucked the book under my arm.

"Send in Nurzhan as you leave," she said, so when I passed Nurzhan on the stairs I told her that Zivar wanted her.

Back with Tamar, I leafed through the book, squinting at pages. "Have you ever heard stories about places a long way away?" I asked. "Zivar wants to hear them." On that journey, Photios had found a man who spoke a little Greek, badly, who had served as his guide. They'd seen amazing creatures: huge striped cats so big they could eat a human, and giant gray animals with noses like long ropes that they could coil and uncoil like we might grip with our hands. It had gotten unbearably hot while Photios was there, and then rained so hard he thought they were all going to drown.

"I've heard stories about a land with no night," Tamar said.

"That's impossible," I said.

"Well, maybe. I heard it years ago from one of the kitchen slaves, who claimed to have heard it from a man who'd been there. A trader-explorer, like Photios. He was there for a week, or so he thought—it was hard to mark time without night, but they slept and ate each day, and that's how he counted—and the sun never set. It did get a little dim at times."

I shook my head. "I think he was pulling her leg."

"Probably. But I bet Zivar would like the story. What's that sound?"

We paused and listened. It was coming from outside and was not wind, or the clatter of sleet hitting our shutter. It was a tap, tap, tap, quite steady.

"Thaw," Tamar breathed. "The snow is melting. It's finally almost spring."

# CHAPTER TEN

*I*n one of Zivar's letters from Photios, he described a pretty land, somewhere south of us, where spring arrived in a single decisive burst. The snow melted away, the migratory birds returned, the flowers bloomed. Here, there was a thaw, then a freeze when all the melted snow hardened overnight into pure ice. There were more snowstorms, and more melts. Then there were days of rain, which finally slacked off, and the muddy hills turned green. The days grew longer.

Tamar and I argued, as spring advanced, about what to do. She still thought selling me into slavery in the mine was a horrible idea; I still hadn't thought of anything better. At her insistence, we both tried to speak to Prax, in dreams, but couldn't find him on our own. If I were going to speak to him, it would have to be for real, face-to-face.

With the first thaw, travelers began to pass through Casseia again—first a trickle, then a flood, like the melting snow. Tamar and I decided to wait until the mud had dried out a bit. "If we need some money, we could sell the packhorse," Tamar said.

"I think we need the horse more."

"We need a way to feed the other horses," Tamar said. "And ourselves. Money for bribes might be nice..."

"We can let the horses forage, since we're not in as much of a hurry."

"Yeah, well, what are *we* going to eat?"

"Oh, I don't know..." I shrugged; the spring wind brought the scent of wet mud through the window, and it made it hard to think of anything other than getting onto the road again. "Do what you think is best."

I went out to exercise the horses. When I returned, I heard a voice coming from the open door to our room as I approached from the hall. Some instinctive nosiness from my days as Kyros's spy made me slow and soften my step, to listen in. "—whether she's interested or not," a voice was saying. Nurzhan, I thought it was. "If she's with you, then excellent. If not, we still want you."

"I don't think I understand what you want me *for*," Tamar said.

"For our Sisterhood," Nurzhan said.

Another servant spoke. "Sorceresses do not run their households very well. The calmest and most logical sorceress still has days when she would throw herself down from the high tower if someone took her up there."

"Think how they run their Empire," Nurzhan said.

"We have control over Zivar," the other servant said. "We take care of her, and she serves us. That's the natural order of things. There should be a ruler, and the Weavers should serve her, and should be taken care of when..."

"...when they're too crazy to be trusted with a glass of tea, let alone an Empire," Nurzhan finished.

"That's the natural order we're working to restore."

"You." Tamar's voice was frankly disbelieving. "You expect me to believe..."

"It was actually Zivar's idea, some years ago," Nurzhan said. "We think she's forgotten about it, though."

"Everything has to start somewhere. The Sisterhood started with Penelope, and her apprentices..."

"Right," Tamar said.

"We have *many* friends," Nurzhan said. "We're not alone."

"Think it over," the other servant said.

"Why approach me, and not Lauria?"

"She's one of *them,* now."

"But—"

"You'll see," Nurzhan said. "She seems perfectly fine right now, but in a few weeks, a few months— fever, melancholia. You'll have to take care of her."

*It won't happen,* I told myself.

"In any case, you're one of us. You have been one of us all winter. Lauria, well, she came with you, so if she wants to be part, we'll accept her."

"What do you want from me?"

"To carry the word."

"We're trying to *free* slaves, not recruit them for your plot."

"The servants we speak of don't want to join the bandits. Surely you've met a few..."

I thought of Zarina. *She would be in her element in the home of a lone sorceress.* Tamar may have thought of her, too, because I heard her murmur reluctant assent a moment later.

"Think it over," Nurzhan said. I could hear the sound of someone standing up, and I slipped swiftly back down the stairs, so that I could pretend that I was just coming up and had overheard nothing. I saw Nurzhan and the other servant coming out as I approached; they gave me a bare glance and a courteous smile, and I knew that if I hadn't overheard I wouldn't have suspected anything.

I waited that afternoon to see if Tamar told me anything about her conversation that afternoon. She didn't. She told me nothing that night, either, and nothing at breakfast, though she was quiet, her face thoughtful.

When I was working for Kyros, this sort of information would have been squirreled away. I never would have told the person I'd overheard that I'd overheard her, though I would have taken careful note of whether or not she'd come clean to me, all so that I could report as fully as possible to Kyros when I was done. Gathering information for myself was harder. I realized that I didn't care whether Tamar was going to tell me on her own—I just wanted to know what she thought of the proposal. "Hey," I blurted out after an implacable Nurzhan brought our breakfast and left again. "I overheard you yesterday."

Tamar quickly pasted a look of surprised innocence over her features, then shrugged and dropped the pretense. "I thought as much. You've had this expectant air ever since."

"So . . . what do you think?"

"Are you asking whether I want to join their 'sisterhood,' or just what I think?"

"I guess I just want to know what you think."

"Well, they're right that sorceresses are an intemperate lot. If it weren't for the magic, they never could have created and held an Empire. Then again, if it weren't for the magic, they wouldn't be, well ..." She threw up her hands in a shrug. "I thought about it all night. But I guess the fact is, I still feel Alashi, even though we walked away. And what serves the Alashi better? A fractious, weak council running the Empire that threatens them? Or someone like Nurzhan?"

"Would Nurzhan have the sense not to invade Alashi territory?"

"If she needed karenite to feed her pet sorceress ..."

"She could *buy* it from the Alashi with a lot less trouble."

"Perhaps. But I'm not certain of that. The Sisterhood is dependent on karenite; without it, there are no more spell-chains, no more magic. Even if they had a formal truce with the Alashi, you *can't* let your enemy control something you need that badly. The Alashi can never trust the Sisterhood, or anyone who relies on the Sisterhood. Not unless a whole lot of karenite suddenly turns up in Persia."

"I can't imagine that they haven't looked for it there."

"Me either."

"So ... no. I'm not joining."

I sighed, feeling both a little disappointed and a little relieved.

"But I think I may ask them for more information, because who knows, it might be useful."

Tamar did not invite me down to the kitchen with her when she went to have one final chat with Nurzhan, so I followed a few minutes later, planning to eavesdrop.

But as I passed the receiving room, I heard a hiss and turned to see Zivar. "Come for a walk with me," she said, so I put on my boots and we went out.

The city streets were paved with stones, but still covered with a layer of slick mud. Here and there I could spot patches of dirty snow. "The walls of my house have ears," Zivar said after a little while. "I wanted to talk privately. No, not about the conspiracy." She glanced at me, her eyebrow tilted up; I knew I looked surprised. "Of course I know about the Servant Sisterhood. I have ears, too, and they don't always know that I'm listening. They're right, in a sense. The Sisterhood makes for a strange empire. No, I don't care about that. I want to negotiate with the Alashi."

"For karenite?"

"That would be part of the arrangement, of course. I want to ask for shelter with them. Asylum. I want them to protect me from the Sisterhood, and in exchange my aerika and I will serve them."

"That would..." I tried to imagine making this offer to the eldress. "That would be a very strange arrangement. Some of them worship the djinni."

"Don't most worship Prometheus and Arachne?"

"Yes, but..." My words stumbled to a stop. "Well, they might take you up on it, I suppose. Maybe."

"Will you negotiate as my representative? I do not wish to go there unless I have promises of safety."

"Um, that would be hard." I found myself flushing. "You were right, I was cast out. You might ask Tamar... though she threw her lot in with me..."

"Ah." Zivar gave me a shrewd look. "Well, then. I suppose this was a rather useless conversation."

"Send your man," I said. "The one who explores. They're always happy to see merchants."

"Ha. Photios, you mean? I suppose I could send him. I don't exactly trust him."

"Do you trust me?"

"You and I are of a kind. You have seen the borderland, and heard the singing of the aerika. You aren't Greek, and you're outcast from the Alashi. Two mice, passing through a forest full of owls."

"There are more than two mice in the world, though."

"Yes, true enough. So, green mice, then. The only two green mice in the world."

"So far as we know."

"Yes. Well, since you can't go to the Alashi for me, perhaps you can keep your eyes open for green mice. You never know what you'll find, until you look for it."

*T*he day we departed, Zivar and all her servants came out to see us off. Zivar gave me a small book of paper bound with leather. "You can write, as well as read, I assume? Then as a favor, it would please me a great deal if you would write descriptions of anywhere particularly interesting you should happen to travel. It is possible to have packages delivered through the Sisterhood of Weavers—the Temple of Athena in any large city can arrange it. I would be in your debt. It can be convenient, to have a sorceress in your debt." I bowed, and took the book. "I should add, packages sent through the Sisterhood are sometimes examined."

"I will be discreet in any messages I send," I said.

Zivar turned to Tamar. "I really do wish you the best," Tamar said to her, before she could say anything. "I hope you have enough spell-chains soon."

Zivar nodded a little hesitantly, then withdrew to her house. The stable hands brought out our horses; they were ready, our belongings loaded.

"Think about what I said," Nurzhan whispered to Tamar, and opened the door.

*I*t was strange to be on the road again, with our string of horses. We had to travel slowly just to give ourselves a chance to get used to the saddle again. "I could use some of Maydan's salve," Tamar muttered our first day.

We stopped to rest at the inn where everyone else had gotten sick, though we didn't eat any food. Instead, I put a little bit of the stew into a leather pouch, thinking that I would bring it with us. No one got sick that night, but if it was left to spoil . . . But after a couple of days, it smelled terrible and attracted swarms of flies. I ended up throwing away the entire pouch. I still thought that poison was a good plan, but I wasn't carrying rotting meat the whole way up to the mine.

"Maybe we can find a diseased animal and sell it to the guards for food," Tamar suggested once we'd left the stink behind us.

"How would we know that they wouldn't feed it to the slaves instead of eating it themselves? If it were obviously sick . . ."

"There are ways of hiding sickness . . ."

"How suspicious would that be, though, to walk up and knock on their door to sell a lamb?"

"Well, if we posed as merchants, with a *lot* of different stuff . . ."

"Like slaves?"

"Shut up about it, Lauria, all right? I'm not going to

sell you. We could have a lot of stuff, including live-stock, and then throw in the sick lamb as a gift at the end to close the deal, 'for a nice dinner tonight.' Then be sure not to eat any ourselves, wait until everyone goes down sick, and raid. I think poison is a good idea; we just need to think of the best way to do it."

"What if we can't find a sick lamb? And what if it doesn't make anyone sick?"

"Well, you know, that would be a much worse problem if we started this by *selling you to the mine*. If it doesn't make anyone sick, we go away, wait a month, then come back with another round of things to sell. We can do it twice, three times, as many times as it takes to make everyone ill."

"They're a suspicious bunch."

"Yeah, well, let me know if you think of a better plan—and selling you into slavery is not it," Tamar said. "I want to free Sophos's slaves first, anyway."

"That's because you don't trust this plan to work. You want Sophos's slaves free in case the mine guards get suspicious and kill us both."

"Yeah, well, that's true, so I hope you think up a better plan between now and when we go to the mine."

"How are you going to free Sophos's slaves?"

"I'm going to talk to Jaran. Actually, what I would really like to do is have *both* of us talk to Jaran. Do you think we can try that tonight?"

I shrugged. I hadn't tried to go to the borderland, on purpose, since the night I'd visited Zhanna. It hadn't plunged me into darkness like the day I'd tried to bind the djinn, but I couldn't shake the sense that I'd just gotten lucky that time. "I guess we can try," I said. "Tonight, then."

We camped that night. I had expected our yurt to smell mildewed from its winter folded up in a corner, but it welcomed us with the scent of wool and woodsmoke. We made ourselves porridge for dinner over our campfire, and then settled down under our mound of blankets. It might be spring during the day, but nights were still cold. "This will be easy if we go to sleep touching," Tamar said, so we snuggled against each other. "Don't worry about finding Jaran. I think I can get both of you. Just try to stay in the borderland when you get there."

The borderland was quiet tonight; I felt as if I stood on the very edge of rippling water, unable to move away but desperate not to get wet. I was alone: no Tamar, no Zhanna, and thankfully no Kyros. *Don't think of him; it might draw you together.* I thought of Tamar instead, and after a moment that stretched for what seemed like a week of nights, I found myself standing in Sophos's harem, with Tamar and Jaran. Tamar clasped my hand, and his, holding us in place with raw concentration. "We're coming," she said to Jaran. "If you and the others would be free, we can get you to the Alashi."

"How will we break out?"

"Can you think of a way?" Tamar asked.

"Kill Sophos," I suggested.

"And his guards?"

"You outnumber them."

"They have weapons."

"We can't free you without your help," Tamar said. There was a pause.

"It's going to take us time to get to Helladia," I said.

"Weeks still," Tamar said.

"I can kill Sophos," Jaran said. "But I'm not sure what to do next. What about his guards?"

"Well, think of something," Tamar said. Things were fading around us. "We'll talk again soon..."

Tamar groused about Jaran as we rode the next morning. "So he doesn't know what to do after he kills Sophos. And I should? How am I supposed to know what he should do next?"

"Should he free himself?"

"We're meeting him halfway! We can get him to the Alashi! I think I could break just *Jaran* out without help from the inside, but to get the rest out..."

"Well, it's not like we can go in and work on the inside like I did to get Burkut," I said. "Either of us would be recognized."

"True enough." Tamar sighed. "In fact, just the thought of being near Helladia makes me queasy. I'm afraid somehow...well."

"I know."

"But if I have to..." Tamar straightened up. "I want to get them out, all of them. I am *going* to get them out, even Aislan, even Meruert's baby."

"Boradai?" Boradai was the elderly woman who acted as housekeeper and mistress, keeping the slaves in line.

"Ugh." Tamar wrinkled her face. "Boradai...I don't know."

"She should be sold to a sorceress. She'd like Nurzhan's idea."

"Ha. If only we could somehow get her on our side. She'd probably be an asset to Nurzhan's conspiracy, they could send her to some sorceress who needed a firm hand. But she's happy with the power she has, and clings to it like you'd cling to your shelter in a storm."

"Does she have a weakness? A soft side?"

"Boradai?"

"A child?"

"No, she's barren."

"A lover?"

"N— yes, actually. Or maybe, once. I heard rumors."

"A man, or a woman?"

"A man; that's why she knows she's barren. They were separated, oh, at least ten years ago. Well before I came to live there."

"Why were they separated?"

"It was a strange story." Tamar spread out her fingers against her horse's withers, thinking hard. "I didn't meet him, remember, I had it in bits and pieces from the other slaves. Boradai was a harem slave herself, a *long* time ago—not for Sophos but for some predecessor of his in the post. When she was still fairly young, though, there was an outbreak of smallpox, and she survived but was badly scarred."

"So then what?"

"Aislan has always hoped to win her freedom with her beauty. If Boradai had such hopes, they were shattered, of course. But she still knew how to dance, and various other arts, if you catch my meaning. And she had no desire to be put to work in the kitchen. So as she recovered from her illness she made herself useful in the harem, teaching dance and so on. And eventually she was put in charge of that, and of other things."

"What about the lover?"

"Oh, yes. Well, she's *ugly*, you know, and I don't know why any man would fall in love with her personality, so it's not like she would exactly have her pick. Still, there was a man who worked around the household fixing things that broke, and *somehow* they fell in love."

Tamar's tone was so disbelieving I felt I had to offer Boradai at least a small defense. "Love can be a mysterious thing."

"Apparently she'd break stuff that he'd have to fix, to spend time with him." Tamar shook her head again. "Anyway, one night there was an escape, and it turned out that Boradai hadn't stopped it because she was in her lover's arms. There was speculation that the lover had distracted her on purpose, but Sophos must not have thought so because the lover was just sold. He said that Boradai was quite useful in the harem, that she did an excellent job, and he didn't want her distracted, so he sold the lover and bought a new slave to fix things. This one was repulsed by Boradai's scars, and in any case I think she was still pining for her old lover."

"Where is he, do you know?"

"I have no idea."

"Do you think Jaran would know?"

Tamar started to shake her head, then paused. "Who knows? I'll ask him. Tonight."

*H*is name is Alisher," Tamar said. "And he was sold to an inn, actually, in Elpisia. But I don't see how this is going to help us. If we free him and bring him along, do you think Boradai is going to turn on Sophos and help us out?"

"Maybe," I said.

"What's she going to be able to do that Jaran can't?" Tamar scratched her head. "I mean, really,

Lauria, why are you worried about being nice to her? Boradai is as bad as any Greek."

"She's still a slave."

"So? Even if she wants to be free, I wouldn't want her on my side."

"Would you want Nurzhan? Boradai is the Nurzhan of Sophos's household."

"I suppose. But it's been over ten years! Do you really think she even still cares about Alisher? He probably has another lover by now. He probably has kids."

"If he does, we'll have to think of something else."

Tamar shook her head, bemused. "Well, at least it should be easy enough to talk to him. We can just get a room at the inn. But it's Elpisia! You know half the city."

"Not that many people," I said, though my stomach churned at the thought of going back there again.

"You know what would make sense?" Tamar said. "You stay outside the city and I'll go in and get the room. Talk to Alisher, see if he wants out, whether he wants to help us, and whether he still cares at all about Boradai."

I hated the idea. "Stay outside?"

"Yeah, you know, like *I* did last fall, remember? You had all sorts of excuses for leaving me behind. Well, now you have a good reason to stay behind yourself. Maybe it's not half the city, but how many people in Elpisia *would* recognize you? Even pretending that Kyros didn't live there. There's your mother, right?"

"Yes," I said, my voice a little faint.

"Everyone in Kyros's household. Some of the guards from the garrison. All your old neighbors..."

"I could pull a scarf over my face."

"You're going to sit in the common room of the inn

with a scarf on your face? Yeah, *that* wouldn't be conspicuous at *all*."

"I could stay in our room..."

"Face it, Lauria, you'd be more of a hindrance than a help."

"You're enjoying this," I said.

"What does it matter? I'm *right*."

I fell silent.

"I'm *right*," Tamar said again, and I grunted reluctant assent.

When we reached Elpisia a few weeks later, spring was well advanced. We found a concealed spot along the old riverbed, and it occurred to me that it had been almost exactly a year since I had tracked Alibek to a spot much like the one we were hiding in. The realization made me jumpy.

We'd spent some time on the way up working on Tamar's appearance: new clothing, careful styling for her now-shoulder-length hair. She dug the forgotten face paints out of my pack and painted her own face, trying to look older. When she went into Elpisia she would be posing as a part Greek, part foreign trader. I thought the results were mixed, but she definitely didn't look like a runaway slave anymore. Looking her over, I was startled to realize that she was getting taller.

Now, in the late-afternoon sun, Tamar dismounted to give me a quick hug good-bye. "I'll talk to Alisher tonight and come back tomorrow morning. I'm only going to break him out if I have an excellent opportunity. Otherwise we'll figure something out. The wall probably still needs fixing."

"Probably."

"Sit tight," Tamar said. "No one's going to recognize me. I'll be back in less than a day."

"I know." Tamar hesitated a moment longer, so I added, "Good luck."

I tucked myself down into the rocks and sat on a folded-up blanket. The horses drank from the trickle of water where the river had run, then began to munch on the green vegetation that had grown in the spring rains. It was all heartbreakingly familiar, and I tried not to think about how my entire old life lay beyond a crumbling wall less than an hour's walk from where I was. *It's not my old life. It's someone else's old life. Someone I don't even like very much anymore.*

Night came, and I slept, and dreamed.

Perhaps it was my nearness to Elpisia, but I dreamed of my mother. As with some of my early dreams of Kyros, I was uncertain whether we faced each other through our dreams, or if I was simply dreaming of her.

In the dream, I stood in the doorway of her apartment and she pulled me inside. "*Lauria.* Darling. Where have you *been*?"

I stepped inside. "Mother . . ."

"Let me take your coat."

"There isn't time . . ."

"There's all the time we need. Shhh, shhh, sit." She stopped tugging on my coat, and instead pushed me gently into her chair and poured me tea that waited hot on the stove.

"Is Kyros—" I glanced around wildly. "I know that you are Kyros's mistress. I know he's my father. He—"

"I know you had a falling out, darling. Shhh, don't worry yourself right now. He's not coming." She poured herself tea as well. "He had a very bad headache this afternoon and went home early. He has a remedy he takes for his headaches, and it makes him sleep very soundly. Too soundly to dream. *He's not coming.* So sit with me awhile."

The tea burned my lips. I set it down. "Will you come with me?" I asked.

"Come with you where?"

"Away from here. From Kyros."

"Where have you *been,* darling?" she asked. Her anxious fingers plucked at my clothes. "I knew you would be gone for a while, but you *vanished.* Kyros stopped speaking of you, and I could tell by his eyes something was wrong..."

"Kyros won't hesitate to use you against me," I said. "He can't take you hostage right now because he can't speak to me. He doesn't know where I am."

"Where *are* you?"

"I can't tell you, either. Kyros would have it out of you."

My mother's lips tightened. "You should have more faith in me," she snapped. "You are my *child.* I would never betray you to Kyros."

"I'm not saying you'd go running to him, I'm just saying that he's a hard man to keep secrets from."

"Well, you're right about that. Still, you can trust me." My mother drained her teacup and said, "I'll tell you something he doesn't want you to know. He taught me how to bring you here."

"What?"

"He taught me the trick. I know it now. He's been wanting me to do this for a while now, but I've been pretending to be a slow learner." She gave me a satisfied smile. "I think he's convinced I'll never get it. But I waited; I knew some night he would have a headache and I would have my chance. And so it happened." She squeezed my hand. "Now, darling, *tell me where you are*. I just want to know that you're safe."

"As long as Kyros doesn't find me, I'm quite safe," I said, though this was a blatant lie.

"Darling. Come back to me, we'll go to Kyros together. I'm sure we can work things out . . ."

"No!" My hands closed over her wrists. "I *can't*. Listen, I can tell you everything that happened, but you'll have to promise to leave. To come with *me*, somewhere safe, away from Kyros . . ."

"*Where*? To the Alashi? I have no wish to spend my life on horseback with the bandits. Tell me, darling, do you think I would fit in there?"

I imagined Janiya's likely reaction to my mother. Would they try to make her join a sword sisterhood for the summer? Teach her to ride and fight? I pictured my mother holding a sword gingerly in her soft hands, or learning to shoot a bow. "No," I said. "You wouldn't."

"Well, that was a fast answer," she said. "Where do you think you're going to take me, then?"

I was silent.

"If you don't know where you're going to take me, I'll stay here until you think of something. I've always fancied a trip to Penelopeia. If you'd like to take me there, I might go."

"But Kyros . . ."

My mother shook her head. "Kyros is no threat to me. No! Don't interrupt me again. I've known Kyros for over twenty years. You may think you know Kyros, but I *know* Kyros. He might send you a message that he'll kill me if you don't come running back with your tail between your legs, but he'll never do it. Never."

She gave me a kiss on the cheek. "Darling, I miss you. Come back to me. If you're close by I can tell you when it's safe..."

"I'm a long way away," I said. "A long, long way. Halfway to Penelopeia."

My mother sat back, her eyes sad. "Well, then," she said. "I do hope I'll see you again someday."

I wanted to leave her with something, but I knew she would take the words *I love you* as a poor substitute for *I'm coming home.* I closed my eyes for a moment, remembering how I had summoned a tent the last time Kyros had found me in my dreams. "I have something for you," I said, and opened my coat. Dozens of white roses tumbled out, filling the room with their sweet scent. Their soft petals rose up in a cloud around both of us, and then I was awake, my pulse racing, waiting for Tamar's return.

*I* saw Tamar coming at dawn—and to my shock, she had another person with her, an older man, his graying hair touseled and dusty. Alisher. She waved when she saw me and turned briefly to Alisher—telling him my name, I thought—and his eyes glinted a little as he turned back to me.

"How did you get Alisher out?" I asked Tamar when she reached me.

"They sent him out on an errand right at dawn—a friend has a broken bucket-crank over his well, and they offered Alisher's services to fix it." Alisher had a wood box tucked under one arm, I noticed—his tools.

"Did you arrange the broken crank?"

"No. He gets sent out to fix things a lot."

Alisher had graying hair covered in a layer of fine

dust, rounded shoulders, and a tired face. I looked him over, wondering what he could ever have seen in Boradai; I'd found her ugly and frightening. "So, um," I said, trying to think of a way to ask.

"We found each other late in life," he said with slow dignity.

"Right," I said, embarrassed by my own transparency.

We mounted up. Alisher was stiff but more competent at riding than I'd feared. We set out toward Helladia, casting nervous glances back, but there was no sign of pursuit yet.

Our trip to Helladia was slower than we'd become accustomed to. Alisher never voiced complaint, but his hands would go white as he gripped the edges of his saddle. Also, the horses tired faster with an extra rider. Finally, we were out of grain for them, and had to allow them plenty of time to forage.

I grew agitated as we rode, and our slow pace seemed nearly intolerable. I dismounted a few times to run ahead; eventually I always had to stop to catch my breath, and Tamar and the others would catch up with me. Alisher's look was a little bemused and a little scornful; Tamar looked worried.

Whenever I had to pause to catch my breath, I would find myself thinking about Sophos. *No one will lay a hand on you. I will not forget again, my lady.* I shuddered, remembering the way the drugged wine had made me clumsy. Sophos's sweat, the grunting noise he'd made. *The knife, for a moment, within my grasp. He won't escape me this time.* I tasted bile for a moment and swallowed hard.

I had threatened Sophos at the time. *Kyros will kill you. I'm going to tell him I want you castrated first.* I'd believed with all my heart that Kyros would take bloody retribution against Sophos. He hadn't. That had been one of the locusts that had eaten away my trust for Kyros. *And I don't regret it. This way I'll get to kill Sophos myself.*

"How are we going to do this?" Tamar asked me as we settled down the first night. "We've got Alisher now, so . . . do you want me to try to send a message to Jaran?"

"I was thinking maybe I'd go in when we got there," I said. "During the night, of course, and climb in to find her." *And then find Sophos . . .*

"I'll tell Jaran," Tamar interrupted. "He can tell her, and see what she says."

Tamar spoke with Jaran, in the borderland; Jaran spoke with Boradai. ("Tell him not to, you know, bait her," I said, once it was clear that Tamar was set on not sending me in to find her. "He's not an idiot, Lauria," she said.) We moved in toward Helladia during the day. Two hours' ride from its walls, we found a lovely place to hide. In a valley in the hills between Elpisia and Helladia, we found a cave large enough to conceal even our horses if we wanted to bring them in with us. The brush was thick and you'd have to be a skilled tracker even to know we were down there. Fortunately, it was warm enough now that we wouldn't freeze to death without a fire.

Tamar shook me awake partway through the night. "You were right," she said.

"About what?"

"Boradai. Jaran says to go outside and wait somewhere visible; she's going to send a message."

My curiosity warred briefly with my distrust for Boradai, and then I started to leave the cave. Tamar caught my arm and I shook her off. "I'll go out by myself," I said. "You wait here. I think I want to be a little way away from you and Alisher, in case it's a trick."

I came out of the cave and made my way up from the brush, to an outcropping of rock. The moon was up and nearly full. It was a good night for an escape, I thought. The air was crisp and cool this time of night, but I could smell the day's heat seeping out of the rocks around me.

And there: the messenger in the air. "Djinn," I said. "Who sent you?"

"The holder of the chain," it said. I thought I was going to have to drag out a description, but it added, "The woman called Boradai. Are you Tamar?"

"No, I'm a friend of hers. Did she send us a message?"

"Yes. Here is what she said: 'Tell them that we are ready, and there is no one within these walls to hinder our escape. All the guards within the walls are dead, but there are many more guards outside. Now what?' "

Now what? The djinn waited. *No one to hinder our escape* ... I wondered if they'd killed everyone within. *No time to ask.* The djinn could bring them out easily enough, but it would be best not to attract too much attention. "Tell Boradai this," I said, and cleared my throat, arranging my disordered thoughts as carefully as I could. " 'Boradai, you have a spell-chain, and a djinn at your disposal. Tell the djinn to follow my instructions. I will have it construct a palanquin like a sorceress would use, and send it to you with the palanquin. Have the slaves get into the palanquin and the djinn can carry it back out. The guards will see the palanquin and assume it's a sorceress visiting Sophos. But be warned, if you try to save yourself but not the rest of the slaves, Tamar and I will make you regret it.'" I nodded, and the djinn vanished. *Now for a palanquin,* I thought.

"A palanquin?" Alisher said in frank disbelief when I scrambled back down to the cave. "It's not something you just throw together!"

"With a djinn..."

"Maybe you can have it go steal one," Tamar said, her voice a little doubtful.

"I'd rather not," I said. "The sorceress might send djinni of her own to come looking."

It was back. "Boradai has sent me to you," it said. "She says to do whatever you ask, other than to slay someone."

"First, find me a wagon," I said. "Just beyond the windward wall of Elpisia there is a place where the army leaves things that are broken past repair. Find me a wagon, or something like it—a big box made of wood. Big enough to hold twenty people if they're crammed in tight. Sturdy enough that it won't fall apart in the air. If you see one, pick it up and bring it to me, and set it carefully on the ground over there. If you don't see one, come right back here."

The djinn vanished, and we waited.

"This isn't going to work," Alisher said.

Then, in the distance, we saw it. "The guards in Helladia are going to see it," he added.

"It's too dark," Tamar said. "Besides, we're a long way from there, I don't think they'd see it even in daylight."

"It's going to drop it on our heads!"

"No, that would go against its instructions..."

There was a great crash and rattle as the djinn set the wagon down into the brush. I climbed up to examine it. The boards were loose and the sides were partially rotted; the wheels, of course, were totally useless. For our purposes, I thought it would serve. "Now we need fabric," I said.

"It's not going to look like a sorceress's palanquin," Tamar said.

"It doesn't have to pass for one up close. It just has to fool the guards who catch glimpses of it."

Tamar nodded thoughtfully. "Send the djinn back to Boradai," she said. "She'll be able to send us cloth."

The djinn vanished with my message and I turned to Alisher. "What do you need to make this safe to ride in? If it's being carried by a djinn?"

He inspected it—skeptically, but after a moment he took out his tools. "It's warped out of shape but should hold together. I'll just knock a few boards back into place..."

The djinn returned with yards and yards of fine cloth. I unrolled it and wrapped the wagon; Alisher used a few small fasteners to pin it into place. We mounted a couple of sapling trees like tent poles at the corners of the wagon, and pulled the fabric over the top like a roof. When we were done, it was a clumsy, bright thing, but from a distance—in the dark—it would pass as a palanquin easily.

"Right," I said to the djinn. "Take this to Boradai. If it has to make multiple trips, it can—no one's going to get in the way when they think a *sorceress* is involved. Carry it *gently* and set it down *carefully*."

The djinn whisked off the makeshift palanquin; watching it go, my doubts were calmed. It was dark enough that it was barely visible. Even once the sun came up, it would be a tiny dot of vivid color up in the sky, just like any other palanquin.

We waited.

And there it was, coming back. It touched down lightly and two dozen former slaves stumbled out, none people I knew. No harem slaves. Some looked like they were dressed for stable work, others like they had worked in the kitchen. All were jumpy and confused. "Tamar!" one of the women exclaimed, spotting her. "Where have you been? *What's going on?*"

"What happened?" Tamar asked her.

"Boradai woke us up a few hours ago and herded us into Sophos's dining room to keep an eye on us. Boradai had Sophos's spell-chain and she said we all needed to just sit tight and she'd get us out of there. And then she made us get into the wagon—" The woman clutched at Tamar's arm in horror. "It was carried by a bound djinn, Athena save us all. But it didn't drop us, and here we are."

"I think it's going to take two more trips," Tamar said to me. "Can we send it right back?"

I nodded. "Go ahead," I said to the djinn, and it picked up the palanquin, vanishing quickly from sight.

"Now what?" one of the slaves was asking. "Now what are we supposed to do?"

"It's up to you," I said. "If you could reach the Alashi safely, would you like to join them?"

There was a pause, and one of the older stable hands asked softly, "Would they take me? At my age?"

"I don't think your age will matter," Tamar said.

"I had a brother go to the Alashi, years ago," he said. "At least, I like to think he made it."

"What if we don't want to?" asked the servant who'd known Tamar.

"What if we liked things the way they were?" asked another, her voice surly.

"They're never going to be the way they were," Tamar said. "You're part of a slave revolt now, like it or not. But if what you really want is to be a slave again, well, we'll see what we can do. And if you don't want to join the Alashi, you could head south on your own and look for work. Just be careful, because if you're recognized . . ."

Muttering. The palanquin was back. "Boradai is getting nervous," reported one of the men as he climbed out. "She thinks one more trip will do it."

No harem slaves in this load, either. We sent it back and waited.

"I wish I'd gone with it," Tamar muttered. "I *hate* waiting."

There was nothing for it, though. I looked at the eastern sky, wondering how close we were to dawn. The horizon still looked dark to me, but it couldn't be that much longer. *And once they're all here, morning will be very close. So then what? Hide them all here through the day, or start straight into the desert? We'll be pathetically easy to spot . . .* I started trying to calculate whether we could have the djinn steal one of the huge sky-boats used by merchant companies like the one Zivar backed. With one of those, we could take everyone to the Alashi in one trip.

There: the palanquin was returning. Everyone fell silent as it descended; it was overloaded, I realized when I saw the sides bulging from misplaced elbows, and when it touched the ground one of the boards split with a crack that made everyone jump. But the harem slaves spilled out, along with some strangers. And last of all, Boradai.

She was as ugly as I remembered, but her pock-marked face held vivid triumph. One hand clutched the glittering spell-chain. She strode forward, looped the spell-chain around her neck, and said, "You'd better not have lied about Alisher."

He had been half hidden behind the crowd of servants; now he stepped out shyly. They didn't rush into each other's arms; he was too reserved for that, and she was too proud. But her eyes grew very soft, and he swallowed hard. They clasped hands and did not let go.

Meanwhile, Tamar greeted the other harem slaves. I remembered a few from my time there: Jaran, the shaman; Meruert, who now held a plump baby in her arms; Aislan, the old "favorite," who looked bewildered and not entirely pleased at this turn of events.

Jaran approached Tamar, a faint smile on his face. "I have a present for you," he said, and held out a leather sack.

Tamar opened it and recoiled as she looked inside, then swallowed hard. "Lauria, I'd say this is for you, too," she said, and upended it. Something roundish hit the ground with a soft thud; it took me a disconcerted, horrified moment to realize that it was Sophos's head. Sightless eyes open, mouth agape.

I sucked in my breath; my first reaction was simple horror and disgust. It rolled toward me as it landed and I jumped back a step, which made Jaran chuckle drily. I realized that I was shaking—not just my hands, but my whole body. *Dead, he's dead, he's dead. And I didn't get to kill him.*

I looked up to meet Jaran's eyes. It was Jaran who killed him; that was why Jaran had had the privilege of carrying the head to Tamar. Despite his snicker a moment ago, he was regarding me with curiosity and at least a hint of respect. *I was not Sophos's only victim,* I thought, and wondered if Tamar regretted not having been the one to kill him. *She's probably just glad that he's dead.* I'm *glad he's dead, foul rapist that he was.*

"Thank you for the gift," I said, and my voice was steady.

"You're welcome," Jaran said, and his look now was a little questioning. Sophos's nose was against the dirt; with his toe, Jaran rolled the head so that it faced the sky. "I waited until he was done with me, then cut his throat when he was, you know, in a fine mood and ready for a good night's sleep. It was the sort of opportunity that only a concubine would have."

"You had a knife," I said.

"Thanks to Boradai."

I nodded.

Meruert stepped over the head to embrace Tamar and give her a kiss on the cheek. I saw Aislan on the fringes of the crowd of escaped slaves, trying to hide her obvious fear. Her eyes narrowed with puzzlement when she saw Alisher, then widened when she saw Tamar. When they swept over me, I saw only vague puzzlement; I was fairly certain she didn't recognize me at all.

"How safe are we here?" I asked Boradai.

"The guards from town will probably come into the house looking for Sophos soon," Boradai said, her eyes glinting. "They'll be like sheep without a shepherd, though, for a while, running around. Most of his officers were at dinner last night. We killed them all."

I glanced at Aislan, wondering if her officer had been among the slaughtered.

"Where are you taking us?" one of the other servants asked.

"Yes, and why? None of us are worth a great deal..."

"My daughter lives back in Helladia. Can you go get her, too?"

I gestured for silence and after a few moments was able to get everyone's attention. "Look. You're free. We freed you. You can do whatever you want right now. If you'd like to join the Alashi, we'll get you to the Alashi. If you'd rather be a slave, we can figure something out. If you don't want to be a slave *and* you'd rather not join the Alashi, well, we can probably figure something out there, too. Think about it."

There was an outbreak of chatter. I went to speak with Boradai, who still held Alisher's hand. She was the keeper of the spell-chain. Whatever we ended up doing, we were going to need her help if we wanted to use the djinn.

"Jaran said there was another option," she said, narrowing her eyes as she looked at me.

"Yes." I glanced around. "Let's go for a little walk. I don't want to be overheard."

Alisher came along, of course; so did Tamar. "You've heard it said that sorceresses can be either the best mistresses, or the worst," I said. Boradai nodded. "There are some with no family to keep an eye on things, whose servants keep an eye on them instead. Tamar and I met one, down in Casseia. Her servants confided that there is a conspiracy of such servants. I could...put you in touch with the servant we met. She could arrange for you to become the housekeeper, I think, of a sorceress. Then it would be up to you to manage things to keep her alive and in line. It's a task I think you would be good at."

"What do these servants want?" Alisher asked. "I mean, eventually."

"They want the Empire, I think. They expect to rule it through ruling the Weavers. I don't know when." I thought about Tamar's comment that the Alashi would not benefit from an Empire with reasonable rulers, then shrugged it off. Tamar wasn't saying anything, so I wasn't going to worry about it.

"Alternately, while you hold your spell-chain, you could go anywhere. You could resettle in some foreign land, you could become merchant traders . . . the spell-chain gives you many options, if you aren't afraid to use it."

"I'm not afraid of much," Boradai said, her hand caressing the beads.

"No," I said. "I can see that."

We walked back to rejoin the group and I drifted from cluster to cluster, listening. Some were eager to go to the Alashi and trying to persuade their more timid companions that they would love life among the bandits. Others were depressed, some crying. "How *could* she," I heard someone saying. "He *trusted* her, trusted her more than any Greek should probably ever trust a slave . . ."

I looked at Boradai. "You could have done this years ago," I said.

"True," she said. "But I didn't know where to find Alisher. Sophos made noises, occasionally, about buying him back, if I worked hard enough. I knew he was probably lying, but there was always that hope. Even if I found him and somehow got him out, I couldn't see myself among the bandits—learning to ride horseback, at my age. I couldn't get the necklace without killing Sophos, and I wasn't the one with the best opportunities. And I wouldn't have chosen to involve anyone else. Too messy, too complicated."

"It worked, though."

"Yes. Every concubine had a knife last night, save for Aislan."

"You were quite sure none would put it in *your* back, then."

"Oh, no, I kept a careful watch on my back. But they weren't fools. They did as they were told."

The eastern sky was lightening to gray. I strode back over to where the rest of the slaves waited. "Right," I said. "If you know for sure that you want to join the Alashi, go stand over by that tree." I pointed.

Jaran strode over, unhesitating. Meruert tagged after him a moment later, then a large group followed. Then a few others, one at a time, like lost sheep looking for the comfort of their herd. *The Alashi are going to want to kill both me and Tamar for this,* I thought.

There were perhaps twenty left. One was Aislan.

"Where would you like to go?" I asked them.

"I'd like to go back to Helladia," Aislan said.

*Her officer must be alive,* I thought. There was an outburst of fury from the slaves who wanted to join the Alashi. "You'll need to wait a few days," I said. She inclined her head. "And I can't guarantee your safety."

"I don't need your guarantees," she said.

"Right. The rest of you?"

Three of them had some idea about starting a merchant company. They were going to head south. Six more didn't know what they were going to do, but seemed to think that they'd be able to come up with something. At least it wasn't winter, so they wouldn't freeze to death. "Steer clear of Elpisia," I advised them.

There were eight slaves who wanted to remain slaves, and one more who simply didn't care what we did with him: we could abandon him to the mercy of the Helladia garrison, it seemed, or sell him to the mine; he didn't care. The first eight pleaded with us to find them a kind master, someone who would take care of them when they were old and sick. There were calls of derision from the Alashi-bound ex-slaves, and one of the eight burst into tears.

"How the hell are we going to manage this?" Tamar asked me. "Are we seriously going to, you know, *sell them* into slavery?"

"I guess we'd better. I don't know how else we're going to find them a kind master." I thought about Solon, and his treatment of Burkut. Maybe we could send them to Solon. Actually, that wasn't a half-bad idea, except that they clearly would never make it on their own. *I* couldn't very well take them there myself. Maybe Tamar could do it.

That left nearly forty people who needed to get to the Alashi. I turned to Boradai. "I have a favor to ask."

"You want me to use the spell-chain, don't you," she said.

"Yes. Two more trips with the palanquin."

"I don't think it's going to make it. It's falling apart."

"Maybe we can have the djinn steal a wagon from the garrison. Or from Sophos; he had a wagon. What ever happened to Elubai, anyway?"

"Coughed himself to death, last winter. Sophos's wagon would work. We don't have to worry now about the garrison realizing that something is wrong in

Sophos's house, but someone might watch to see where it goes..." Her eyes went absent and she touched the spell-chain. The djinn appeared, hovering in the air. "First, don't hurt anyone. If you'd have to *hurt* anyone completing my instructions, then stop and come back here. Now, back at Sophos's house, there's a squat stone building with a broken door. Inside is a wagon. Go get the wagon. Pull it out, then lift it into the air. Take it high in the air—above the clouds. Once it's above the clouds, carry it to us. Don't bring anyone with it. If there's someone inside it then leave and come back. Don't damage the wagon. Set it down as gently as you can, on the flat spot of ground over there." She glanced at me, as if to see whether I had anything to add, then said, "Go now, and perform my instructions."

"You're very good at that," I said.

"I've spent years managing slaves," she said.

It took a long time for the djinn to set the wagon down, once it was in sight. "As gently as you can" was apparently "so carefully and slowly that it will take a full hour to make the final landing." It was full day by now, but there were clouds, heavy with spring rain. I thought they'd burn off by noon, though. We'd best hurry.

"I think we can get twenty people in there if they pack in tightly," Boradai said. "They're not going to like sitting on the edge as it flies through the air, though."

"They'll manage," I said.

"Someone's going to have to ride along to tell it where to go," Boradai said. "That's not going to be me."

"I'll do it," I said.

Boradai shrugged. "All right. And then I will have repaid you for my freedom, and Alisher's—by helping you to free the rest." She spoke firmly, but the question lurked in her eyes.

I nodded. "The debt will be repaid." *And now let's do this, and do it fast.* I rounded up twenty of the former slaves and everyone climbed into the wagon, sitting on the floor or on the laps of their friends. "We're going up to the steppe," I said. "Last chance to stay behind."

No one moved.

"The djinn is going to carry us up. If you're going to die of fear, then climb out now."

Murmurs, but no one moved.

I had to sit on the wagon seat, to see down and direct the djinn. I climbed on and sat down. *This is no good. I could fall off.* I borrowed some of the cloth from the old makeshift palanquin and tied myself on, wrapping the silk around my middle and testing it with a tug. Tamar came over and bound it a little more securely, then pinned it in place with a brooch shaped like a tree. I blinked at it, then remembered where it had come from: it was the brooch given to us back in Daphnia by the crazy sorceress who wanted to buy our karenite. "Hurry back," she whispered.

None of the former concubines were on this load; they wanted to stay with Tamar for as long as possible. "Right," I said. "Djinn, are you there?"

A shimmer in the air. "Yes."

"Did Boradai tell you to obey me?"

"She said not to kill anyone, but that other than that I should do as you say."

"I think I'm ready. I want you to lift the wagon as you would a palanquin. Make sure no one falls out while we go, but I want to be high enough that the clouds hide us from anyone below. Then fly us north, up to the steppe. Head northwest from Helladia, and tell me if you see a large gathering of people below us."

The djinn picked up the wagon; I swallowed hard, as it felt as if my stomach was back somewhere on the ground, probably flopping around on the grass like a beached fish. We went straight up. One of the slaves was counting out loud as we rose, and she reached one hundred before we stopped going up. I clutched the handles and looked down, trusting that between my death grip and the wrapping of cloth, I wouldn't fall. The ground was a terribly long way away, and it was a relief when we were swathed in cloud and I couldn't see it anymore. Without really intending to, I imagined the fabric snapping, my grip failing . . . I sat back, swallowing hard. My mouth tasted very sour and the fall was much too easy to picture.

Now we were moving. *Too fast.* I wanted to scream at the djinn to slow down, but instead I forced myself to wait a moment or two. My hair was blown back by the wind, whipped into knots, even as short as it still was. The wind stung my eyes. The slaves in the wagon bed cried out. When I twisted around to look at them, they had ducked their heads down and covered their faces. Good idea. Now I knew why palanquins were always covered in silk, but it was a bit late for me. I let go with one hand. The cloth held me firmly in my seat, so I shielded my eyes with my free hand and watched as well as I could.

There were no landmarks, and I realized that it was going to be very hard to know where the djinn was taking us. But the Alashi should be having their spring gathering right now—that would make it easier. Tamar and I had left Helladia last spring, then walked roughly northwest for five days before running into the gathering. On horseback, we probably could have done it in a day, if we'd pushed the horses hard, but it would have been a long day. Carried by the djinn—it felt many times faster than the fastest galloping horse, but so high up, exposed to the wind, anything would have felt fast to me.

I remembered that day months ago when Zivar had dragged me out of bed to run frantically around her courtyard. *The secret of flight. This isn't so bad,* I thought. *I can trust the cloth to hold me in place . . .* Then, without warning, the djinn suddenly pulled us up, the height of a small house. I heard screams from the wagon box. "Why did you do that?" I hissed.

"Bird," the djinn said.

We had leveled out. But a few minutes later we bumped, then dropped a bit before steadying. "Wind," the djinn explained that time.

Back in the wagon box, I could hear someone sobbing; others were praying out loud. A gust of wind caught our side and made the whole box sway. I wondered why sorceresses never had this problem while traveling by palanquin. Or maybe they did and I just didn't know it. I didn't remember anything like this the time I'd flown with Kyros, but maybe that was why Kyros didn't like to fly . . . I grabbed the bar with the hand I'd been using to shade my eyes, then stretched the cramped fingers of my other hand. "How far have we come?"

"A few hours' ride."

It had been much less than a few hours. I sighed and reminded myself that I was going to have to do this *again.*

Another bump and sway, and somebody in the wagon box threw up. Of course, they threw up right in the wagon box, since they were (understandably) afraid to lean over the side. A few minutes later, someone else threw up. I wished I could cover my ears and hum to block out the sound. They were going to be as ragged and pathetic a group as any others who'd reached the Alashi, even if they got a short ride rather than a hard slog through the desert.

Rain began to fall. We were within the cloud itself, and the rain here was like thick fog that soaked us to the skin. I shivered, wishing I could go huddle with the others in the wagon box. At least there were enough holes in it that it wasn't filling with water.

It was another hour or two before the djinn said, "There are men below."

"Take us down again, slowly and quietly."

I could hear someone speaking Danibeki; what conversation I could catch assured me that we'd found the Alashi. "Back up, and a little ways away. I don't want to land in the camp."

Up again, over a hill, down. "*Carefully*," I hissed, but our landing was still rough enough to leave me bruised. The refugees tumbled out of the wagon, desperate to get away. I didn't want to untie myself, so I watched as they all climbed out.

One of the younger women turned back. "My lady, we don't know your name. When they ask us who freed us, what should we say?"

I laughed. "They'll like you better if you freed yourselves."

"That would be a lie. I never could have made it on my own."

"Then tell them Boradai freed you. That's the truth, after all."

"I've never liked Boradai. I'd rather you get the credit."

"Believe me, the Alashi are annoyed enough at me already."

She was puzzled, but shrugged and turned back to the others. "Thank you," she said. "I hope Arachne and Prometheus guard your path."

"I can use all the help I can get."

I didn't stay to watch them approach the Alashi camp; I didn't want to be nearby when the Alashi came looking. "Take me back to Boradai," I said. Then, hesitantly I added, "As fast as you can."

I had thought that if the djinn's top speed was too fast to be comfortable, I could always shout at him to slow back down...but this turned out not to be so easy. The wind was screaming in my ears, and I had to let go of the handholds and shield my face with both my arms. We plunged at some point and I thought I heard the squawk of a startled bird somewhere behind us, or perhaps the djinn was just enjoying the opportunity to torment me. "Slow down," I tried to shriek, but the djinn must have been able to avoid hearing me because our speed did not decrease.

Finally we stopped and hovered in the air for a moment. "Soft landing!" I managed to spit out. We plunged for an unending moment, then slowed and settled back on the ground as lightly as a blown feather.

My hands were so cold I could hardly bend my fingers; Tamar untied me and let me climb down to rest for a few minutes. The sun was up, but the clouds hadn't burned off yet; all that excitement in so little time. "The wagon needs to be cleaned," I said, and collapsed, shaking, to the ground.

"You shouldn't have to go twice," Tamar said. "I can go this time."

"No—it's all right. Perhaps this time I'll bring a bucket for people to pass around as they vomit. Keep the wagon a bit cleaner..."

"What do you think we should do with Sophos's head?" Tamar asked.

"What does Jaran want done with it?"

"He said to ask you what you thought."

"Huh." I wondered if it was still lying on the ground, staring up at the sky. "If I could, I'd leave it on Kyros's desk like a paperweight."

"Oh, I like that idea," Tamar said. It wasn't until I heard her talking to Boradai that I realized she was actually going to carry through on it. *This is probably a bad idea,* I thought. At least I'd have a chance to rest while the djinn ran its grisly errand, but...I stood up and saw the head rising up into the air. *Too late.* Boradai could always call it back, but I didn't want to ask her for a favor, not when I'd stated just hours ago that her debt was repaid. I sat back down to rest while I could.

All too quickly, the djinn returned. Jaran approached me as I stood up. "I'd like to ride where I can see," he said. "Can I sit beside you?"

"I guess so. Tamar can tie both of us on."

Everyone climbed on—including the one who'd insisted he didn't care what happened to him. Apparently he'd changed his mind. "Last chance to get on, if you want a fast trip up to the steppe," I called. "Last chance to get off, if you don't like being carried by djinni."

"Wait just a moment," one young man pleaded, climbing out of the wagon. He ran over to where the eight who'd chosen to remain slaves were waiting. A few minutes later, he returned with an older woman held firmly by one arm.

"It's her choice," I said.

"She's choosing to come with us," the man said. She nodded reluctantly. *Well, if she decides she really wants to be a slave, the Alashi will oblige her,* I thought. They settled into the bottom of the wagon box. Tamar brought fabric over and bound both me and Jaran to our seats. I wished I had time to rig some sort of hat or veil, but wound up wrapping a scarf around my head and pulling most of it over my face, tucking it in as well as I could.

It was easier this time, now that I had some idea of what to expect, from the lurch in my stomach as the djinn lifted us up to the screams of dismay from the wagon box as we started to move. I didn't have to try to watch over the side, since the djinn knew where we were going. "Try to vomit in the bucket," I suggested. "It'll keep things cleaner."

Jaran was white-faced but kept quiet as we started flying—no screams or vomiting. After a while he turned toward me. "So we met, last year, but I can't say I really knew you very well," he said. He had to shout to be heard over the wind; it wasn't exactly a private conversation. "The djinni had a little bit of an interest in you even then, though."

I wasn't sure what to say to that, so I made some noncommittal noise that was lost in the rush of air.

"Have you figured out what you were meant to do, yet? Freeing slaves, is that it?"

"I'm going to free the rivers," I said, the words slipping out before I thought the better of it.

"Really? How are you going to manage that?"

"I don't know."

There was a pause, and Jaran gave me a surprised shrug. "Well. I was going to tell you that I thought you were crazy, but the Fair One seems to think you really will." He still sounded doubtful, which was reasonable, since if I hadn't been fevered, I would have thought it was a crazy idea, too. It took me a moment to remember that the Fair One was the djinn who spoke with him sometimes.

"When are you going to free the rivers?" Jaran asked. Behind us, we heard someone retching. I hoped they had the bucket handy.

"I need to free Prax first," I said. "I'm not sure how I'm going to do that, either."

"Prax is the mine slave?"

"Tamar told you? Did she tell you my idea? She doesn't like it very much."

"She said you had an idea, but it was crazy and she wasn't going to help you with it," Jaran said.

"We can't talk to Prax because he's not a shaman. My idea is to poison the food of the Greek soldiers and help the mine slaves escape while they're sick. But to gain access to the food, to talk to Prax, we need someone who can actually go down to the mine. I thought maybe I could have Tamar sell me into slavery there, and once I'm there . . ."

"That is a stupid plan," Jaran said.

"It's the best I've come up with."

"Well, it's no wonder Tamar didn't like it."

"Tamar's idea was to dress as merchants and bring lots of things to sell, and then to throw in a sick lamb as a gift at the end, in the hopes that would sicken them."

"Sounds like a better idea than yours."

"Well, except that the mine guards are suspicious of anyone coming. If we brought *slaves* to sell they'd never question it, but even if I were willing to sell people to a mine, we're short of money right now. And I think we're running out of time."

We fell silent for a little while, listening to the sobs and retching of the slaves in the back of the wagon. My ribs felt bruised from the binding cloth, and my hip bones hurt from bumping against the seat. *If I do this again, I hope it's in a nice, cushy palanquin, with a real sorceress telling the djinn what to do.*

"The Fair One likes your plan better than Tamar's," Jaran said. "I can't think why."

"Maybe she knows it will work."

"Maybe."

"Or maybe she thinks I deserve it. I'm the reason Prax is there. Did Tamar explain that part to you?"

"Huh." Jaran let out a very dry chuckle. "One of Sophos's girls was sold to a mine once. It was sort of my fault, though not entirely."

"I saw her," I said. "Well, maybe I saw her. She was in Sophos's mine. I saw her when we passed through, on our way to Sophos's house. Elubai tried to scare me by hinting that I'd be sold there, too, if I didn't behave."

"She was sort of like Aislan, but more vindictive. Aislan was a favorite, but she knew she was better off with us than against us, you know? The other girl ... well, she was just trouble. She would spill all sorts of things to Sophos just to make the rest of us look bad— and to make herself look good. She didn't realize that just because Sophos will use your loyalty, doesn't mean that he's loyal to you." He used his free hand to rub the back of his neck. "I made it look as if she'd stolen something from Sophos. I didn't intend for her to be sent to the mine, just for her to learn a lesson about what Sophos is capable of. But he decided to make an example of her. I never saw her again."

"You mean you haven't seen her again. She was still alive a year ago. Maybe you'll see her yet."

"I suppose. If I were a better person I'd try to free her."

"You're only indirectly responsible for where she is."

"Well, you didn't sell Prax to the mine, did you? Kyros did."

"I returned him to Kyros. He was smart and capable. I think he'd have made it to the Alashi."

"But he wasn't so smart and capable that he wasn't caught by you."

"Even a capable person loses some of the time," I said.

We lapsed into silence again.

"Tell me about killing Sophos," I said eventually.

"What do you want to know?"

"All of it."

"Boradai gave me a knife," Jaran said. "And... Well. Sophos is a man who likes to see people in pain. Or he *was* such a man, rather. That's why he summoned Tamar so often. It was always rape, with her, because she never got used to it."

"What about you?"

"I was more used to it than Tamar. But..." He laughed a little, under his breath. "I'm the bastard of Sophos's commanding officer. So he liked to use me because in some strange way it felt like he was . . . Well. There's a drug that's used to make people sluggish; they gave some to you before you were sent to Sophos." I remembered that vividly—the bitter aftertaste of the wine, the clumsiness of my limbs. "Last night Boradai slipped some into the wine, after warning all the concubines not to drink any. So everyone was a little slow, though I don't think they realized it. And she gave us all knives. Sophos took me back to his room early and barred the door. I'd had all sorts of ideas about stabbing him somewhere creative—no one so much as twitches at the sound of a scream from Sophos's room. But when it came right down to it, I simply took my first and best opportunity. There's a great big vein in your leg, near where it joins the rest of your body. I took out the knife and cut him there as deep as I could. He bled out in a matter of moments. Boradai wanted the head, to give to Tamar, so after he was dead I cut it off. Then I used his water to wash up, and waited for Boradai to come find me and tell me it was time."

"Did you leave anyone there alive?"

"Sophos's wife got wind of what was happening and took the children and hid somewhere. We didn't waste any time trying to root them out—we were pretty certain they couldn't get to the garrison to alert the soldiers, but they'd have fought like rats if we'd cornered them. I'm sure they've come out by now."

"There must have been guards who weren't with concubines last night."

"Yes, but Boradai knew precisely where they'd be. She summoned them one by one to different spots, and we took turns jumping them." He shook his head. "I never would have thought it would be possible to sub-orn Boradai."

"She said she didn't know where Alisher was. Yet you knew."

"The Fair One knew. I saw no reason to tell her." Jaran shrugged. "What are you going to do now?"

"I guess Tamar and I will try to find homes for the eight . . . seven . . . who want to remain slaves."

"Good luck with that."

"I know of a good place to sell them, but I'll need to find someone else to take them there."

"I suppose." Jaran stared at the horizon. In the east, the sky was beginning to turn a lighter violet. "Suppose I came back with you. Told Tamar I was going to help you with the next step, then slipped away with you some night and sold you to the mine."

"Tamar would kill you."

"She'd have to catch me, though. She might kill *you* once you were out."

"Why are you offering?"

"Because the Fair One likes the idea. Then again, it's possible she just doesn't like you and wants to see you suffer. But since you're volunteering . . ."

"All right, then," I said. "Come back with me. You can tell Tamar that you're going to stay with us to help us. She'll be so happy to see you again, she won't ask too many questions."

The wagon stopped moving. I peered down over the side. "Let's go west just a little," I said. "Right, that flat spot there. Take us down, gently, and put it there."

The landing was gentle enough not to break any-one's bones or split the wagon in half. The miserable ex-slaves all scrambled out of the wagon. I saw Meruert, with her baby. "The Alashi are that way," I said, pointing. "The first group should have found them by now. They're not going to be overjoyed to see you, but stand your ground."

"Are you coming, Jaran?" Meruert asked.

"Not right now," Jaran said. "Maybe I'll be back in a month or two."

Meruert nodded. "Good luck," she whispered, gave us each a kiss on the cheek, and followed the rest.

Back in the air, I clung to the idea that we would be home soon. "Not as fast as last time," I said. "But *almost* as fast as you can. Get us back to Boradai."

The last of the mist was vanishing when we landed. The waiting group was much diminished now. The former slaves who wanted freedom, but not with the Alashi, had struck out on their own some hours ago. Tamar still waited, of course, and as predicted, she was delighted to see Jaran. Boradai had waited for our return, Alisher at her side. The former slaves who wanted to be resold—seven of them, now—waited in the shade, a forlorn-looking lot. Aislan waited in the shade, too, a contemptuous smile on her face.

"Jaran came back to help us," I said by way of explanation. Tamar didn't question his return, just helped untie us from the wagon and gave him a hug. Boradai watched with a faint smile.

She approached a few moments later. "I have an idea that would be to our mutual benefit. Those seven—" she gestured. "They asked to stay in slavery. They will need to be sold. Let me take them; I'll sell them. The money will assist me in making my way in the future."

I glanced at Tamar. She didn't like the idea, but neither of us had wanted to deal with trying to sell the slaves. "A kind master," I said. "I had an idea of a man just west of Daphnia ..." I told her about the farm and where to find Solon.

Boradai nodded. "I'll take care of things. But you have no objections; you're not going to try to claim them."

"I'd really just as soon stay out of the business of selling slaves."

"Understandable." She turned toward the slaves. "Right, then. Into the wagon, all of you." There was grumbling and dismay—they had hoped to *avoid* another experience with the djinn—but they obeyed. *There are some who really are happier this way.* I thought of Burkut, of his miserable death.

Boradai and Alisher climbed up into the wagon and bound themselves to the seat. I watched as Boradai fingered the spell-chain. They rose up like a basket being lifted by its handle, and then flew away from us toward the rising sun. From the ground, it looked like such a *pleasant* way to travel ...

I turned back to our horses with immense relief. "Jaran, you can ride Kara," I said. "I'll take Krina again."

*I* dumped the bucket of vomit and washed it, then picked up the bag that had held Sophos's head. I started to throw it away, then remembered an old soldier's saying, *death breeds death.* Rotten meat might make the mine guards sick; would it make them even sicker if the rot came from human blood? I looked in the bag; there was blood and fragments of skin and bone inside, and it already had a smell that made my stomach queasy. Rotten animal meat smelled bad enough. Rotting human flesh ... I swallowed hard, then rolled up the bag, wrapped it in another bag, and packed it.

Jaran was still wearing the light, impractical clothes of one of Sophos's concubines. I dug through my bag. I would need to share my clothes with him, as he was much too big to fit in anything of Tamar's. The end result was that we both looked like ragged vagabonds, but neither of us looked like an escaped harem slave. "Is it safe to set out?" Tamar asked. "Surely the soldiers in Helladia know by now what's happened . . ."

"It's not all that close . . ."

"But they would recognize Jaran." He nodded agreement. "I think we should stay here, at least until night."

I thought I would fly to pieces from impatience, as I waited through the rest of the day. We sat in the cave, along with our horses. Tamar and Jaran chatted quietly with each other; I paced. Aislan sat near the back of the cave, because Tamar didn't trust her near the front.

I wondered what the soldiers would make of the situation: Sophos dead, the slaves vanished. If they'd caught a glimpse of the makeshift palanquin, they might think a rogue sorceress was involved. With any luck, the Sisterhood would blame the Younger Sisters and our enemies would distract themselves fighting with each other.

Night fell; the moon was full tonight, so we could ride, slowly. We packed up and mounted; Aislan stayed in the back of the cave, as if she thought we'd simply forget about her. "Aislan," Tamar called, just before we set off, and she reluctantly came out. "You can do whatever you want now. Go back to your lover in town, run away to the Alashi, whatever." Her voice was kind, kinder than I would have expected; Aislan had never been very nice to Tamar back in the harem. "I hope you find what you want. Whatever it is."

We pushed the horses, traveling through the night and into the morning, trying to put distance between ourselves and Helladia. Then we gave the horses an afternoon to graze and rest, and made camp.

I sought the borderland that night, and tried one last time to find Prax. The djinni had taken me to find him once; surely I could find him again. He had tried to kill me, and had drawn blood—had that created a thread between us that I could use to find him? I found the borderland easily enough, and touched the spot on the back of my arm where he'd managed to cut me. *Prax*, I thought.

I stood for a long moment on the dark plain; then the world tilted, and rippled around me, and suddenly I was watching a woman on a horse, from above, like a bird. *Or a djinn.* It was day, and I recognized the horse—it was Zhade, my old horse, from when I worked for Kyros. That was when I realized that the woman was me: I was seeing myself, two years ago. I was looking for Prax.

I drew breath to shout at her—at myself—but no sound came.

She dismounted. *I saw movement*, I remembered. She approached cautiously, her hand on her sword's hilt. For a moment, even though I knew what had happened, I thought that she wouldn't see Prax, and would continue on her way. But no. There was a faint sigh of triumph, and she reached for him.

Prax uncoiled from where he'd crouched, a broken shard of ceramic jar in his hand. "You're going to regret finding me," he snarled, and lunged. He moved fast, and with utter ruthlessness—he knew he couldn't afford to hesitate. The Lauria I saw below flung her arm up to shield her body, and yelled out a curse as the shard scored across her arm, cutting deep enough to draw blood. She drew her sword.

"I'll die before I go back there," Prax spat.

"No," Lauria said, her voice perfectly assured. "Kyros wants you back alive, so I'll bring you back alive."

Prax lunged again—a mad tactic, his stub of a makeshift knife against a sword, but Lauria stepped to the side, grabbed his outstretched arm, and knocked the shard from his hand with her own sword's hilt. Then she brought the heel of her boot down on it, crushing it into the dirt.

Prax crumpled. He didn't cry, but I could see the defeat in his bowed shoulders—I'd seen it that day, too. I'd known that he'd give me no further trouble. I swallowed hard, and the world tilted around me, giving me a look, just for an instant, into the old Lauria's triumphant eyes. Shaken with a blind surge of anger, I wanted to hurt her—kill her, even, or at least terrify her. In the strange landscape of the borderland, I felt my anger go out like an arrow . . . and then, a moment later, as I hovered on the edge of waking, felt it return, and strike me, like an arrow in the gut.

*Oh gods. I don't know what I just did, but it wasn't good.*

To my relief, someone was shaking me awake. It was Jaran. "Now would be a good time, if you're ready. If we're close enough."

*I'll need something that reminds me of Tamar.* Shaking off my dream as well as I could, I took my knife and sawed off the very edge of her coat, then knotted it tightly around my wrist, like the scraps of sister cloth that had been given as bracelets, back among the Alashi. The sister cloth had hair in it. I didn't dare pluck a hair from her head, for fear of waking her, but I found a stray hair on her bedding and knotted that around my wrist as well. As for my own possessions— I would have to leave my sword here. Perhaps Tamar would find a use for it. I left it, sheathed, by her blankets, the hilt near her hand.

We slipped away on foot, leading Kara. Dawn came when we were a mile out from the entrance to the mine; Jaran looked me over. "Take off your boots," he said. "Those are way too nice for a slave who's being sold."

"Give me your sandals, then."

We traded shoes. My boots were too small for him, and his sandals were too big for me, but they were close enough to serve.

"Could you ask the Fair One whether Prax is still alive?" I asked. "Could *she* carry a message to him?"

Jaran pursed his lips as he worked my boots onto his feet. "She is not my servant; I am hers. She likes the idea of you going into the mine. I don't think she'd want to send you in if Prax were already dead, but I don't think she'll carry messages, because she wants you to do this."

"Why?"

He shrugged wordlessly. "The djinni have their own plans."

I stood up. "Do I look all right?"

"You passed as a slave in the harem ... mostly. Here you'll be a slave in trouble, so any misbehavior will be written off as something that needs to be beaten out of you."

"I think I'll try not to get in trouble."

"Good plan." Without warning, Jaran backhanded me across the face, knocking me down.

"You son of a . . ." I scrambled back from him, rubbing my cheek.

He shrugged. "Look, do you want to pass, or not? If you're a slave in trouble, you'll have at least one bruise."

"You could have warned me!"

"Sorry. I thought this way would be easier for you." He took a rope out of the saddlebag and tied my hands together, then tied the other end of the rope to the saddle. "I'm a merchant from a caravan. You went missing briefly last night—when we found you, you said you were lost, but I don't believe you. I'm making an example out of you." He jerked his head. "Last chance to back out."

"Let's go," I said. My head was spinning. "Where are you going to go after you sell me?"

"Up to the Alashi," Jaran said. "If I go back to Tamar after this, she'll kill me."

I'd been flying high for days now, and it had served me well. As we approached the mine, though, I felt my good spirits beginning to fall to earth, like a spider descending from its web. *This will work,* I told myself, trying to reassure my own doubts as we walked. *Will work will work will work.* If not, well. *I'll feel really stupid.* I touched the packet of rotting flesh. *Arachne, let this work. Prometheus, let this work.*

"Stop!"

There was a wall around the mine, well maintained and carefully guarded. Jaran reined in Kara and she backed up a step; I had to skip to the side to avoid being stepped on. "What do you want?" the guard called down.

"I'm selling a slave," Jaran said. "Are you buying?"

"We're always buying. This has certainly been a good week!" There was a pause, and then the door swung open and an officious-looking little man came out to look me over.

"Why are you selling?" he asked.

"I need the money," Jaran said. I waited for him to tell the rest of the story, but apparently he was angling for a better price. The guard didn't notice.

"What do you want for her?" he asked.

"I'll trade her to you for 150 pounds of grain for my horse," Jaran said.

"A hundred," the guard countered, though this was an absurdly low price.

"A hundred forty-five," Jaran said.

"Done," the guard said with a shrug, and sent for sacks of grain to hand over on the spot. Jaran untied my rope from the horse and tossed it to the guard. *The Fair One thought this was a good idea,* I reminded myself, and followed the guard through the gate. He kicked the door shut behind me.

*This will work,* I told myself again, but I could hear the vulture of darkness settling around me. The arrow of anger I had fired at myself had struck my heart. This time, I would be facing both the real darkness and the darkness inside.

# CHAPTER ELEVEN

This was a gemstone mine. I could see two slaves turning a crank to draw something up out of a narrow hole in the earth. My first horrified thought was that this tiny passage led to the mine, but then they grabbed a bucket of water and dumped it into a brick-lined shallow pool in the ground. Other slaves knelt beside the pool, scrubbing the loose rocks. The washed rocks were tossed onto broad sheets of linen, then sorted through under the sun by more slaves. The larger chunks were broken into smaller chunks by slaves working with hammers on big rock slabs, then washed again. If they were finding anything valuable, I didn't see it. A few glanced up to see the newcomer, but I didn't see Prax.

A hill rose up to our west, and a tunnel had been dug into the hill. I could see two slaves coming out with a wheelbarrow full of rock chips, which they dumped into the pile of stones to be washed. The soldier led me into the side of the hill. "Down," he said.

The opening was larger than the well, but not by

enough. A ladder led down into the darkness. *You can't be serious,* I thought, but he clearly was. I began to climb down. The daylight disappeared, replaced by the dim flicker of lamps. "Fresh muscle," the guard shouted down the hole. "On her way down."

My legs trembled as I went down into the darkness; my palms were slippery with sweat. *I don't need a dark bird this time; I'm meeting the darkness on my own feet.* I told myself that I was meeting the darkness on my own ground as well, but I knew that was a lie. For a minute or two of climbing, I could see nothing at all, and hear nothing but my ragged breath and my borrowed sandals hitting each rung of the ladder, but then I saw a grayish flicker, and I could hear the *clink, clink, clink* of hammers working against rock.

When I'd joined Sophos's harem, I'd been given a disdainful welcome from Boradai, and then instructions from her and Tamar. Here, as soon as I set foot on rock at the bottom of the mine, the guard gave me a hammer, and put me to work.

*Is Prax here?* I tried to look around, only to get a rough shove in the back hard enough to knock me to my knees. "Quit stalling," the guard said.

There were only two guards down here at the bottom of the mine. They had twitchy hands that seldom left the whips they carried, and short swords. *I can look for Prax later,* I thought, swallowing hard, and climbed back to my feet to get to work.

We chipped rock away from the walls of the tunnel, piece by piece, carrying the chunks in baskets to empty them into a barrel that was pulled up on chains. In the lamplit shadows of the mine, all the rocks looked gray. I hoped they didn't expect me to actually spot gems.

In the dust and the dimness, and my own interior

bleakness, the other slaves all looked alike to me, too. Until the person next to me hissed, "What are *you* doing here?" I looked over. I didn't recognize him at all, but he was cleaner than I'd have expected, wilted like a spent flower but not yet hardened. Fresh muscle, like me. Why did he know me? Then I realized—he was one of the seven, one of the ones who'd chosen to return to slavery. *Oh, gods. Boradai sold them here? But...but...*

"It *is* you," he hissed. "This is *not* what we asked for, you lying, foul..."

"I know," I said. "Shhh, the guard is looking at us."

He lapsed into frightened silence. After a little while he said, "Sophos was a fine master. A good man. He treated me well."

"Sorry," I muttered.

"You should be. I never asked for your help."

"He had two faces. You saw the nicer one."

"It wasn't that hard to stay on his good side. You were with Tamar, weren't you? She was uppity. Thought she was too good for anyone."

Our eyes met in the dim light and I knew he saw my disgust, as I saw his anger.

"I'm going to free you again," I said.

"Sure you are. Did you bring a djinn?"

"No, but I'll free you without one."

"Sure you will." We heard a guard approaching and fell silent. The guard stood directly behind me for a long moment; I redoubled my efforts with the hammer, breaking chips loose from the wall. I thought I could hear the guard's breath, feel the heat of it against the back of my neck. I didn't dare look; he would take that as an invitation to draw out the whip, and with eight fresh slaves this would be a convenient time to make an example of someone. Anyone. I was one of the weaker new slaves, a good choice should they decide to beat someone senseless—or worse.

Finally the guard moved on.

"I never wanted freedom," the man said. "Never."

"Sorry," I muttered again. thinking, *shut up, already.*

"Sophos fed me, he gave me a roof over my head. I was warm in the winter and had water to drink in the summer. You took my home away from me. And now, *now,* thanks to you, here I am." He swung the hammer up and against the wall with a particularly vicious clink. The force of the blow shook a basket's worth of rock chips loose, and he knelt to gather them up and dump his rocks into the barrel. When he was back, he gave me another venomous look and said, "This is all your fault."

"You're here because *you* chose slavery," I hissed. "You were gifted an opportunity that many people die trying to get, and you chose slavery. So don't whine to me because it didn't work out the way you'd hoped."

"You promised a kind master."

"Did I? Well, I gave Boradai the name of a man who would have bought you and treated you kindly. She sold you here instead. Blame her."

"Boradai—"

"—is a free woman now."

"But—"

"When we were standing outside Helladia you were free. You didn't have to go with Boradai. You put yourself in her power. *Your* mistake."

"I hope you rot in hell."

"We're already in hell. If you're lucky, I'll get us out."

I wondered where Tamar was, right now—what she'd done when she woke up and found us gone. *She'll go back to the Alashi*, the darkness whispered. *She's stuck around out of loyalty, but after this—this betrayal—she'll shed you like the deadweight you are. You're on your own.* I shook my head. I could trust Tamar; she was out there, waiting for night, and we'd manage this together. She'd had plenty of opportunities to leave me if that's what she wanted to do.

*Not since winter ended, though.*

I could trust her.

*You used to say the same thing about Kyros.*

Tamar was my blood sister.

*Kyros is your father.*

When the shadow had fallen over me in the winter, I had taken to my bed and scarcely moved until it lifted, finally, weeks later. Here I didn't have that luxury. I had to keep moving, keep the hammer moving, keep my mind working on our escape. I'd forgotten, during my months without the shadow, how hard it was to *think* in the darkness. It felt as if weights were chained to my mind, at least for any reasoned thought. My fears—about Tamar abandoning me to my stupidity, about Kyros finding me, about Prax killing me—continued to chase each other around and around like little yapping dogs.

Someone up above struck a large bell; around me, everyone gathered up their stone chips into their baskets and went up, one by one, to dump them into the barrel. I followed. The barrel went up, lifted on chains by slaves turning the crank somewhere above. Then it came back down with a steaming pot and a stack of wooden bowls. A ladle for each of us; everyone slumped against the wall to eat. I'd hoped for stew, but what came out of the pot looked like cooked horse grain. I was still hungry enough that I scraped the bowl clean to get the last of it.

As we were bringing back our bowls, I heard a quiet voice say, "I heard someone say your name is Lauria." I turned—it was Prax. *He's still alive*—but his eyes burned silently, and I swallowed hard, wondering what I could say with the guards so close.

Nothing, as it turned out. I was shoved back to my spot, Prax was shoved in another direction. Anything I had to say to him would have to wait until later.

I picked up my hammer. My hands were beginning to blister; my arm muscles were sore. As I swung it, the yapping dogs started up again. *Even if you can swing it now, what about tomorrow, what about the next day? This plan was doomed; you only came up with it as a way to atone by dying. So let them make an example of you. Prax will see, maybe he'll be satisfied. But it certainly sounds easier than swinging that hammer one more time, doesn't it?*

*Prax. He hates you, and for good reason. He has every right to hate you, far more than the whining bastard on your left has. Even if you want to help Prax, why should he listen to you? Maybe as soon as the guards are out of sight for the night he'll pick up one of these hammers and beat you to death.*

*Well, if that's what he wants to do, I guess I'd better keep swinging this hammer so that the guards don't kill me first. Prax sure has a better right to kill me than the guards do.*

*And then Tamar will try to find you tonight, and . . . what? If you're dead, you won't be able to talk to her. She'll think she just didn't find you, so she'll stay close, and try again . . . and again . . . How long before she*

*gives up? How long before one of the detachments
from the Greek Army stumbles across her and kills her
out of suspicion that she's Alashi?*

I tried to clear my mind, as I would when I was meditating, but the fears crowded in anyway, swarming
through my thoughts, nipping at me. *Tamar,* I thought,
swinging the hammer with a clink against the rock
wall. *Tamar. Tamar. Tamar. Tamar.* I focused my mind
on her name like a bead on a chain, willing that to banish the other thoughts and worries. I could do nothing
more until evening, nothing more until I'd spoken with
Prax and—I hoped—Tamar. *Wait until evening.*

*W*e heard another bell. Up went the rocks, and
down came dinner—more gruel. Our hammers went
into the barrel with our empty bowls to go up. *I guess
Prax will have to kill me with his bare hands.* Down
the ladder came the slaves who'd worked that day
washing rock chips. Down came a barrel of blankets—
one each—plus a pot to piss in. Up went all the lamps
save one, leaving us nearly in darkness as the barrel
was pulled back to the top. Finally the guards went
up the ladder, and last of all, the ladder itself was
pulled up.

It was a remarkably secure prison.

As the guards were leaving, the slaves from up top
were looking for places to lie down and sleep for the
night. The slaves from below were waiting, though,
and I thought I knew why.

Prax approached me from the back of the mine as I
stood, gaping up at the hole where the ladder had
been. "You are the Lauria I remember," he said.

"Yes."

"This makes no sense. You weren't owned by Kyros. And half a dozen from the line swear they saw you last week, a free woman. What are you doing here?"

"Looking for you," I said.

"Why?"

"Because I want to give back what I took from you."

"Are you *drunk*? What the hell do you think you can give me here?"

The slaves from above had gotten back up to listen, and there was a ripple of hard amusement at Prax's question.

"I mean, *really*. Do you see a way out of here? Do you see a ladder? Every slave is put down here at night."

"I have a friend on the outside," I said. "A shaman, and my blood sister. Once we know what we're going to do, we can have her come and let us out."

"There is a wall. There are guards. They are constantly watching for bandits, and you think your friend has a chance?"

"I think she'll have a chance if we can poison the guards." I pulled the packet from my pocket. "Who cooks for the guards?"

A long pause. Then... "He does," Prax said, and pointed.

I held out the packet to the man. He was cleaner than the rest. "Would you use this?" I asked.

"What will it do?"

"Make them sick." *I hope.*

"If I make them sick, they'll take away my job and send me back to the bottom of the mine."

"No they won't. Because while they're throwing up, my blood sister will come throw down the ladder, and we'll come up and kill them all, and escape to the Alashi. And then we'll *all* be free."

The cook looked at Prax. Prax looked at me.

"I swore last fall that I would free the people I sent back to slavery," I said. "I found Nika, and took her to the Alashi. I took Uljas to the steppes. And...and Burkut as well."

"What happened to Burkut? You're trying to hide something," Prax said.

"Burkut died. He was free, but he died." I waited for Prax to say something. When he didn't I went on. "I don't know where Thais is. But I spent all winter trying to think of a way to free you. I thought that if I was willing to risk everything by going inside, I might be able to help you get out. And all the other mine slaves."

"Why?"

"Do you really need to know the answer to that?"

Prax stepped close to me and for a moment I thought he *was* going to try to kill me with his bare hands. I could smell him, fetid and sweaty with a faint odor of rot and death. His breath was terrible. "I dreamed of you, some months ago," he said. "We faced each other, and you promised to free me." I nodded. "So tell me. Why? And why now, and not two years ago when you took me back to Kyros?"

"I was Kyros's servant then." I swallowed hard. "Now...now I am Alashi." *And always will be. No matter what they say.*

Prax's eyes swept over me and he nodded, finally.

"There are two guards down here during the day," I said. "Why not kill them and break out, even without poisoning their food?"

"The ladder is pulled up unless someone needs to go

up or down," Prax said. "Also, there is air to breathe here at the bottom only because a djinn blows fresh air down a shaft. If they sent the djinn to do something else, we'd all suffocate."

"What about the slaves above?"

"There are far more than two guards on top," Prax said. "They protect the mine from bandits. They could certainly fight off slaves."

"Well." I turned back to the cook. "Will you put this in their food? It's possible that it won't do anything at all."

He took it, crumpling it in his hand and hiding it, finally, inside his shirt.

Prax took his blanket and lay down in the tunnel. "You probably need to sleep now," he said. "Speak with your blood sister. Then tell us if she's willing to help us."

I wrapped my blanket around me, then lay down and closed my eyes. Around me, I could hear the shuffle of other slaves settling down. The tunnel floor was cold, even through the blanket, and uneven. And despite my exhaustion, I couldn't fall asleep.

I rose, finally, and sat up, leaning against the wall and trying to meditate. Around me, in the dim light, I could see silent humps, the sleeping slaves. Then Prax sat up and came to sit next to me.

"I couldn't sleep my first night here either," he said. I thought he was going to go on to give me grief—after all, it was *my* fault he'd wound up here—but he just scratched his knee, his eyes a little distant. "The floor is awfully hard."

"I need to talk to Tamar," I whispered.

"Maybe tomorrow night."

"I gave the cook the packet..."

"Well, and tomorrow night we'll know if it's worked."

My eyes felt like they were crusted with sand; I was so tired, I couldn't understand why I hadn't been able to just *sleep*. "Why are you being kind to me?" I blurted, resting my forehead against my knees.

Prax shrugged. "Why not?" When I didn't answer, he went and lay back down. After a few minutes I lay down again as well.

I slipped into a gray twilight sometime very late in the night, but I couldn't find Tamar, or she couldn't find me; I thought I heard the echo of her voice, but I couldn't make out her words over the clatter of a bell. Then the ringing of the bell woke me, and I was back in the mine.

We ate breakfast below; more cooked horse feed. Then a different group of slaves went up to work on the surface for the day. We rotated, apparently. I wondered when it would be my turn to go up, and hoped that I wouldn't have the opportunity to find out. Prax was down with me, still. He worked beside me today, his eyes on the rock as he chipped away.

"How much of what we're breaking here is gems?" I asked as we worked.

"In a good week we find a handful. Up above, they get a bonus if they find any. Extra food. Down here, they don't expect us to be able to spot anything. There was one time, though, that someone found a big swath of something in the rock—they had us chip away the rock around it to pry it all out, and then everyone got the rest of the day off."

"When was that? Recently?"

"No. I don't know when it was. Maybe last spring? Or last summer. It's hard to keep track of time."

I wondered what had kept Prax alive, all this time. How he'd survived the work, the hunger, the abuse. He was rail-thin now, hard and spare; anything extra he had had been burned away, eaten by the darkness. He saw me looking at him and returned a measuring look before going back to his task.

The hammer was rubbing blisters onto my hands; I tried to change my grip, but that helped very little. I thought about tearing loose some strips of cloth from my shirt to pad my hands, then discarded the idea. *Just endure it,* I thought. *Either we'll escape and I'll have time to heal, or I'll die anyway. Attracting attention from the guards now isn't worth it.* By the time we stopped to eat lunch, my hands were slick with blood.

I watched carefully to see what the guards were eating. They had a separate meal, which they ate, leaning against the barrel and chatting with each other. I wondered if the cook had slipped the packet in. The guards didn't seem to find anything wrong with the food. One glanced toward me as the meal was ending and I quickly looked away.

Not quickly enough. "Hey, girl," the guard said, ambling toward me. I looked down—then, afraid the guard would be angry at me for not answering when he was clearly talking to me, I looked up again. I stood up and instinctively tried to square my shoulders and straighten up before thinking, *no, he wants me to cower, just give him what he wants.* It didn't matter. I could smell my own fear, and I'm sure he could, too.

"What did you do to piss off your old master, anyway?" The guard wasn't fat, but he was fleshy, and soft, for a soldier. Stark contrast to the hungry slaves. His clothes were dirty, but pressed and mended. No doubt some privileged slave had laundry duty.

"I don't know," I said, my voice ragged.

The guard poked me in the chest with the handle of his whip, hard enough to knock me back down. Then he uncoiled his whip and lashed me once on the legs. The tearing pain caught me by surprise and I yelped like a puppy. "Sure you know," the guard said. "They all know. Are you going to tell me now?" The whip snapped out again and I cringed, trying to pull away with nowhere to go, biting back my own sobs. He wasn't hitting me hard; I knew that. From his perspective, this wasn't punishment, but teasing.

"I'll tell you," I said, my back pressed against the tunnel wall. "I can tell you my guess."

The whip snaked out one more time as I was saying that and I almost broke down into sobs before I got some sort of shaky control over my voice. "I went for water and got lost. He must have thought I was trying to run away, since we were so near bandit territory. He said he would make an example of me, so he sold me here, not even for a very good price, to be rid of me. To make sure everyone knew."

"Got lost. Sure you did." The guard nodded, and for a moment I thought he might press the issue, but he'd tired of his sport. "What are you all gawking at?" he roared, and everyone picked up hammers and went back to work.

My hands were shaking, and my legs, but the tears dissipated as I let the darkness swallow me again. *Nothing matters, nothing matters, wait it out, wait it out.*

Before I had left with Sophos, he had promised that I would be treated respectfully—that he wouldn't forget that I was a free woman. Then he'd raped me. But that had happened just before I left Sophos's house for the Alashi. For most of my time with him, I'd thought myself untouchable; my fear had been feigned. Here, I was truly a slave. Reflecting on that even briefly made the panic rise up in me like the urge to vomit. *There's only one way out now. Only one way out. So keep going.*

The guards did not look ill. Not even slightly. Maybe the evening meal would be different? Dinnertime came, we ate again, and the guards and the ladder went up. All eyes turned to the cook.

"I put it in the noon meal," he said. "That stuff you gave me. It smelled terrible, I thought they'd all notice, but no one complained. But they're not sick, either. It didn't work."

*It didn't work.* I felt dizzy with dismay.

"We need a stronger poison," Prax said. "We'll mix together the stuff in the night pot tonight. Scoop out a little, let it sit in a packet for a day, then try giving them that." He squeezed my shoulder. "This will work."

"Why are you so certain?" I asked him as we lay down for the night.

"The djinni promised me I would be free," he said softly.

"Are you *sure* it was the djinni?" I asked.

"Are you thinking of the dream where you came to me? I'm not thinking of that. This was different. Not long after I first came here, I decided that I'd rather die than remain a slave. I didn't want to be beaten to death—too painful—so I didn't dare just stop working. Instead, I stopped eating. For two days; no one noticed. Then that night, a djinn came to me and told me that I needed to eat, and survive, and trust them, because I would be free. I asked when, and the djinn wouldn't tell me, but it did say that an Alashi woman would come and lead me to freedom. I thought that was strange. I didn't know a great deal about the Alashi, but I did know that they *never* free slaves. You're supposed to free yourself, and then if you reach them, they figure you're worthy. The Greeks say the Alashi sacrifice newcomers to their gods, but they don't, really—the desert does it for them."

"But I'm not Alashi. They cast me out. Alibek..." I trailed off, not wanting to tell the story. "They took my vest," I finished, lamely. "I'm not one of them."

"You said yesterday that you were Alashi."

"It was the easiest way to explain. And—I am more Alashi than I am anything else, even if they don't want me anymore."

Prax almost smiled. "The djinn meant you."

*I* could see Tamar, but she was a terribly long way away, across the steppe, riding her horse. I shouted her name, and she turned toward me, but though she urged her horse forward she grew no closer.

"We're going to poison the guards," I shouted. "Once they're sick, we'll need you...we'll be trapped, below the ground, we'll need you to lower the ladder..."

She was still distant, but I could see her face, tight with fear. "Can you hear me?" I shouted. "Do you understand? Please..."

She was yelling something back, but I couldn't hear her; the wind whipped her words away. They reached me, finally, echoing in my ears as I woke up. *I'm going to kill you for doing this to me. You and Jaran both, I'm going to spit you on sticks and leave you for the vultures...*

I lay awake in the dim light of the one lamp. *Tamar
wants to help. She must be willing to help, because I
have to survive this in order to give her the satisfaction
of killing me. But that's not what she'd have said if she
heard me. If she'd heard what I said, she'd have given
me more of an answer.*

*Maybe she heard me just as I woke, the way I
heard her.*

*The message got through.*

*Surely it did.*

There was nothing I could do about it, not lying
awake. Even after dozing off into fitful light sleep, I
wasn't able to find Tamar again. I thought I heard
Kyros's voice, in the distance, but I couldn't be sure.

*I* woke for real sometime before the guards came
down to wake us. Prax had taken a stick, stirred together the contents of the night pot, then scraped the
revolting result out onto a scrap of cloth, and set that
aside in a corner.

"The guards are going to smell that," someone murmured. "What are you going to say when they find it?"

"Lauria can say that she was sick during the night
and soiled her clothes," Prax said calmly. "She's feeling
well enough to work this morning, though."

The cook came over to stare dubiously at the shit-
smeared folded cloth. "Do you really think they're not
going to *notice* if I put that in their food?"

"Put in only what you think you can get away
with," Prax said.

"And you think it'll work this time. What if they
*catch* me?"

"Take care that they don't. But I think it will work."

Prax caught the man's eyes and touched his arm. "The djinni have said that we'll be free."

The cook nodded, trembling a little. We were going to let it sit for a day; hopefully he wouldn't drop dead from sheer nervousness in the next day and a half.

"Did the djinni really promise that everyone here would be free?" I whispered as we took our spots and picked up our tools. "Or just you?"

"I see no way that I could be freed alone," Prax said. "It's everyone or no one, don't you think?"

"Some could die," I said.

"It will do him no good to think about that."

It would do me no good to think on it, either, but that's what I did for much of the day. I found it hard to imagine this working well enough that no one would die in this escape attempt, and I saw no particular reason to believe that I would be one of the survivors. The melancholia made me *slow*. My thoughts had no clarity and my wit no quickness; surely I wouldn't be any better at avoiding a swinging sword.

Even after a mere two days underground, the sunlit world had begun to seem strangely far away. The rock was real, the task was real, the pain in my hands was surely real, but the open air, the steppe, freedom... they seemed much farther away than a hundred rungs of ladder.

The day passed, somewhere above us. With no sun to follow across the sky, my only hint was my increasingly hollow stomach. But our lunch arrived, finally, and then our dinner, and then people were descending the ladder and blankets were passed out.

I'd hoped, desperately, that I'd be able to speak with Tamar again tonight, but instead I found myself aching and sleepless, my mind lurching in slow circles like a dying animal. I sat up, finally, and leaned against the wall. The pebbles on the floor had begun to poke into my sore muscles, and my entire body felt bruised.

Something lifted my hair—a stray breeze? No. A glimmer in front of me, pale in the shadows, a djinn as miserable as the rest of the mine slaves.

"You're the djinn that brings us our air," I whispered. "I can't free you. We'd die before morning."

"You can't free me now," it whispered back. "But I will be free, like you. You will set me free before you go. It was promised."

"What was promised?"

"You were promised. I've seen you in the places that only we can go; I've seen your face, I've heard your name." Another feathery brush against my hair. "We aren't supposed to share our secrets with you, but they've left me here, abandoned me in the darkness, and I don't care anymore what they say. *You are ours.* You are the one who will free me. Promise me, promise me ..."

"Can you fetch me something that will really make the guards sick? Real poison?"

"No. I am bound tighter than you are."

"You're talking to me, though."

"I can wander the mine freely, but I am bound below the surface."

"I think you're as crazy as I am."

"The slavers think that my land is dark, they think that darkness is what we need, what we like. They are wrong. They see nothing, *nothing*! They don't know what our land is like. We are not creatures of darkness. We are not creatures of stone, of caves."

"Neither am I."

"No." Another touch.

"I will free you as soon as I can."

"They won't want you to. The others here. *Keep the spell-chain. Use it.*"

"I know. I'll free you anyway."

"Promise."

"I promise." It was a foolish thing to promise, but I could no more turn away from the djinn's plea than I could turn away from Prax, now. "Once I can, I will free you."

My hair whipped briefly around my face, and then the djinn was gone. I wondered how close we were to morning, and after a while I lay back down. I did sleep, and I even dreamed, but I didn't remember the dreams in the morning.

*T*he cook took the new packet, slipping it under his clothing and giving Prax one more terrified look before he headed up the ladder. "Lunch pot," Prax whispered to him. He glanced at me, and I nodded, thinking, *I can't bear any more waiting. Let this work. Please, please let this work.*

I'd been staying as far away from the guards as I could, but after lunch, I found a spot to work on that was near enough that I could listen to their conversation. I was hoping desperately for indigestion, at least; a lack of appetite, the cold sweat and headache of looming illness. They weren't much for talking, though; they paced up and down the line for much of the afternoon.

Finally, though, they took a tea break, lounging against the wall for a little while as we kept working. "Anything new on the rider?" one of them asked the other.

I felt the sweat on my arms turn cold. *Tamar. Is this Tamar?*

"Well, from what Therapon could tell, it's only the one. If she's a scout for a bandit raid she's a long way ahead of the rest."

"Maybe she's planning to break in and rob us in our sleep?" They both chuckled at that.

"Word is, she's to be brought in if you can catch her. She's got a fast horse. Probably tomorrow the word will be, *go catch her.* There's no way she's out riding for her health. She's up to no good."

They put their cups down, with that, and a moment later the whip snapped out against my leg. "Teatime's over," the guard said, and I realized I'd slowed my pace, trying to listen to their conversation. "Back to work."

So. There it was. *She's here, but we're almost out of time.* I wondered if she knew they'd seen her, knew they were after her. *I have to dream tonight. Have to. Have to warn her.*

*T*he cook was shaking and pale when he came down. "I'm not doing this again," he said when the guards were gone. "They tasted it, you fools. They *knew* something was different."

"Did they eat it anyway?"

"Yes, but that was lunch, and are they on their knees vomiting? Some poison!"

Everyone looked at me. Including Prax. *Just admit defeat. You've lost. You are lost. What are you going to say now?*

*If I don't give them hope, right now, they will truly be lost.*

"I have another idea," I said. "But it needs to be day. For now—sleep."

It was enough. Barely.

Prax came to speak with me, once all was quiet. "I don't have a plan," I whispered before he could ask. "I don't have an idea. I lied."

"I know."

"The djinn that brings our air stopped to speak with me last night," I whispered. "Last summer, there was another djinn that helped me." The djinn bound in the bandits' spell-chain had promised me that if I would free it by breaking the chain, it would move the bandits somewhere far away from us before returning to its home. "We made a deal," I said after a moment. "I freed it by smashing the binding stone of its spell-chain. It helped me. I could free the djinn that brings our air. Maybe it could do something..."

"Do you know where the spell-chain is?"

"No. But I could free it another way. It's ... hard to explain."

I saw Prax's hair move, ruffled slightly in a stray breeze that touched nothing else. "If I freed you, could you help us, if you chose?" I asked the djinn.

"No." The hiss was tinged with regret. "I would be home, and not here. And you would suffocate here in the darkness, and I would be an outcast forever, for sacrificing your life for my freedom."

"If we freed you during the day, what would they do then? Would they bring us up, or let us die here?"

"I think they'd bring us up," Prax said. "It would cost them a lot of money to replace all of us, and it would shut the mine down for weeks. They're always buying. But they'd keep a close eye on us."

"For how long? It would take time to get a new spell-chain. Perhaps they'd get careless."

"Perhaps . . ."

"Tomorrow," the djinn hissed, and was gone. I felt my resolve harden. *Tomorrow. One way or another.*

*T*amar was with me; she was in my arms, like a lover. "You have to leave," I whispered, and her arms tightened around me. "They know you're out there, they're going to capture you if you stay. Pull back, at least. You can still help us once we're all out."

"You're going to need my help to get out."

"No, I have a new plan. But you need to be sure they don't catch you—if they do, it'll all be over."

"You don't think I could talk my way out?"

I thought that over. "No."

"I'll bear that in mind."

"Tell me you're going to take my advice," I said. "No more hints. *Tell me* what you're going to do."

"Don't worry about me."

"They haven't caught you already!" I said, horrified, but the dream was fading.

*I* woke feeling grimly certain that Tamar *was* in the hands of our enemies. I watched the faces of the guards for clues. *They're smiling. They have her, and that's why they're smiling.* I tried to position myself near them again, to listen. They seemed a little groggy, though, as if they *had* been sick the night before, if not as incapacitated as I'd hoped. They paced and watched us; conversation was minimal.

"Hey, girl," one of them said. I thought from my

hunger that it was late morning, but I wasn't sure. I kept my eyes on the rock, hoping they meant someone else.

"Yeah, I mean you," he said, and I turned. He nodded. "Come here."

I dragged my feet. "We've got a special task for you," he said.

"A special privilege," the other said.

"Do this right, and we might let you spend tomorrow upstairs in the fresh air. Would you like that? You know, you get a piece of cheese if you find a gem. Or a slice of apple. You'd like that, wouldn't you."

I swallowed hard and nodded, keeping my eyes on the ground.

"Well, then. Let's show her what we've got. No, wait—first, have your hammer ready." They snickered. I shrugged and raised my hammer.

One of them had his tea glass upended over something; he lifted it, and I saw a tiny spider, no bigger than my thumb. I remembered, last summer, Zosimos telling us about this, after Tamar freed him from the mine. It was a good amusement to force the slaves to kill spiders, knowing that many worshipped Arachne. No doubt they weren't sure whether I worshipped Arachne or not—or else they'd caught Tamar and were trying to use this to know if I was Alashi. Surely any Alashi would hesitate to kill a spider.

*I am a child of the djinni.*

The spider was scuttling for the shadows fast enough that I didn't think I could actually get it with my hammer, so I stomped on it with my foot.

"That's one dead spider," said the guard who'd first taunted me. He bent over it, and I saw the back of his neck, exposed: pale skin, the bony spine jutting out.

*My chance,* I thought, and not trusting my sluggish mind to consider the consequences fast enough, I simply swung my hammer, as hard as I could.

The hammer sank into bone and flesh with a crunch. He was far more yielding than the rock wall, and my stomach twisted. He was a man, but he was my enemy, and I knew that I couldn't afford second thoughts.

Prax—had he seen this coming? How could he, when I hadn't known until just now that I would do this? Prax had his own hammer in his hand, and he leapt forward, swinging it into the face of the other guard. Another crack and a crunch, a second swing—his cry was cut off even as he voiced it, and a moment later both lay still.

"Are they dead?" someone whispered.

I flinched from touching their bodies, and Prax did it, feeling for breath and a heartbeat. "This one's dead. This one isn't, but I wouldn't expect him to wake again in this world."

"They'll leave us to die," said one of the men who'd gone with Boradai. "Even if there *were* a ladder, they'd see us coming up and kill us all..."

"They're not going to leave us to die." I swallowed hard. *Just keep lying.* "This was all part of my plan. The spider, that was a surprise, but it worked out well, didn't it?" Nervous murmurs of agreement. I looked at the body and the unconscious guard. "I know how to use a sword," I said, and took one.

"I've swung one. Once." Prax took the other. I remembered the cut he'd given me when I took him back to Kyros and didn't argue.

*We need to get to the top. That's the next step. How? The barrel of rocks that will go up at lunchtime.*

"Right," I said. "Prax and I can hide in the barrel. We'll pull a sheet over us and pile rocks on top. When it gets to the top, we'll come out, kill the guards, and kick the ladder back down."

"Kill the guards?" Prax said.

"We can do it," I said.

"*Then* what?"

"How many guards are there in all?"

"About twenty."

"Eighteen, now," I said. "There are a lot more of us than there are of them. We're going to do this."

Above, we heard a gong. "That's the signal for lunch," Prax said. "Normally everyone would dump in their stones now."

"Let's get in." We both fit, barely, our limbs twined together like lovers instead of old enemies. I wedged my sword in, point down, so that it wouldn't cut me or Prax, and Prax did the same thing with his. Someone stripped a shirt off the dead guard and we pulled it over us like a taut roof; a thin layer of rocks was carefully piled on top.

"The slaves will know something's going on. We're going to be much lighter than the rocks."

The slaves clustered around us. "If the unconscious one stirs, hit him on the head again," Prax said.

"We can do this," I said. "Trust us." I could smell their fear, but there wasn't anything I could do about it now. "If we don't succeed in this, what will happen?" I whispered to Prax, in the dark.

"Something like this? At best, they'll pull out the djinn and let everyone below suffocate. At worst, it'll be an uglier death. No mercy, not for something like this. And for us..."

"I don't want to know. Shut up." I closed my eyes. "Djinn, are you near?"

The touch, like a feather. This time I reached back. "Return to the silent lands, lost one of your kind, and trouble us no more," I whispered.

A moment of exhilaration. In the darkness, I thought for a moment that I could see a glimpse of the place the djinn came from, through the gate in my heart. And the djinn—I saw the djinn, like a wild-eyed woman of ragged flame. It hesitated for a moment in the doorway, turned back, grabbed my face, and kissed me full on the lips. It was like being kissed by a whirlwind, or by the sun. I felt a moment of intense heat, and all the breath went out of me. Then it was gone, and I was in the dark again, in Prax's lap, his arms wrapped around me.

"Are you sure that was a good idea?" Prax asked.

"No. But this way we guarantee ourselves no stragglers. And the Greeks can't pull the djinn out of the tunnel to use it against us."

A shrug. And then another gong, and the barrel began to move.

It was a curious feeling, being lifted up like that. On one hand it reminded me of the trip in the makeshift palanquin, carried by the djinn; on the other hand, it was much slower, with many jerks, each of which threatened to leave the contents of my stomach on my lap. *How are we even going to know that we're at the top?* But we slowed, and then stopped. "Be ready," Prax whispered, as if I needed a reminder. Then, "Now!"

I leapt to my feet; Prax followed as soon as I was off of him, stolen swords in our hands. Whirling, I saw a guard, and lunged, trying to run him through before he even knew what was happening. *Djinni guide my sword*... His stunned cry choked off in a gush of blood from the slash to his neck. *Well, or guide Prax's sword. Really, either is fine.*

There was only the one guard. Only the one! The ladder was rolled up on a spool; I unbuckled the belt that held it in place and let it unroll to the bottom of the tunnel. "Start up," I called down.

Prax leaned past me and called down the shaft, "The djinn is gone. Come up if you want to live."

"Is there usually only one guard?"

The two slaves shook their heads. "There's usually three. They pulled two out to go out looking for bandits, I think."

Had Tamar not been caught, then? Or maybe she had, and had sent them out looking for a nonexistent bandit tribe to better the odds against me.

The ladder and barrel were inside a cave in the hill. This was probably to keep rain out of the mine, but for the moment they also gave us a hiding place. We waited while the slaves climbed up from below. When I realized that no one was bringing up their hammer, we lowered the barrel again, shouting down to put the hammers in there if they weren't going to carry them up. I wanted more targets than just me and Prax, whether the other slaves liked the idea or not.

The slaves climbed up steadily, but it was going to take a long time—and once up, everyone had to let their eyes adjust to the daylight just inside the cave. *How are we going to even fight out there?* When about half the slaves had climbed out, another guard came in looking to see why the rock wasn't being delivered, and we struck him down, too. *Four down. Sixteen—or so—to go.*

"How many more do you think will come looking

before they start to wonder what's going on?" I asked Prax.

"One more, if we're lucky."

"Let's wait a little longer. Give our eyes more time to adjust."

The last of the slaves were coming out when the next guard approached. He hesitated well short of the door and called, "Methodios? What the hell are you doing?" Pause. "Methodios?"

I turned to the slaves. "There are sixteen guards left. Each of you has a weapon. Kill all the guards, and we will have a stable of horses to take us to join the Alashi. *Go.*" I turned to the door and ran toward the guard with drawn sword.

This was the first guard who was actually prepared to be attacked. His sword was out by the time I reached him, and it was clear very quickly that he was a much better swordsman than I was even when I was not hungry, bleeding, and half blind from the bright sunlight. But Prax was on my heels, and three more slaves armed with hammers, and he fell beneath our blows like a felled tree.

"Come on," I shouted. "You know who your enemies are. *Take them down!*"

The rest of the guards knew now that something was horribly wrong, and were running toward us from their positions along the wall. One was pulling out a spell-chain, and I felt a malicious sense of triumph that I'd denied them that weapon, at least. The slaves who were sorting rocks began to pick up large chunks of stone as their own weapons. From the corner of my eye, I saw the cook running out of the tent with a large butcher knife. There were slaves who were falling back and doing their best to hide, but most were fighting like rats in a tunnel.

*We can do this. We're going to do this.*

In battle with the Alashi, I'd always felt a mixture of terror and exhilaration. Exhilaration that I was fighting my enemies, sword in hand, free to defend myself in any way I could. Terror because I was usually facing a better fighter than I was. Now, the heat of battle was in my blood, burning away the shadow, at least for now. I caught a guard across the wrist with my sword; he fell back a step, then was forced to the ground by my allies with hammers. Another guard had a long spear, but someone threw a hammer at him hard enough to knock him off his stride, and then he was lost, fallen.

Then we heard a horn, blasted long and loud. *Summoning back the ones who rode out looking for bandits. Shit.*

There was no time to think about it. There was only time to raise my stolen sword to defend myself against the next guard, to hope that the slaves with hammers would be able to overwhelm him before he killed me. There could be no retreat here. There was nowhere to run. We would kill or die until only they, or only we, were left standing.

Then suddenly there was no one in front of me. I looked around wildly, just in time to see arrows. The remaining guards had scrambled up on to the wall, lined up beside each other, and were shooting down at us. "Spread out," I shouted. "Scatter!"

We needed something to hide under, or behind. I found myself with Prax and one of the slaves who'd gone with Boradai, behind a building I thought was probably the kitchen. "We could hide inside," the slave panted. I noticed that he still clutched his hammer, and that it was red with someone's blood.

"They'll trap us there," I said. "Burn it down around us."

"But out here—they'll circle around to the other part of the wall. Shoot us down. How are we going to get out of here? How can we fight against bows?"

"We should move now," Prax said. "Charge them before they get a chance to spread out."

In the shelter of the building, my blood was still racing, but my mind had slowed again. I had no idea what to do. On the other side of the building, I could still hear cries of pain; not everyone had found shelter. *We need to get out of here. We need to kill those guards before we can get out of here. We need to protect ourselves from the arrows . . .* "Is there anything we can hold like a shield?" I asked.

"The pans for sorting the rocks," Prax said, pointing. The pool of water for washing and sorting was a short sprint from where we sheltered, across open ground.

"This is all your fault," Boradai's slave said, turning on me.

I closed my eyes. "Shelter in the kitchen if you want. I'm running for a shield, and then toward the guards with the bows. I don't see as we really have much of a choice."

We ran for it—Boradai's slave following along with me. I snatched up a tray, unscathed, and held it up like a shield, then whirled around, trying to see where the bowmen were now, where I needed to hold the shield to protect myself. *Come on. Come on. Djinni help me, have they spread out already?*

But no more arrows came.

"Lauria! Help me close these doors," a familiar voice shouted.

"Is that your ally on the outside?" Prax asked.

I ran toward the gate. It *was* Tamar, still clutching her bow. "What," I gasped, helping her to pull the gate shut. "How...?"

"There are more out there, hunting the bandits they thought I might be scouting for. But we can close the doors and shoot down at them. Who knows how to use a bow?" she shouted down at the slaves who were stumbling out from their makeshift hiding spots. "Come on, surely some of you must have seen one used. Get up here!"

"The rest of the guards...?"

"There's no time..." Tamar glanced over the wall, then shrugged. "Yesterday evening I rode up to the gate and told them I represented the Younger Sisters, and was here to make them a very lucrative offer for whatever karenite they were finding."

"Karenite? They mined gems here!"

"I figured that surely they found karenite occasionally."

"Did they really believe that you were a sorceress? You're not old enough."

"I had that spell-chain you made back in Casseia—I linked the two ends together and kept it as a necklace. They didn't get a good enough look at it to see what was missing. If they'd asked for me to summon my djinn, I'd have given them a stern look and said that my aeriko was *already on an errand* that was far more important than any silly games for their benefit. Anyway, when I realized you'd made your move, I was in a private conference with the officer in charge. I stabbed him in the heart before he knew what was going on, and then got my bow and found a spot where I could be useful. And I think I *was* pretty useful, taking out the five men on the wall like that." She looked over the wall again, then eyed me. "And *you* didn't think I could talk my way out if they caught me."

I knew what she wanted and was more than happy to provide it. "I was wrong. Oh, was I wrong!"

"You're lucky, did you know that?"

"I am far luckier than I deserve."

"And don't you forget it. Now go get the bows and see what you can do about teaching a bunch of slaves to defend a fortress."

Prax was already pulling bows loose from the twitching fingers of the fallen guards, and digging out the quivers of arrows. "I've never used a bow before," he said.

"You'll be great at it. It's not that hard." We found three more slaves who were willing to give it a try—the nervous cook was one, to my surprise, and one of the others was one of Boradai's.

The wall was built to defend the mine against bandit raids, and provided shelter for us to crouch behind while occasionally leaning out to shoot arrows. "Put your bows down," Tamar said. "Wait until I give word to pick them up. There's no point in shooting at them until they're within range."

We could see them coming, now, five men on horses riding together down the road. Tamar's own bow was in her hand, the arrow ready. "Right," she said as the men slowed to a walk. "Pick up your bows..."

Another pause. I heard one of the horses snort.

"Arrows ready..."

The men came to a dead stop, staring at the closed doors.

"Now," Tamar whispered. Her arrow hit the lead horseman square in the chest; the rest of the arrows went wild. I'd expected them to charge forward to come to the aid of their fellow guards, but instead the four survivors wheeled their horses around and ran, as fast as they could, in the other direction.

"We'd better get out of here," Tamar said.

"First—" I grabbed her arm. "Prax, this is Tamar. Tamar, this is Prax."

"It's a pleasure to meet you," Tamar said.

Prax gave her a slightly hesitant nod.

"Where's the stable?" Tamar asked. "We'll make better time getting out of here if we've got horses. Unless you're hiding a djinn up your sleeve..."

"I freed the djinn."

"You did? Well—good."

We climbed down from the wall, and for the first time, I had a moment to survey the damage. My elation began to fade. Of the mine slaves, fully half had been killed or were dying; of the survivors, most nursed an injury, minor or severe. Some of the slaves knelt over the bodies of friends, trying to stop the bleeding, or whispering to them to open their eyes. Others stood stunned, blood-slicked hammers drooping from their hands, waiting for me or Prax to tell them where to go next.

"Have you had enough of slavery?" I asked. There was no response. I looked around, wondering about the slaves Boradai had brought here. I could see at least one dead on the ground; another was standing, shocked and empty-handed, in the courtyard. The one who'd whined to me my first day held a blood-soaked hammer and looked like he was actually ready to climb on a horse and find the Alashi. "Listen up," I shouted. "We're leaving as soon as we can get the horses ready. We, as in me, Prax, and all of you." There was still no response.

I turned to Tamar. "Get the horses ready. I'll send someone to help you if I can figure out who's taken care of the horses." And then I went to the cook. "It's time to go," I said. "Do you know anything about horses?"

"No." His voice was shaky.

"Riding isn't that hard, honestly. Do you want to go wait by the stable?" I moved on to one of the slaves who stood with a bloody hammer, staring in horror at the blood on his hands. "You can go wash off, if you want, and then get ready to go. Freedom is within reach." He seemed as half-asleep as I felt, and I shook his arm gently. "We need to hurry. But we're going to make it; the desperate part is over." I went next to one of the ones who knelt beside a body on the ground. "We have to leave the dead. Even the dying. Freedom is within reach, but we need to hurry . . ."

A ragged line was forming beside the stable; others were following my lead, gathering their friends, washing their hands, getting ready to go. "Find water-skins," I told one of the men who looked a bit less lost than the others. "We're going to need water."

"Have you had enough of slavery?" I asked one of the slaves who'd gone with Boradai.

It took more time than it should have, precious minutes when the four surviving guards had gone to get reinforcements, but then we were picking up the waterskins and the sacks of food, loading up horses from the stable, and then setting out, over the hills and away.

# CHAPTER TWELVE

There was no real hope of *hiding* that night, just hope that it would take the surviving guards time to stumble back, convince someone to take them seriously, bring reinforcements. *If they come after us, we're dead.* Following the lead of Prometheus—*rob your enemies*—we'd taken bows and swords from the fort, but I was the closest thing in the group to a competent swordsman. And Tamar was the only one who was good with a bow. *The djinn promised that Prax would reach freedom, so clearly we're going to survive, because he'll die with the rest of us if we're attacked. Then again, it's possible that* this *counts as freedom.*

*Well, there's nothing I can do about it, so I might as well stop worrying about it.* Somewhat to my surprise, I was able to thrust the fear aside and think about other things, like finding water and reaching the Alashi.

"Are they still at Spring Gathering?" I asked Tamar.

"Probably. It hasn't been that long since we freed the harem. I know it feels like months." It did, in fact.

"*Someone* will still be there. There might be groups that have left for the summer..."

*Groups.* The sword brotherhoods and sword sisterhoods. Janiya, Zhanna, Ruan... *Don't think about what you can't have.* I swallowed hard. "Maybe someone closer?"

"Maybe. I'm going to try to ask a djinn."

I lowered my voice. "If the Alashi were annoyed with us for sending them freed slaves before..." I looked around the camp.

Tamar followed my gaze with a smirk. "*You* didn't free them and *I* didn't free them, though we provided some important support at times. *They freed themselves.* If they hadn't picked up those hammers and gone after their masters, we'd be dead and they'd still be slaves."

"I kind of forced their hand. If you're told to fight or die, and you fight, is that taking your freedom?"

"Hell, yes. Besides, they didn't *have* to fight. If they'd come up and then hidden in a corner and waited for the fight to be over—it's awfully expensive and troublesome, killing all your slaves. You kill the leaders, you make examples of anyone who might have blood on their hands, you beat the rest and you send them back to work."

"You're probably right."

"Probably? You should just learn to trust me on some things, Lauria." She was still gloating over her ability to fool the guards.

"How did you know they wouldn't just say, 'Oh yeah, we've heard of the Younger Sisters, and we're turning you over to the Sisterhood, who we're loyal to'?"

"Well, I didn't know for sure. It was a calculated

risk. But the Younger Sisters are clearly causing all sorts of trouble for the Sisterhood; he'd have been a fool to just discard my offer out of hand. I thought the spell-chain would boost my case, and also I told them Melissa had sent me, since we know Lycurgus's friend is involved with the rogue Weavers. I stirred in a little flattery. I'd figured out by then that they were finding at least a little karenite—not a great deal, but some—and I told him that they were finding more than any other mine, and if the Sisterhood of Weavers said otherwise, they were lying to him. I thought it was possible that the Sisterhood had hinted to him that they thought maybe he was pocketing some of it and re-selling on the black market. And sure enough. The Sisterhood should be more careful about alienating their servants. Just look at you; you were loyal to them once and they screwed it up."

I laughed a little at that.

"So what did Prax think of you? Are you friends now?"

"He didn't try to kill me, like Uljas said he was going to."

"Well, clearly Prax is smarter than Uljas."

"Either that or he saw that I was his most likely way out."

"Have you talked to him since we made it out?"

"No, I haven't."

"Maybe you should."

"I think it's his right to approach me. Or not."

"Coward."

I shrugged.

When I slept that night, I had a vivid dream. All my djinn-sent dreams were strikingly vivid, but this one left the others behind. The light was bright enough to make me wince, the sounds loud, realer than real. I felt someone gripping my hands tightly enough to cause pain, and when my eyes finally adjusted to the light, like they had when I'd come out of the mine, I saw the djinn I'd recently freed. It looked like a woman, facing me, gripping my wrists. "I have a message for you," it said, very simply. "I was sent to tell you this. The slave you seek, Thais, is in Elpisia; she's owned by Zopyros."

Then it vanished, and the dream vanished, too, and I was awake in my blanket, cold with sweat. *Elpisia? We went down to Casseia to look for her and she'd been bought by someone back in Elpisia?* It fit with what little we knew about what had happened: she'd been bought by a Greek officer who'd taken her somewhere far away. Zopyros was one of the officers from Kyros's garrison. If he'd wanted Thais, it was strange that he wouldn't have bought her in the first place, but thinking back to her escape, I was pretty sure Zopyros had been away at the time.

Even if she was in Elpisia, why would the djinni suddenly decide to hand me information on a plate? *This is a trick, they're up to something,* I thought, but as the melancholia faded, I'd learned to distrust my own distrust. *Tamar didn't leave me and wasn't betraying me. I'll go to Elpisia, carefully, and take a look to see if Thais is there. Maybe she is, maybe she isn't. It's worth a look. I certainly don't know where else to find her.*

The journey across the steppe was going to take some time. Tamar knew where to find water; that was our salvation. I vividly remembered our desperate search for water after we escaped together from Sophos. The memory made me thirsty enough to want to drain my waterskin just thinking about it.

I was beginning to itch, though, wanting to go find Thais. After a half-day of travel I asked Tamar what she thought. "You're needed here, as a guide. I'm not. Alone, I could make it back to Elpisia in just a couple of days. If Thais is there, if she wants to come with me..."

"I don't want you going without me," Tamar said.

"Just because I needed you at the mine, as it turned out, that doesn't mean I need you holding my hand in Elpisia."

"You'll need me for *something*. You'll need me to find you water, if nothing else."

"I'll carry water. It doesn't take that long—if I have two horses, one for me and one for Thais..."

"No. Just no."

I brooded about it through the afternoon. As we were cooking up a pot of lentils to feed everyone, she turned to me and said, "Promise you won't just take off."

"What?"

"Promise you're not going to do something *stupid* like leave in the middle of the night. Do I need to re-cruit future blossoms to set a guard on you? Because I'll do it."

"Are you trying to humiliate me to death? What did I do to deserve this?"

"You snuck off in the middle of the night last time, that's what you did to deserve it. Now promise."

"I promise not to sneak off in the middle of the night," I said.

"Or during the day," Tamar said doggedly. "Promise that you will not sneak off."

"I promise not to sneak off, day, night, or twilight," I said.

"Good, because I'll come with you to Elpisia. It's not going to take all *that* long to get the new blossoms up to the Alashi."

"New blossoms?"

"Well, what else are you going to call them? I refuse to call them escaped slaves. They're not any kind of slaves any more. They're Alashi recruits. Blossoms."

"I don't know if I'd call Prax a blossom to his face. But it's up to you, I guess."

Within a day, though, I heard everyone using the term, with a delight that surprised me. I remembered hearing *blossom* mostly as an insult, mostly from Ruan, but the former mine slaves were apparently pleased to have a term for themselves that didn't include the word *slave*. The spring flowers hadn't faded in the summer heat quite yet, and some picked flowers as they walked, making wreaths to crown one another as we lay down in the grass each evening.

I barely saw Prax for several days; I'd begun to think that he must be deliberately avoiding me. But on the fifth evening, he approached me with a wreath of his own in his hand. "Lauria," he said in greeting, his tone a bit offhand.

"Prax," I said, and nodded. "I haven't seen you much."

"No," he said, and stood awkwardly for a moment. "Let's go for a walk," he said. "It's impossible to have a private conversation with dozens of eavesdropping blossoms an arm's reach away."

*Well, if he tries to kill me, Tamar will make him sorry.* I followed Prax out of the camp.

"After you brought back Uljas, he said he was going to kill you," Prax said when we were out of camp. "Did he try?"

"No. Not exactly. He said he's going to kill me if he ever sees me again. That's what the Alashi are going to do, too, so..." I shrugged. "Hopefully it won't come up. Did you ever swear you were going to kill me?"

"Well, I gave it a try, don't you remember?"

"It healed without a scar. But yes."

"I was angry after you brought me back. But after the djinn spoke with me... I knew it was meant to be. Especially when I saw you again. Look at what we accomplished."

"Half the slaves died."

"But *all* of us would have died, in slavery, eventually." He shook his head. "How the Greeks will rage over this!"

"Even the Alashi would call this a successful raid," I said. *Aside from losing half our people.*

Prax nodded, his eyes glinting a little in the light. "Anyway. We've talked a bit about the Alashi, these last few days, and what's waiting for us there. Tamar told us a little, and I knew a little more. We know we're going to have to pass tests; they'll split us up as much as they can. But once we've all been initiated, we want to form our own subclan. The Gulzhan, soul-of-a-flower clan."

"That's lovely," I said.

"And whether the Alashi like it or not," he said, "you're a member." And he set the wreath of flowers gently on my head. "The other Alashi can cast you out; they can threaten to kill you. But someday we will have our own camp, and our own elders. And you will always be welcome among us."

I was speechless; I tried to swallow my tears, and realized that if I said anything at all, I would break down completely. So I was silent. After a long moment, Prax gave me a nod, brushed one of the loose flowers back into place against my hair, then rose and walked back to the camp.

The next day was the first really hot day—hot enough to make everyone miss the coolness of the deep mine, if not the mine itself. A whisper of haze burned off within minutes of sunrise, and my head ached by noon from heat and brightness. When I saw someone approaching, I thought at first it was a mirage, my sun-dazzled eyes creating a person out of windblown grass and shadows. Then I heard the exclamations of others, and I realized it was a person approaching on horseback. Then she grew closer, and I realized it was an Alashi woman, her sword tied into its sheath and her bow unstrung.

And then I saw her face, and realized that it was someone I knew: Zhanna. My heart leapt, seeing her again.

A hush fell over the group. Zhanna gave the blossoms a friendly smile; they returned looks of stark terror. With a shrug, she slowed her horse to a walk and came up to me and Tamar.

"I'm just ahead of the rest of the Sisterhood," she said, speaking very softly. "We know you're coming, and with whom. The eldress would like to speak with Tamar. She'd probably like to speak with Lauria, too, but since you're to be killed if we get our hands on you . . . Janiya sent me ahead to warn you. Tamar needs to stay here or we'll have to ride after both of you. Lauria needs to go."

*Surely I'll have a moment . . .*

Zhanna met my eyes and shook her head regretfully. "You need to go *now*," she said.

I mounted Krina. Tamar gave me a look of chagrin. All these promises not to sneak off, and now . . .

"I have enough water to get back, if I'm traveling alone, and quickly," I said.

"Elpisia," she said. "Wait for me there."

And I left, my heart pounding.

The ride back to Elpisia was quiet; I'd thought that Tamar might catch up with me, but she did not. I thought that she was probably being taken back to speak to the eldress of all the Alashi, probably to discuss our current project. I wished I could see it, because I didn't think Tamar would be the least bit apologetic. I'd hoped that Tamar might visit me in dreams, but even when I went to sleep clutching my talisman of rag and hair, I couldn't find her.

Perhaps this was in part because I'd begun to have trouble sleeping. If Krina had been willing, I felt like I could have traveled all night as well as all day. The lingering fogginess in my head from the melancholia was completely gone. I felt perfectly alert, clearer than I had ever felt before.

Reaching the dried-out riverbed near Elpisia felt oddly like coming home. I'd been back here so many times now, with Tamar; I holed up in the same spot we'd used last time, so that Tamar could find me easily. There was still a little water in the bottom of the riverbed, but it would be gone in another week. Still, Krina could drink, and I could drink, and we could wait for Tamar. I could go into Elpisia and free Thais, and we would take her up to the steppe, and . . .

And then what?

*And then free the rivers,* my mind whispered. *Just as you decided. Someone has to do it, so why not you? Free the Syr Darya, free the Amu Darya, and with the*

*rivers' return the power of the Weavers will be ended.
That's what everyone says, and their belief will make it
true. We'll return to our ancestral lands, no longer
scraping out a living on the steppe, we'll overthrow the
Sisterhood and the Younger Sisters and the servants
and all of them. The rivers will make us free . . .*

Tamar was going to think this idea was completely
crazy.

*Well, and she'll probably be right.*

But freeing an entire mine of slaves, that was crazy,
too, and we did it.

Night fell, and the moon rose. I went down to drink
more water; I felt as energetic as if I'd just risen, so I
groomed Krina again. She was amenable to this, though
she snuffled me gently as if to say, *go to bed, silly human.* I lay down on my blankets for a while, then got
back up and sat outside, listening to the wind riffling
through the grass. *What if Tamar isn't coming?*

*Don't be ridiculous. Of course she's coming.*

*What if the Alashi make her stay with them?*

I wanted to scoff at that idea. I could guess why
they'd wanted to speak with her—probably to tell her
to quit freeing people that they then had to deal with.
And I could guess that she would tell them to get
stuffed. But I wasn't sure what they'd do then. Let her
go with a shrug? That didn't seem likely. Keep her prisoner forever? That also didn't seem likely. Kill her? *We
only kill bandits, rapists, spies, and traitors.* "Troublesome former blossoms" wasn't on the list. But if they
were frustrated enough, would they try again to pretend that she had been in league with me? *Over
Janiya's dead body.* But what *would* they do with her,
and how long would it take?

By morning, I had decided that I couldn't wait here.

Someone might already have noticed Krina; someone could come at any time to investigate. *I'll cross the wall tonight and find Thais. Once we're out, we'll move somewhere farther away. I'm not sure we can safely cross the steppe without Tamar to find me water, but at least we can get clear of Elpisia. This isn't a safe place for me.*

As I did every time I visited Elpisia, I thought about going to my mother. My thoughts traveled the well-worn paths of worry. *I have nowhere to take her, no safety to offer her. Her best defense is innocence. I have to stay away. And if I visited her, we'd only fight anyway…*

Night fell. I headed to the wall; it was as easy to climb as I remembered. Over I went, through the streets, to the house of Zopyros.

Thais had been a harem slave, like Alibek. Remarkably beautiful, she had apparently seen her chance one day and slipped out. I suspected that she'd had a confederate planning to bring her supplies. She'd holed up like Alibek, but with more water and an icy confidence that hadn't entirely broken even when I pulled her out and took her back to Kyros. At my suggestion, he'd asked if she had a confederate; she denied it, and he decided not to pursue it. I'd been a little frustrated by that, at the time, but had moved on to my next assignment.

Zopyros's house was a narrow city house, several stories high. The upper windows stood open to the cool night air. I could see lights burning in several of them, and after an hour or two of patient watching, I actually glimpsed Thais in one of the upper windows. My breath quickened. *The building across the way… if I could get up on that roof, maybe I could see in…*

It took some climbing, but I found a way up and crawled carefully across, trying not to make too much noise. I lay down at the edge of the roof.

*Oh, perfect view.* I could see right in the open window. Thais was brushing her hair and talking with someone—I couldn't tell if it was Zopyros, but she certainly had a more comfortable job than a mine slave. Then again, Kyros always had a soft spot for beautiful women.

*So close, and I'm so close to done.*

I waited for a time, wondering if I would have the opportunity to speak to Thais. My thoughts began to race again. Waiting patiently grew increasingly difficult, but I forced myself to lie still. Then a wave of dizziness washed over me. I closed my eyes for a moment and was jolted suddenly into a vision. *Am I in the borderland?* I wondered. And then, *Am I dreaming? Is this a dream from the djinn?*

I saw the eastern mountains and heard a distant roar. Then, crashing down like the end of the world, I saw the water. *The Syr Darya. The river returns.* The wall of water was like a moving mountain itself. I'd heard stories of snowslides in the mountains in winter, and this made me think of the stories I'd heard, only larger. *The river.*

And then I was back on the roof, and Thais was alone. *This is my chance.* "Thais," I called softly, trying to shake off the vision and focus on the world around me. "Come to the window."

Could she hear me? But she came over, peering out into the darkness.

"You ran away once. Would you still like to be free?"

"Who asks?" she said.

"Someone who can help you."

Her face was suspicious.

"Listen to me," I said. "Can you slip out? I may be able to help you climb down, if you need to. And I can help you reach the Alashi. If you would still like to go there."

"Wait for me on the street below," she said, and drew back inside the window.

I climbed down one wall, slithered down another, and dropped, finally, to the street. And waited, in the shadows, across the street.

After a few minutes, the door opened, and Thais stepped out into the street. She looked straight at me. I stepped out of the shadows and looked back, expecting her to say, *I remember you* or *what are you doing here*? Instead, she said, "Come closer."

I stepped forward into the light spilling from the doorway. Thais reached out and traced the line of my jaw with one finger. Her hands were clean, and soft. She remembered me. I was quite certain of that.

"Will you come with me?" I asked.

Thais tilted her head and gave me a slow, triumphant smile. She took a deep breath. And then her hands locked on my wrists and she shouted, "*Zopyros!* Come here, there's a bandit—*Zopyros!* Hurry!"

I tried to tear away from her, but she clung to me like a burr. "Why are you doing this?" I hissed.

"I'd rather see you dead than have anything else in the world," Thais hissed back. Zopyros's men were pouring out into the street, surrounding me, dragging me into the house. "She offered to take me to the bandits, if I'd run with her," Thais said. "Bandit—thief!" She loosed me, finally, and fell back a step, smirking.

"Do you know who she is?" It was Zopyros, shouldering his way to the front.

"Her name is Lauria," Thais said. "She used to serve Kyros. I don't know *who* she serves now."

Zopyros looked me up and down. "Lauria," he murmured, and nodded recognition. "Kyros will want to hear about this, I think."

"He's up with the army..." someone said.

"No, not anymore. He came back just yesterday." Zopyros jerked his head at his servants. "Bring her, and let's go."

*E*ven late at night, there were lights burning within Kyros's walls, and a slave opened the door promptly when Zopyros knocked. I recognized the doorkeeper, and I could tell by the way his eyes widened silently that he recognized me, too. His eyes flicked over me, Zopyros, the guards that flanked me, and my bound hands. Then he stepped back silently to allow us inside.

Within the walls of the courtyard, it was tempting to imagine, just for a moment, that nothing had changed. I could smell the roses grown by Kyros's wife in the garden, and hear the splash of the fountain, and a chorus of crickets. I couldn't resist a glance up toward the room I'd once thought of as mine; it was dark and shuttered. Kyros's office stood open to the cool night air, and I could see a lamp burning. The slave hurried inside to announce us. "Kyros would like to see you right away," he said, stepping out.

"I'll bet," Zopyros muttered. Leaving his burly guardsmen in the courtyard, he put a firm hand on my arm and steered me into Kyros's office.

Kyros looked older than I remembered, and smaller. His hair was thinner. Still, he summoned his old smile when he saw me pushed through the door. "Ah, Lauria," he said, as if he'd been expecting me. "We have a great deal to talk about. Sit down, please." He turned his attention briefly to Zopyros. "I greatly appreciate this. Come back tomorrow."

Zopyros bowed and accepted the dismissal. I sat down awkwardly, my hands still bound in front of me.

"Well," Kyros said. "This is not how I expected to see you again."

I said nothing. The first rule of gathering information was to let the other person talk. Unfortunately, Kyros knew the same rule, because he fell silent, and looked at me expectantly. Finally he said, "I think you're supposed to give me your report. Aren't you?"

I decided to go with the story I'd worked out in my head all those months ago, and stick to it. I cleared my throat. "Alibek got away, from whoever you sold him to. He ran to the Alashi, over the summer, and joined them. In the fall, when my sword sisterhood rejoined the rest of the Alashi, he recognized me. I was cast out; I was lucky to escape with my life."

"Why didn't you come back here?"

"I thought there was still hope for my mission." My voice sounded a little stronger to me. *I can do this. I can convince him.* "Because of Alibek, they knew that I worked for you, and that I took people back to slavery. So I decided to track those people down, break them out, and take them to the Alashi. I had this idea that they'd be singing my praises, and that the Alashi would take me back."

"Ah." Kyros sipped some tea. "Do go on," he said, when I didn't.

"Given the importance of my mission, the cost of a few slaves seemed ... well, pretty insignificant."

"Quite."

"I had to take some time off during the winter, but I got them all out of slavery. Thais was the last." *Was going to be the last. Why didn't she want freedom? Even Uljas chose freedom over vengeance.*

"Ah." Kyros smiled faintly. "Perhaps I should have mentioned, back when you worked for me ... You were correct when you suggested that Thais may have had someone helping her on the outside. It was Zopyros. He'd tried to buy Thais, I hadn't wanted to sell, so he encouraged her to run. He was going to set her up in some other city, and visit occasionally."

"And now he owns her."

"Yes, I sold her all the way down to Casseia, to punish both of them, really. But he found her! Quite a determined man. And then you found her as well, but I've always known that you were determined." He nodded, still with that faint smile. "I was a bit chagrined when I saw that she was back in Elpisia, but Zopyros is quite useful to me, so I'll hold my peace for now." *He would hold a grudge, as well, I knew; Kyros could hold a grudge for decades, even if the object of the grudge never knew it.* "Now, then." Kyros riffled lightly through the papers on his desk. "I had a report of you, some months back—where was it? Yes. Solon. He said you'd made yourself rather useful."

"I did my best," I said.

"You were alone with him on multiple occasions— no *companion* keeping an eye on you. You could have taken the opportunity to send me a message."

"I didn't know whose side Solon was on."

"You also saw Myron. Again, no message."

"I had reason to believe I was being watched."

"My aerika," he said. "What *did* you do with my aerika?"

I shook my head, giving him a bewildered stare. "I haven't seen either of your aerika since I left the Alashi. That didn't really surprise me, though—after all, you didn't know where I was. I assumed you would want me to complete my mission, if there was still hope. I thought there was. I *still* think there is . . . eventually."

Kyros had leaned back with his cup of tea. "Yet you don't expect me to trust you." He nodded at my bound hands.

I looked down as if I was just noticing that I was bound, and let my shoulders twitch a little. "I have been living on the wrong side of the law for a good long while," I admitted. "Do you mind?"

For a moment I thought he was going to. But then he met my eye and shook his head with a faint smile. "Lauria, I had you watched."

Watched. "By . . . whom?"

"By my new aeriko. I had a hunch you might have gone to Casseia, and come spring, it found you on the road. You left *Sophos's head* on my desk. Perhaps you freed his slaves to win your way back into the graces of the Alashi—it pleased your companion, after all. But I know from my watcher that leaving my friend's head on my desk was *your* idea."

"He raped me," I said, my throat thickening against my will. "You *sent* me to him, and he *raped* me." I struggled to get control of my voice, and thought frantically for what to say next. "I thought I'd make sure you knew I'd taken care of it."

"Yes. But then you had yourself *sold* to a mine. Surely, my dear, if you thought you could turn to me, you wouldn't have chosen such a risky way to free one slave."

"You didn't think I'd be able to get out?" I narrowed my eyes. Another thought occurred to me. "If you knew I was there, what I was planning, why didn't you intervene?"

"The mine was tapped out. The men who worked there...unreliable. Besides, we lost track of you for a time."

"I've been sitting outside the city for two days. Why didn't you just come find me if you wanted to talk to me?"

"I was waiting to see if you would come to *me*. Which you didn't."

"No. My companion is a shaman. Djinni do favors for her sometimes. I always have to assume I'm being watched."

"Even in your dreams."

"*Especially* in my dreams."

Kyros sighed. "Lauria, I wish I could believe you. But I've been in contact with the Sisterhood. The high magia believes that you're no longer loyal to us. She ordered that if I could lay hands on you again, I was to have you executed for banditry."

I caught my breath. *He can't kill me. Not Kyros.* He met my eyes; he could see my fear. I wet my lips. "You always said I was your most trusted servant. What will the others think? Myron, your other servants? If you have me killed—if you refuse to trust me—"

Kyros had a faint smile on his face. I knotted my icy hands into fists. "Perhaps you're right," he said. "I tell you what. I'll take you to Penelopeia, and let you speak with the high magia yourself."

*He's not going to kill me.* Relief flooded in; my bound hands trembled. But—"Penelopeia?"

"I'll send the high magia a message, and I expect she'll send a palanquin. As much as I hate flying, it's the only reasonably efficient way to get to Penelopeia." He clasped his spell-chain, whispering under his breath. The chain looked familiar, but I definitely recognized the djinn. It was indeed the chain Zivar had made. I wondered if he knew this probably meant that the Sisterhood considered him *unreliable.* I couldn't hear the message, though clearly the djinn could. "It will take some hours for the palanquin to arrive." He rang a bell that rested on his desk. "In the meantime, why don't you go get some rest."

A guard appeared at his door—a stranger to me, to my relief. I stood up, awkwardly, and just before the guard escorted me out, Kyros gestured for him to wait. He drew a sharp knife, and cut the rope that bound my hands. "I'm sure you're not going anywhere tonight," Kyros said.

I was escorted to—of all places—my own room. It had been aired out, and the bed made up with fresh sheets and a warm quilt. Lamp in hand, I took a moment to look around. Everything was where I had left it, even my leather-bound book of paper, which rested on a shelf beside my bed. A cup of warmed wine waited on my desk, but I left it untouched; the last thing I wanted right now was wine.

I peered out the window. I saw no one out there, and for a brief moment considered climbing out my window and trying to escape. But surely Kyros wasn't that stupid. There would be a dozen guards; my attempted escape would be final proof that I'd changed sides. Though since Kyros was not at *all* stupid, in fact, surely he knew that in any case. I wondered why he hadn't executed me, as the high magia had ordered. Did I have information he wanted? That the high magia wanted? Or was it fatherly sentiment that had caused him to spare me?

I lay down on the bed and closed my eyes. Could he see into my dreams? It didn't matter; I still had to try to talk to Tamar. I touched my talisman as I tried to sleep, and after a little while, actually succeeded in drifting off.

I had come to think of the borderland as a shadowed, misty place, but tonight, like the night I had met the djinn, it was dazzlingly bright. *I'm seeing it like the djinni see it.* But where was Tamar? Then I glimpsed her, like a mirage of water on the endless plain. I opened my mouth, but all that emerged was a whisper.

Tamar was speaking, but I couldn't hear her. I tried to picture her by my side, whispering in my ear, and for a moment the borderland rippled, but then I felt a jolt and we were far away again. She cupped her hands around her mouth to shout, and a moment later the words reached me: "Come back to the Alashi. They will take you back!"

"Kyros has me," I said, but knew she couldn't hear me. "It's too late."

Tamar started to shout something again, but the dream was coming apart like crumbling clay. The light was scattering around me, dazzling my eyes; I could hear a roaring in my ears like rushing water. I clenched my fists, trying to draw the world together again by pure strength of will. Instead, it began to spin around me. I focused on my most important goal—reaching Tamar. I needed to speak with her, and something told me that this might be my last chance.

Then all was still. I stood in Sophos's courtyard, holding my torn shift around me, the wind freezing my feet. Tamar faced me, the strong-willed but terrified slave child she'd been that night. Our eyes met, and I knew that I had one heartbeat more to say whatever I wanted to say.

"I love you," I said.

*A* servant came to wake me while it was still night; I was already awake, sitting quietly in the chair by my old desk. Kyros waited for me below, in the courtyard. "Did you sleep well?" he asked.

"Well enough." Remembering my own lies, I said, "It's nice to be home."

Kyros raised an eyebrow at that. "Indeed. Well, perhaps we'll be back here soon."

I forced a smile. Kyros had given me a home, once; I'd believed myself bereft of it when I'd turned against him. Now—Tamar was my home, wherever she was.

Playing the stoic, tolerant father rather than the boss or the prison guard, Kyros shepherded me to an elaborate palanquin of violet silk. The palanquin I'd ridden in with Kyros before had been a tiny, spare device by comparison, with its cushioned seats and curtained windows. This palanquin was like an enclosed flying room. The floor was carpeted, the walls hung with silk, and we would recline on cushions as we traveled. "You'll get to see Penelopeia from the sky," Kyros said, nodding toward the curtain on the side, tied back with a ribbon. "I expect you'll enjoy that."

*Penelopeia.* The home from where the Weavers had sprung forth. Casseia might be a city built by the Weavers, but Penelopeia was the city *of* the Weavers.

*Surely,* whispered the mad flooding river part of my mind . . . *Surely, this is where they will keep the spell-chain that binds the Syr Darya.*

*Because the rivers are meant to return.*

*And you are the one who is meant to free them.*

*This is the madness talking,* I thought, stepping into the palanquin and sitting down on the silk cushion across from Kyros. *This is the cold fever, which I know is racing through my blood just as it takes Kyros's wife, and Zivar, and all the failed apprentices of the Weavers as well as the sorceresses themselves.*

*Perhaps it is madness.*

*But I'm going to free them anyway.*

# ACKNOWLEDGMENTS

Many thanks to my excellent editor, Anne Groell, and to Jack Byrne, my agent.

For ongoing critique, encouragement, and camaraderie, I'd like to thank the members of the Wyrdsmiths writing group: Eleanor Arnason, Bill Henry, Doug Hulick, Harry LeBlanc, Kelly McCullough, Lyda Morehouse, and Rosalind Nelson.

For a hands-on lesson in jewelry making and an introduction to synesthesia, I would like to thank Elise Mathesen, whose stunning necklaces helped to inspire my image of the spell-chain. CuChullaine O'Reilly of The Long Rider's Guild answered questions for me about horses and long trips on horseback. And Dr. Lisa Freitag answered questions for me about food poisoning (as well as various other medical things). Of course, all the things I screwed up anyway should be blamed on me, and not on any of the generous people who took the time to answer my questions.

Thanks to my beta readers: Michelle Herder, Rowan Littell, Catherine McCubbin, Curtis Mitchell, Fillard Rhyne, Bill Scherer, Blake Scherer, and Karen Swanberg.

A very special thank-you to my awesome husband, Ed Burke, who is a phenomenal husband, father, and human being. And hugs and kisses for both my little girls, Molly and Kiera.

Finally, this book is dedicated to my parents, Bert and Amy Kritzer, who encouraged my obsessive reading habit from an early age, going so far as to install a little reading light in my favorite reading nook: behind one of the living room chairs, in front of a heating vent. I first started saying I wanted to get a story published when I was about seven years old. My mother shrugged and said that if I wrote a story, she'd help me figure out how to submit it. It was a few years before I took her up on that, but even at seven, I appreciated the offer.

## ABOUT THE AUTHOR

NAOMI KRITZER grew up in Madison, Wisconsin, a small lunar colony populated mostly by Ph.D's. She moved to Minnesota to attend college; after graduating with a B.A. in religion, she became a technical writer. She now lives in Minneapolis with her family. FREE-DOM'S APPRENTICE is her fourth novel, preceded by FREEDOM'S GATE, TURNING THE STORM, and FIRES OF THE FAITHFUL. You can visit her website at http://www.naomikritzer.com.

Don't miss the thrilling conclusion to

The Dead Rivers Trilogy

# *FREEDOM'S SISTERS*

## *Naomi Kritzer*

## Coming in Summer 2006 from Bantam Spectra

Turn the page for a special preview.

# FREEDOM'S SISTER
## Coming Summer 2006

**Tamar**

*W*hen I rode into the camp of the Alashi spring gathering, I tried to sit tall and hide my fear. *You're as good as they are,* I imagined Lauria whispering to me. *Look them in the eye. You have nothing to be ashamed of.* And I wasn't ashamed. I was proud of what Lauria and I had accomplished. We'd freed well over a hundred slaves. I took a deep breath and raised my head.

The Eldress had summoned me. *But what is she going to do with me?*

First, apparently, she was going to make me wait.

Janiya, the leader of the sword-sisterhood that Lauria and I had ridden with last summer, had escorted me back, leaving the rest of her sisterhood as escorts for the mine slaves. We dismounted, let a girl lead our horses off to get water and sat down in the shade near the Eldress's tent. I glanced around covertly. Lauria and I had arrived at the end of the big spring gathering and left just before the big fall gathering. The noise and activity around me was both achingly familiar and deeply foreign.

Janiya looked me over. She hadn't spoken much on the ride back. Now she cleared her throat and said, awkwardly, "You look well."

I looked down at my muddy trousers, and my worn, dusty boots. Lauria and I had bought ourselves new clothes when we'd come into some money; they were worn almost to rags now. My hands were filthy, my nails ragged, and I imagined that my face and hair were similarly disreputable.

"You could use a bath, but that's not what I was talking about," Janiya said, and I looked up, surprised that my thoughts had been so transparent. Her lips quirked. "You look very confident. You look like a woman who can stand on her own and defend herself. When I first met you . . . well, you looked like you would be willing to fight until the last drop of blood had left your body, if you had to, but you didn't look like you believed your efforts would *matter.*"

I let out my breath in a brief, voiceless laugh. "It's good to see you again," I said. Janiya looked pretty much as I remembered—maybe a little more gray in her hair.

"It's good to see you, too." Janiya clasped my hand briefly. "I wish . . . " She let the words fade, unspoken. *I wish I could see Lauria again, too.*

"Why does the Eldress want to see me?"

Janiya shrugged, though surely she knew what this was about. My guess was that this was about the slaves that Lauria and I had freed. *The Alashi do not free slaves. We welcome those who free themselves.* Maybe the Alashi didn't free slaves, but I did.

Janiya glanced over at the Eldress's tent. "It's time."

The interior of the tent was dim, and surprisingly cool in the afternoon heat. It took a moment for my eyes to adjust. When I had arrived with Lauria a year earlier, we had been brought to the Eldress, who had listened to our story and accepted us as "blossoms," provisional members. Now, though, there were eight old ladies sitting in the dim interior, and five old men. One of them sat directly opposite the door, on a raised, cushioned platform; her white hair was braided and wound in a circle around the crown of her head. She wore a long dress, a vest so richly embroidered you could barely make out the black cloth underneath, and a necklace that looked like a spell-chain, though when I looked for a piece of karenite that would imprison a djinn, I didn't see one. From the way the others looked at her, and looked at us, I thought that they were probabaly the clan elders. I bowed respectfully; the Eldress gestured to a spot near the door, and Janiya sat down so I sat beside her.

"Good afternoon, child," the Eldress said, her voice much kinder than I had expected. "You've come a long way since I met you a year ago."

I didn't know what to say to that, so I gave her a stiff nod.

"I apologize for bringing you back against your will. Zhanna has brought me the information that you and your blood-sister have passed to her, but I wished to speak with you in person." She fingered her necklace. "I have been told that when your blood-sister was trying to bind djinni, you were able to stop her. Is this true?"

This was not the question I had expected. "For a time," I said. "First, I doused her with cold water to distract her, so she hid from me. So then I went to the borderland, and waited for her there. And I was able to force her back out."

Murmurs, around the circle.

"I was a Shaman's apprentice. Zhanna's, and before that, Jaran's."

"Yes. Jaran." The Eldress raised an eyebrow, and

*now* came the challenge I had expected. "The Alashi do not free slaves."

"I am not Alashi. I left when you exiled my blood-sister."

Janiya, who was the one who actually had exiled Lauria, bit her lip and looked down.

"You *chose* to leave," the Eldress said. "You could choose to come back."

"Why?"

"To teach." That was one of the clan elders, a man I didn't know. His voice was a soft growl. "To teach the Shamans how to guard the borderland and the djinni, so that we can lay siege to the source of the Sister-hood's power."

"I'm still not convinced that's a good idea." That was a clan eldress with only one eye, and a scar that stretched from forehead to chin. "That will just prove to them that we *are* a terrible threat to them, that they *must* move against us."

"They're coming, whether we act or not."

"You don't *know* that."

"They're moving the army up! What else could it . . ."

"All right," the Eldress said. "I've had enough of this. Back to your clans, all of you. I want to talk to Tamar alone. No, Janiya, you can stay. Sit down. The rest of you . . ." She gestured, and after a moment or two, they rose and went out, still arguing. The tent was very quiet with them gone.

"It's been like this for days," the Eldress said. "I'm sure you can imagine. Now. Tell me. Do you think you can teach other Shamans to do what you did?"

"I don't know. I could try. But—" I raised my chin. "I don't want to stay here. I want to be with Lauria. Are you going to keep me here by force? Or . . ." *Or are you going to let her come back?*

"You have a great amount of faith in your sister."

"Lauria can free bound djinni by touching them. If they come close to her, she can send them back to the borderland. That's *really* what you should have your Shamans learn to do."

"Really? Well, the djinni must want her where she is, then, because they said nothing about trying to bring her here. But they told me to bring you. They said that *you* would know something that would help us."

"I know something that will help you?" I shook my head. "Well, I can try to teach the Shamans the trick of guarding the borderland. But I have to admit, I agree with the elders. I don't see how it would help us.

"What is it you want?" I asked. "What is it you want me to do?"

"Teach the other Shamans how to guard the borderland, if the skill can be taught," the Eldress said. "Then . . . we can give you karenite, enough to enslave an entire army of djinni. Use it to sow discord among our enemies."

"Alone? I'll be robbed by bandits."

"Of course not alone. Janiya can go with you."

Janiya's head snapped up; she had not expected this. "But my Sisterhood . . ."

"I will arrange for another to lead it in your absence. You walked among the Penelopeians once, Janiya. You can do it again."

"We'll need a third," Janiya said. "Someone who could pass as Greek."

"Perhaps Alibek," the Eldress said. "I will consider it."

"You're forgetting something," I said. I raised my chin. "Lauria."

"I did not forget your sister," the Eldress said. She

rose from her seat and opened a wood chest that sat nearby; from inside, she drew out something black. She shook it out, and I realized that she'd taken out two black, embroidered vests. Mine, and Lauria's. "I had Zhanna give these to me, some weeks ago." She handed them to me and sat back down. "Yours is yours again, if you want it. Lauria's can be hers again, too, if you give it to her. Her fate is yours to decide."

"She can come back?" I asked, just to be sure.

"Yes. She can come back. As Eldress of all the clans, I grant amnesty to Lauria. She came among us as an enemy, but I believe that she had sincerely turned against her old master, and was ready to become one of us in truth and not just as a tool." She leaned back and looked at me; her eyes were unnaturally pale, I realized, a pale blue like the sky. "You will be initiated as one of the Alashi, before you go. If you choose, Lauria can be initiated in absentia, just as Burkut was."

That night, I held Lauria's vest and tried to find her. I'd tried to find her at night while I was traveling with Janiya, as well, but I hadn't been able to. Tonight, I saw her, but far away. It was like seeing a Lauria made from smoke and fog, and I kept thinking she would disappear altogether.

"Come back," I said. She didn't seem to hear me, so I shouted. "Come back! Come back to the Alashi, they will take you back!"

Lauria shook her head; I couldn't hear her words, but I thought I saw her lips move to say, *too late*.

"I'll help you free Thais, but come up to the steppe first," I shouted. "You can come back, the Eldress has granted you amnesty."

The wind whipped across the steppe; I saw Lauria

stop shouting, and close her eyes in concentration. For a single heartbeat, the wind died, and I found myself standing in Sophos's courtyard. Lauria stood before me as I had seen her the night that Sophos had raped her—shaking with cold, her torn clothes bloody. She looked into my face and her lips parted. "I love you," she said, and vanished from the borderland like the flame of a blown-out candle.

**Lauria**

*T*amar," I whispered, though I had found myself in
mist and shadow, and searched for Tamar in
vain. Someone was nudging my ankle. Kyros.

"We're almost there," he said. "I thought you might
like to see Penelopeia from the sky."

I blinked and looked around. I'd nodded off against
the cushions of the palanquin, sometime during the afternoon. I'd started out feigning drowsiness to avoid
talking to Kyros, and I must have fallen asleep for real.
I sat up and stretched. The cushions under me were
damp from sweat. All the curtains were drawn; Kyros
feared flying, and hated looking out of the palanquin.
*Well, he doesn't have to.* I drew the corner of the curtain aside and peered out.

We were still high up. Looking down, I could see
golden fields. Further away, something vast and dark
caught the afternoon sunlight in rippling sparkles. I
caught my breath and squinted, wondering what it
could be. Blowing sand? Some sort of shiny rocks?

"It's the sea," Kyos said, though he hadn't looked

out, only at my face. "Penelopeia is on the shores of a sea."

"That's all *water*?" I stared at the glittering expanse.

"Salt water," Kyros said. His voice was a little amused. "You can't drink it."

That was even more difficult to grasp. Salt was a precious, scarce resource. "There's salt in it? Can they get the salt out?"

"Easily enough, but the Empire gets more of its salt from the salt flats east of here."

I looked out again. *All that water.*

"How much further to Penelopeia?"

"We'll be there soon," Kyros said. "Before sunset."

It was difficult to believe that in less than a day, we had traveled a distance that should have taken weeks.

Kyros had his feet kicked up on a bolster. I glanced at him again, wondering if he was going to ask me questions, but he appeared to be deep in thought. I looked out the window again.

I thought I could see farms now, below us. There were houses, surrounded by fields. The dark ribbon that ran alongside the farms was not, I realized, a river, but a wide, well-kept road; there were people traveling along it, with horses, wagons, camel trains. I had been studying the ground for so long, trying to pick out details, that I was startled to see movement out of the corner of my eye, in the air. I looked, expecting a bird, and saw something that looked like a flying barn, or a very large flying box. An aeriko caravan, I realized, shipping apples one direction and grapes the other. It was painted bright yellow with a blue design.

"Your mother would be shocked by your hair," Kyros said.

I touched the cropped ends. "It's grown out a lot." I scratched an itch. "I think if my mother saw me now she'd want me scrubbed raw and picked free of lice before she let me kiss her." *I'll certainly look the part of a bandit, if I get taken before the High Magia like this.*

Kyros chuckled a little and fell silent again. I sat back against the cushions and tried to practice, in my mind, what I would say to the High Magia, but my thoughts kept skipping ahead to when she didn't believe me. Would she have me executed? Or tortured like a captured spy? *Like the captured spy I am?*

What did I know? The locations of the Alashi camps, last year. But even a djinn could find that out; they didn't need me for that. How to infiltrate the Alashi, the tests I'd had to pass. The beads. I grimaced inwardly at the memory, but I was almost certain that the precise tests varied depending on what the leader of the Sisterhood or Brotherhood thought you needed to learn. Or the Clan Elder or Eldress, if you joined the Alashi in the winter, or were too young or too old to go fight.

I knew that the Alashi had karenite, but the Sisterhood knew that already. I knew something about the karenite trade in Daphnia—the names of the two sorceresses who bought, or tried to buy, my karenite. *I could turn them over, I suppose.* I knew about the Servant Sisterhood and the Younger Sisters, but little beyond the bare fact of their existence. There was Zivar, of course. Zivar, who'd been born a slave and then managed to pass herself off as a Weaver's apprentice. *The green mouse. The only other green mouse in the world.* They could potentially wring information about Zivar out of me, but I doubted that the Weavers cared particularly where Zivar came from. She made spell-chains on command, and handed them back over, at least for now. She was useful. Her origins were unimportant.

*I could tell them about Lycurgus.* Lycurgus, Kyros's cousin, was supposedly the steward of a farm owned by the Sisterhood. Tamar and I had taken Uljas there, looking for Burkut. Lycurgus had been drunk most of the time, and I'd realized while there that he'd been skimming farm profits to help the Younger Sisters. *That's the sort of information I could give Kyros to convince him that I really was on his side all along.* I didn't really care whether I condemned Lycurgus or not; I had no fondness for the man. Solon had been kind, and far more competent. And loyal to the Sisterhood.

If I were talkative enough, could I convince them I really had stayed loyal to Kyros?

*They'll believe me. Of course they'll believe me.* I knew it was the cold fever whispering in my ear, but I embraced it because the alternative was dispair. *They'll believe me because I am the one meant to free the Rivers. I can only do that if I'm alive.*

"Can you see the towers yet?" Kyros asked.

"Towers?"

"Well, you've been to Casseia, you know the sort of thing I'm talking about. Casseia has one tower, built very tall by aerika. Penelopeia has over twenty towers like that. You should be able to see them soon."

I leaned a little further out the window and squinted my eyes. I *could* see something up ahead, barely visible against the blue sky. As we got closer, I could see the towers more clearly—first two, then six, then more. They spiked up towards the sky like glittering needles, and as we grew closer I realized that some were partially clad in polished copper and brass. *They must have aerika who do nothing but polish the metal.* It was an appalling display of power. Zivar had told me once that she never felt that she had enough aerika, though she lost a bit more of herself every time she did a binding. I was certain that the metal-polishing aerika had not been bound by women like the High Magia, but by their apprentices and lesser sisters, acting on orders.

The sun was low in the sky. We were arcing down, now, and I thought I could see the Fortress of Penelope, the palace where the High Magia and some of the other most highly placed of the Sisterhood lived. White marble walls, partly clad, like the towers, in polished metal. A lower tower had a glowing light inside like a beacon, and I wondered if the fire was tended by a human or a djinn. *An aeriko. I need to remember to use the Greek words.*

The aeriko set the palanquin down gently in the courtyard. Slaves were already waiting to help each of us out. I felt a little light-headed and accepted the arm offered to me. We were in an inner courtyard of the palace, large enough to accommodate several more palanquins. A fountain splashed lightly in the center, and the walls were decorated with mosaic images of Athena.

Kyros was having a quiet conversation nearby; then he stepped over and said, "I've arranged for you to have a bath before you're presented to the High Magia."

*Presented to.* Like a gift. I felt a little ill, but followed the slave who led me to a room of warm water and herb-scented steam. If I had any hope of an opportunity to run later, I needed to restrain the impulse to run now. *There is nowhere to run to anyway. I am in Penelopeia, in the Fortress of Penelope.* I wondered what Tamar was doing now. The realization of how far away she was made me slightly dizzy. *Weeks . . . months of travel.* I tried to tell myself that I would see her again, but for the moment, all I could do was submit to the ministrations of the slaves as I was immersed in water, scrubbed clean, and picked free of lice.

Once I was clean and dressed, I was escorted to one of the many interior gardens and left to wait . . . and wait . . . and wait. The night sky was dark; the courtyard was lit with torches. They'd dressed me in linen, with a light wool shawl for warmth, and sandals. I realized that my last material link to Tamar had been severed. The little talisman I'd made for myself, threads from her clothing knotted around my wrist, had disappeared in the bath. *We are blood-sisters. They can't ever truly separate us. Even if I can't find Tamar, when I go to the borderland, she is a Shaman; she will be able to find me.*

My new clothes felt all wrong. Foreign. Everything was foreign. The night was warmer here than it had been back on the steppe; the breeze had a strange misty softness, rather than the brisk edge I expected. There was a salty smell in the air, along with the perfume of the orange tree that hung low over the courtyard foundation, and a warm, spicy smell that wafted from the doorway. Tea, I realized a moment later. The guard there was drinking tea.

I couldn't sit. I paced, instead, back and forth in the courtyard. In addition to the orange tree, there were copious flowers, even this early in the year, including some blood-red blooms shaped like a candle's flame. I forced myself to slow my step and study the flowers, as a way to calm my mind, but it did little good.

The guard in the doorway was female, I noticed. Last summer, Janiya had confided in me that she had once been free and a guard employed by the Sisterhood of Weavers in Penelopeia; they had their own elite cadre of women guards. I wondered how many of the people in the Fortress of Penelope were women. There was at least one man, Kyros, but I'd seen no others. The sorceress I'd studied with during the winter, Zivar, had permitted no men in her house, not even slaves. Surely some of the sorceresses here were married, though . . .

The guard cleared her throat. I looked up, and she beckoned; it was time to go. She stood back to allow me to go first; she followed behind, as if she thought I might flee. *Maybe that means that there is somewhere to go? Or perhaps she always does this . . . .* Despite her boots, her step was quiet on the marble floors. The corridor was lit with oil lamps. I wondered if they were tended by human servants, or aerika.

At the end of the corridor, we reached a closed door made from heavy wood. The guard rapped on the door, and someone inside swung it open. The room was warm, and moist with the smell of breath and sweat, as if it hadn't been opened for days, even to let in the cool evening air. There was a long table, with chairs clustered at the other end. Kyros sat in one, and a thin older woman sat in the other. Her hands were folded over each other on the table; her fingernails had been allowed to grow extremely long, and had been painted. They made me think of blood-stained claws. Her face was deeply lined. She was dressed in red silk that matched her claws, and had a gold bracelet that looked like a serpent coiled around her upper arm.

Looking at her, I could see the cold fever lurking, but it did not master her—not today.

"So," she said. "You are the spy."

I swallowed hard. "Kyros sent me . . ."

". . . to spy, yes, of course, yet you didn't just say

*yes, I am the spy.* That's very interesting. Why didn't you?"

"Because . . . because . . . Kyros has lost his faith in me."

"Really? He seems to have a great deal of faith in you." She glanced at him dismissively. "More than I think is warranted. He brought you here, had you bathed and given fresh clothes, as if you were truly *his* spy, returning from the field, ready to report. Strange. We sent him orders to have you executed."

"But I—"

"Do you have anything *useful* to report? Anything that Kyros doesn't already know? You were out of contact for a while, but then he sent an aeriko to watch you, so I can't imagine you have all that much."

"Lycurgus," I sqeaked out.

"We already know about Lycurgus. I'm done with you." She gestured, and the guard stepped forward, laying her hand on my shoulder.

"Wait—" This was happening so fast. "I tried—it's not my fault—" I wondered if they would use a sword, or a rope, or some more gruesome death. *Let it be over with quickly, if they're going to kill me . . .*

The sorceress had started to turn away; now she turned back, and looked me straight in the eye. "Kyros clearly wants you spared, so we'll leave your neck intact for now. Take her to the pit." She turned away again.

"Kyros," I said. "KYROS!" I caught a glimpse of his face, his eyes wide and worried, and then other guards came, and I was swept away with them like a twig in the tide.